Star 111

LUTZ SEILER

Translated from the German by Tess Lewis

nyrb **New York Review Books** New York

This is a New York Review Book

published by The New York Review of Books

207 East 32nd Street, New York, NY 10016

www.nyrb.com

Copyright © 2020 by Suhrkamp Verlag Berlin
Translation and afterword copyright © 2023 by Tess Lewis

Originally published in German as *Stern III* in 2020.
All rights reserved by and controlled through Suhrkamp Verlag Berlin.
First published in English in the UK in 2023 by And Other Stories, Sheffield.

Library of Congress Cataloging-in-Publication Data
Names: Seiler, Lutz, 1963– author. | Lewis, Tess, translator.
Title: Star 111 / by Lutz Seiler ; translated from the German by Tess Lewis.
Other titles: Stern III. English
Description: New York City : New York Review Books, 2024. | Series: New York
 Review Books classics
Identifiers: LCCN 2024003216 (print) | LCCN 2024003217 (ebook) | ISBN
 9781681378534 (paperback) | ISBN 9781681378541 (e-book)
Subjects: LCSH: Families—Fiction. | Germany—History—1990– —Fiction. |
 LCGFT: Domestic fiction. | Novels.
Classification: LCC PT2681.E529 S74713 2020 (print) | LCC PT2681.E529
 (ebook) | DDC 833/.92—dc23/eng/20240315
LC record available at https://lccn.loc.gov/2024003216
LC ebook record available at https://lccn.loc.gov/2024003217

ISBN 978-1-68137-853-4
Available as an electronic book; ISBN 978-1-68137-854-1

Printed in the United States of America on acid-free paper.

10 9 8 7 6 5 4 3 2 1

For my parents

I am twenty-eight, and practically nothing has happened.

RAINER MARIA RILKE
The Notebooks of Malte Laurids Brigge

THE CABLE ADDRESS

Carl's train stopped well before the station, accompanied by a metallic stuttering and juddering as if his journey's heart had suddenly stopped beating just before arrival. Outside, a sea of crisscrossing tracks and behind them, the Wailing Wall. The Wailing Wall was a kilometer-long brick facade that demarcated the Leipzig station grounds from the city, pierced by strange, honeycomb-like openings through which a street, buildings, and sometimes even people were visible. For some reason, it was not uncommon for trains to stop here, outside the station, the destination in view, for minutes or hours; it was like an old complaint, a familiar song. The travelers' gaze inevitably fell on this wall—hence the name.

The morning after the telegram arrived, Carl had set out for Gera. He wore a clean pair of jeans and his old black motorcycle jacket with the diagonal zipper across the chest over a freshly washed shirt. He owned three of these collarless work shirts, identical shirts with thin, pale blue stripes from his time as an apprentice bricklayer before he began his studies. He'd even trimmed his hair a bit, laboriously, with dull nail scissors—shoulder-length would have to do. He was returning home like someone long-lost, at least that's how he saw it for a moment. Most castaways were stranded only after their return—that's the saddest part of those stories. Once home, they could not adapt to life on the mainland. The many obstacles, storms, years—all the loneliness, which, ultimately, turned out to have been best. Often, they were unable to tolerate mainland food or they died because of their excessively long hair, which they had to display

9

at local fairs to make money, and which, one night, when they were asleep, would wrap itself around their necks like a noose . . .

Outside, the conductor walked the length of the train, swearing and knocking on the windows of each car: "Off the train, everyone off!"

They were on an old outer track with a temporary wooden platform. Technically, it was not a platform, but a ramp through which grass grew and a few young birch trees protruded sideways, apparently impervious to waste oil and excrement. The birch leaves glowed yellow. Carl saw this glow and heard the rap of his steps on the wooden ramp. Like convicts, they trudged single file toward the station on a narrow walkway between the tracks.

The dimly lit concourse surged with people, a billowing motion, shouting and braying. Again and again, the loudspeakers, which transformed every word into a muffled, hollow dream language, a single, completely incomprehensible call, repeated: "Uh-uck!"

The object of their siege was the express train to Berlin, a string of eight or nine grime-encrusted carriages with nicotine-yellow windowpanes. On the evening news the day before, there had been talk of additional trains and further provisional border crossings, along with repeated formulaic appeals for calm. A few of the Berlin-bound managed to scale the greasy carriages and launch themselves headfirst into the overcrowded compartments through the skylights. A scene out of Bombay or Calcutta—in the Leipzig train station it appeared excessive, like part of an overblown choreography, out of place and on a large scale.

Carl slowly pushed his way through the crowd. His bag kept getting caught. The strap cut into his shoulder and seemed about to tear. He immediately regretted having dragged all his papers and books along—how stupid, how thoughtless of him. Several expletives rang out, his face was pressed into the coarse felt of a jacket that promptly made a feral sound—then something rammed him in the chest. He fell, dragged down and twisted by the weight of his bag. Someone who surely was just trying to catch him hit Carl's face hard with the flat of his hand; Carl tasted sweat and lost his bearings.

"Uh-uck! Uh-uck!"

The cry now came from on high. It was the voice of a drunken giant babbling down at them from the soot-blackened cathedral of the station, but his dwarves no longer obeyed.

"My bag!" Carl shouted when he came to.

"Which bag, young man? Do you mean this one?"

The bag was still there; more precisely, he was lying on it. For a moment Carl saw nothing but faces bending over him, tense but controlled. It's joy, Carl thought, pure joy. But he couldn't actually tell what emotion was controlling them, if it was, in fact, still joy or already hatred.

"Do you need help?"

A girl, sixteen at most, was offering him a handkerchief. As always, Carl was surprised by the gleaming red, that fresh, slightly unctuous substance that couldn't possibly have come from him: blood.

"Will you be alright?" The girl touched Carl's arm. He saw her round face and in it, her eyes, very light and watery, as if blind.

"No, you have to stay with me. Forever."

"Thanks. You'll survive."

He made his way outside along an empty platform. He tried not to pay too much attention to the blind girl (she wasn't actually blind), but she stayed with him, holding his arm. They were a couple, at least until Carl collapsed onto a bench.

"Are you also going to Berlin?"

Carl tilted his head back and felt it in his throat—a warm thread that unspooled from somewhere on the roof of his mouth and, strangely enough, burned a little. He had to swallow, again and again, but it still hung there. Since he was a child, he often had nosebleeds. Back when these things mattered, he used to impress his friends by being able to stop the bleeding with a single blow of his fist to his forehead. It was a boxing trick. He rammed the ball of his hand against his forehead, or the blow glanced off it. The impact had to be forceful, making the head jerk backward. It was all in the jolt. If you were too timid it didn't work.

"No, I'm going . . ." He shook his head gingerly to stop the spinning before his eyes. The girl remained standing next to him for a while. Carl considered what he could ask her but then, suddenly, she was gone, and he murmured his answer: "Home. I'm going home."

Centimeter by centimeter, the express train to Berlin pulled away from the platform. The overcrowded carriages slid past. Someone hollered, "Arrivederci, you bum!" and a spontaneous chorus struck up the song that Carl only knew in his grand-mother's melancholy rendition: "I'd love to stay a bit longer . . ." Carl watched the train leave. The departing chorus passed the ramp with the glowing birch trees, which began waving shyly and tremulously.

The word *bum* was still buzzing in his skull. A bum was some-one with a bloody nose, squatting on a train platform that no trains left from. Someone who has no idea where the journey is headed, thought Carl.

He pulled the telegram from his bag. It was just a note, hand-written, with a stamp below the writing. In the lower right-hand corner, the operator had noted the date and time: 10 November, 9:20 a.m. "we need help please do come immediately your par-ents." No reproach, no mention of his months of silence, only this, a cry for help. Just that weak little word *do*. Carl could hear it, in his mother's voice: "do come." He pictured her hurrying downhill into town, with short, brisk steps, he pictured her dictating the address, filling out the telegram form, meticulous but also tense, nervous, which is why she forgot the salutation, and he pictured Mrs. Bethmann, the woman at the counter, counting the syllables. Even these days, when the most unimaginable things were happening, the "cable address"—as those behind the post office counter called it—still worked.

Carl had to admit that he hadn't been particularly worried—parents were solid ground, unassailable, the home turf you could retreat to in times of need. Missed, yes, it was odd, he *missed* his parents and not just this past year when he'd only seen them one single time, no, even before then, always, actually, he had always, always missed them.

He looked for the track on which the southbound trains usually ran, to the region on the border between Thuringia and Saxony from which his family came—"where the fox and the hare bid each other goodnight," his father's favorite expression for "in the middle of nowhere." When he was a child, every night before he went to sleep, Carl had imagined foxes and hares slowly gathering at the forest's edge to say goodnight. Sometimes there were other animals in the mix, all different kinds of animals, and sometimes a few humans who were good friends of the animals. All these gentle, clever creatures gathered in one particular, moonlit spot at the end of the day—a silhouette of raised muzzles, raised heads and a single chorus: "Goodnight, you hares from Gera, you foxes from Altenburg, you ravens from Meuselwitz, goodnight!"

PART I

BEWILDERMENT

Carl couldn't remember who'd first suggested "going out for a few steps," his father or his mother. It wasn't unusual. He followed behind, his parents in front, as always. His father had just turned fifty, his mother forty-nine. His father had become slender, the brown leather jacket, the drooping shoulders, gray hair thinning on the back of his head—Carl had never seen him this way. They walked along the Elsterdamm from Langenberg to the Franzosen Bridge, their traditional walk along the river. There were hundreds of photographs of it in the family album, neatly glued and meticulously captioned by his mother: the six-year-old in a collared shirt and bow tie, his eager smile and large, eager teeth—Carl on his first day of school. Then the fourteen-year-old with a pageboy haircut and a serious, dismissive air. Next to him, his mother, her hair in a chignon, wearing a Corfam coat, autumn '77. And so on, along the timeline through all the years and seasons until today, which no one photographed. On their right, the lazy flow of the Elster, its moldy bank and the Langenberg meadows. His father stopped, turned and said, "Carl."

It would be nice to relate that a wind suddenly rose in the Elster Valley, blowing along the river, or that there was a peculiar sound, maybe a kind of whistling, a thin, soft whistle from the meadows that is heard only once every fifty or one hundred years: "Carl . . ."

His parents wanted to go. To leave the country, in short.

A soft whistling, for example. Carl looked around and it was suddenly as if this (their) world of river and path had only been set up provisionally (not for eternity) and as if it now (like everything else) (obviously) had to be dismantled and stashed away, as if it had (from one moment to the next) become irrelevant and worthless. "That's not how we meant it," Carl's mother would have interjected if there had been the opportunity but there was no pause in the sequence, just bewilderment. Carl's single sentence, bumbling, stammering, like that of a helpless, frightened child whose parents are suddenly no longer adults: "I think you're underrating the whole, the whole—I mean, *the whole homeland thing.*" It was strange for him to say it, he wasn't used to talking to his parents like this; something had been turned upside down. They walked on upriver in silence—mother, father, child amid all the shams of their abruptly obsolete, discontinued life.

There was no conversation at supper, either. The mood was tense, and Carl started to consider it all the result of a bad hypnosis and he didn't want to be drawn in any further. First, they had to eat, then clear the table and wheel everything back into the kitchen on the serving trolley, a small, two-tiered cart with a chrome frame. The muffled rolling sound it made on the carpet, long familiar, the soft clatter of the dishes as always, as if things could only stay this way forever—after all, that's what everything here had been set up for. The cart was lifted over the doorsill in the hallway, this was his father's job, but today Carl leaped up to help him, carefully, so that nothing slipped off. "Now there's someone who sees what work needs to be done," was his father's highest compliment.

Like two children, they pushed the trolley together down the hallway and into the kitchen. Carl felt helpless but he lent a hand and was suddenly overcome with a feeling of homesickness, with a longing for homecoming, for rest, sleep, the return of the prodigal son, something along those lines. Longing for that exhaustion that descends like a seizure, which only ever struck him here, at home, on his childhood sofa: "Oh Carl, why don't you stretch out for a bit? And here, take the pillow. Do you need a blanket? Here, take the blanket . . ." First the pillow, then the blanket, which meant: defense against all self-doubt, the obliteration of all distress.

When Carl and his father returned from the kitchen, his mother was on the sofa. She seemed nervous and fitfully crossed her legs. These days she wore her hair short and smooth like a young boy's, which made her look even smaller than she was. Still, it was easy to see how much strength there was in her, how much determination. His father held him by the arm.

For a moment, it looked like they were only play-acting: sudden departure, parting, escape—and the papers on the flat surface of the secretary, lined up parallel to the edge. They reflected the light from the small fluorescent tube covered by a shade and Carl had to close his eyes for a moment—land certificates, deeds of transfer, a gift deed form certifying that *all this* would now belong to him. Carl Bischoff, the only child of Inge and Walter Bischoff, born 1963 in Gera, Thuringia, "currently a student"; "student" was only written faintly and in pencil.

"It would be nice if you could look after the place, that's to say, we're asking you to." Or: "Could you look after the place, that's to say, we'd like to ask you to."

Later, Carl couldn't remember the exact wording, just "ask" and "look after" and that he had allowed the *handover*, which in the moment had a solemn aspect to it, to happen without resistance, at least without any mention of his own plans. The brute force of incomprehension left him at a loss for words and eclipsed everything else.

That little word "why?" presented itself but was not admitted, on the contrary, "why?" and any answer, Carl sensed, would only lead deeper into that state of unreality that, it turned out, became absolute when he learned that his parents planned to attempt their *departure* (that's how they referred to it) *separately after Giessen.* From the central transit camp on, they would initially each try on their own, in order to "double our chances." That's how his mother had put it and that was the name: "Central Transit Camp." She was trying to keep her voice steady, but Carl could hear that *separately after Giessen* had not been her idea.

"We've thought it over carefully."

And then: "Your mother always wanted to leave."

Carl didn't have the slightest doubt that Inge and Walter (since adolescence he was in the habit of calling his parents by their first names) belonged in this house, in this life and no other, which is why he started in on the dangers and risks, of which he only had vague notions. His mother looked at him.

"And you, Carl? Where have you been all this time—without a single word? Do you have any idea how worried . . ."

Then the handover.

A tour of all the rooms, the new oven's features, the electrical wiring and the fuses, their farewell to it all. An envelope lay on the secretary. "Five hundred marks," his father said.

"Any other questions?"

It was already late evening when they returned once more to the garage, down in the valley, next to the railway embankment. For a while, they stood next to each other, their hands in the cone of light cast by the workbench lamp while Walter explained how the tools were organized. That summer, a few important and rare pieces had been added to his collection, including an ignition timing mechanism and a distance gauge with twenty tabs (0.05 to 1 millimeter), priceless tools. There were larger, cruder tools on the metal shelves, but the valuable ones were hung on the wall over the workbench with rubber straps made from preserving-jar rings or mounted on brackets Walter had made himself from narrow slats rubbed with recycled oil: tools of various sizes, ordered in increasing and decreasing sizes that, together, created a kind of landscape (a homeland), gleaming and cool.

Carl's father wasn't wearing his overalls, which he usually put on when he was in the garage, just an apron, the gray, knee-length apron that was reserved for work on the house. He picked up one of the new socket wrenches and simulated its use. The raised voice, the pauses, the "so" and the "then," the tone of his detailed explanations and the message that hadn't changed since Carl's childhood: the world demanded concentration—and patience; the world was rickety, fragile, in a questionable state, but it could be repaired.

"Do you know how long it takes to set up a collection like this?"

"Quite a few years," Carl replied.

"A lifetime," his father said.

As a sign that he understood, Carl fingered the tabs on the new distance gauge. The thin steel was slightly flexible and rather greasy. The grease smelled sweetish, edible . . . Here in the garage's dim light, with a tool in his hand, Carl could have begun speaking, confiding in his father, suddenly it seemed possible, this was the opening made only for that. He could have recounted what had happened to him in the past year (*befallen* him was the old, more precise word). The breakup with H. and why he'd stopped going to class and why he had hidden himself away from the world.

He wouldn't have told his father everything, of course. His attempt with the pills. The Kröllwitz Clinic. The empty days.

He pictured it: his father's worried expression, but no reproach; a nod, a pause—

"Finally, one more thing about the car."

Carl put down the tool. His father asked him to get behind the wheel of the Zhiguli. He turned on the ignition and pointed to a small light below the tachometer that lit up or not depending on the motor oil, but Carl had already stopped listening to what his father was explaining.

They sat next to each other in silence for a while, in the semi-darkness of the narrow precast concrete garage, and Carl was unable to imagine his father's life. Walter's hand lay on the black imitation leather dashboard, right in front of Carl's eyes. As if he wanted to show Carl his hand one last time in farewell, how his hand looked exactly like his son's and not only in its shape, the lines on their palms were identical; the same history was written in their hands.

"You don't drive up to the gates of a refugee camp in your own car, I expect," his father said, then fell silent. The tool landscape shimmered in the rearview mirror. Carl realized that the distance that usually stood between them was suspended.

"No, I . . . I know," Carl stammered. That was all.

His father seemed to still be pondering, but then he got out of the car and Carl rested his arms on the steering wheel.

As a child, he would sit for hours behind the wheel of the Zhiguli, making rumbling sounds; clutch, shift, gas. A light went on in the apartment building across the way. Effi lived there—Effi Kalász, with whom Carl had been in love since eighth grade without ever telling her.

A STORY

Carl slept in his childhood room, on the so-called *teen bed*, an orange and green striped sofa bed. Back then, just before his fourteenth birthday, his parents had redecorated his room. He'd been surprised by the unannounced disappearance of his fold-down bed, which could be turned into a cabinet during the day very easily, and that his mother never missed an opportunity to call "very practical and, most importantly, space-saving." In fact, the new furniture left only a narrow path from the door to the window, under which stood Carl's desk. The disappearance of the fold-down bed and the appearance of the teen bed signaled (still) the end of his childhood.

Carl looked around. The only books in his parents' house (aside from his father's reference books on computers and programming languages) were now kept on the shelf above the teen bed: the Meyers encyclopedia in nine volumes with the one-volume supplement, a Duden dictionary, a dictionary of foreign words and two small encyclopedias (one of nature and one of history). Everything else was unchanged. Also unchanged was the play of light and shadows on the room's ceiling, the street noise and the voices from the entrance lobby. Someone had spray-painted "The revolution will prevail" in red on the base of the apartment block across the street.

Before he fell asleep, Carl heard footsteps overhead, heavy steps, not the steps of a girl: Kerstin Schenkendorff, the daughter of the man who kept the *Hausbuch*, a log of all the building's tenants and their guests. He lived in the apartment above them, she was a few significant years older than Carl; what had become of her? He remembered the night of the story. Inge and Walter had gone out, which rarely happened. Carl counted as one of those children parents proudly call "sound sleepers," but this time there had been a monster, a dragon chasing him unrelentingly and with an enormous appetite. Carl screamed and woke, drenched in sweat. He ran into his parents' bedroom, but it was empty. He ran through the apartment: no one there. Only the dragon, still hiding somewhere, so Carl had to escape but the apartment door was locked. He'd pounded on the door and called, maybe even screamed, and then, at some point, he heard Kerstin Schenkendorff's voice outside on the stairs. She spoke to him soothingly, calmed him down, and asked "if a story wouldn't be nice?" Carl crouched in his pajamas, he pressed his ear to the

23

door, snuggled up to it (dear door) and heard the soft rustling of the house, then, behind the door, the story that Kerstin started telling him, and kept on telling until he fell asleep.

The next morning, Carl drove his parents to the border. Even before the sun rose, his father had brought the car up from the garage and set the keys next to Carl's plate. Carl saw the keys and he felt a certain pride although he knew that what was happening could only be wrong. Weren't they his parents? With their quiet, daily life organized down to the smallest detail along with a particular love of order and repetition? A few platitudes from his schooldays drifted by: "the historic situation, the historic moment . . ." The historic moment has turned your heads, was Carl's view, but he didn't say it. He did not feel superior, but rather at a loss.

One possibility was to keep thinking of himself as *their child*. Parents knew what they were doing and sooner or later the wisdom of their decisions would become clear. It would emerge, just as it always had. And after all, you could look at it in a completely different way: in their own way, Inge and Walter were contributing to the revolution that was taking place everywhere. They stopped showing up at work, they left their positions and prepared their escape, if you wanted to call it that. His parents! They were the unlikeliest refugees Carl could imagine.

The matter of the accordion was upsetting. His father had dragged the old, black case with the instrument up from the basement. He had attached straps that enabled him to carry the bulky monstrosity on his back. He wanted to take it with him, that much was clear, but what for? Carl knew that the instrument belonged to his father, but he'd never seen him play it. Like so much that was stored in the basement, it came from a distant past that was shrouded in darkness.

"Why do you want to schlep that thing along, Walter?" Having to ask this question was unpleasant for Carl. It was as if he were holding a mirror up to a child and running the risk of making him unhappy in a single blow.

"To play now and then," his father replied. "I think I'll take it up again."

It was the usual breakfast: fresh butter, sliced cheese and warmed rolls from the Gera bakery cooperative, where his mother had worked (until the day before) in a four-person department that was responsible for creating new recipes. Four gourmets, as his mother emphasized, including two pastry chefs (the way she pronounced *Konditoren* sounded like *Doktoren*), masters of the trade with decades of experience. Her job was to save costly ingredients by calculating an "ersatz." Apple seeds instead of almonds, for example. Green tomatoes instead of candied lemon peel, and so on. Over the past years, the term "substitute" had been substituted for "ersatz." When the small group sat together, racking their brains over what could be *substituted* for what, Inge took notes. Carl's mother was the secretary, and she wrote everything down, even the most far-fetched suggestions. They often held very long and serious discussions before finally drawing up the "substitution calculation." On the day of the tasting, they would meet again. Naturally, they didn't have enormous expectations (as his mother put it), but they did harbor a certain hope (utopian, not easily justified, perhaps the kind fostered by alchemists at the end of their experiments when they're about to lift the lid). Each of them had, nonetheless, gone to great trouble, thought long and hard, and taken a risk.

"Then you look away and chew," according to Inge's rendition. "You chew and can't bear to look each other in the eye, and no one wants to say anything."

Carl's mother found it painful. She had learned her skills from her mother on the farm. Even as a girl she had enjoyed baking and did it often—twenty kinds of cake for each celebration, which were then set out on cake boards as big as cartwheels in the vaulted cellar, on what they called the cake rack. Carl remembered it well—the peculiar *Huckelkuchen* ("bumpy cake," which was also called "camel cake"), the legendary cheesecake (a legend they all rehashed every single time) and the search for the shelf with the chocolate streusel cake, which was the most important for the child Carl.

In his father's opinion, it was a matter of crossing the border as fast as possible. Walter talked about Willy Brandt's speech in front of the Schöneberg town hall. It was in all the papers. Something in the speech had revealed to him that the border would only stay open for a short time. He explained it to Carl with the laws of fluid mechanics, "all you need is a little bit of physics, a simple trick, to relieve pressure." And the Russians are still here, too, after all. That was his strongest argument.

He had chosen Herleshausen for the border crossing. That's where buses would be leaving from and there was also a train station nearby. Rain had started to fall during the night and was now streaming down. Carl's mother said, "The sky is weeping." She saw it as a sign—of what exactly remained her secret.

They spoke little during the drive, the discipline of flight and concentration on what was most essential prevailed. Carl was the driver of the getaway car and in the car were two refugees who had to be smuggled westward. Strange: it was his father who was sitting in the passenger seat. And the woman in the back seat was his mother, who was checking the documents one more time, all stowed away in a plastic bag and secured with a rubber band.

"You're driving too far to the right. You're driving in the middle of the road again, Carl. Not so fast, please . . ." Nothing, not a single remark. Carl waited for one, after the Hermsdorfer interchange, he even wished his father would make a remark.

The gentle pull of the Thuringian hills on the left and right of the highway. The view of the road, with the spidery tar-patched cracks in the concrete. The Zhiguli ran over large black spiders along with the gaps between the slabs, the rhythmic beat of the tires—a jungle noise and a strange thought: maybe what he had done in his life so far wasn't so wrong and pointless after all. It was just my own way of driving, Carl thought, to put it very broadly and simply.

Part of their *preliminaries*, as Carl's mother described it, involved getting new and better glasses from Wunderlich Opticians on the Sorge (the main boulevard in Gera), for the fine print in the masses of forms she believed they'd be required to fill out *over there.* "Bärbel, I'm taking a cure and need a pair of glasses," was Inge's explanation to her optician, who had filled her request almost overnight. Inge had also bought two sturdy backpacks, the ones called hunter's rucksacks, "because, and this is important, you always need a hand free on the go, you understand Carl?" She was agitated and kept repeating the sentence: "You always need a hand free." She had drawn up lists and imagined various *situations*. One of these was that "in the camp" she would wear pajamas at night instead of a nightgown as she usually did; the toilets were surely out in the hallway, at the end of some corridor, maybe even in a courtyard you'd have to cross at night, perhaps under the eyes of a camp guard or other refugees drawn outside by the dozen simply out of excitement. And yes: there would be queues for everything, to get food, to get passes, for every stamp and every certificate. "But now we have to see it through, one way or another, you understand, Carl?"

Her self-confident demeanor, her way with words. Carl knew that nothing held his mother back once she had set her sights on

27

something. The neighbors all liked her, even Schenkendorff. Oh, all the friends, colleagues and neighbors who now, after decades of tried and tested fellowship, had to be left behind without a word, no goodbyes, no farewells, no notes with homemade biscuits wrapped in a napkin that his mother had always gladly left on doorsteps and work desks as "a little token," as she put it.

Giving everything up, leaving.

Although what was happening was weighty and life-changing, Carl later had only vague memories of their conversations; maybe he was in shock. He accepted their decision, he respected it, what else could he do? And finally: who could know what would prove right or wrong in the end?

On the evening before they had chatted about this and that, but not about anything that would have made things clear to Carl. There were a few useful phrases at the ready—"imprisoned an entire lifetime" and so on, which was generally accurate, but his parents did not use them, that wasn't *the reason*. Carl understood that there had to be *more* to it, something that could blow it all up (and did blow it up), even though they had long ago worked out a plan for the rest of their lives. It was surely stored away safely somewhere with their documents, on the bottom of the box in the secretary or some other such spot.

It became ever clearer to Carl that he basically knew very little about his parents and only carried around a few faded, childish images from the album of his schooldays and adolescence. Had he ever really thought about them? Was it children's obligation to think about their parents when they became adults? And if so, when should they start? Were the mid-twenties already too late?

He stared ahead at the roadway. The Thuringian hills to the left and right. My parents are leaving the family home—a very odd and sad sentence at this moment. Before, leaving was reserved for the children. Children went out into the world, not parents. And then the parents worried about their children, and so on.

The border crossing was crowded: passersby, the curious, lines of cars and streams of pedestrians—the country seemed to be dispersing in a giant migration. Among the crowd there were more than a few with rucksacks and suitcases, strong, young travelers who seemed to have met here by agreement and be supporting each other. There was no one his parents' age. With the large, black accordion case on his back, Carl's father looked like a displaced person trying to save one of his household effects. Fittingly, the ruins of an unfinished highway overpass rose from the valley. "They can keep building now," his father murmured. It was an odd remark, since he assumed the border would be closed again soon. In the background, at the foot of the watchtower, soldiers stood holding their machine guns non-chalantly in front of their chests and Carl secretly agreed with his father: the whole apparatus could be put back into operation at any time.

Once more, Carl offered to drive all the way to Giessen, to the central refugee transit camp. His father looked at him as if through a tunnel. Spontaneous alterations were out of the question—on this point, at least, the course was familiar. His parents' lives would change, forever, that much was certain, but the upheaval was following the old rules. And it wasn't clear that they would ever see each other again.

Then the goodbye. A temporary parking lot, actually it was just part of a field, muddy pastureland, dark, gloomy soil. His parents wore their green plastic rain ponchos from their mountain holiday in the High Tatras, which covered their rucksacks and made them look like cosmonauts preparing to set foot on a strange new planet despite adverse conditions. "What wonderful trips we've taken!" This exclamation followed every holiday. His mother also wore her Tatra hiking boots made of brown buck-skin (the thick soles, the jagged tread), and only then did Carl notice that under her gray sweater vest, she was also wearing the checked hiking shirt she had bought in Tatranská Lomnica, not far from the Slovakian mountain hut they rented for many years, settling in with a trunk full of soup packets, canned cheese, and homemade liverwurst. His parents had always been very frugal. Now they were leaving everything behind and taking on the West. Like one of their hiking tours.

Finally, they hugged Carl: stiffly and somewhat reserved, their cool, damp rain ponchos like a final rejection, entirely unin-tended, and maybe that's why he had to fight back tears. When he started the car, the waving began. His parents waved and when he drove away, they were still waving, and in the rearview mirror, Carl could see them, still waving, and he waved, too, his arm stretched out of the window, letting his sleeve get drenched in the rain. Waving until the one leaving has disappeared and then a bit longer for good measure—that was the family tradi-tion. Later, in a dream, Carl saw them all standing there, waving, his parents in their place and he in his, at great distances from each other, and each in their own lives: I'm here, that was me, goodbye my dears.

"Our parents should have a better life." Something was wrong with this sentence.

THE CHILD CARL

The short hallway, the wardrobe's dull sheen, and in the dim light his mother's summer coat, watching him mutely. For a while, Carl padded from room to room and sank into the absence: walk, don't think. He breathed in his parents' smell. He tried to be as quiet as possible.

In front of the television, the two chairs upholstered in black and red bouclé. To the right of the television, the cabinet with the record player, the anti-static cloth folded neatly next to the unit. The replacement cloth, unused, in a plastic bag behind it. Strangely, all these things were still there, stoically continuing their existence.

The bedroom was basically taboo, the parental zone. Carl sat on the bed (on his father's side) and pulled out the drawer of his nightstand. He was a child again, home after school, looking for the Polish playing cards with the four aces (four women), who were *topless* as soon as the card was tilted slightly.

"What business of yours was it to look in the drawer, Carl, explain yourself."

He stood up and tried to smooth the bedcover. Even moving a chair required overcoming resistance. He didn't just drag it across the floor, he lifted it, carefully.

On the evening news they showed a map with the new border crossings. The trains of the German National Railway were said to be "at two hundred percent capacity" and photographs of the train stations were shown. For a second, Carl thought he saw himself in a crowd of people. In two rapid steps, he reached the window. The neighbor's lights: they were still on. He closed the curtains and turned off the ceiling light. At midnight, a recap of the past days. He remembered the warning his father claimed he'd heard and had to admit that Willy Brandt had chosen his words very carefully, almost as if the speaker were secretly leaving open something pivotal. As if the whole thing could still turn out to have been a great bluff. At the end was a report of unrest in several units of the National People's Army and the camera pensively panned along the walls of the border dog kennels at Potsdam-Wilhelmshorst. They were surrounded by tall pine trees on which lay the warm light of

31

the setting sun. A primeval forest, for which Carl felt a brief longing.

He had to hold his position and "secure the hinterland," that was the agreement in short. He would stand by in case help was needed; in any event, he would wait for word *from over there*, as his father called it. "You're the rearguard, Carl, as it were."

The rearguard. The word annoyed Carl, but he had ultimately agreed. What else could he do? He didn't understand exactly what was happening to his parents, but the sincerity and gravity of their request was clear. It was the least that he, *their only child*, could do for them in these unfathomable days—the very least.

Carl found his mother's old typewriter in one of the linen cupboards and he set it up on the writing desk. It was a Consul. He liked its heavy, semicircular casing. It was cool to the touch and gleamed in the light of the small neon lamp. Typing took effort, each letter a hammer blow—the sound of steps overhead, someone said something, muffled voices. He tried at half-strength and the writing faded.

It was a kind of a poem about a soldier who passed through the Straits of Gibraltar alone in his U-boat. There were five lines in it that Carl liked a lot—as if written by a stranger. He recited the lines again out loud, and the image of a completely different life flashed before his eyes: he had five lines that granted him permission. He stood and paced around the room; a warm feeling of happiness.

Next to the typewriter lay a few books he had brought with him: Anna Akhmatova, René Char, Gertrud Kolmar. He wrote down excerpts in his notebook. Copying was a way to get closer to the sacred. It was the American method. A kind of religious service. Afterwards, he read his own poem again. There he was, underwater, on the bottom of the sea, with his "Nautilus." He was utterly alone. Solitary and silent, he passed the Moroccan roots of Africa. It was still good.

Two days later: "There will be no return to the prior state of affairs." Carl wondered if his parents were following the news and if they might possibly (consequently) correct their plans and decide to turn around and return to Gera. He wished they would, then the doorbell rang.

He was in the hallway on the way to the kitchen. Alarmed, Carl stared into the semi-darkness over the door. The bell was old, electromechanical, a tiny clapper that beat rapidly against a bowl-shaped piece of metal, a kind of bell. After the clapper stopped, there was a lingering sound, the bell rang—and rang. It was this sound that hung in the air, swelled and gained an audible outline. An outline of the furniture and coats in the hallway and now even of Carl himself, he could feel it on the cold edges of his ears, he'd *become audible*.

"Carl, open up! I know you're there."

Schenkendorff's asthmatic voice, like an avalanche of small, dusty gravel. Carl's ears seemed frozen, seemed to have grown in the hallway and all of a sudden weren't small anymore, but expansive and full of hidden corners. I know you're there: suddenly he was the child Carl again, hiding because he had "neglected his homework," the child who had caused trouble in school, "undisciplined" and "at risk of being held back," as Mrs. Klotz, his homeroom teacher, had described him. One evening, she had shown up at suppertime . . .

"Carl! Is everything alright?"

Part of the "strategy" was that Carl (if possible) would not talk to anyone, at least not for the first few days. "We need the head start," his father had said—or something to that effect. His job at the Gera data processing center (he programmed the large computers) was the reason for the secrecy. He was a person *entrusted with secret information,* that was the official designation. Carl did not believe that his father harbored concrete fears because of this. He just wanted some breathing room, to gain distance, Walter had said. All in all, it would simply be easier if their disappearance remained undiscovered in the building for as long as possible, easier for them and for Carl.

"I'll be back, Carl!" Schenkendorff called.

The next morning, he slipped two sheets of paper under the door, like in a movie. It was a form for registering arrivals and departures in Gera-Langenberg and the district of Gera with the police. Carl wondered if Schenkendorff had known everything all along.

Later, that evening, Carl pushed the chairs and the table against the wall and laid out two long rows of pages on the orange-brown carpet. He left a path between them so he could walk up and down and inspect the writing.

He now saw that the poem about the soldier in the U-boat could be improved here and there. But the rhythm was good, and he had caught the underwater feeling. The right mix of longing and desolation, at least it seemed so to him. Not out of personal experience or because he was living through something similar (in a broad sense)—this thought would not have occurred to Carl. On the contrary: the man in the U-boat was poetry and if it was poetry, then it had nothing to do with his own (trivial) life. It was the other world, the one that was worth the trouble (none other was). Carl dreamed of the day when he would manage to write a great, authentic poem. Something as great as T. S. Eliot's *Four Quartets*, for example.

The carpet was too soft a surface to write on. Here and there the tip of his pencil pierced the paper—tiny holes.

"Breathing holes," whispered the child Carl who had been crouching next to him the entire time. "Breathing holes for your poems."

"Do you think that's good?"

"Yes."

"And what do you think of the poems?"

The first days in Gera: no news, no letter.

Conscientious parents, always reliable.

Separately after Giessen.

He tried to picture it. Some camp, a sports hall maybe, or a defunct railway station, somewhere in the north. Camp beds and cotton blankets, near the sea, high and low tides. What would they live on? They didn't have any relatives in the West, no acquaintances, none of the care packages that imported jeans, coffee and the bewitching odor of the West that so many people talked about. And no Western money either, of course, never. Only the provisions in the hunter's rucksack. His father's heart medicine, did they think of that? Many who left had some kind of address. Maybe they weren't particularly welcome, but they had an initial goal, a name, a street—instead of a train station or a reception camp. He pictured his parents, side by side, diving into a thickening fog of confusion.

Once a day, Carl crept down three flights of stairs to the mailbox and often a flight further down to the cellar where the preserves and cider were stored, hundreds of jars and bottles on metal shelves, provisions for the rest of his life.

When darkness fell, he would go out on the balcony to smoke. From the balcony, there was a view far into the Elster Valley. To the left was his old school. He just had to lean over the railing slightly to see it: two stories, long, brightly lit corridors between the rooms, the physics lab, the chemistry lab, Bunsen burners. Class started at ten minutes to seven. First the short warning bell, then the long final ring. At six thirty, breakfast—his parents had already left for work. Two rolls, already spread with jam, coffee substitute and milk from the blue thermos (the blue

35

thermos from his childhood, he suddenly saw it, alarmingly distinct, with the small dent, the chipped enamel, the slightly loose, unevenly stained seal on the screw top) and next to his plate, his mother's daily note:

"Dear Carl, Good luck with your physics assignment. Concentrate hard and avoid careless mistakes! Please light a fire when you get home, and don't forget the ashes . . ."

No letter, no news, day after day. When Carl was tired and distracted, he occasionally thought: they'll never leave. But they had left. Parents, to whom nothing really serious could happen. Separately after Giessen.

The refrigerator and the freezer were well stocked, the provisions from their old life, enough for weeks, months maybe. His mother had divided everything into servings, in milk cartons she had cut open neatly and washed thoroughly. From the faded blue script, Carl recognized that the cartons had been reused several times. He deciphered the words "Milking Parlor," words he liked. The combination of milk and parlor—now that was clear and powerful poetry. Each carton was sealed with a small rubber band. A small strip of cardboard with the contents and date was inserted under the elastic. He contemplated the frenetic handwriting slanting into the word's progression. *Refugee script*, Carl whispered into the freezer compartment and with a jolt the refrigerator sprang to life. In the appliance's drone he could hear his father's admonition to keep the door open as briefly as possible, not longer than two or three seconds: "You should know what you want beforehand. Concentrate."

After three weeks in Gera, he had to admit that he was no longer fit for anything. He could only manage to read for a few minutes, then he had to get up, to move. Because he didn't want to meet anyone or speak to anyone (especially not about his parents having disappeared without a trace), he only left the apartment at night, like an animal leaving its den under the cover of darkness. Sometimes he roamed the Gebind, that was the name of their neighborhood, seven *Altneubauten* apartment blocks, four stories tall as always, plus a few other buildings, rising in tiers on the hillside toward the forest. And sometimes he walked along the river, following their old walk to the Franzosen Bridge. He saw the shimmering black water of the Elster and up ahead the silhouettes of his parents, the leading man and lady of family traditions. He saw how his mother put her arm around his father's waist, laughed and pulled him close. Even as a child, he had not only felt boredom on their Sunday walks along the river, but also a certain sadness, about which he knew nothing specific. Maybe it was that he only ever followed the unit his parents formed from a certain distance, he slunk after them (so to speak) and so was left alone with the river, in which his fantasies drifted, whirled around, and, in the rapids, went under like an overloaded raft . . . When the stream of his thoughts grew too frenzied, he stood, rooted to the ground, and had to breathe, breathe, until it all calmed down again. Meanwhile, his parents drew ever farther away with the confident, perfectly matched steps of a thousand walks together.

He drank too much and talked to himself. He went to seed and did not write a single, serviceable line. Instead, he watched television all day and all night. The headlines and reports were always new, always more incredible: a call for a general strike and former government officials put under house arrest, some already in prison. The old order was falling apart with breathtaking speed. Accompanied by hard cider and preserved plums. The border dog kennels with the golden pines were still worth a report. In the kitchen, dirty dishes piled up, rubbish littered the floor, the smell of rot. At night, Carl tiptoed down to the cellar in his socks and noiselessly returned upstairs with fresh plunder. The cider was extremely sweet and gave him a heavy, piercing headache; maybe he drank too quickly.

Now and then, Carl lingered a bit downstairs. He felt listless and needed a rest before climbing the stairs. It was as if his parents' sudden departure had sucked all the available strength from him. Separately after Giessen. The missing persons reports increased: people from the East who had disappeared into the West without a trace, gone underground. People from the East who left their mothers, fathers, husbands and wives (and, yes, their children, too), crossed the border westward and vanished. This was *the* opportunity to change their lives. First the Iron Curtain, now a golden bridge. How easy it must be to do away with a few of these adventurers and freedom seekers, to bury them if some advantage could be drawn from it . . .

Should he drive to Giessen? Request an inquiry with the refugee registry? Or just start by filing a missing persons report? A hundred thousand people were underway, allegedly. A hundred thousand since the border was opened.

"You don't drive up to the gate of a refugee camp in your own car,"—*that's just not proper*, is how Carl had understood his father. It was in keeping with his respect for the process of escape in uncertain conditions. But above all, as Carl saw it, it accorded with his trusting nature—his confidence that a certain (good, proper) conduct would elicit a certain (good, proper) reaction. And maybe he was right. Maybe this kind of humility and penance was necessary for a refugee from the East. As extraordinary as the step they had taken was, and as chaotic and audacious as it all seemed, they wanted to do it *respectably*. They wanted to be good refugees, which made Carl's heart constrict. His poor parents. They would never make it. They weren't callous enough, their elbows not sharp enough. They weren't familiar with the worst things, they were too old, too fragile, too vulnerable, and they were schlepping a large, black case around with them.

Only now, down in the cellar, standing in front of the shelves of cider, did fear reach Carl. That is, it had been there for a while, the whole time, in fact. It squatted in the Anchor-brand canning jars, in the canned blood sausage, the pears and plums, it crouched in the dark corners and smelled of rat. It gnawed at the piles of old newspapers, chewing the paper into tiny shreds and spitting them out. It devoured the cyanide lures and didn't die, on the contrary, it grew.

Carl had lit a candle (the light hadn't worked for years) and leaned his back against the coal shelter. His gaze fell on his grandmother's armoire, which at some point had been brought down to the cellar and stowed between the potato clamp and the storage shelves. One corner of the armoire was charred. As a child, he had tried to set it on fire, dreamily and with great patience: Carl-the-stupid-child liked to stare into small fires, absently, without a single thought. On the wall facing him hung the large panel of his model train set, shrouded in ancient sheets. Through a gap you could see a landscape, a train station, little plastic people with their feet glued to the surface. All these things were composed of fear. Somewhere out there, history was raging, and his parents were roaming around in the middle of the turbulence.

MAGHRIB AL-AQSA

Sayings were in the air: "One after another." Or: "A fool takes on too much at once." And again and again, in his mother's warning tone: "You can't have everything. You can't have everything."

Carl let the apartment deteriorate, maybe that's why it started to exert pressure on him. It demanded of him, simply put, that he maintain the old life, as a stand-in. Afternoon coffee at the table in the front room at 4:30, bath day, garage day, and so on, the only possible sequence in this place. "We're abandoned, too, understand?" The television armchair by the window had spoken (his father's chair) and it wouldn't calm down, so Carl began talking to it: "Why it happened this way, I mean, what they *really* have in mind—we don't know. It's a kind of secret, you see, their life-secret."

Schenkendorff had slipped new forms under the door. On these, Carl's name was already filled in, the address, too, very neatly, in capital letters with a ballpoint pen. A fourteen-day registration deadline.

What was the point? It would have been easier to take the forms, exchange a few trivial words, and make something up. Carl realized that he was ashamed. He was ashamed that his parents had left "under the cover of darkness," as the neighbors would put it. After a few decades in the community, they'd simply disappeared without a word.

Because he refused to live according to the apartment's customs, there were mishaps. In the kitchen at night, in the dim light: he held the spoon upside down and the chalky liquid of a medication he'd wanted to take dripped from the dome of the spoon onto his shirt. Nothing serious, but the little accidents accumulated, creating a hostile atmosphere. A glass shattered and right away Carl stepped on a shard with his bare foot. He was seized with anger. Out there, borders were falling and he was stuck in Gera-Langenberg. Abandoned by God and the world, and above all by Walter and Inge. It was the first time that he felt the seed of offense.

He went into the kitchen, pulled aside the curtain and peered down the street. In the entire building (three staircases, four stories), only one family had a telephone line—the Schulers, who received the emergency calls. "Only for true emergencies, please," was the stipulation. If Mrs. Schuler appeared at your door, you knew that *something had happened*, and over the years it became impossible to see this neighbor from the next staircase without picturing some misfortune coming (or remembering a past misfortune). When Mrs. Schuler left her apartment, she usually had her dog with her, a wearied terrier mix whose head always sagged and who never barked. His entire life long, Carl would picture misfortune every time he saw one of those shaggy dogs—mute and with drooping ears. But snuffling and shameless, too.

The street was empty, and no phone call was good, very good actually. He had to learn to control his feelings; he shouldn't be so sensitive. Next to the sink stood an open bottle of cider. Carl finished it off, quickly, as if there were something he finally had to finish, then went to bed. It was late afternoon. He pulled the Meyers encyclopedia off the shelf and read. *Morocco*: Maghrib al-Aqsa (Arabic, "the western place"). Officially al-mamlaka al-maḡribiyya, kingdom in northwestern Africa. History, geography, Middle and High Atlas Mountains and "beyond the Atlas range, past a fringe of oases, the transition to the Sahara." There was a small map indicating natural resources, climate zones and the largest cities. Carl read the names out loud. Agadir, Tangier, Marrakesh, Fez, and then he repeated again and again: Fez, Fez. "Everyone has only one song," Paul Bowles, who lived in Tangiers, once said. Café Hafa, Pension L'Amour, tin roofs, cats, the Maghribi sun—his dreamed-of life, it was happening there. "That's where it will be," Carl whispered and fell asleep.

He dreamed of Corporal Bade, who counted seconds in the voice of a talking horse. A good thirty seconds and the guard had mustered in full uniform—field packs, steel helmets and weapons. Carl reported for duty and the horse began to whinny: "Eeeeeffffffiiiii—the only woman Soldier Bischoff eeehhver loved, or whaa-aat? Riiiiight, soldier? A good fuuuuck? Did you fuuuck Eeeff-fi?"

41

When Carl woke, bathed in sweat, it was midnight. Why did he dream of the army? As so often, in situations in which he felt confused and disoriented, stories from his past resurfaced: on the one hand, the perpetual longing for solace and redemption; on the other, bad decisions, missed opportunities, magical moments wasted—all those promising occasions before they had passed.

In his socks, Carl padded down to the cellar and returned with two fresh bottles. He was on the third floor (the Koberski family to the left, the Dix family to the right), when the door above sprang open—Schenkendorff! This time, he was waiting for Carl. Carl began to sprint, three steps at a time, but he slipped just before his goal. He threw the bottles into the air; it was a reflex. He tumbled into the apartment, kicked the door shut with his heels and hit his head on the wooden coatrack—all in a single movement.

For a moment, there was complete silence. Carl's ears became ice-cold.

From somewhere above his head, the doorbell's ringing rippled out over him. It carefully outlined his motionless body on the hallway floor. Effi knelt down on the other side of the door and asked "if a story wouldn't be nice."

"Yes, a story, please," Carl whispered.

"You do understand that things can't go on like this, Carl."

"No, Effi, not like this."

"Now listen."

ZHIGULI

First Carl drove to the post office on Zeitzer Strasse and explained to Mrs. Bethmann that all mail sent to his parents' address should be held at the branch to be collected: *poste restante* was the word. He filled out the relevant application, a short form.

"Poste restante," Mrs. Bethmann repeated, revealing a strip of her large white incisors.

"And for how long, Carl?" She was a beautiful woman about his mother's age, maybe a bit younger, her jet-black hair in a ponytail. When he was a child, she reminded Carl of Mireille Mathieu, who at the time was called the "sparrow of Avignon."

"Two months, maybe? Until the end of January? And I'll call regularly, here at the post office, I mean, to find out if anything has been received. Would that be possible, Mrs. Bethmann?"

Carl's embarrassment was palpable. On top of that, her inquiring look at the lump of bandage over his eyebrow. Mrs. Bethmann was in his mother's exercise group, ten or twelve women who met every week in the school gymnasium at seven in the evening on Thursdays—that alone would have been reason enough to ask about his injury. Carl took her silence on the subject as a sign of solidarity, rather than disapproval or indifference. She silently wished him luck and she surely also wished herself luck and maybe all the other residents of Gera-Langenberg as well. They'd all withstood life together up to this point, after all. It was as if the world were in an extremely sensitive, free-floating state, Carl thought, as if they'd only just begun to exist. Right here, right now, at the post office telegram counter.

From the post office, Carl drove back to the garage. Driving did him good. Finally he was responding to the great movement, which had seized everything and upended it, with his own movement. Carl had just turned off the road when a former classmate appeared; it was H. Strangely, H. had a dog with him that moved very slowly, as if in slow motion, with a half-hovering, half-shuffling gait. Its eyelids were oddly swollen, almost squinting. It headed straight for Carl, who took fright and sped up.

43

The white car with orange racing stripes on the roof and sides—seventies style. For a moment, Carl wondered if the Zhiguli had been *transferred* as well and now belonged to him. Surely not. And why not? Because the car was his father's, because the car was his father, and so on. A faint prickling slowly circled the arch of his left eye socket. It went away, then returned, but didn't grow stronger. It was just his eyebrow, a laceration, nothing more.

The windowless depths of the garage, the shimmering tool landscape on the walls, like a long sunken treasure. Yet only five weeks at the most had passed since his father had last adjusted the carburetor and bled the brakes. The endless care and maintenance. Garage Sundays and their liturgy.

Carl had his own, smaller toolbox of scratched green metal and his own *work blanket*, which he packed in the trunk of the car. It couldn't be a bad idea to have a blanket along with a sleeping bag, and just to be sure he chose a few extra, very useful tools and added them to his toolbox. Among them, the large, wooden-handled screwdriver and the feeler gauge. His eyes fell on his masonry tools, his old work bag, yes, why not, he packed it and various additional items (even his father's garage shoes) and tried not to put too much thought into it. He wasn't in any condition to do so. Was it possible that he'd never see his parents again? Carl swallowed and spoke loudly into the trunk: "They're doing well. They're doing well."

After midnight he parked the Zhiguli on top of the hill near the edge of the forest so that it couldn't be seen from the apartment block. The mailbox was empty. He immediately started cleaning the apartment, as thoroughly as he could. He tried to restore the old order, down to the last detail, as if nothing had happened. Everything ready and hospitable: welcome home, dears! He was fantasizing. He washed the dishes and carried the empty bottles back down to the cellar. He didn't linger, no extra farewell for the model train or the charred armoire. A small bloodstain on the hallway carpet, hardly noticeable.

The building was silent when Carl drove the car up to the door. For the final stretch, he turned off the motor and let the car glide. He opened the trunk. In the hallway stood a few things he had selected for the *trip*—or should he call it something else? Like a thief, he furtively carried the things downstairs, including his mother's portable typewriter, as well as a shoebox filled with maps and a few portions of frozen meat. He simply grabbed a few items, almost in a panic, without any thought or planning.

Finally, he crept back upstairs one last time and sat at the desk. The faint hum of the small, hidden fluorescent tubes. When he was a child, Carl had believed that a light always shone in his parents' secretary—a warm and cozy place where life was sustained, even overnight, so that it would still be there the next morning and could continue on and on, forever.

He wrote a letter to Storost Boarding House in Halle and asked the caretaker to pack the rest of his things in a crate. The lease for his room ran until the end of the year and strictly speaking there was nothing there that meant anything to him. After abandoning his studies, he had sold his most valuable possessions, piece by piece, to get by. First the shower unit, then the record player and finally—unbelievably, actually—his very first typewriter, an Erika, which had been a Christmas present from his parents, Christmas 1985, sold off in spring of 1989. And what he was doing now, wasn't that also a kind of betrayal? Desertion of the rearguard? Surrender of the hinterland? Or was he following their example? At least he still had Mrs. Bethmann, the sparrow of Avignon, whom he could call every day. And he had the Zhiguli. He would "look after it," as his parents had put it.

The very last thing Carl did in Gera: he took a clean sheet of paper and wrote to Effi. It was a final farewell in the form of a love letter. He told her that she would always be the only one for him. It sounded a bit too grandiose, given that they'd never been *together*—and never would be either, Carl thought. "How did you manage to appear to me constantly these past days?" He felt very close to Effi in that moment, even though it was just a letter, just the faint rasp of his hand on the paper, the gentle friction of writing.

It's certainly easy to claim that this was due to the mood of the times, to the hypnosis of departure. But in that moment, in that final minute at the desk in the apartment of his parents, who had more or less forced him to drop them off in a strange, damp meadow (with nothing more than a hunting rucksack on their backs) only to disappear without a trace, it was different. It was their strangely distant, decisive and, how should he put it, self-sacrificing conduct (that's how Carl experienced it now), that demanded a new truthfulness from him.

PART II

BEHIND THE SCREEN

A man stepped out onto the street heading toward the city center and raised his arm. It was three o'clock in the morning. Without a word of thanks, he got in the car and leaned back in the seat. They drove for a time without engaging in conversation. "Stop just up ahead," the man ordered and stuck a bill rolled into a cylinder the size of a cigarette between the heating vent louvers on the dashboard. Carl had heard about illegal cabs, but never imagined it would be so easy.

Just before Alexanderplatz, he turned onto a street that seemed suitable at first glance. It was called Linien Strasse. Only two streetlamps were working in the first hundred meters, and Carl parked the Zhiguli somewhere in the half-light between them.

The neighborhood was filled with three-story housing blocks from the fifties, maybe even from the thirties. With their dirty, plaster exteriors, they were ugly but at the same time familiar and trustworthy. Pigeons flew in and out of the semicircular dormers, also not a bad sign. But, most importantly, this neighborhood was quiet; it was downright *silent* even though it was right in the center of the city. Only at the last moment, already half-asleep, did Carl notice the disturbing noises—laughter, shouting and desperate screams that reached him from some nightmare.

In the first days, Carl made a few small rounds. He explored Berlin, but always returned to Linien Strasse to sleep. He drove to Kastanien Allee, which until now he had only known as the title of a book of poems, and he walked around aimlessly for a while. Carl was on an expedition. He could feel his heartbeat. Somewhere here, behind these facades, those good poems had been written and published in literary journals with titles like *Liane* or *Mikado*. Searching for their particular essence, Carl scrutinized the people on Kastanien Allee, in a respectful way— even though in Berlin such politeness might look foolish. In fact, he spotted more than a few who had that look of absolute necessity in their eyes, the necessity that could make a writer; and one or another of them already seemed deeply immersed in his or her solitary "I must," Rilke's dictum, which Carl, too, had followed ever since he'd come upon a volume of the *Letters to a Young Poet*. At the same time, Carl had the feeling on this street of being in a reserve, a district that was not easily accessible. In any case, he preferred to approach it carefully, not to rush anything. He heard the sound of his footsteps on the sidewalk's granite paving stones and understood how odd it was (in light of what was happening to him just then) to maintain the idea of a proper sequence, and this made him smile. "At four thirty in the stairwell / of 30 Kastanien Allee, there was a fleeting smell / of dead mice *lost in thought*." Carl knew the smell, dead and lost in thought – these were the first lines of *Kastanien Allee*, not a bad beginning for a volume of poetry.

Every evening, just before six, Carl phoned. For his calls to Gera, he used a post office on Kollwitzplatz that he had noticed on one of his forays through the streets of good poems. For long-distance calls, it had a narrow wooden cubicle with a tiny window in the door through which you could see the counters. Every time he called Mrs. Bethmann, she had a kind word ready for him.

"Your parents' letters are surely being held temporarily some-where, in some postal warehouse or other at the border. That certainly wouldn't be surprising, Carl, in all the chaos."

"Yes, of course. Thank you, Mrs. Bethmann." He took a deep breath and pressed the receiver to his ear.

"Where are you now, Carl?"

Her voice sounded like it was coming from the middle of a snowstorm, from somewhere, in any case, that seemed much farther away than Gera. Carl was not used to phoning (to talking into a machine). It annoyed him. Ultimately, you didn't know if the other person truly existed.

"Carl?"

Now and then, he picked up taxi fares. Either it happened without trying or all he had to do was drive slowly through the streets and, with his head angled slightly, look at the passersby on the sidewalk with some interest. His vague intention to earn some money as quickly as possible had soon taken shape. Gas cost 2.50 marks a liter, and his reserves (the 500 marks from his parents) would be used up in a few weeks even if he were frugal.

The Wilhelm-Pieck Strasse that ran parallel to Linien Strasse (its quiet backstreet) proved fruitful. This was particularly true on nights Jojo was open. Jojo was on the lowest floor of a new, red-tiled building—two aluminum-framed windows, neon lights and a disco ball. Only once had Carl pushed his way through the sticky, completely packed rooms and made it to the bar that stood behind a glass partition covered with posters. These posters didn't advertise bands, just DJs with names like Trent, Heretsch and Pichground. They didn't serve beer, only wine and mixed drinks. The woman at the bar wore a dove-gray top covered with small zippers. "Ice?" For a moment, Carl had no idea what she meant. The option of ice cubes in his drink was a novelty. In honor of Hemingway he drank something called Cuba Libre, Club-Cola with Wilthener Goldkrone brandy—he recognized the label in the dim light. Almost everything was mixed with Club-Cola and there were bouncers everywhere, at the bar, at the door, even on the dance floor. Club-Cola, order, and baby faces: they wore their hair above their foreheads cut short and straight, long in the back, and the outline of giant combs protruded from the pockets of their marbled jeans—it was all detestable. Right behind Carl, a fifteen-, maybe sixteen-year-old girl was dancing. She spun around and looked at him, her arms (wings) raised helplessly, her eyes half-closed. "She's like the wind."

Carl felt old and dirty in Jojo and he was sweating because he didn't want to take off his leather jacket. It wasn't just that he was out of place there, it was more than that. For a moment, he had the sneaking suspicion that the world he belonged to had furtively disappeared and he was one of its remnants, a rotting piece of driftwood on the great, broad stream of the new times.

In the morning, Carl aired out his car. He carefully rolled up his faded cotton sleeping bag, wiped clear the fogged-up windshield and put the seat back upright.

"Piss off!" was written in the dirt on the rear window. The idea that someone was looking at his face at night while he was sleeping was unnerving. And didn't people usually write "pig" or "wash me" instead? On top of that, did people usually leave a signature: "Milva"—who was that supposed to be? Carl briefly considered covering the car windows with towels (which he didn't have) at night or taping up newspaper (which he could get ahold of), but not being able to see what was going on outside spooked him even more.

For the first time, it was completely clear to Carl that he didn't know anyone in Berlin. He only knew a few poems that had been written here; nothing else had pushed him to come. Yes, to some extent he was imitating his parents' self-imposed exile—as if that were also a way (the real way) to be a good son after he had, in defiance of all agreements, abandoned his post in the hinterland.

Like his parents, he had his sights set on no address; he had left without a destination, just some fantasy in mind, but no bed.

For breakfast, he walked to a bistro on Alexanderplatz where he could use the toilet to wash and brush his teeth. The bistro was below the Presse Café, a meeting place for people who looked like they knew their destination.

The bistro was actually too expensive for him and there were hardly ever any other customers, but it was the first place Carl went to after he arrived in Berlin, so he remained loyal. He ordered scrambled eggs with brown bread, which the waiter toasted to rock-hard slices and Carl softened again with butter, jam and eggs. He was served at the counter; Carl liked this at first (he found it cosmopolitan), but later didn't. This had to do with the waiter and his big-city arrogance. His eyes were full of disdain. He deplored the tousled hair that hung down past Carl's shoulders; he deplored Carl's unshaven, sleepy face and everything else about him that was easily scorned: the motorcycle jacket, the unkempt fingernails, the toothpaste-flecked pouch with his toiletries, etc. Carl was sure the waiter was cheating him in some way or other. You too will hear of me one day, Carl thought. "One day" was the date when his first book would appear; Carl dreamed of that day. After a few visits, he managed to take his plate and retreat to a seat at the window.

He took out his notebook but as soon as he opened it, he felt tired and couldn't think of a single thing to write. His last entry: "It will take your whole life, absolutely every moment from the day you were born. It wants to call the shots without revealing any more of itself—simply demonic!" What happened if it wanted you and you weren't suited? An aberration, a false connection? Maybe at twenty-six he was already too old to seriously go about becoming a poet.

Carl awkwardly fished a ballpoint pen out of the hole-ridden lining of his motorcycle jacket and wrote:

12 DECEMBER

On the other side of the intersection lies Alexanderplatz. There is no greater desolation.

Two days later, the temperature dropped to five below Celsius. Carl sat in the Zhiguli with a bottle of brandy, picturing a film about gold prospectors in Alaska. A careless, inexperienced prospector who had almost frozen to death is revived with brandy. "Take a swig of this," a flinty but good man says to the half-frozen prospector. Then the bottle is brought to his mouth and at first it looks like the man is being forced to drink against his will, as if a certain amount of effort is required: small, burning sips, heavy breathing. Gently but firmly, a small dose of consolation is poured into him, you can read it on the two men's faces, most clearly in their eyes. The consolation is pivotal.

Before going to sleep Carl whispered, "Take a swig of this," to his pale reflection frozen on the windshield where the Klondike story was playing. That evening he didn't turn on the reading light over the dashboard – he was exhausted and wanted to remain hidden. "It's better for the battery too," he explained softly and stowed the bottle. His cheek touched the brown leatherette of the seat back, stitched in broad stripes. It was ice-cold. He pulled in his knees and bunched his sweater under his head. He envied the couples that passed by on the sidewalk. He listened to the melody of their conversations and to the sounds of the trams, first a dull rumbling followed by a high note on the curves, then quiet again. He pictured his parents from a distance: in a long, dark column in the snow, wearing army backpacks and hiking boots; his father carrying a small coffin on his back, the accordion; a strenuous climb on a mountain path, farther and farther west, following the call of gold.

Carl thought of Effi and pleasured himself. It went very quickly. He was freezing, only his forehead and his dick were hot. Maybe he had a fever. As he was falling asleep, he heard a woman's footsteps. The hard, metallic metronome of her heels on the pavement, tack-tock-tack, just-fuck-off. Then laughter and screaming again, but they were just practicing, they practiced far into the night—the day before Carl had discovered that the fortress-like facade on the other side of the street was the back of a theater called the Volksbühne.

The cold woke him around four o'clock. Half-asleep, he crawled forward, cranked the seat back upright and started the engine. He could rely on the Zhiguli's heater, built as it was for Asiatic winters. "Better than Mercedes," his father had said.

He drove with his left hand on the steering wheel. His right rested on the gear shift's dark knob. It was a pleasant, fluid drive. The Zhiguli practically rolled on its own and Carl could daydream. He liked the sound of the radial tires on cobblestones, so he sought out cobblestone streets—up and down the gloam of Schönhauser Allee, for example, with the rumbling and grumbling under the cobblestones' skulls, until he warmed up. And with the rumbling, the dull ocean sound of the fan, wind and warmth on his cheeks. The Zhiguli ran as if on tracks that Carl had laid out ahead and the warmth enveloped him. It was pleasant and he felt almost as if he were asleep again. At some point he turned on the radio and the windshield turned into a television screen. Someone on the radio said that repairs would cost one billion, that would be the price for the broken-down East. At the words *one billion* the speaker's voice started to glow. Carl could hear the glow and a pre-Christmas light fell on the steering wheel's chrome-plated spoke. Carl wondered if he was part of the calculation, *included in the cost,* and if so, at what value.

In the news there was a report on new border checkpoints. It was often hard to work out which street in the West was an extension of which one in the East—Carl had learned this in his cabbing. The connections had been lost somehow. Again and again you came across dull, empty spaces, old wounds suddenly reappearing: half of the city was a knotted landscape of scars. Carl turned the radio dial. It was intoxicating to drive this way. The windshield showed a film about streets and facades starting to remember how things used to be, what it was like to be a complete city, undivided, and that was the moment when someone said Carl's name over the radio. Carl was startled. He braked and skidded over the cobbles to the side of the road.

". . . Radio P . . . is Radio P . . . ellow sol . . . our meeting pl . . ."

He tried to tune in better but lost the signal. He attributed it to his fever, if it was a fever. To his left a subway train rumbled in the depths and in the next moment the voice returned. A long list of names was being read out, monotonous and full of pathos, as if it were a list of victims or missing persons. At some point Carl realized that these were street names, house numbers, addresses, a front line.

Then it was over. Carl rolled down the car window, took a deep breath and steered the car back onto the street. The meat in the car trunk gave off a terrible smell; Carl found it hard to get rid of the meat. Simply throwing it in the garbage would have been sacrilege and another betrayal. That's what was so confusing about his sudden lack of parents: he reacted like a child. He still wanted to be a good son, a good orphan, Carl thought, and immediately felt ashamed of this nonsense.

The third Sunday in Advent. Shortly after midnight Carl bolted awake. His entire body trembled. Around him reigned deep, shadowless darkness. Once, when he was a child, dried pus from conjunctivitis had so completely encrusted his eyes that he woke in the morning but could only stare into the swaying darkness behind his closed eyelids. A few seconds of mute panic, then his scream: "I'm blind!" He lay in bed, screaming, and didn't understand that the necessary action for sight (opening his eyes) hadn't even been taken yet.

Another attack of the chills. Carl pulled himself together and felt for the cigarette lighter. The small ring immediately began to glow. It wasn't him, it was Berlin. Berlin had reverted to a primal state of utter darkness, "a time before God," Carl murmured and resolved to write this down later, but he forgot.

He peeled himself out of his sleeping bag, which took determination even though the faded cotton fabric didn't really warm him. He felt ill. When he opened the passenger door, something fine and damp silently slid onto his lap—snow! It had snowed. "We're completely snowed in here outside, Zhiguli and I." The last radio message, we're all in despair down here on earth. A pigeon flew over the street.

It took a while for Carl to lock the car and shake off the sense of being in outer space—his hands shook. He had to walk, to get moving and he stamped a Young Pioneers song into the sidewalk: "Take wing, white dove, bring peace . . ." He slipped and had to giggle, then he began to jog.

Even the lobby in Jojo was crammed with people. You had to press the back of your hand, an arm, or your forehead against the glass of the front door for it to be opened. To get in, you had to show a stamp on your skin somewhere. Carl realized that he had no chance of getting in that night. Still out of breath, he turned into the entrance of the next courtyard to relieve himself somewhere. The steam from his urine enveloped him and as he gradually regained full consciousness, he heard fine, melancholy music. Carl pushed through the shrubbery that overran the courtyard and approached the side wall. The music grew louder, someone would say something and another person would answer very calmly, in short sentences, but it was not a normal conversation.

"What have you been doing all these years?"

"I've been going to bed early."

Again, music.

Carl noticed a steel door, gray and edged with rust, all but invisible. A few seconds later he was standing in front of the man who went to bed early. His figure seemed to undulate slightly when Carl entered. Then Carl was grabbed, not roughly but firmly.

It felt good to give in. It even felt good to fall to the floor. He landed on a heavy piece of cloth, maybe an old velvet curtain. The dusty smell of stage sets, perspiration and stale air. To the right and left of him, a few people cuddled together. The cinema auditorium must be on the other side. They were looking at the film's mirror image. The crafty pack in its den, Carl thought.

Although it wasn't especially cold behind the screen, Carl got the chills again. It was unpleasant because during the quiet scenes you could hear how he froze. He clamped his teeth together and contracted his muscles. Someone stretched out a hand toward him and very quietly asked a question. The hand was cool and smelled of nicotine and a mixture of light oil and rust, a construction site odor, fundamentally familiar.

"Yes," Carl replied.

His eyes gradually got used to the darkness behind the screen, but he didn't dare turn his head to the side. He recognized a curtain with the inscription "theater 89." Because of the film he hadn't understood a single word, but he wanted the hand and the concerned voice to stay, so he quietly repeated once more: "Yes."

The small, cool hand slowly began to roam over his body. It was not a caress; there was no particular tenderness in its movement. It was rather a kind of anamnesis, an assessment of his outline, his dimensions. It was a measuring, an evaluation, done carefully and without haste. Carl accepted the hand. He didn't move but eventually it became unavoidable. He had swelled under the hand and met it with a small movement. The hand disappeared immediately, and Carl felt the withdrawal. He had grown hard, partly of stone, which surely had something to do with his fever; in a few seconds he was going to explode. The hand had realized this. It returned and calmed him.

"Oranienburger Strasse," whispered the voice he now felt deep inside, the hand's voice.

"Yes," Carl whispered and fell silent.

For a length of time that was difficult to describe exactly, his cock lay in the small, cool construction site hand. For a long time, the hand simply held him firmly but then it serviced him with a craftsperson's skill in a strong and well-balanced fashion.

ONCE UPON A TIME

When Carl woke, he was lying on a rough mattress which gave off an animal smell; he was drenched in sweat. He could vaguely make out a doorframe with a dwarf leaning nonchalantly against it. At the head of the mattress stood a glass of milk. It was a jam jar filled to the brim with milk.

"A small greeting from the future," murmured someone he couldn't see or who was only in his mind. Without a second thought, Carl picked up the glass of milk.

"Where are you from, Zhiguliman?"

The milk was rich and tasted good. Carl drank the entire glass and closed his eyes. Again, he pictured the crafty pack. The film was over and they apparently assumed he was one of them. Perhaps simply because he had come in through *their door*, right into their hiding place behind the screen. Only later did Carl realize that it must have also had something to do with the film they had seen together. Suddenly there was a connection, a shared destiny—that strange word, which no longer struck him

59

as overblown. But above all it was connected to the woman who held him by the arm as if he were a war invalid and pushed him out into the cold, dark courtyard.

"You can always tell the winners at the starting gate," she repeated, and laughed. She was wearing a crudely sewn fur cap and a dark blue winter jacket, like the ones Carl knew from construction sites, along with felt boots and a wool skirt (unless it was a very long sweater), under which she had on black wool stockings, maybe several pairs over each other, which preoccupied Carl pointlessly in his feverish state. She was not tall, but she was sturdy. She was called Ragna, sometimes Reggae, too. Her face was white with large, smooth cheeks. Carl had never seen such fair skin before. Then there were her eyebrows, thick and black, as if drawn in ink.

The whole pack wanted to *go for a drive*, which was impossible, but then again not entirely impossible. They jumped around the Zhiguli like children and brushed the snow off of the windshield. The snow hadn't stuck anywhere else, and it didn't feel very cold anymore, not wintery cold anyway. Maybe it had only snowed on Linien Strasse, on the Zhiguli. Because it's Russian, Carl thought and longed for snow.

They cheered and shouted when the shock absorbers bottomed out. Carl found the muffled banging painful. Every blow to the chassis was a blow to what he was supposed to be protecting as the rearguard or hidden reserves or whatever. He tried to drive carefully but the street was in terrible shape and everything blurred by fever. Six people sat on the back seat, next to and on top of each other. In the passenger seat sat a large, broad-shouldered guy, who gave Carl directions. Maybe he was their leader. His name was Hoffi. Ragna called him the Shepherd. On the Shepherd's lap sat a boy with steel-blue hair, beating some crazy rhythm on the dashboard. The glove compartment sprang open and Carl's toiletries tumbled out and the blue boy caught them. He waved Carl's toothbrush triumphantly in his fist. "Let's drive to Vegas and scrub the sun!"

"Easy now, Kleist," the Shepherd said and held the boy gently in his arms. Now he was the giant with a bird in his hand, taking great care not to break its bones.

". . . scrub the sun," the bird crowed again and everyone laughed.

"Up there on the left," the Shepherd ordered. He looked for the cigarette lighter. Carl turned the ceiling light on: a flash of metal-rimmed spectacles and a beard that tapered to a neat braid, into which the pits of some fruit had been woven—Carl's last clear image on that night. Then a passageway, some hole in the wall. In his fever, Carl thought the crafty pack had just set him to the side (disposed of him), the dying animal in a corner.

Now and again, Carl woke from his feverish sleep. Ragna stayed at his side when he had to make his way to the toilet. She supported him to some wooden lean-to and, yes, she assisted him (or he imagined it). He heard her speaking softly to him but he didn't understand a thing. Someone answered, maybe him, maybe another person. Then darkness and silence returned.

The room was low-ceilinged and not particularly large. When Carl raised his head, he made out the silhouette of an enormous, upholstered chair that resembled an electric chair from an era long past. The little person, he recognized now, was a large package of toilet paper that had been torn open. There were two small windows, covered with bedsheets, just below the ceiling. On the other side of the room was a rusted construction lamp. Next to it stood two dully gleaming appliances on wheels that turned on and off with a soft clicking noise. Later Carl remembered most clearly this barely audible clicking and how it had calmed him. At the time, he wasn't familiar with the term "oil radiator." What he saw were light-brown friends on wheels with glowing, red eye-lamps, warm metal sheep that gleamed in the dark, gleamed and clicked and radiated a profound confidence.

After three days, his fever had been sweated out. Something was happening to his mattress; someone was trying to push him off it. Carl spun around and saw the animal. Its head hung over him, very close and inquiring. It looked him directly in the eye, not aggressively, merely surprised: the bristly white hair, the extraterrestrial pupils—a goat, without a doubt.

"'From the ruins risen newly,' as the old song goes!"

Hoffi, the Shepherd. He pulled the bedsheets off the window and opened it. Fresh, cold air streamed in, a streetcar trundled past, footsteps, the sounds of the city.

"Come, Dodo!" He pushed the goat aside with his arm and handed Carl a newly filled glass.

"Goat milk, my friend! It heals everything. Measles, diarrhea, depression . . ." He crouched next to Carl and laid a hand on his forehead.

"Do you think you can stand, Zhiguliman?"

The goat had taken a bite out of the ticking and was trying to eat the straw out of the top of the mattress. Carl saw its extended muzzle, its powerful teeth. Its coat was snow-white.

"You're lying on Dodo's fodder."

"On her fodder?" It was the first thing Carl had managed to say. He had started speaking again, but it was more of a croaking.

"On her winter feed. And now we'll go get some breakfast, too, Zhiguliman. Did you like the milk?"

He wore a cloak, a kind of poncho, and a brown sweater vest with a V-neck into which he had stuffed the braided end of his beard. In his left hand he held a small pail and in his right an iron rod that ended in a sharp hook, with which he scratched the goat's back. "Come, Dodo, come." Carl listened to the mesmerizing softness of his voice. Assisi of Berlin, Carl thought. The saint dexterously caught the ring on the goat's collar with the hook of his halberd. A quick, energetic tug and together they left the cellar.

"Dodo loves the salty taste," the Shepherd explained. "Sometimes it's seaweed. Straw or seaweed, saturated with the sweat of sleep, of dreams, of screwing, soaked with the juices of illness and the exhalations of the final moment—the salt of life, you could say, understand, Zhiguliman? Dodo is hooked on it. She chews and swallows it all and makes her magic milk out of it."

"Straw to gold," Carl replied quick-wittedly. For this kind of repartee, he was actually never quick enough but sometimes he just blurted things out, a found moment. The Shepherd turned to face him and smiled amicably.

"There's just one problem: humanity wants to die on spring core mattresses! That is, straw is rare, increasingly rare. That's why we're collecting these mattresses on our forays, more or less on the side. It's the best fodder in winter, that's all."

Their path led from cellar to cellar and Carl soon lost his bearings. It was hard enough for him to stay on his feet. What hadn't escaped him was that the Shepherd kept mentioning the word *Assel*, woodlouse. He called the whole thing *the woodlouse*. It was a code, no doubt, maybe an alias, one of the things that Carl didn't understand here. Maybe I should be on my guard, Carl thought, but he felt too weak—and he was hungry.

In the courtyard, the Shepherd released the goat from his hook and it immediately disappeared into a dilapidated side building. Carl only registered many of the details later: the old coach house, the sheds and the so-called park, a kind of jungle over which a dilapidated wing of the building towered. "This old building is Dodo's domain, both her stall and her climbing rock, a place of complete and utter freedom."

They crossed a large terrace, from which a door led into the main building. The water on the terrace was frozen and crunched softly under their shoes.

*

Too many details for Carl to process in his state: first a woman had come up to them and given the Shepherd a quick but tight hug. She wore a thick turtleneck pullover and wide-leg pants: she was very elegant.

"Lil sis, this is Zhiguliman. He lives with us now, more or less. And this is Irina, the Princess of the Oranienburgers—and my sister," the Shepherd explained without looking at Carl.

"Do you feel better?" the woman asked and examined Carl.

Her glittering eyes, her long blond hair.

"What's your name?"

"Carl. Carl Bischoff, I was . . ."

"Let's get something to eat first," the Shepherd interrupted him and even though Carl kept talking, mostly to express his gratitude (he nearly bowed, in fact), and even though Irina gave some kind of answer, the table remained very quiet. As if they'd only spoken in their thoughts or as if the questions were first gathering elsewhere. The bubbling sound of boiling water evaporated the last of his anxiety and spread warmth. Things were cozy, pleasant, and there was the smell of coffee.

They sat around a thin table, placed diagonally in the room. Carl had seen a few of the faces in the rearview mirror, insubstantial, blurry. He recognized the girl they called Ragna—she had been looking at him then very directly and attentively. She had placed her fur cap before her on the table like soldiers did. Carl saw her jet-black hair for the first time.

The room was large and expanded in the glare of the gallery lighting—small spotlights screwed onto thin wires extended over the counter of an open kitchen. In the light, the pack seemed like a random group of people, in any case not of the same type, thought Carl. Irina, or the Princess, circled the table and poured from a glass pitcher. She touched each person briefly; she laid a hand between Carl's shoulder blades, very lightly, as if in passing, completely naturally while she was turned away, talking to someone else, explaining something. Everything about her exhaled generosity. "I haven't been in the city very long," had been Carl's last sentence and it now echoed constantly in his mind. He felt dirty and he probably reeked of goat.

The breakfast was unusual. A few things that Carl had never seen before stood on the table: for example, something that Irina called a *starfruit* and next to it, so-called *avocados*. They were cut in half and the Shepherd squeezed lemon juice over them. The avocados had large brown pits, which the Shepherd put in his mouth, sucked clean, then spat out and stowed in a small inner pocket on his poncho.

For a while they quietly discussed their concerns and paid no attention to Carl. The main topic was the building. The Shepherd had divided the residents into three groups: "cooperative," "odd" and "intractable." The cooperative ones had already made their basements "available." Then they discussed other buildings and, if Carl understood correctly, the savviest way to take possession of them.

The man sitting across from Carl stood up without a word and started cooking fried eggs. He wore heavy work boots (with steel-capped toes), black pants and a brown tracksuit top zipped up to his throat. His name was Henry but the Shepherd only called him "the good painter." As evidence, he had shown Carl a painting. It hung to the right of the passageway to the front room, bright with morning sun, and so Carl couldn't see the painting clearly in the backlight. It was an animal in motion, a galloping creature that stormed through the air into the room, toward the viewer, on legs or stumps which streamed with something like blood; the energy of its forward momentum was so strong and realistic that Carl found it hard to turn his gaze away from it.

With everyone's eyes on him, the good painter brought the frying pan to the table and slid fried eggs onto the plates, silently and solicitously. Carl was fascinated by how calm and even his movements were. A man named Hans made a joke, but the good painter merely smiled and stayed focused. As if every fiber of his being kept him in contact with the real, with the secret center of this world. He is already very far advanced, Carl thought, he carries it within. And I'm outside somewhere, in the void. None of his verses could stand beside the galloping animal.

"Maybe you'd like to bring some of your meat in and cook it?"

Irina had suddenly addressed Carl. Her hand touched his arm and Carl blushed.

Of course they'd smelled it.

"I think it's . . . not very fresh anymore."

"We could still use it as feed when the border dogs come," Hoffi murmured.

Whatever the Shepherd had in mind, he was serious. He didn't joke about the meat and Carl was grateful to him for that.

"Meat and tools. You have a ton of tools in your trunk, Zhiguliman. Do you know how to use them?"

"They're my tools."

"Your tools." He nodded with satisfaction. "Good tools, right, Ragna?"

Ragna nodded too. She had hardly said a word for all of breakfast and hadn't looked at him either. Carl swallowed and took a deep breath . . .

"No, no, Zhiguliman, you don't have to explain anything here. More than a few people are on the move in this freshly liberated city. The whole world is being parceled up anew these days—but if you're looking for something permanent . . ."

The Shepherd looked him in the eye. The expression *something permanent* hit home for Carl; maybe he wasn't the great adventurer he thought he was.

". . . then unfortunately there wouldn't be any place for you here, Carl."

He had called Carl by name and said "unfortunately."

"What do you think, Ragna? 20 has also already been allocated but we'll think of something, won't we?" He smiled—open and gentle. It was a victor's smile but without any hint of scorn or superiority. "As a worker, as a traveling worker, you've earned our solidarity, Zhiguliman."

After breakfast, Carl had showered in Irina's bathroom, which was along the terrace. He also left a few pieces of clothing there to launder—the Assel-Princess had offered. She had come into the bathroom and seen him naked; it didn't matter. It was as if he were already part of the pack, as if he were of the same breed. Everything seemed already embedded according to a long-standing plan and leading toward the only logical conclusion. It was a strange feeling. It was the presentiment of a legend (if there is such a thing, thought Carl), on the point of taking him into its profound, all-embracing "once upon a time."

Before they left Oranienburger Strasse, Ragna led him downstairs again, back to the place the Shepherd had called the Assel. Something made it clear to Carl that his feelings for Ragna were improper and misplaced. Maybe it was her felt-booted gait, her wool stockings, her low, hoarse voice. Or her fur cap that looked like it had been made with a stone needle, a rare object passed down from ancient and early history, a den for her pitch-black hair, coarse and warm.

"Some of the tenants are very old. Irina takes care of them, talks with them, runs errands, does their paperwork. They haven't come down here for a very long time. Most of them have transferred their cellars to Irina and the Shepherd, for the most part voluntarily."

They crossed the courtyard and came to a small porch with a half-height lean-to. It was more of a hatch, a cabin door, and behind was a narrow flight of brick stairs leading into the depths. Carl saw Ragna's hand feeling for some old-fashioned light switch. It was this hand. How could he get her to take up the measuring again? He longed for it. Or, no, that was a lie, he craved it, like Dodo craved the salt of life, Carl thought.

"Basically, it's this entire basement floor. To make it easier for the tenants to understand, Irina calls it a place for meeting and exchange. And why not? A little market, natural products and goat milk for vegetables, free trade, without money, an anti-capitalist underground kolkhoz, so to speak, that, too, would be possible in a stronghold of the aguerrillas."

Carl heard this strange word for the first time. Ragna said it in a near whisper, as if she were telling a secret.

The large part of this basement had no light. Ragna explained that the room where Carl had sweated out his fever had once been a small apartment with a hair salon: "But then, in the fifties, a law was passed that officially forbade living in basements. The hair salon shut down, as did the small egg shop opposite." She pointed into the darkness. "The egg lady is still alive, in the building next door. A very strange, evil woman."

"Evil?"

Ragna kept talking, softly. She showed him the door to Dr. Fenske's cellar. "Fenske went to school with Günter Grass, in Gdansk, at least he claims he did. And now he refuses to share his cellar." Carl thought about the connection while Ragna took a small knife from her bag and picked the lock. "It's the biggest room down here, with a vaulted ceiling. It used to be part of the left wing of the building, which was torn down after the war, at least the part above ground."

Carl could see a row of crutches propped against the wall and a jumbled collection of boots covering part of the floor, like a fragment of a mass exodus.

"Those are just left-foot boots," Ragna whispered, "leather and rubber boots. Irina says he collected them in the streets after the war. She says the crutches come from Gdansk and the boots from Berlin and Fenske doesn't want anything changed down here. Irina is still negotiating with him. I think she'll manage, she has these skills . . ."

"What skills?"

They were standing in the light of a construction lamp and Ragna explained to Carl what would need to be done, the sequence of the construction work: masonry, wiring, installation. It sounded presumptuous. Like felt boots on thin ice.

"Brandenburg-style," Carl said, to show her which of them was the bricklayer. Ragna just nodded and laid her small, cold hand on a brick that protruded slightly from the rough wall. As soon as she touched it, a few greasy, shiny gray bugs crept out of the sandy caulking.

"Woodlice. Endless woodlice. They're everywhere down here," Ragna whispered. "And they seem to like our bricklayer."

She looked at him and for a moment, Carl imagined creeping inside her, into this woman of fleece and wool, and disappearing there forever.

27 RYKE

Elderberry and birch trees, undergrowth. A copse had grown up in the bomb crater and a narrow path led through it to the house. Without hesitating, Ragna stepped into the thicket and Carl followed her. She carried a brown leather bag with copper clasps, a kind of midwife's bag. Something glittered on the path, a multi-colored stone, a piece of tile maybe. The brushwood grew almost up to the apartment building, only to the left of the door to the stairwell was there a small, paved area with three ashcans and a fire pit encircled with temporary seats, fruit crates and stones.

"Where the watch sits at night," Ragna murmured, but Carl was sure he had misheard her.

Even in the copse, Ragna had begun walking stealthily. She was now bent forward and treading lightly on her feet. They climbed down a half-collapsed outside staircase and crossed the building. The basement corridor was flooded. "It wasn't always like this," Ragna said as if looking back over decades. "The ground here is just hard-packed dirt, like in the olden days." She balanced on a few fieldstones that stuck out of the water like smooth, round skulls. Carl braced himself and felt the wall's streaky dampness; a smell of rot and mildew hung in the air, and they had to breathe it in.

At the end of the corridor was a flight of stairs that led back up to the ground floor in a second courtyard. Actually, it wasn't so much a courtyard as a shaft, a ravine. They crouched there for a while and observed the building. It looked dismal from the back, crumbling gray, as blank as a gravestone from which time had washed away the inscriptions but not the bullet holes. "Only the rear building survived under heavy fire," Ragna whispered. Garbage lay strewn all around, overgrown with stubborn brown weeds that looked particularly lush and gave off a greasy gleam. It's all ugly, Carl thought, but still, it felt good to sit next to Ragna, shoulder to shoulder, backs against a shed wall, on this dirty stretch of moon surface. She had pushed back her cap and he wanted to kiss her right then.

Ragna pointed to a couple of windows on the fourth floor. "How do you like it here?"

The woman in the half-open doorway wore a dressing gown of thin silk and carried a child in one arm. For a while, she just stood there, short, slender and blinking, then she gave Ragna a hug and Ragna kissed the baby's head. The door closed and Carl stayed behind alone.

The stairwell was ice-cold. All the doors had two eyes, small, glass portholes at chest height, probably an early form of peephole. Most of the eyes were taped up or painted over, everything looked temporary and worn-out. The glass was missing from the woman and child's portholes (there was no name on the door); she had stuffed a colorless rag into the opening, maybe a diaper, Carl thought. The walls of the stairwell were plastered with posters from the floor to the ceiling. They were eaten away by saltpeter—strangely, they were mostly filled with fruit motifs: posters with gleaming cherries, apples, plums, out of which mortar crumbled. Also peculiar was the strong rope (more of a cable) that ran up all the floors, loosely wound around the banisters.

"This is Arielle," Ragna said, and Arielle took a half-step out of the door. The thin silk dressing gown over her chest had slipped a little. The baby was tugging at it. With impressive nonchalance, the young mother asked if he was alone or *en famille.*

She's nineteen at the most, Carl thought. He stared past her but could still see her well; he also saw the mess in her entryway. Something told him that the baby had just nursed, the warmth the mother and child radiated, perhaps, that so-called "milk radiance." They had slept before the baby nursed. They'd been at home the entire day and at that moment a certain sadness reigned. And there's something else I can't quite read, Carl thought. It was written in the waves of warmth. It was a clear, enticing, almost naive frequency, easy to catch, probably even through the wall.

My parents have been missing since right after the opening of the border, that is, I'm alone now and am looking for a den for just me and my writing, in my search for the transition, more precisely, the passage into a poetic existence.

"No, I'm alone," Carl said, but didn't stop there. He repeated the dumbest sentence in his head, only, in fact, because it was ready and waiting, because the dumbest things always swim on the surface of the mind: "I haven't been in the city long."

Without waiting for his answer, Ragna had snapped open the clasps on her midwife bag and turned to face the neighboring flat. Carefully, as if she were starting a complicated ritual, she pressed her hand to the door right between the two glass eyes and listened. Evenly breathing silence, which meant the flat was healthy. In the next step she explained to Carl what it was necessary to pay attention to before opening a flat (she called it "opening")—the case history, as it were, "which we'll skip now, of course, because in this case it's known," Ragna said. "It certainly is," Arielle said and gave the baby, who was asleep, a kiss.

Ragna's lesson also had a theoretical, more bureaucratic part, which concerned the water supply, the electricity, and the relevant housing administration, in this case it was Alscher, Ragna told him, Alscher Property Management, specializing in Jewish property. "On the one hand, this means that next to nothing is done for these buildings, to say the least. On the other, it means that no one has monitored these buildings very closely and now they are essentially left to themselves, like leaky, derelict boats foundering in the sea of this city, and at some point they sink, with or without their crew—which makes no difference to *them*, but it does to *us*, understand, Zhiguliman?"

She pushed her Stone Age cap off her forehead and smiled at Carl. She had said "the least."

Smoothly, Ragna took this and that tool from her bag, approached the door and simulated its use. It was the final and shortest part of her instruction. At the end, she took a step back and handed Carl a pry bar.

"A good lever and the way you go at it, I mean *with feeling*, that's the whole secret."

The door panel was loose. Carl rattled it tentatively. It was a test, a competition between workmen. Now he could show that he was up to it—a childhood and youth in the garage, then on construction sites . . . While he had a crack at the door,

Ragna lectured him on the characteristics of door locks from the turn of the century, the upkeep of which requires "only a little knowledge," something no one is prepared to muster even though all it takes is a single drop of quality oil "now and then." Now and then a small, firm, cold hand, thought Carl; fundamentally, every manual skill has a sexual core, a context that eventually becomes invisible and is lost, the way the languages of defunct professions gradually fade and then are completely forgotten. What would come was a world without handwork, an artificial world, ultimately without bodies. The door panel bounced against the frame with a hollow sound, a cry rose, a shadow descended:

"First the crowbar! Drop the crowbar!"

The man had flown down the stairs, his hand on the railing, on the rope to be exact, he used it like a sailor and brandished a metal rod.

"Drop the crowbar!"

"You mean the pry bar," Ragna countered without batting an eye.

"Very well, Miss Pry Bar!" The steel rod clanged against the railing.

"Sonie!"

"Arielle?"

He was no longer young but looked like a boy, like a knight's page. His hair was the same length all the way around his head and smooth.

"This is Ragna, from number 20, and this . . ." Arielle lifted her head with a jerk, but squeezed her eyes shut at the last moment. For a half-second, she looked at Carl's face with her eyes closed.

"From number 20?"

A brief silence set in. The baby started to whimper.

"It's too cold here for . . ." With her free hand, Arielle brushed her shoulder-length hair behind her ear and vanished.

"Arielle." The man named Sonie no longer seemed wild or imperious but insulted. The tip of his steel rod was forged into a small barb, like the one Carl had seen on the Shepherd's pole in the Assel—maybe it was the weapon of the day. An image of a smithy flashed before Carl's eyes, embers and the smell of sweat, "be the anvil or the hammer" . . .

"From number 20," the page repeated and brushed the hair from his forehead. Carl saw his light eyes, the crazy gleam and the sternness in their depths. Arielle and Ragna had ignored him, even though *he* was the guardian of this building.

They conferred for a while. Their discussion wasn't about Carl, the pry bar or the flat; they'd ostensibly resolved that. Once again, *buildings* played a role, addresses threatened with demolition, "the whole street, all the way to the water tower," Sonie whispered, his voice trembling. "They start with those streets that are wide enough to set up cranes for new buildings. First Oderberger Strasse, then Ryke Strasse, that's their plan." Ragna said something about needing "good people" now and her gaze fell on Carl. "Good people, good weapons," the page repeated. The Shepherd's name came up several times: Hoffi, short for *Hoffnung* or hope. Hoffi, the Shepherd, who had the connections (all the way to the "round table in the head office") and the secret demolition list, with which everything could be substantiated.

"On Christmas Eve, our battle begins," Ragna whispered, "do come by."

Sonie tapped the barbed end of his rod softly against Ragna's midwife bag.

"You don't need that here. I have a key. I have keys to the whole city."

In the apartment, Carl found a few things that had been left behind: an armoire, a broken bed frame and an old black and white television, its screen facing the wall as if it were ashamed of something.

It was a dark one-room flat with a tiny hallway, which also opened onto the kitchen. In the kitchen stood a workbench, a massive thing made of oak boards and steel angles that almost completely filled the small room; otherwise, there was nothing. Only a few odds and ends, walnut shells, paper wrappers from eucalyptus lozenges, and under a sink mounted unusually high on the wall there was a small, dirty stool that was almost indistinguishable from the reddish-brown tiles. The half-sweet, half-sour smell hanging in the room reminded Carl of his grandparents' bedroom, where on holidays he had slept next to his grandfather in the double bed after his grandmother's sudden death. He remembered the brown curtain on the window to the courtyard, which was always kept closed, even during the day, and the chamber pot under the bed, which his grandfather often forgot to empty; he thought of his fingers in the cold urine when at night, enveloped in darkness, he tried to pull the large enamel pot quietly out from under the bed, only as far as absolutely necessary, only to realize after all that it wouldn't be possible to use it just once more . . .

"Christmas Eve, in the afternoon," Ragna had said very casually, almost coldly. She had pulled the pencil from her cap and written the address for him on the wall.

Right now, the most important thing was the stove. The tiles over the stove door were broken and provisionally covered with clay. Cinders were encrusted on the grate and the ash pan was full. Fortunately, there was also a coal box with a few briquettes and bits of wood. Every movement elicited a faint echo in the room. Carl tore a few empty pages from his notebook and stacked wood on the paper and then, for starters, he very carefully put two briquettes on top.

He closed his eyes and felt the warmth on his face like a caress. He pictured the writing desk in Gera, its eternal light; he pictured

Ragna, the pack and Sonie with the key, which Carl now held in his hand—my key, my flat, Carl thought. It had turned out that the door was merely shut, not locked. The previous resident, a man named Lappke—a paper sign with his name in childlike handwriting was pasted over the bell—hadn't seen any reason to lock it.

After the coal had caught fire, Carl went to get his sleeping bag from the Zhiguli. He emptied the trunk and carried everything upstairs. He crossed the copse; the shards on the path shimmered the word SALVE, now he recognized it. To the right of the entrance, the remains of a small wrought-iron garden fence were deteriorating. Behind the fence lay a few crooked borders of beds or graves.

The door clicked shut and Carl was suddenly filled with the soothing foreignness of the place. The sound of his footsteps on the tiles and their clear echo inside him: he could feel it from the crown of his head to the soles of his feet, a current of beneficial, calming solitude.

He went into the room, pulled the mattresses (foot, middle and head sections) out of the broken bed frame under the window and set up his bed in the middle of the room. They were straw mattresses, Dodo's fodder, Carl thought. Out of the corner of his eye he caught sight of a large, gray pile of debris, a soft wave of ancient dust billowing sluggishly above the floor, a fluid mesh of spiderwebs, dirt, and hair; Lappke's hair, Carl thought and it didn't bother him. He added the last pieces of coal and listened to the soft rumble of the fire—there is no lovelier sound. He resolved to stay awake a bit longer so he could close the stove door at the right time, but then he fell asleep.

BLACK AND WHITE

The connection was shaky on this day. "A forwarding request," the sparrow of Avignon repeated. The voice of the woman in the Gera post office sounded different than it usually did.

"Ryke Strasse, postal code?"

"One-zero-five-five," Carl replied, "thank you, Mrs. Bethmann."

"Then I'll forward the letters to you right away . . ."

"Letters?"

"Three letters, Carl! From your mother, three at once!" She chuckled contentedly. "They must have gotten caught up somewhere, in a mail car on the border, perhaps, on some railway siding—you know, Carl, the German National Railway is not exactly a marvel these days . . ."

Carl stared at the stone floor of the post office through the small window in the telephone booth: black and white. You preserve something in your thoughts, Carl thought, in your mind's eye like an object, but underneath, far below, the little black squares swim in their own world. He closed his eyes. He didn't mind the tears; he was alone, he was hidden here.

"Carl?"

On the way home, he bought paint—one color for the walls, one for the floor and a small bottle of nitrocellulose lacquer, with which he neatly labeled one of the empty mailboxes (the one that was the least rusted and dented). He wrote very carefully in dark blue capital letters: BISCHOFF. The name of the father, the mother, and the son. This brought them together again. He made an effort to fasten the box, which hung half-loose from the wall. In the end, he broke off a small branch from one of the elder bushes in front of the building and jammed the box's flap shut. He could feel his father looking over his shoulder. "No lock, Carl?"

Although he didn't know what the letters said, he felt relief. He had abandoned his post, he had deserted, but from now on, he would be a good son, a good son at a distance.

Carl spent two afternoons whitewashing the wallpaper in his flat (glueing loose strips back onto the wall), and on the third he started painting the floor, as best he could, with a color called oxblood. The rough, worn flooring drank up can after can of the blood. Under the oven lay a few bricks, old firebricks perhaps, cloaked in a gray mass of spiderwebs and dust that looked like the fur of a mangy old dog, lying in wait for Carl to stretch out his hand.

Two or three forays through the abandoned contents of derelict buildings in the surrounding courtyards was enough to collect what he was missing for the time being. Normally, he would have found it shameful, or at least unpleasant, to drag his loot home through the streets in broad daylight, but it felt like he was only watching it happen. He had the room, and he had the right.

For the first few days, Ryke Strasse had been shrouded in fog and so Carl had only made out the vague outline of the broad, squat, round tower, posted like a reliable old watchman at the end of the street, watching him sternly but not unsympathetically. With its stubby chimney at the peak of its conical roof, Carl had taken it for a remnant of an old fortress. As the fog cleared on the horizon, a second guard suddenly appeared at the back of the first, soaring and unmistakable—the Television Tower. "I see you," Carl whispered. He was surprised. Connecting these dots, Ryke Strasse continued much further, essentially through half of the city and into the sky. A red light flashed up there, or no, rather a whole row of lights were flashing, Carl now realized. When he was a child, he'd found the Television Tower bland and boring, but from this angle, he liked it.

*

When Carl entered his building, he always forgot that first there was a step down, even though it startled him to the core every single time; first this step into the abyss (a hundredth of a second that went straight to his marrow), then the sight of the small, neglected herd of mailboxes in the entrance corridor, and among them, the one now named BISCHOFF, which was waiting for the three letters.

His loot included: a chair, some tableware, a good aluminum pot and, yes, even a picture—it showed a flute player who wasn't playing his instrument, just gazing in front of him with his head lowered. Carl liked it from the moment he saw it. The most valuable item: a food-encrusted two-burner stove top, which he carefully cleaned and set on a small rusty frame next to the sink, across from the workbench. It worked and Carl was proud of it.

Lappke's workbench (the bench for working, Carl thought) was four meters long and almost one meter wide—everything he owned fit on it: his mother's typewriter, his few books, a pile of blank paper and the pile with his poems. Pile was a bit of an overstatement. Since he had started writing, he'd never exceeded twenty. He had twenty poems, no more. When he finished a new one, it took only a few days (sometimes just a few hours) until he had to admit that one of the older poems simply no longer held up. Twenty poems weren't enough for a book, when you figured that a volume of poetry had fifty poems on average. Fifty! Inconceivable. How could anyone write fifty good poems, good enough for a book? But he would never have a greater, more rewarding goal, and it wasn't actually a goal, it was his life. After everything had been put in its place, Carl freed the flute player from his ugly frame and hung the picture over the workbench.

That evening, Carl counted his money, the few notes he had left. He sniffed them and spread them flat. He'd piled the coins in one-mark stacks. The coins smelled of aluminum and old sweat, the notes smelled of fear. That vague fear of not making it in life, of failure: "He just wasn't cut out for it." And so on.

He opened his planner diary. The depressing little columns of numbers: like a numerical refrain on every page. Here he could track how his funds had shrunk. The few illegal taxi fares hadn't even covered his expenses—breakfast in the bistro, drinks at night, along with chocolate, gas, cigarettes . . . Life on the street had been expensive, but from now on he would be frugal. He could eat breakfast *at home*, he didn't need to go to the bistro. At home: where his toothbrush newly stood on the wobbly sink at the back, in a coffee cup from some other flat, thoroughly washed.

Up to this point, money had hardly played a role in his life, as very little as there had been. Instead, there had been the feeling that, in any event, it would be enough. That he wouldn't have to starve, for example. Now it was necessary to find a more serious job. He wouldn't have to pay rent for now, but he'd soon have to register his electric meter, as a roommate or under the cover of some other made-up story. Processed cheese, mixed fruit jam and brown bread were cheap, and ever since he could remember, a roll cost fifty pfennigs, which meant that, at this rate, he could manage for a while. Only coffee was expensive (and indispensable), 8.75 marks for 125 grams. The question of money. It was the second most important question. After the question of whether he was a poet. Or could become one.

There was a vegetable shop on Sredzki Strasse, at the corner of Kollwitz Strasse, that had very few vegetables but did have cheap canned soups, and there was a grocery store a little farther away, on the other side of Prenzlauer Allee. And there was a baker around the corner. Carl took a sheet from the stack of blank paper and drew up a weekly chart with taxi days, writing days and set times for reading. Although his appointment on 24 December was already on the wall in the entrance hall (he hadn't painted over it, just around it), Carl also wrote it in his planner: "Ragna, 20 Schönhauser." Didn't that sound wonderful?

He could hear Arielle speaking to her child and he pressed his ear to the wall. He heard her steps and her strangely isolated (smooth, plastic-like) voice that seemed to bend inwards. He had fantasies about Arielle. He absorbed her radiation.

Every evening at bedtime, Arielle sang to her child and soon Carl was taking care not to miss the goodnight song. Her beguiling singing—Carl's ear grew ice-cold on the wall and by the end felt frozen. In the morning, they met on the steps but she quickly slipped past him, her face hidden behind the baby. Instead of Arielle, the child had looked at him with a calm, skeptical look.

Soon it became clear that there was one room he and Arielle shared: the toilet. It was one floor down with a narrow window facing the front, onto the copse and the street. Basically, it was the only truly bright room, although naturally it wasn't a proper room at all, just a cabinet with a wobbly toilet bowl and a floor covered with candle stumps and empty cardboard toilet paper rolls, which you could move your feet back and forth on when you sat there, gazing out over the tops of the birch and elder trees.

The cold was the biggest problem. The coal merchants of East Berlin were closed until the new year and, in any case, Carl didn't have a coal card to show them. He had seen someone was inside the shop at Schiele Bulk Coal & Briquettes, but the glowering man hadn't opened the door, he'd just waved his arm threateningly, as if scaring away a dog. In the merchant's window hung a greasy scrap of wrapping paper with a special offer on bundled coal in indecipherable handwriting.

"I believe everyone here has a basement." After this phrase, Arielle squinted so hard, she had to close her eyes again.

"Cold, isn't it?" She looked at Carl with her eyes closed and he was touched.

Sonie's nameplate on the third floor was engraved with *Sonie*, "never-so." Under his name was a small photomontage, a stylized queen of spades whose upper half looked rather sweet and lower half rather diabolical.

Sonie obligingly told Carl how to get to Lappke's basement. "Where the skull is hung at the end of the passage. I'll explain the rest of the building to you after the holidays," Sonie said and brushed his ponytail off his forehead. Carl had learned that he was a kind of caretaker for the building, the house elder, as it were. "With the oldest face," Sonie had said.

Lappke's basement: a layer of sludge made from wood shavings and coal dust, nothing else. Someone had fastened a sheep or pig skull over the open gate. Carl crouched down. It was all foreign—and silent. A room full of absence that invited him to stay. You could linger here, crouching in the half-light, in the coal sludge, without thinking or feeling anything in particular, without any distress at all: this was what he had felt from the beginning, outside, in the copse, what struck him to the marrow, the allure this house emitted.

With his bare hands, he dug a few chunks of coal out of the morass and wiped them clean (again with his bare hands), then carried them upstairs in his tool bag to dry them out. It was fine to scrabble in the mud, pleasant even. It was housing and housing was part of the preparations that he had to make *for the (main) thing.* He was on the right path. It's as if I'm already writing, Carl thought.

PART III

GIESSEN, RHEINE, DIEZ

The letters look tired, Carl thought. The envelopes (crumpled and worn) bore a few puzzling stamps that pointed to detours. Carl wondered if they'd been read, if people were still allowed to read letters or retain them or make them disappear, surely they were. His mother had put a zero before the Gera post code (as a child, Carl had always understood posed code), which looked strange to him until he realized that it was an "O" for *Osten*.

The familiar handwriting, delicate and treasured. Before he could start reading, Carl slipped into a brief mental absence, an old reflex triggered by the sight of her handwriting. Once again, he was the child who would find a note from his mother next to his plate at breakfast before school and (without reading them) lose himself in line after line of elegantly flowing curves and loops.

The first letter seemed to have been written in a state of great agitation and confusion. It contained a fragmented description of her first stops in the West, a muddled sequence of places, which Carl later tried to untangle in a sketch. What emerged was the image of a large circular movement over hundreds of kilometers, first northwards to the Dutch border, then back southwards along the Rhine, "our emigration," as his mother had begun calling it. Carl pinned the page with his topographical sketch above his workbench, next to the flute player: "The Way of My Parents." He didn't quite know why he had given his drawing this (oddly stiff) title, it was probably not abnormal after not hearing from them for such a long time, after they'd disappeared for so long: he now had hold of them; he could keep an eye on them and no doubt the prosaic word "way" was nothing more than an attempt to soften things, to establish a level of normality and not have images immediately spring to mind of particular stories that began with an unfathomable (bad) decision and then led, step by step, to an inevitable catastrophe. Only later did Carl recognize the word's ambiguous overtones—yes, his parents were a-*way*, away on their way, maybe forever.

The Bischoffs spent the first day after crossing the border in the Giessen transit camp. The Giessen train station had been gracious in its announcements over the loudspeakers: refugees from the East had what they called the opportunity to telephone free of charge from the station post office; blankets and bags of food were being distributed in the waiting room. An iron pedestrian bridge led directly from their train platform over the tracks. From it, they could survey the wide queue of people that stretched from the station to the camp. "A stunning sight," Inge wrote to Carl, who could hear her voice as he read, a faint exhortation in each sentence, directed partly to herself, partly to the world. On the other half of the bridge, separated by a grille, several locals—people from Giessen—passed them. "I saw their faces, Carl, the looks they gave us. I'd have liked to explain everything to them, I was ashamed."

Inge and Walter on the run, or how else to describe them? For hours they did not advance a single step on the grilled iron bridge, from which they could see over the tracks and far out into the countryside. The Giessen train station seemed to have been built on a mountain. A young woman next to Inge had burst into tears because, all of a sudden, she no longer knew if she was doing the right thing. Inge Bischoff gave her a hug. There were discussions among those waiting over how one should conduct oneself in the camp and what was most important. There was one *know-it-all*—"there are always such people," Inge wrote Carl, she liked to categorize people: there were experts, posers, shysters and so forth, but there were also hard workers and those who were "totally fishilant" (Carl never completely understood this Thuringian transformation of "vigilant," it was one of her particular expressions)—there was, then, this know-it-all who claimed there were good days and bad days to arrive at the camp. Sunday was one of the bad days.

To the left of the camp's entrance gate hung a panel with numbers. Numbers 4 and 5 were lit. The interior courtyard was full of people. Then the throng in Building 5—an overcrowded corridor, shouts and questions, forms and questions, desperate questions, meal tickets, ashtrays, ten, twelve rooms, each room wielded power over one of the indispensable authentication stamps. Surrender and invalidation of your identity card: was this really necessary? A strange moment for Inge. In some of the rooms, the faces of the officials were barely recognizable, they were all smoking. Soda bottles, scraps of food and overflowing ashtrays on the tables. Her way to the West led through smoke-filled rooms.

Inge and Walter met again in the camp's courtyard. The caravan of buses in the courtyard, like metal segments of an endless snake. They opened their backpacks and exchanged a few things. Then Carl's father said he had to go back to room 503 one more time. Then Carl's mother said, When you get back, I might be gone already. And there she stood, near the buses in the turning loop, alone in the chaos.

An older man with a megaphone and a flat, leather bus-conductor's bag climbed onto one of the buses. Still partly winded, he started his speech: They should all keep calm. Everyone here in the camp was "making every possible effort." Back then, in '45, they would have managed as well. This did not reassure Inge, on the contrary, it sounded as if she were emerging from a war that was lost forever. Maybe that is how it was. She turned her eyes from the bus yard to the valley, a large, broad valley, the twilight, Hessen, that's Hessen, Inge thought, wasn't it incredible, but actually the mountains looked Thuringian, like lost territory.

A caravan of seven or eight buses slowly rolled out into the night. After all the exertions, it felt good to sit in the warm, dimly lit body of the bus, it soothed Inge to rest her head against the cool window and even though there were no announcements and no one knew where they were headed, many of the passengers fell asleep immediately.

Their destination was Rheine, somewhere in the north. After a few hours, the buses rolled into an expansive army compound with barracks as far as the horizon and steel bunk beds. There was a storm. The young woman from the iron bridge did not leave Inge's side. She now seemed almost too weak and distraught to stand, so Inge brought dinner to her in the barracks. The next day she had disappeared. No one knew where she'd gone. "She was younger than you," Inge had written Carl. Carl's mother was the oldest woman in the camp. "I'm the camp elder, as it were, Carl. But I don't mind."

In Rheine, there were new forms to fill out and a man who explained everything to them, loudly and clearly, point by point. On the wall behind him hung a sign with gold letters: *Damloup Military Barracks, Dorenkamp.* Good German infantry, the know-it-all said, but the man sitting next to Inge shook his head: "Army airfield." Like schoolchildren, they sat together at long tables, filling out their forms.

"After German nationality, write 'Yes,'" said the man who was explaining everything. Inge gave the person next to her an uncertain look and wrote Yes. Yes would be better than No, that much was clear. An advantage of which they'd not been aware (until then)—a present. A map as tall as a man hung next to the food counter in the canteen. Captioned FEDERAL REPUBLIC

OF GERMANY, it was festooned with blue-headed pins as if it were tracking the chaotic advance of a front line or were some kind of voodoo charm. Everyone crowded in front of this map, plates in hand. The know-it-all had called the map the *distributor*. Sooner or later, each person discovered the location of his or her next lodgings and they stared at it, as if the small, blue pin might reveal something about what awaited them.

"I believe I could feel at home even in an airfield barracks if it were bright, neat and clean," Inge had written Carl. He heard her voice in this sentence. It was thin, shaky, and emerged from the thickening fog of confusion. Why had she written this to him? Just to reassure him? Carl realized that his parents' emigration had not followed a carefully considered, well thought-out plan.

Their departure was sudden, the very next night. There were hectic announcements and Inge, who'd kept her hunter's ruck-sack *packed and ready to go*, leaped into one of the buses. Inge Bischoff had always been active; runs along the Elster, upstream to Köstritz and back, once in a while she had even been the trainer for their exercise group; now it all paid off.

They drove along the Rhine to Düsseldorf. Inge looked out into the darkness. The river had to be out there somewhere. She whispered her wishes to it. She was still the girl from rural east Thuringia, in the stalls with the cows, out in the fields at harvest time, then secretary, stenographer and finally co-inventor of ersatz recipes. The local good soul.

In Düsseldorf, a special train was ready but only at midnight did it receive authorization to depart. It was very quiet in Inge's compartment. They were all tired. When they were in motion, a soft, refined voice over the loudspeaker announced the places slipping by invisibly outside. "We are now passing Bonn station." "Andernach to the right, in the direction of travel." It sounded unbelievably tender. Inge and her traveling companions looked at each other and couldn't help but smile—the things they do here. "That's the West for you," someone said, "only in the West."

In Frankfurt, Inge was the last one to leave the compartment. It was four in the morning. The largest stamp right on the first page of her documents read "Osthofen Transition Housing," but the address of their emergency housing was The Farmer's Tavern, 8 Berg Strasse, in Diez. "I was surprised," Inge had written Carl, "that suddenly I was the only one heading for Diez and basically I had to backtrack a long way, to the northwest. From Giessen to Diez, wouldn't that have been shorter? In the end, there will be a reason for everything—and farmer's tavern sounds better than hostel, doesn't it?"

Her train wouldn't leave for three hours and since she was sitting there, on the right platform, she used the time to write a letter. "How are you doing in Gera? Well, I hope, dear Carl. Take whatever you need from the preserves. You know how thankful we are. Aside from me, there's no one on the platform, just a man photographing me from every possible angle. He doesn't say a word, he just takes pictures of me and . . ."

Carl skimmed over the last lines. He folded the letter—his fingers were cold and stiff. Giessen, Rheine, Diez—only Osthofen was familiar. It was where the concentration camp in Anna Seghers' *The Seventh Cross* was located. He remembered this from German literature class. Seghers had called it Westhofen. She'd changed East to West.

Inge's second letter was sent from Diez. "All our trials make us stronger. I'm filled with an incredible strength, Carl, and we know exactly what we want, you see?" No, he did not. In fact, the opposite seemed to be the case. There was something his parents were keeping from him, something his mother wasn't telling him.

She was now living in the Farmer's Tavern, a two-story inn with side wings. The road ended only a few meters behind the inn, at a cliff face that rose forty, maybe fifty meters and divided the upper city from the lower. The cliff's darkness colored everything, the neighborhood, the street, one's thoughts.

Inge had a room at the end of the hallway, right over the restaurant, with her own washing facilities. When she first arrived there was tremendous noise in the bar, shouts that were clearly understandable even outside. Inge opened the door and someone roared, "Another old lady on the run from her old man!" Then silence returned. Behind the counter, the innkeeper looked at her. Inge handed him her papers (basically, she was proud of her *legitimization*), then she said it: "I need a two-person room. My husband will be joining me soon." It was an intuition, a kind of self-defense.

Her first days in Diez. Registration office, Montabaur employment agency, and forays through the city, which Inge called her "reconnaissance walks." She explored the streets and surveyed the faces of Diez. Something inside her had changed. It was only November, but what would Christmas be like? Where would they put the tree?

She walked to the bridge over the Lahn. She stared into the current and let her mind drift. The more perfect the banks of the Lahn looked to her, neatly enclosing the river, the slate-clad gables of the houses and the castles in the mountains (the silvery slate gleamed in the last light of the day), the less she felt she had any right to them. This beauty was part of another world, one to which she did not belong. I'm a complete stranger here, Inge thought, I'm out of place. She had imagined certain details and situations but hadn't known anything. She had turned her back on her past and suddenly found herself up in the air. She thought of Walter and regretted having separated in Giessen. She looked down at the dock with the paddle boats and imagined a message in a bottle "with all my thoughts and feelings, Carl."

In the letter, Inge was confiding in him. She drew close to Carl in a way that was unfamiliar to both of them. Then she seemed very distant again and sometimes Carl felt that the lines he was reading were like a report from a stranger who knew a few things about him from his childhood and recent years, and otherwise knew how to impersonate his mother—a stab in the heart. Carl turned in alarm: no one there to chastise him for this mortifying nonsense. No: Inge was his mother and he loved her. "I love my parents, just so that's clear," he whispered. If he were ever to tell this story, he would begin with that sentence.

Twenty meters from the "Swimming Pool" sign, Inge had asked a man in his garden the way to the swimming pool and burst into tears. The man had invited her inside and asked how he could help her. His name was May, Mr. May, he was a retired schoolteacher, and he repeated his offer of help. Afterwards, Inge felt much better. She continued on to the swimming pool, where she then sat (even though the weather was too cold for it) in a wicker chair and gazed out over the empty meadow at the river.

She wanted to be very frugal, never more than five marks for any purchase was her motto, and these, for the most part, consisted of apples, soap, some basic cosmetics. Meals were provided in the Farmer's Tavern, with portions weighed out. Tea and bread were free of charge. She wanted to learn; one new thing every day was her goal. She observed how to release the carts in the supermarket from the chain and figured out how to flip open the telephone books in the phone booths: there's got to be a trick to it, she thought, and she figured it out. It was a victory. Then she telephoned the transit camp in Giessen to inquire about the location of her husband: no one knew exactly where Mr. Bischoff had ended up.

Inge had quickly gotten used to the noise in the restaurant; by midnight at the latest someone would take up the dirty song: "There is an inn on the Lahn . . ." Inge hoped that it wasn't about this particular inn, The Farmer's Tavern.

Every morning at eight o'clock, she had shown up at the Diez branch office of the Montabaur employment agency, but there was never any work (especially not for creators of Christmas recipes without almonds or raisins), which is why she'd started going door to door. It was very unusual and she felt it clearly: where did she come from, what business could she possibly have being here in Diez on the Lahn—and so on. Some didn't say a single word, mistrusting her motives. Her request for work seemed suspicious, preparing the ground for some con, perhaps, or for robbery. There had been warnings about just such things recently. A few people realized that she was from the East and pulled her into their houses, into strangers' hallways. Inge faced their emotion (yes, she really did come from *there*, straight out of the *zone*) and reassured the stunned; she let them hug her and drank schnapps or café au lait. "Can you drive a forklift?" a man in the mail-order house asked and Carl's mother had inexplicably answered, "Yes."

"After all, Carl, I do have my driver's license."

She didn't get the job, so she started cutting the hair of people in the Farmer's Tavern for two marks. "Just to bring a touch of style," Inge wrote. She hadn't ever learned how to cut hair and at first it was just one woman from Leipzig to whom she brought a touch of style, but word spread. Inge had cut her son's hair his entire childhood, his and his father's, often on the same day, on Haircut Day (same day, same cut). Carl had even written a poem about it, which he would never publish even though he liked it, mostly for its (very exaggerated) simplicity and concision:

the little slave

in this exceptionally
narrow kitchen my
mother cut

my hair. first
i always had to
shift to the left for

the right side and
then to the right for
the left side.

No wonder, then, that an image of the kitchen in Gera-
Langenberg flashed in Carl's mind as he read the letter from
Diez, that immortal kitchen, but now it wasn't anymore—it
was abandoned and betrayed, by every one of us at that, Carl
thought. In the Farmer's Tavern, too, there was very little room
for cutting hair: a side room off of the restaurant, just a niche,
actually, where a few of the emigrants or migrants (no one was
able to explain the difference conclusively) regularly gathered,
"at least those here who really want something," as Carl's mother
noted in her letter. They discussed the situation and shared their
experiences while Inge "gave them a cut" and took care that no
hair fell in her customers' beer. She was the oldest in the building, the oldest of the refugees, pushing fifty, she could cut hair,
people trusted her.

After these gatherings ended, she swept the dull floorboards,
dumped the hair into the bin, drank the remains of someone's
beer (in one swig) and went up to her room, where she picked up
her pen and noted down everything she'd heard in the conversations: everything she'd heard, everything she'd seen—it might
be important *for future purposes.*

What she liked best was going into the garden centers because
of the smell of fresh earth, which did her good, but also made
her cry. Inge bought herself a plant. Back at the tavern, she made
friends with Mrs. Glatt, the woman who served meals, with
whom she exchanged a few sentences every day, bending down

and speaking through the serving hatch. Long tables were set up in the breakfast room and soon everyone had their regular place. Some chewed silently, some talked the entire time, becoming very verbose, and some went straight from the breakfast table to the bar and started drinking.

After a few days, Inge had cut the hair of almost every resident in the Farmer's Tavern and had brought out a very particular resemblance, which served only to enhance something they all already had in common, something fundamentally unmistakable and yet hard to describe. The innkeeper, who never missed an opportunity to allude to the stigma of their Eastern origin, called it the *emigrant cut*. In this respect, Carl thought (bent over his mother's letter from Diez), when I was a child, I also had an emigrant cut, the most striking feature of which is a perfectly straight diagonal line, sloping sharply over the ear to the chin—a specialty of his mother's that outlasted several eras, beyond all fashions and customs, proof of her stubbornness. You carry the stigma long before it's given a name, Carl thought, and seen in this light, maybe it had always been a question of leaving, even in her narrow kitchen in Gera-Langenberg, maybe all those haircut days over so many years were just preparation for leaving one day, for *emigrating* as his mother liked to say.

In Limburg, Inge visited Mrs. Glatt, who proudly showed her a certificate with the title "Best Neighbor." Inge only learned later that you could find them, ready-made, in stationery stores. Mrs. Glatt drove her around Limburg, but Inge could not appreciate the city's beauty. "I couldn't bring myself to go into the cathedral," she wrote Carl. "I just couldn't. I always need to be outside, in the fresh air, out in the open."

The innkeeper at the Farmer's Tavern called Inge "tricky." He would lie in wait for her and was often drunk.

"Those who can't make it in Diez, are sent to Osthofen," the innkeeper grumbled in her ear. All the guest rooms were full, so he was converting the attic—in the hope of more migrants. The ceiling over Inge's bed caved in from the construction. Ashen, like a violent ghost, the innkeeper had looked down on her in the night.

"Well, when is he coming, your husband?"

"Soon, very soon."

FIVE PIECES OF COAL

When Carl woke the next morning, he was lying on the bare floor. Two of the three sections of his mattress had slid all the way to the hallway doorsill. The foot end was still in its place— the floor of his room must have a slope.

"So that can happen here too," Carl whispered. His throat was sore. He remembered the rope he had picked up on one of his forays through the city. It was a cheap, fuzzy rope rolled into a ball no bigger than a tennis ball. He unwound it completely and began tying the sections of the mattress together like parts of a raft. It wasn't easy but he had time. Finally, he had succeeded in doing something practical again, something that worked in the real world, even if in a world where people had long been sleeping in beds, but then that wasn't one of the truly important things on the way to a poetic existence.

He placed his sleeping raft in the middle of the room, pushed the frame of the old black-and-white television up to it and tied the raft to it. The television was a Stassfurt model from the sixties. His grandfather had owned one. The Stassfurt was not only a good mooring, its nice, heavy wood case also served as Carl's night table, on which he could put a glass of water or books and a notepad, in case he thought of something in the middle of the night that he needed to write down right away.

For days, Carl had been working on one and the same poem. The title was "The Friederician Child". In actual fact, Carl didn't know what that was supposed to mean ("friederician"—there was probably no such word), but even in the hundredth version, it still sounded promising and like something that *he absolutely must write*. It was the language that captivated him (it downright detained, imprisoned him), the sound of certain words and connections he couldn't let go of, not for anything in the world, even though they were completely abstract and actually had no meaning (something he only understood later). Some indefinable force had toppled a child into a deep well but now the child was slowly climbing up, coming closer, growing larger, overwhelming. Carl could see him and his enormous, moon-like face . . . It was absurd, utter nonsense if you examined it closely, but Carl couldn't let it go. He had to speak into the well, as if his words and the sound of them would be lost forever if he didn't keep hold of them, at least until he had created it: the absolute poem.

Hardly any of the oven's warmth reached his workbench. The kitchen window was drafty. He saw it in the flicker of the candle's flame, but also felt it on his face and hands, faint waves of shivering. The door to the street always stood open. It would become stuck (as if frozen) and snow drifted in. Winter also held sway in the stairwell.

Christmas would have been a good opportunity to suspend work on the "child" for a day or two, to get some distance (to put it aside a while), but there he was again, shifting words and syllables here and there since morning, always the same ones, rarely bringing anything new to the poem. He had finally decided to leave the house, "a few steps in the fresh air can work wonders" (again, his thoughts slipped into his mother's words, where could she be now, on Christmas Eve, and where was his father, and what should he think about this Christmas, which they wouldn't be spending *en famille*), when there was a knock. Someone was knocking at his door.

It was Arielle. She held a package, loosely wrapped in news-paper, in front of her stomach. It looked heavy and yet she was making an effort to look elegant.

"Merry Christmas!"

The package started to slip and Carl saw that it was coal, high-quality briquettes—large, pitch-black and gleaming. As Carl set them down carefully before the oven, he read the stamp: REKORD.

"These ovens, in any case, can't hold more than five at a time. You have to be careful and it would be better to use less wood, it burns too hot and the firebricks are already cracked . . ."

She circled his room, stretching her head upwards and at the same time tilting it slightly, a gesture from the avian world, her long neck and her slender, hooked nose seemed made for it. She had put her hair up and was nicely dressed in white jeans and a turtleneck sweater. She'd prepared herself and didn't squint. Carl thought, she has a good heart, or something to that effect.

It was clear that Arielle didn't know much about ovens, but Carl was impressed by her self-confidence, or, more exactly, by the great conviction with which she put up her front. The whole performance felt artificial and each of her movements appeared planned, fragile and open to attack. Everything about her seemed highly vulnerable and elicited an emotion that Carl hardly wanted to acknowledge and yet that is exactly what touched him, what captivated him about Arielle and, how should he put it, *freed* him. She simply came to see him in his den with a welcome present. She didn't know anything about him and very little about ovens. She strutted around his apartment, looked around, touched a few things and talked as if everything in the world was now clear.

Carl spooned the precious coffee into two cups and poured water over it. Arielle pointed at the brown spots on his kitchen ceiling. Mold was visible in places and some whitish wood. "The drunk likes to shower late. He gets in the shower and falls asleep. After a while it overflows, some runs down on your side, some on mine." She said it as if it were something that would connect them from now on. "It doesn't stop on its own, you have to go up there." She stretched out her arm, placed her hand on the wall between their apartments and looked at him intently. While Carl wondered what message might be hidden in this look, Arielle seemed not to know how to complete the gesture with her hand and just stood there, leaning on the wall. There weren't any seats Carl could offer her, just the mattress-raft.

"You have to go up and pull him out, otherwise it doesn't stop."

"What?"

"The water, the shower."

Carl handed Arielle her coffee and released her from her paralyzed nonchalance. He was grateful for her helpfulness and he would have liked to hear a few more pieces of advice. He'd have liked to spend Christmas with her, why not, just like this. Arielle stood in front of the workbench.

"You write."

"Yes." Admitting it to her was easy.

"Read something."

"No, I . . ."

"How about this one? Five pieces of coal for a poem."

Carl knew that reading aloud was out of the question, but he wasn't embarrassed in front of Arielle. He read standing up, next to her, leaning against the workbench. His voice caused a faint echo in the room. Even as he read, it was clear to Carl that the poem wasn't good enough. He almost stopped reading.

"That's nice. Could you read it one more time?"

"No."

"Then I have to go now—to being good neighbors!" She raised the coffee cup without looking at him. She went to the sink and wanted to rinse out the coffee grounds but Carl stopped her; he touched her hand and for a moment they were close.

"Would you give me something to read?" She gestured at the small stack from which Carl had taken the poem, the stack of so-called finished texts. Carl's sense of mastery had vanished. Without a doubt, there were better poems in there than the one he had read for her.

Arielle thanked him and Carl had to watch her fold the sacred paper with the finished poems several times and stuff it into her jeans pocket. He stood in the hallway for a moment, listening to her footsteps. She didn't return to her apartment next door but went down a few floors, where a door opened for her.

Confused and without a thought in his head, Carl felt his way back into his kitchen and opened the cupboard. Until now he had avoided looking closely at the contents of this cabinet, built into a niche beneath the kitchen window in each of the apartments in the rear building to serve as a refrigerator or small larder. Carl wasn't particularly squeamish, but this cupboard filled him with disgust. Like the space under the oven (where the dust creature lurked), the kitchen cupboard with its two hinged doors was one of the untouchable places where the legacy (spirit) of the previous tenant Lappke lived on. Carl was prepared to respect it, which meant ("turning the argument on its head" as his father liked to say) that he could never completely take possession of the apartment on Ryke Strasse. He saw three shelves, wrapped in greasy lining paper, which Lappke (or someone else in the cupboard's prehistory) had tacked to the undersides. In the back, Carl saw a hole, half a brick wide, opening onto the courtyard outside. It was plugged with rotting rags that didn't completely fill it, so a few thin rays of daylight illuminated the contents of the cupboard. A small, icy draft of wind blew into Carl's face.

The right side of the cupboard was bare, the left side was crowded with a throng of soot-covered containers. They were the Anchor canning jars, the kind his mother used (had used in her previous life), jars of preserves. This recognition helped Carl overcome his disgust for a moment: he carefully pulled out one of the jars and held it up to the light. At first sight, it seemed to hold a small, mummified figure, a wizened lump. Carl cleaned the jar and recognized plums that had fused into a creaturelike clump under a centimeter-thick crust of sugar and mold. Without thinking, Carl tugged on the flap of the sealing ring and the glass lid with the anchor symbol was released with a soft whistle. Carl took a spoon and gingerly scraped off the top layer that covered the clump, its seal almost as tight as if it were a second lid. Then Carl tasted it. The fruit still seemed to be good. The liquid was viscous and the plums almost liquid. It tasted—strange. Sweet. Like a liqueur. And by the second spoonful, Carl could already feel it.

PLEASANT PLACES

The pack's den—Carl had pictured it differently. The building was neither hidden, nor was it unremarkable. On the contrary: its dark gray gables of raw brick dominated the area and diagonally opposite was a subway station. The windows on the lower floors were barred and the curb smelled of gasoline.

"Password."

Carl looked up. It was Kleist, the glowing blue of his hair.

"Is Ragna there?"

"Password, dumbass!"

"Which password?"

Kleist thrust a brandy bottle with a rag stuck in it through the bars. "I'll light you on fire, you dumbass!"

At the same moment, as if the hand with the bottle belonged to a large, all-encompassing mechanism, Ragna came out of the building.

She smiled, but only for a second. "Christmas is too much for Kleist." Something about her had changed.

Despite her felt boots, she looked almost elegant as she preceded him with short, determined steps, in her wool stockings. A Christmas tree decorated with aluminum spoons hung upside down from the ceiling in the staircase. Squared timber and steel tread plates were stacked in the passageway to the courtyard. Two men were cutting holes in the wall right behind the door. It was ice-cold inside the house. A few dogs ran toward them but then swerved into one of the apartments; someone who wasn't visible had called the animals with a sharp command, a single syllable, which Carl tried to memorize.

Ragna explained the works being done, calling them "defensive measures." She led Carl upstairs, to her own door, as if he were an important guest. "Next door to me lives Henry. We all call him the good painter, but you already know that. And above us, up there on the bridge, behind that steel door . . ." she pointed at the stairs leading up and Carl obediently looked in that direction, "begins the world of technology, Little Frank's realm. He's our signalman—Save Our Souls until doom comes, understand?" On the way downstairs, she listed the names of the other tenants, which Carl immediately forgot. The Shepherd lived on the bel étage.

Almost all the doors stood open, maybe that was one of their rules. With half an eye, Carl registered holes in the walls and ceilings through which ropes were strung like suspension bridges. The fourth floor was the exception: two official tenants with valid leases (from time immemorial) lived there with doormats and slippers for the basement in front of their doors, relics from a long-gone era, according to Ragna, a time of laws and regulations that had lost a bit more validity with each passing day and had become almost incomprehensible and, yes, completely meaningless.

"In the beginning, we broke into their apartments too, inadvertently, of course. Naturally we apologized at once," Ragna explained to Carl. "And now we help each other. It's all about being good neighbors—and about solidarity. Demolition is scheduled for February: 20 and 21 Schönhauser, bam! Will you be with us when the battle begins, Zhiguliman?"

Carl didn't know what to answer. Ragna led him back down to the ground floor and then out into the courtyard, where a large pile of debris and chunks of concrete was stored. "The Wall," Ragna murmured, pointing at it.

"*The* Wall?" Carl asked.

They passed a Russian jeep. It was a GAZ 69. Carl reached out and touched the cold metal. He knew the model from his time as a driver in the army. When he was a soldier, he had driven an IFA W 50 and later a ZiL, a Soviet mechanical wonder.

The back of the courtyard bordered a completely dilapidated greenhouse; a row of gravestones with an unknown, angular script were propped against the wall of the neighboring courtyard. "Hebrew," Ragna told him and pointed to the grounds behind the wall: "The Jewish cemetery. They used the stones here for all sorts of things. The cops have their station in the Jewish old-age home but none of them know that." Carl thought of the movie behind the screen. Looking at the stones, he could suddenly hear the film score, the music was coming from the gravestones.

Through the back door they entered a shop that had once sold cut flowers and plants, "wreaths and floral arrangements for the graves." Ragna was making an effort to speak loudly and clearly and all of a sudden—but only for a moment—it all seemed ridiculous. The shelves held hydropots. One large shelf was filled with dried brown flower arrangements—the yellowed white of the bows, the silvery script:

In Loving Memory
For Everything There Is a Season
Miss You
Adieu

The ground was littered with small, pale yellow paper sachets of plant food, partly torn. As white as flour, the fertilizer dusted the floor. "For everything there is a season" had been one of his mother's favorite sayings—when I still knew her, Carl thought. For a moment he saw her on the banks of the Lahn with a funeral ribbon around her chest, *Adieu.*

While waiting for everyone to arrive, the pack argued over slogans to hang on large banners over the building's facade: *No one leaves willingly* or *The buildings for those who live in them* or *Education is domination.* Ragna did not join in. She sat next to Carl on the empty sill of the shop window that had been pasted over with newspapers and peered through a tear at the street outside—her face was white as snow, as if she hadn't seen a ray of sunlight for weeks. Carl deciphered the arc of writing on the plate glass: *Floristeria—Flowers, Wreaths & Arrangements.* It was very warm in the Floristeria, almost hot. Carl noticed a train-car radiator on the floor, the glow of its electric coil shining through the protective grate. Kleist was resting one of his boots on the grate and the leather sole was smoking.

The discussion soon turned to defensive measures, then to sourcing provisions and drinks *in case of emergency.* A woman who was called Mother Suse boiled water in an aluminum pot with an immersion heater. She handed Carl a coffee in a plastic cup encrusted with brown, and gave his head a gentle rub.

The Shepherd was the last to appear. He raised his arms as if he wanted to bless the world. His poncho looked ceremonial. His beard had been woven into a loose braid in which a piece of amber glinted. Around his neck he wore a leather band. He now stood in the center of the room, at his feet the crafty pack, a few whom Carl didn't know, fourteen, maybe fifteen, people in all.

"Why do I in this new world . . ." he looked around questioningly, "cheer on all anarchy unfurled?"

Cheers and applause, a dog started to bark and was immediately silenced.

He went up to Mother Suse and tenderly placed his large hand on her belly. His clothes smelled of the stall, each of his movements gave off an animal essence; without a doubt, the Shepherd smelled of Dodo. On his way back to the center of the Floristeria, he knocked Kleist's foot off the heater with a single, well-aimed kick; he appeared deft and superior. Kleist stretched his mouth into a grin, but it wasn't a smile, just a baring of his teeth.

"We don't need favors. It's always the same old story." Hoffi shook his bearded head sadly. "Taking possession of the building on Christmas Eve—it's no present!"

Carl felt a sense of embarrassment. He tried to be less conspicuous and slid from the sill of the display window to the floor. He crouched there with his back to the wall in the semi-darkness and started piling up the sachets very carefully, like a drug dealer. "Went to a hairdresser in the West," hissed the girl sitting next to him on the filthy stone floor with both arms wrapped around her knees. Her small, shaved head was wreathed in an aura of cold disdain. Ragna's hair was, in fact, different. Carl only saw it now. As always, she was wearing her fur cap, but what stuck out from under it gleamed softly and the tips curled under slightly. She looked like Mireille Mathieu on the La Paloma, Adieu album cover. Or like Mrs. Bethmann from Gera in a cap, Carl thought, and it warmed his heart.

"From this very street, Goethe left the city after only a few days here," the Shepherd pointed at the Floristeria's papered-over shop window, on the other side of which lay Schönhauser

Allee, whose cobblestones had murmured Carl to sleep only several nights earlier, "but we are staying here. And these aren't the *Tame Xenia*, my friends—this is *our fight*."

Carl looked around; no one seemed to know what Xenia was supposed to mean or what the Shepherd was alluding to, but maybe he was mistaken, it was all so strange. Ragna was a kind, warm creature, a kind of Berlin Daniel Boone, but the bald girl, for example, was a warrior and Kleist a madman and the rest of the pack (with their torn clothing, sweaters cut under the sleeves and on the sides, lace-up boots, chains around their hips, matted hair, hoods, and black crosses painted on their bare forearms) seemed ready for military campaigns that were very far removed from the territory of poetic life. In any case: his hair was also long and shaggy enough to hide him when he bent over the plant food and his fingernails gleamed black from digging out coal. "Cold water is best for washing off coal dirt," his mother always said, "cold water and Fit dish soap." Carl had bought some Fit, but he would also have needed a brush. Too many things.

The agenda was only a suggestion, the Shepherd stressed, "because no one here wants a new hierarchy, not what Ragna recently reported after her foray through buildings in the West, the buildings of the so-called squatters. But we have to arm ourselves, too! Prepare, defend, freedom takes work!"

"Freedom *is* work!" the warrior next to Carl hissed, spraying some of her poison. Like an experienced teacher, the Shepherd waited until calm returned, then read out the agenda, which Mother Suse had been holding ready for a while:

"First: Carl Bischoff. Second: contacts, neighborhood, outlines, and flyers. Third: ammunition, military advice, and defense. The issue of the dogs. Fourth: Little Frank's research report, item: police radio, item: telephone chain, item: Radio P and thought broadcaster." He handed the sheet of paper back to Mother Suse. Radio P—Carl remembered.

"Furthermore, I propose that in these pivotal days, we meet every evening, all of us! I propose we use the Floristeria as our headquarters."

An argument immediately broke out over whether the flower shop was suitable, particularly from a strategic perspective, given that it was on the ground floor, facing right onto the street, and on top of that only fifty meters from a station of the People's Police. On the other hand, there was the easily surveyed wasteland of Senefelderplatz and in back, a good jungle-like escape route through the Jewish cemetery and the so-called "Jews' Path" (Hoffi called it "the last dirt road in Berlin"), which led to Kollwitzplatz and so on. After a while, the Shepherd raised his hand. The metal frames of his glasses shimmered nervously and something glinted on the leather band around his neck, a large ring like the one Carl had seen on Dodo's collar. Maybe it was the heat: once again the room was spreading its former greenhouse atmosphere, its stupefying climate of chlorophyll and humidity; Carl absentmindedly sprinkled the contents of one of the sachets into his coffee and drank.

"Before we decide, I propose we close the public part of our meeting—Carl, please!"

As if he'd had his eye on Carl for some time, the Shepherd strode quickly up to him and offered his hand. Carl took it and Hoffi helped him up. For three, four seconds, Carl's hand lay in the Shepherd's large, rough hand, which didn't let go even though Carl had been on his feet in the middle of the room for some time. Despite his apprehensions, it wasn't unpleasant, quite the contrary. And a short time later, Carl couldn't have said who had held on to whom for so long. It was the power of acknowledgment that washed over him in those seconds like warm rain on a drought-stricken land.

The Shepherd started introducing Carl. A few details were exaggerated, and some were false. The high point of the

Shepherd's account wasn't their meeting behind the screen of theater 89, nor was it Carl's move to Ryke Strasse ("Carl's accommodation in one of our vacancies," as he put it), but the tools in the trunk of the Zhiguli:

"Our friend here comes to Berlin with a trunk full of tools. He's a traveler. He travels through the world. He is *a worker*. A man from the working class. He's a bricklayer by trade . . ."

The Shepherd paused and looked around. An ancient standing lamp was hauled into the dim shop and turned on. The lampshade was torn. The silver on the ribbons glowed, *The Lord Has Taken.*

"It's surely not an exaggeration to say," the Shepherd continued, "that these days no other trade seems as valuable and worthy—since the Wall fell, we need bricklayers! More urgently than ever."

He made a sweeping gesture that encompassed the flower shop, Schönhauser Allee, and half of Berlin.

"This building is just the beginning. Everything is falling apart. We have to act faster than the occupiers and their speculators. Their money will come. It's sitting there ready, by the bagful, impatient. But we know the score."

Carl saw that the Shepherd was pleased with his speech. From outside came the noises of the street. A rustling swept through the tangled needles of the funeral floral arrangements that had begun to shrink in the heater's warmth. The rustling hummed in Carl's skull, probably an effect of the fertilizer. The Shepherd turned his head in the lamplight. He looked eerie, like a giant bat.

"Here is the secret list . . ."

He pulled a sheet of paper from the lining of his poncho and unfolded it. "These are the addresses."

He waved the sheet triumphantly and began reading, slowly, emphatically, like a poem, repeatedly punctuated by Kastanien Allee, often Schliemann Strasse, Duncker Strasse, Oderberger

Strasse and occasionally Ryke Strasse. It was the list of abandoned houses that had been sentenced to death, including entire
streets that had been slated for demolition for years. It was the
list Carl had heard that night on Radio P.

Each new address increased the discontent in the flower
shop but only a few expressed it openly, led by Kleist with his
war whoop and the girl with the shaved head: "Let's be the par-
tisans of these buildings! Remember Arkady Gaidar! We're no
hooligans, we're no band, we would never shame our homeland!"

They're all versifiers here, Carl thought, all except me, I'm
just fertilizer.

By the end, the Shepherd stood in the room as if dazed, then
he offered Carl his hand. He looked at Carl and, at that moment,
it was as if they were meeting for the first time.

Life is Finite—Memory is Infinite, Carl read as he stepped out
of the door. The gold on the ribbon glowed.

REVOLUTIONARY TRADESWOMEN was written in red paint
over the stairs to the basement. The old, faded letters beneath
it were still legible: Air-Raid Shelter. A stone staircase, a clean,
dry corridor, and in the half-light, arrows shone.

"Here we are." Ragna motioned for Carl to take a step back
and opened the door. The key hung on a leather strap around
her neck.

He lost sight of Ragna for a few seconds, then a single dust-
covered light bulb came on. This was no normal cellar. It was a
vault supported by steel columns with semicircular arches of
brick. Little by little, Carl took in the room, the deep shelves
along the walls and the small, old-fashioned writing desk in the
center of the space with a tatty chair, covered with scraps of fur,
the remains of her old skin, Carl thought nonsensically.

On the desk lay a mountain of oil-covered rags and an
open tool-allocation book, and next to it a sheet of paper with

abbreviations and numbers, partly crossed out or checked. Sums of money, Carl thought. He recognized it immediately. On the floor under the desk were gasoline cans of various sizes, five-liter and twenty-liter. Directly under the vault were a few window or air shafts, plugged up with fresh straw. The shelves to the left held electric saws, hammer drills, angle grinders, and jackhammers. There was even a vibrating plate that must have weighed half a tonne and behind it a complete welding machine, all in all a monstrous, almost terrifying collection of machinery, equipment for a major construction site. On the opposite side of the room were shelves with smaller instruments of all kinds, many of them new or nearly unused, including a few valuable pieces, the finest jointing trowels, soldering irons, neatly polished, spirit levels made of light alloy . . .

"Jointing trowels," Carl whispered incredulously, and Ragna came up next to him. Her felt-booted gait, wool stockings, her low, hoarse voice:

"What do you think, Carl, what will we need?"

There were noises from above, calls, a shout, stamping, the vault vibrated.

"The lines are fallen unto me in pleasant places," Ragna murmured. "From now on, it's their building. They're excited, they want to celebrate, it boosts their morale, you see?"

She said this as if she weren't part of the pack. He looked at her lips, which had closed twice for "boosts" and "morale" and now remained closed. The fertilizer's effect, Carl thought, good thing he'd slipped a few packets into his pocket.

"I'd have liked to assign you a room in our building but for weeks they've all been taken."

It was pure (innocent) desire that now left Carl isolated and pulled him onto its mute, silent ground. There was nothing down below, just Ragna and him and the sense of being absolutely lost. He took her arm and tried to pull her toward him, but Ragna turned her head aside and his kiss met the fur of her cap. A cap kiss, filled with fluff, dust, and an animal smell.

BUCKET BRIGADE

Although no one actually asked him if he was prepared for it all, Carl felt a profound gratitude. The entire pack (except for Kleist, admittedly) simply assumed he was one of them. They'd picked him up, tended and housed him. Through the gray, steel back door of theater 89, he had stepped into their world.

Again and again, Carl imagined how he should have answered the Shepherd surrounded by the pack: Yes, I learned the trade of masonry and have worked as a bricklayer and I'm happy to give back to all of you in this way. However, I'm not actually a bricklayer, I'm a . . . How should he put it? A poet. The good, old, lofty word and its embarrassing pathos. A poet—a madman then, a boaster, a poser, a laughingstock. But what else could he be? I am someone who writes. Writes what? Verse. I'm a writer of lyrics. No one can deny that lyric is an icky word, a word that inspires nausea. "Lyric" has a retching feel to it, by the "ic" the strangulation is complete. A writer of lyrics and his verse—what for, when there are poets and their poetry?

A poet. It was inconceivable but some day he would be in a position to say it. At some point it would be justified. Until then, Carl thought, it could be useful to count for something straight off, particularly now that everything was so uncertain. It was protection, a mask.

In any case, it would have been difficult to explain why he had all those tools with him. He was a traveling bricklayer, what else? Someone on the move. An apprentice in a guild. The journeyman years. Carl remembered the evening in the garage. That strange mixture of sorrow and determination with which he had tossed the tools into the trunk of the car, one after the other, and how he could hardly bring himself to stop. On the one hand: his childhood in the garage and his early apprenticeship, his Thuringian past, which in the moment when his parents said goodbye had petrified into a kind of sham. On the other hand: the Zhiguli, packed and ready to go. The unbridled will to push off, to leave.

It took them less than half an hour to select their tools and load them into the GAZ. That same evening, Carl started work on the Assel, against the wishes of the woman in the fur cap, who wanted to return *to the celebration* on Schönhauser Allee. "Not tonight," Ragna had said. Carl listened, checked his tools and shook his head.

Maybe it was the kiss. Carl wasn't obsessed or unreasonable, but there was an imbalance in his body. He weighed the shovel on his open hand. He felt an unclouded gratitude for the dark, worn wood of the handle: this would be his Christmas this year, this was his present.

He shoveled debris until his hands tingled. He cleared the cellar floor. He breathed dust. Debris was like guilt and the work was an atonement for everything.

Ragna disappeared to find "something edible." When she returned, Henry and the Shepherd were with her. The Shepherd's face glowed. He seemed electrified when he entered the cellar and embraced Carl: "This way, not in any other way, my friend, this way, not any other, guerrilleros!"

Their Christmas dinner: brown bread, butter, and beer. "The perfect feast," Ragna murmured; she didn't have her cap on, just her dusty black hair, and for the rest of the night, the word "feast" circled in Carl's head. Feast, feast.

The Shepherd had brought extra buckets from Ragna's tool archive. His attempt to enlist Dodo as a beast of burden failed because the goat simply stood still and refused to go anywhere. "The goat is stroppy," Ragna called, "she's spoiled, that goat is."

Carl showed them what it means to work. He lined the buckets up in pairs and started filling them. Then he grabbed the handles—two buckets in each hand. Without needing any discussion, they formed a human chain with handover points in the old egg shop and at the small hatch out to the courtyard in back. The passageway was barely wider than an adit and the hatch was just a small access door (a kind of delivery port), against which the buckets collided so that debris and dust trickled into the good painter's sleeves; he didn't mention it. The Shepherd's glasses were covered with a layer of dust and his beard had turned gray, too. He was now a silent, industrious man, without a poncho, without a halberd.

By midnight, they had cleared out around a quarter of the debris. They drank their last beer in silence under the open sky, in the clear, dustless cold of the courtyard. A soft rustling came from the wilderness of Krausnick Park along with the whistling of some winter bird. It was a special moment when Carl announced that he wanted to "finish something." The Shepherd folded Carl in an embrace. Then he turned away and went back to Schönhauser Allee with Ragna.

When Carl returned to the musty damp of the Assel, he was overcome with exhaustion. Fenske's cellar door was open; for a brief moment, Carl stared at Fenske's army of left boots, in the midst of which now stood the two hair salon chairs, they wouldn't have fit anywhere else. "Reinforcements for the one-legged," Henry had said.

Carl scraped at the stone floor for a few minutes (the steel of the shovel blade rumbled in his head, maybe he still had some fertilizer in his blood), then he'd had enough. He simply stretched out on the dust-covered mattress that Dodo had taken bites from.

My sickbed, Carl thought, my first bed in Berlin. In a way
that he couldn't define, he was now at home here in the Assel,
too. Half-asleep, Carl listened to the noises. The good painter
was scraping into a pile the debris that had been tossed through
the hatch. Diligence even in a state of exhaustion was one of
the things Carl had always admired. Not many were capable of
it. He heard the good painter lock the hatch to the courtyard—
without saying goodbye. It wasn't necessary, anyway, because
he had bolted the Assel from the inside. And he had a blanket.
Carl smelled sweat and felt the warmth of the good painter on
his back and then the blanket on his cheek as well.

"Merry Christmas, Carl."

"Merry Christmas, Henry."

Carl dreamed of a glowing red stripe: Irina, Irina, the Princess
of the Oranienburgers. Regal but modest. Without a doubt, she
was the most precious plant in the shop. But no, she was the
florist—Carl recognized that now. And all the others around
her were difficult, wild plants whose cultivation and care she
recorded in a large diary that lay open on the shop counter; it
was filled with numbers and small sketches, anatomies of bone,
wood and screws.

Every morning after lighting the oven, Carl sat at his workbench
and tried to write. In the afternoon, he would descend to the
Assel's catacombs. He didn't think about it much. He followed
the suggestion life had made and it didn't feel wrong.

After a few days, they were finished. All the debris was in
the courtyard. The woodlice scattered in the frost and died,
which reminded Carl of a poem by William Carlos Williams.
Using pliers and a nail, the Shepherd opened the gate in the wall
that separated the courtyard from Krausnick Park. Neglected
for decades, the small park was enclosed by the buildings of
three streets: Oranienburger, Kleine Hamburger and Krausnick

Strassen. A kind of jungle had sprung up between the bullet-ridden facades, but the Shepherd knew of a path and along this path lay a large bomb crater, almost a small valley.

"Maybe we should clear it out first," Henry said, but they refused and just filled it. In the end, the trunks of the birches that had grown on the bottom of the crater were half-covered with the debris from the Assel—up to their stomachs, if that can be said of trees. It was a sorry sight, a moment that renewed Carl's doubts. Of what?

Before beginning the actual construction work, they all gathered for breakfast with Irina. Carl would have called it a site meeting, for the Shepherd it was about "assessing the current situation."

"Guerrilleras! Guerrilleros!"

With the bearing of a general ready to initiate his men into a battle plan, the Shepherd had unrolled a section of wallpaper on Irina's kitchen table and sketched out his strategy point by point on the back. For him, the Assel was alternately a shelter, a stronghold, or a U-boat: "Forty days to launching, that's an ambitious goal." U-boat was his favorite synonym. With enthusiasm, he drew arrows in all directions, indicating the underground passages to other buildings they should consider taking custody of in the future. There was also talk of an existing tunnel toward the Spree that should be made accessible again. It connected with the old surgery bunker of the Charité hospital, which had been hastily evacuated at the end of the war, that much the Shepherd knew.

"The bunker is sealed to this day. Here," he tapped his finger energetically on the wallpaper, "we'll find medicine, morphine, instruments, the whole thing!" He was concerned about "escape routes in combat" and about the battle itself, the "battle for Berlin and its abandoned buildings." Again and again, he called the pack "guerrillas," preferably "aguerrillas," short for *Arbeiter-guerrillas*—"worker guerrillas."

The Shepherd talked rapidly but his sketch was carefully composed, and his presentation was persuasive, even *well thought-out*, Carl had to admit, despite an undeniable element of insanity and megalomania—an aspect that didn't really seem to bother anyone at the table. Maybe because they all know the Shepherd, so understand how to contextualize it all, Carl thought. Irrationality was no flaw at this table, quite the opposite, it seemed to be a requirement for what they were gathered here to do—and maybe it was a requirement for every pack, Carl didn't know. The Shepherd talked: buildings and workers, the right to housing and work, buildings they themselves selected and organized, the emancipation of the proletariat, and so on—this all made sense to Carl, but the aguerrillas didn't. "Hoffi wants to create facts," the good painter had said. "If you don't want power, you won't get it."

In the end, it was something else that seemed pivotal, something they all sensed: the fact that someone here was taking *responsibility*. The Shepherd had *a plan*, that alone was impressive and powerful—and who knows what might come from it. It came down to this "who knows." It sparked an almost unlimited readiness to see, in everything that would happen in the basement of the Assel, not only themselves but also the beginning of a new era: their own era.

The Shepherd talked, he wrote and drew a line diagonally across the wallpaper. Carl listened to the scratch of the felt-tip marker on the paper. He smelled the sharp, poisonous odor of the writing that settled acridly on his mucous membranes. The felt-tip marker was longer and thicker than any he'd ever seen, the first Edding permanent marker of his life.

WORLD ENERGY

In the meantime, Mr. May had *thought of something*. From his garden on the bank of the Lahn River, which was now completely dug up (the clumps of dirt gleamed, plump and satisfied), he led Inge uphill to upper Diez. They walked along a small avenue through a neighborhood of villas and at its end was a modern, white bungalow with a terrace and large windows. At the gate, Inge had read the name Talib. For a brief moment she stood alone on the wide paved driveway with a view of the facing hill, on which two castles and their towers peeked out from the forests (like in a fairy tale); she had not yet been at this high an elevation in Diez.

The Talibs had four children and Mrs. Talib, who invited Inge into the house, was pregnant. She cooked for everyone and from that day on also for Inge, the refugee from the Farmer's Tavern. At noon, they sat together at the table. Before eating, they dipped their hands in a bowl of water and murmured blessings, which Inge (not long after) could softly say with them even though she didn't understand the words. She remembered the time of her confirmation and how she had liked going to church but later (for many reasons) no longer did. "I've been received very kindly here, it is a blessing," Inge wrote to Carl.

Amir Talib had grown up in Syria until his expulsion. He was younger than Inge. He had studied medicine in Jerusalem and worked as a doctor in Tel Aviv. A vigorous man with a precisely shaved goatee, he had been a surgeon in the Diez state hospital for several years now. And: Dr. Talib emanated goodness, warming benevolence, "I feel it through and through, Carl." *Through and through* was another of his mother's typical expressions, Carl recognized her by it.

Inge's job was housekeeping, cleaning, laundry, and whatever else was necessary. She arrived every morning after breakfast and in the evening she returned to the Farmer's Tavern. On her way back she would walk downhill, descending the steep stairs from upper to lower Diez, looking into the illuminated windows. The houses on the right side of the path were built so low into the hillside that she could lay a hand on their roofs as she passed; she patted the houses and read the names on the doorbell panels: Steilschläger, Weidenfeller, Karatag.

She gradually became aware of the neighborhood: the tobacconist on the corner of Berg Strasse, the Rialto ice cream parlor. The ice cream vendor in the Rialto would give ice cream to the begging children, he drove a Kawasaki. Inge briefly envied the children, she caught herself doing it. She praised the motorcycle. Her husband had driven one earlier, "back when we first met," Carl's mother told the Italian man in the Rialto, "an ES 250 with leg wind-deflectors and half-fairing." She had always liked riding on it, especially in the curves and so on, and she fell silent. "We should have worked it out better." The sentence just slipped out and naturally the Italian in the Rialto didn't have a response; he was not suited for that conversation.

Inge washed her own laundry at the Talibs' house, too, which was a huge help. Until then she'd used the sink in her room at the Farmer's Tavern and a large plastic bucket, her first purchase in Diez. She wrote applications on Dr. Talib's typewriter in his office. Dr. Talib would come in and give her tips on what should be included. He smelled of the hospital and operations. Inge could smell his intelligence as if it were something physical and for whatever reason, she always thought of her parents' family celebrations on the farm in the years after the war and how nice it was to be together in the large, steamy kitchen. Suddenly she remembered that she had earlier wanted a daughter, too, a daughter and a son.

She ironed shirts and played with the children. She also took care of the rabbits, two fat, lazy animals who liked to crouch under the ironing board while she pressed the clothing but otherwise never let slip a chance to escape, which always caused much exasperation and shouting that left only the youngest daughter completely unfazed. An ear pressed against the cassette recorder, she listened to the adventures of a young talking elephant who opened each episode with an unspeakable trumpeting blare that cut deep into your brain, taraaah . . .

Inge wrote about all this to Carl, who tried to imagine his mother in her new world. He wondered where her stamina, her staying power came from and how she was able to stay calm despite the fears (separately after Giessen) that flashed now and then through the thicket of her chronological accounts. Carl hadn't lived with his parents in Gera for years, and yet there were moments when he felt like an orphan, abandoned, like a child for whom no light shone in the window. It wasn't their departure or the separation, not that easily named and understood abandonment, it was another: he no longer recognized his parents. He didn't know who they were, actually. With this question in the room, there was not much he could still be certain about (in retrospect). Was everything to date just a kind of fiction? And everything happening now, this so-called reality—was it the collapse of the wall of fictions and the irruption of reality? A confusing thought and Carl had to quickly repeat to himself that he loved his mother, he suffered with her and wished her happiness, *more happiness*.

In the event Inge were transferred to Osthofen, Dr. Talib had offered her one of the children's rooms as temporary lodgings. He also helped Inge in her search for her husband. Through the central transit camp in Giessen, they had managed to find all possible addresses. They drew up a form letter, Talib dictating, Inge typing.

In accordance with her plan to be very frugal on all fronts, Inge Bischoff continued to wear her winter clothes from Gera, along with her buckskin hiking boots with their marked tread. This evidently impressed Dr. Talib and led him to remark, during one of their lunches together, that the Jews, for example, from their very first origins, in the Hebrew bible, that is, were called a *wandering* people—long before being a stranger in exile was understood as a trial or a punishment. In fact, also long before there was any talk of Jews at all. That word hadn't existed, Talib explained, in the time when they were *wanderers*. "Isn't that marvelous?" Talib asked. Inge, who hadn't understood much of what he'd said, nodded and looked at the floor. Talib then started talking about Abraham's travels in the land of Canaan—"Canaan!" the children shrieked.

"It's not the place, it's the wandering that was our founding," Talib said. His wide, Syrian smile radiated waves of warmth, yet Inge felt ashamed. For some time now, she had feared that always wearing the same things, two shirts, two sweaters, in alternation, as well as this pair of (undeniably practical, sturdy, indestructible) buckskin hiking boots, would not reflect well on her. She trusted Talib, but she was also sensitive—and proud.

Dr. Talib began talking about literature while Inge was still thinking about her wardrobe. When she arrived in the morning, she slipped off her shoes, of course, and left them on the light-colored stone floor of the long vestibule. One day Talib had found them there. He had picked them up and carried them into the living room like the prince with Cinderella's glass slipper . . . Neither James Joyce nor Adonis meant anything to Inge. They were *all* wanderers, Talib explained and quoted Yeats, "But one man loved the pilgrim soul in you, / And loved the sorrows of your changing face."

This was too much for Inge.

The next day, she strolled through the neighborhood behind the train station. In a small side street, she found the Diakonia clothing collection site and charity shop. No one noticed her enter. The women in the charity shop were gathered around a large table lit by a low-hanging work lamp, sorting a pile of clothing. Inge's gaze swept over the boxes overflowing with clothing donated by strangers, on the stone floor along the walls. Next to these enormous cartons of dirty, torn cardboard were meters and meters of clothes racks that extended like a shimmering rail into the dim, barely lit section of the shed—at first glance it was a hardly fathomable, depressing sight, as if many people in Diez had suddenly died, people of every age and every size, as if half of the region had perished from some inconceivable illness and this was their legacy. This strange thought occurred to Inge.

She told herself to be reasonable and picked up a gray and white striped pullover. She stroked it and bunched it up loosely, this was *good wool*, but when she slipped it on, the apprehension of death returned, only much stronger than before. Her torso and arms went stiff, she froze with arms upraised, the strange wool covering her face, and she almost burst into tears.

"Feel free to look around," one of the charity shop women called from across the shed. Inge nodded. She didn't move and at that moment another emotion rose in her: a feeling of revulsion and disgust but not for the dead, almost the opposite, in fact, it was disgust for strangers' lives, their smells. "That's not my way, Carl, you know that I'm not choosy." But she couldn't do anything against it.

"Now and then, we get nice things here," the charity shop woman said. She had stepped away from the sorting table and was slowly moving toward Inge, but then, very suddenly, as if she were a diver, she plunged her arms into one of the open cartons and, after a few, rapid crawl strokes, she pulled out a well-lined anorak in Inge's size.

"Something for winter?"

*

121

Although Inge now wore a pair of low-heeled, brown leather shoes from the Diez legacy ("very rarely, actually only in a few cases, is the clothing from dead people," Inge wrote Carl), Dr. Talib brought up the myth of wandering again a few days later. Mrs. Talib had prepared a chicken with potatoes and vegetables and the doctor filled their glasses before raising his: the wanderer soon learns the languages and customs of the places he passes through; comprehension is in his blood, it beats in his heart, in a way, Talib said, and stroked the hand of his wife, who, as always, was seated next to him. First the spontaneous (and most important) understanding, then learned understanding, and finally profound understanding. In this way, the wanderer effortlessly crosses national borders (Talib nodded approvingly at Inge), even battlefields (his wife raised her head and looked sadly into his eyes), whether in Europe, Asia, or elsewhere. The wanderer doesn't just wander, he carries that comprehension that grows with understanding over the borders that our time is so bitterly reliant on. He is the smuggler, the trafficker who pulls the very first wire for hermeneutic current, *world energy* . . .

Talib cleared his throat and continued in a lower voice: often it's very difficult. In Finland, for example, the wanderer takes the shape of forest ghosts, in southern Sweden he is forced to set off whirlwinds, in the west of Germany, he pulls out a pair of scissors and starts cutting people's hair . . .

Inge blushed and the children laughed. Everyone laughed and finally Inge laughed too, a long, relieved laugh.

FROM ANOTHER STAR

When Carl exited the building, he looked left, into a canyon between the buildings that seemed to grow younger from one courtyard to the next and in which a brown birch tree grew, covered with moss or rot, only one branch in its crown glowed white like a flourish.

These were the days of settling in, he gradually conquered his own territory, *my claim*, thought Carl, who liked to think in the language of gold prospectors. His claim was limited and basically smaller than the village his family came from. Behind it lay the city, at his feet, so to speak, but actually in a kind of hereafter, far away. Carl didn't need more, only three or four paths that sheltered him on his walks.

First Carl explored the neighborhood coal yards and their possibilities—Greifswalder Strasse, Schliemann Strasse (where the briquettes were bagged), and the yard on the corner of Sredzki Strasse, which he had overlooked at first because it was closed off from the street by a high wall. But some nights, a truck trailer filled with the black gold was parked on the street outside the coal yard and then it was easy to supply himself.

It was primarily the daily necessities that delimited his territory, which extended to the east past Prenzlauer Allee to the supermarket on Wins Strasse. To the west, it reached the Shepherd and his pack's building on Schönhauser Allee. To the north, only the fifty meters to the other side of Dimitroff Strasse, where the Käthe Kollwitz bookstore stood. The Assel was his outpost. Carl liked heading south best and now, too, he plodded tiredly and dreamily down Ryke Strasse, past the Ryke Retreat bar and the synagogue toward the water tower.

Hardly an evening went by when Carl did not circle the water tower at least once (the *watchman* was his private name for it). This was his first habit as a resident of the neighborhood. The watchman stood on a hill that was overgrown with shrubs and trees, including a single pine, which Carl immediately took into his heart. With its steep rock face and swathes of nettles, the hill resembled an island, which made the tower a lighthouse that had taken the storm-plagued islanders into its cylinder—that is how it must be, not any other way, Carl thought, and in fact there were apartments in the watchman. Six stories of paired windows were set in the brick exterior and through them the tower began to shine at that hour.

Carl stopped halfway and looked up at the hill and the dark outlines of the trees. He watched the pine on the slope, its primeval forest shape and the stiff, almost imperceptible movements of its limbs. And at that moment, he heard it for the first time: the murmur. It came from the depths, the cobblestones themselves were murmuring!

J. Lappke—a corner of the paper sign next to Carl's door stuck up from the wall, like an invitation to finally tear it down and write his name on a sign of his own, but something prevented him. And maybe it was wiser to remain undercover for a while.

On the stairs to the floor above, he'd met Sonie and asked about Lappke.

"We never met him. Died in 1979, that's what it says in the building log. I moved in the year after, illegally, same as you. Lappke's apartment was already empty."

They spoke softly for a while and in the meantime it had grown dark outside. Sonie used the opportunity to instruct Carl on the building's rules: no embers in the ashcan (the smoke gets drawn into the house, the copse could catch fire) and on each trip to the cellar, bring up a bucket of coal for Mrs. Knospe on the fifth floor.

"If Charlotte likes you, you get cake. But we don't do it for the cake. And we take turns shopping for her, in a certain shop, corner of Belforter and Prenzlauer, only there, nowhere else, it's very important to the old lady."

Charlotte Knospe, Charlotte Flowerbud, Carl thought. A name from a novel.

"Go up tomorrow and introduce yourself. I'm sure you noticed the flower beds in front of the building. They're hers. When spring comes, we help her—turning the soil, watering, and so on. And the rope, too, is strung for Charlotte," he reached for the cable along the banister. "She can't walk very well anymore but she still tries sometimes. She rappels down, you could say, but it's more like hopping. She jumps and soars down the steps on the rope. Charlotte is . . . very thin, very light, like a paper doll, understand?"

A lot of information. Sonie looked Carl in the face to check if the new tenant on the fourth floor had understood everything. In response, Carl nodded, what else.

His heart beat faster, closing his own door still filled him with a nervous joy. My door, my apartment, Carl thought. He glanced into the ash-gray courtyard and checked the stove. The damp pieces of coal glowed a poisonous green. They didn't really burn, they just smoldered away, sluggish, without light or heat, and gave off a rancid smell.

"I salute all of you who are damned to the flames," Carl murmured.

"You ssspeak, you ssspeak, you ssspeak a powerful word so casually," came a hiss from the embers. It hadn't sounded dismissive or unfriendly, so Carl took his sheet of paper from the workbench and stuck it onto the stove: he speared the text onto one of the two wires bent into hooks that the stove builder had left, for whatever reason, in the grout between the tiles— in any case, it was definitely too cold to work in the kitchen. He paced around his room for a few turns and murmured the phrases to himself. He circled the mattress-raft and the Stassfurt, and when he passed the stove, he glanced at what he'd written. The sheet wavered in the heat of the tiles, very slightly, like foliage on a tree. It rose and fell with a soft, almost inaudible sound.

That's the most beautiful sound one of my poems has ever made, Carl thought.

His eye fell on the television cabinet, on which he'd put a few books he had borrowed from Potsdamer Platz. Some were still in the plastic bag with the blue lettering: "National Library." Carl admired the golden-yellow building that had landed on the dusty wasteland far behind the prefabricated buildings on Ebert Strasse. To reach it from the East was a struggle, like crossing a desert that was forbidding, cold and, on windy days, covered with gray dust (actually, it was windy there every day, even when the rest of the city was calm), past the container at the border crossing (no one demanded to see his passport there) and past the mound under which, rumor had it, was the bunker. The firewalls, the ruins, the columns of the maglev train—it was like crossing an abandoned test site that was off-limits, Carl thought, a rubble field in which you had to take care not to get lost. If there were ever a specific place, agreed on by both sides for the exchange of ghosts (as for the exchange of agents), then it would have been there, on Potsdamer Platz, Carl thought.

He turned on the ceiling light. His room was mirrored in the Strassfurt's bottle-green glass. And there he was, too, Carl Bischoff, who now approached with one thought: the power cord just reached the socket. It took a moment, then his television casing was filled with a whooshing, whining snowstorm. First the static was very loud, but he was able to turn it down. Maybe Lappke was hard of hearing, Carl thought. Now and then, a shape emerged from the storm, but only for a second or two—"Lappke's ghosts," Carl whispered. Without an antenna, nothing else to see.

Several days later, when he finally realized why humiliating himself would be helpful, he entered a branch of Deutsche Bank on Ritter Strasse, handed over his identification card and was given one hundred marks, the so-called welcome money. It was enough for a small oil radiator, which he put in the kitchen near to the workbench, right next to his chair. There was enough money left for two five-hundred-gram bags of Jacob Krönung, one whole wondrous kilo of coffee.

In the end there was still some small change left that he mixed in with the East German coins in his wallet. He had mistakenly put one of the East German coins on the counter at the bakery on Wörther Strasse.

"You can take that back, young man," the baker's wife had said, "that comes from another star."

BEFORE BIRTH

Carl breathed the acrid odor of plaster into his lungs like an old, almost forgotten satisfaction. The work did him good. It was a more direct and visible expression of his abilities, he felt the dignity that lay in the proper use of a tool and his body gradually remembered every detail, every single movement.

The Shepherd had put Carl in charge and declared himself an underling but not without a reference to "the importance of all work." He philosophized and spoke of the Assel's early days, "its prenatal phase, as it were."

Under Carl's initially tentative and rather tight-lipped direction (he wasn't used to directing others), the crafty pack mutated into a construction brigade. To be sure, nothing in their appearance or demeanor resembled a socialist work brigade, but most of them wanted to work and there were even a few of them who could. The shift began at ten, that was Carl's decision, his first initiative. He knew that this would conflict with the natural rhythm of most of the guerrilleros, but days when you don't accomplish anything before noon are not good days.

Only Ragna, Henry, Kleist, and the Shepherd showed up regularly. Sometimes the fractious bald girl (the warrior) came too. And Irina, who came down to the Assel at least once a day to provide the pack with food and drinks. It was also Irina's job to placate those residents upset by the dull sounds coming from the bowels of their building. With a smile, she followed them on the stairs, explaining and reassuring them, and for the older ones (almost all the tenants were pensioners), she offered to run errands at the grocery store, administrative offices, or the post office . . . Now and then, there were friendly responses: "Well then, I'll just turn off my hearing aid," old Hilsher, the former pastor of the Sophienkirche, called from the fourth floor. "Age has its advantages," Irina murmured and handed Carl a plate with two open-faced cucumber sandwiches. She was both solicitous and proud. Her eyes shone, as did her forehead, which radiated a girlish superiority. The only thing Irina didn't look like was the Shepherd's sister; she's *not really* his sister, Carl thought.

To start, they had ripped out a few wooden partitions covered with whitish mold and removed a thin, mirrored dividing wall from the old hair salon. It felt strange to shatter his own reflection. Shards were strewn everywhere, and Carl carefully scooped them up and carried them out back, as if there were still something there, in the glass, that he had to be attentive to. He initially piled up the shards then came to his senses and threw them in the trash.

They took out the wall between the former egg shop and the hair salon. A lintel needed to be inserted and furthermore the two rooms were not quite on the same level. Carl explained to the Shepherd that leveling them out would require a lot of work and time. Like a building owner who was prepared for *anything*, the Shepherd looked him the eye: "Now tell me, dear Carl—as a bricklayer, I mean—what worker would want to set off on a slippery slope into the future?"

The Shepherd's sayings. Their craziness did not strike Carl as truly alarming, they just touched him gently, rather pleasantly like a cool summer breeze, and above all he sensed the truth hidden behind all the talk of U-boats, strongholds, and aguerrillas, a concern as significant and essential as that hard-to-explain and still indefinite longing that bound them all in those days.

Carl plastered the walls. Now and again Ragna was at his side, as handyman, *my hand*, he thought. Henry shoveled and mixed mortar in a real mortar box with a real mortar spade. The low, muffled scraping of the spade on the bottom of the box—a sound that filled Carl with a profound contentment (it was a there's-still-mortar-there satisfaction, followed by an everything-has-been-used-up satisfaction), tiny snippets of that yet-to-be-described emotional world of a bricklayer at work, a regal subject, but not for Carl who, in short, did not believe in reality, at least not in relation to his writing.

Her tools were good. What Carl couldn't offer from his own collection Ragna took from the revolutionary tradeswomen's archive and they never had a problem sourcing missing equipment or materials at short notice. Hoffi, the Shepherd, delivered the building materials in the GAZ and unloaded them in the courtyard or right outside the window of the Assel, which was at ground level. If Carl stood on tiptoe, he could see the granite stones of the sidewalk (like gravestones lined up one next to the other), and behind them, the street, then the park called Monbijou (they all called it Mombi), and somewhat farther off, Museum Island. "Who pays for all this?" Carl had asked once, casually, as he made a skillful maneuver. "The aguerrillas," was the Shepherd's proud response. Hoffi was often summoned elsewhere for some business, as they called it, and had to leave the site abruptly. Usually it was a man named Hans, a kind of adjutant and confidant to the Shepherd, who called him from the street, his cleanly shaven head appearing at the basement window. He wore leather trousers.

Evenings, Carl and Henry were the last ones in the Assel. They worked, drank beer, and talked. The mortar dried slowly on the damp walls and there were damp patches from which the freshly applied mixture kept slipping to the floor. Carl powdered the areas with unmixed cement. A fine layer at first and then by the handful, like a farmer sowing thick gray dust.

"And that's supposed to help?"

"The cement will draw the moisture from the wall."

"And what if there's a river on the other side of the wall?"

"The Spree? The Spree is a hundred meters away, at the very least."

"It flows by here, underground, you can believe me, Zhiguliman. It's all swamp outside. The Museum Island stands on piles, on supports. The People's Palace does too. Around here, there's no solid ground you can build on."

Carl touched the wall with his fingertips. The river. He would have felt it.

"Let me know when you need me, Zhiguliman."

His trusty sidekick retreated to a corner of the basement and started tearing the empty cement bags into large square pieces of paper. Henry carefully brushed them off, took paints from a dirty shoulder bag he always carried with him (it was a gas mask bag, Carl recognized it right away, a pouch for the mask, a pouch for the filter, part of the basic equipment for every soldier in the National People's Army) and started to paint. Carl watched him for a while, then went to Fenske's cellar and made himself comfortable on one of the two hair salon chairs. He had brought two candles to read by. The construction lamps were being used for the plastering.

There was a short text by Gaston Bachelard, with which Carl felt intimately connected. It was called, "My Lamp and My Blank

Paper." All these books that now enter into our lives, thought Carl. You knew they existed but nothing else about them, just a distant notion now and then. For some of them it was like suddenly getting news from siblings. An intoxicating feeling. As if parts of your own life had taken place elsewhere, somewhere far away. Carl looked up. Fenske's cellar was starting to unfurl its aura: dead men on crutches, feet in boots, disjointed, and Carl, who read, "How good it would be—as well as generous to oneself—to start life over again by writing! To be born in writing by writing . . ."

Carl had to wait for the plaster to dry before smoothing it out. This required patience and was a job for skilled workers only, but still, it did him good not to be alone in the Assel so late at night. Every construction site is transformed after the end of the workday. As with all places that are animated during the day, in nocturnal desolation its contours became more definite, more its own, cool and spectral.

Now and then, Carl left Fenske's cellar to check if *the right moment* had come. He carefully brushed the float over the wall, as if he were currycombing a large animal. He listened to the sound it made, he felt the damp gray skin of the gleaming compound and examined it: the opening and closing of the pores, the slightest shifts, bubbles, full, velvety or lumpy spots, and between them tiny bits of gravel. It was writing, very legible. The woodlice that lived in the joints of the masonry scrabbled constantly through the fresh plaster. Carl pushed them back into the plaster with a light sweep of the float. He had to do it quickly and carefully because often four or five of the creatures ate their way into the open at the same time: "You now have to become petrified, my little friends. In ten thousand years someone will find you and then . . ."

Fascinated, Henry looked over Carl's shoulder.

"Here, for example, Henry."

Carl's float swerved powerfully again and again over one particular area.

"It's good here. Neither too damp nor too dry. You stew it in its own juices, that's the bricklayer's secret."

"The *bricklayer's* secret?"

"Yes, well, maybe it's also something more general, an open secret."

"Is that why you're speaking so softly?"

"I'm not speaking softly."

"You are, Carl, you're whispering."

Carl fell silent. In its own juices. He had never thought *of this*. Only of cracks and clumps.

"I read your poems, Zhiguliman."

Carl put down the float and felt the wall. He would have liked to look at Henry, but he couldn't do it.

"Arielle is—my girlfriend. You knew that, didn't you?"

"No. She didn't . . ."

"There are a few things you don't have a clue about. I'm thinking of Ragna, for example."

Carl dipped the float in the bucket of water, something his instructor had forbidden.

"Ragna? What do you mean?"

"Naturally I'd rather have taken you to Ryke myself, but I had a model that afternoon, the studio was heated, everything was prepared. I've had lots to do recently; a few things are working out really well."

Carl learned that his handyman Henry had started working for a small new press called UVA on Acker Strasse, just a few hundred meters from the Assel, one of the start-ups. He was going to design the covers, the catalog, the ads and so on; he'd be what they'd recently started calling *designers* and: he had passed on Carl's poems.

"There were at most . . . seven poems."

In his embarrassment, Carl couldn't think of anything else to say. His heart was beating in his throat. Something at a publishing house! Something under his name, seven poems by Carl Bischoff from Gera. From Berlin.

"They're really nice, Carl, your lyrical works . . . We should collaborate some time."

He turned away and looked at his cement-bag-paper sketches, mostly heads and a few sheets on which Carl couldn't recognize any outline, just swoops and arcs.

Carl didn't dare express a judgment. In his view, these animals' eyes revealed wisdom; these animals were at one and the same time melancholy, witty, and warm-hearted, if that can be said of sheep and cows. On one piece of paper, Carl had recognized Dodo, looking him directly in the eye.

"Dodo can talk," Henry said.

"Talk?"

"Dodo can do a lot of things. The Shepherd had her in tow back then. He walked through the streets with her, a flag in one hand and Dodo in the other, more or less—Et vive la liberté, if you know what I mean. Apparently, Hoffi grew up with the goat, on his farm back home, somewhere in the north, but no one knows exactly where. He never talks about it."

"He likes animals," Carl countered tentatively, "like you." Carl pointed at the charcoal sketches on the floor.

"Our first plan was a kolkhoz, some cattle, a few stalls in the shed, some vegetables, a small field, maybe in Krausnick Park, there was enough room."

"A farmer in Berlin," Carl murmured, and scraped the blade of his trowel clean with a tile shard.

As they drank the rest of the beer together, they got onto the subject of the worker guerrillas and 20 Schönhauser. Henry called it the "first free building in East Berlin." He was completely onboard and explained the solidarity of it to Carl—Hoffi's principle: that each and every one is equal and equally worthy, although "in the current situation," workers must receive special attention. He doesn't believe in armed struggle, at least not for the time being. "But you have to be prepared." After a while, Carl had drunk enough to ask about money again.

"Two sources of revenue," Henry replied. "First: looting tools. Mostly from containers on construction sites in the West. We break in and done! We've been doing it for a long time. 'Sabotage the breeding ground of capital through immediate redistribution,' that's also part of Hoffi's principle. Second: the Wall, that is, selling it. I'm sure you saw the pile of concrete in the courtyard on Schönhauser. The Shepherd has advance orders and proper contracts. Hans deals with the business side of it. Everything is very well organized. Maybe you heard about the theft of the Wall down in Steinstücken—it took five trucks, the logistics of it . . ."

Henry shook his head and stared blankly for a few seconds as if he himself needed time for it to sink in.

"There are inquiries from firms, even from overseas. They buy large sections, complete, by the meter. These are then set up outside some head office in Cincinnati or at a swimming pool in Sacramento. Private orders are filled too, of course, every little bit helps. Some want their piece of the Wall in a particular shape, that's all I'm going to say about it. We manufacture it in our workshop, discreetly, nicely honed, you can do that with the good cement we have here."

"B 500," Carl said, "best quality."

"In any case, it's a good business and *with that alone* the Shepherd has a lot on his plate, I mean, in case you've got doubts . . ."

The good painter didn't notice, but Carl, whose gaze swept over the freshly plastered wall again and again (yes, he could be satisfied with his work), had immediately noticed a woodlouse that had managed to eat its way through the nearly solidified but not fully cured plaster into the open. The last woodlouse, Carl thought. It was remarkably large, almost as wide as a thumbnail, and its shell was encrusted with lime. Carl pushed some mortar into the hole with the point of his trowel and let the little, gray creature dig.

Henry gathered up his cement-bag pages and stacked them one on top of the other. He carefully stowed his paints in the gas mask bag. Seven poems at a publishing house, Carl thought—there was nothing more he could do for them now. They were on their way. It was a kind of journey that maybe could only happen here, in this area. Seven poems on a desk in Acker Strasse.

Field Street, what a name.

COLLIERY COMRADESHIP

"Why don't you send any news, Carl?"

Carl found it unpleasant to lie constantly and was ashamed about it. Still, he'd been miffed at how rarely his mother engaged with his reports about life at home that he had taken great trouble to invent, and when she did, then only reservedly and superficially. Did it even matter to her at all at this point that he was there in Gera as the rearguard? OK, he wasn't actually *there* and he had certainly sensed the uncertainty and fear in his mother's letters, especially between the lines. Things had turned out differently than she'd imagined. That much, at least, she did confide in him with the intention of "explaining everything" one day.

Until then, the situation would remain the same: his parents were moving through world history. They had set off and were having an adventure; they were the undisputed leading actors of the unfolding events, with all the inherent difficulties, whereas Carl more or less performed services behind the lines, a supporting role, somewhere in the East, in a homeland that was perhaps already half-forgotten.

Carl often backdated his letters by several days to feign a longer postal route. He had to lie about the postmark, too. He invented a central post office in Berlin, where all the mail sent to the West was initially gathered for logistical reasons due to "the new situation." In addition, he had heard on the radio (in the Zhiguli, on his way to the Assel), that letters sent from the East to the West were still being monitored "for the purpose of strategic surveillance." Telephone traffic was also still being wiretapped (by West Germany's secret services), a procedure that, as a man named Kurt van Haaren (the name was pointlessly engraved in Carl's memory) had explained, had "a solid legal justification." All these things take time, Carl thought, but they could, if necessary, be put forward in his defense.

That neither the time nor the place of his letters were in accordance with the truth seemed to him insignificant compared to the energy it took to maintain the correspondence (and with it, the illusion that he was in Gera), including the fictions he had to invent. He often began with trivialities about the neighbors or changes in the area, about new shops from Bavaria that were popping up or strikes in the Modedruck textile company, and so on. And because he couldn't repeat the same stories, he started coming up with a few more specific things, a daytrip to the garden in Kayna (yes, he was looking after that, too) and from there a short hike through Schnaudertal to Meuselwitz, for example. Or taking part in one of Gera's Monday demonstrations. He pictured it and, in a few words, sketched the protestors' path through the city center, down Clara Zetkin Strasse to Puschkinplatz, past the Quisisana restaurant. He described the police officers' restraint (they no longer have much of a say anyway) and the speeches in the St. Johannis Church.

Carl's wrist relaxed, which allowed him to relate individual speeches and add his commentary. He saw brave individuals, people overwhelmed by the unrelenting march of history that was overturning everything in its path. He saw people who were hungry for life, who were embittered, who were filled with hatred. In the end, their call for Germany sounded more like a cry for help, more desperate than enthusiastic, Carl wrote, and it sounded as if they meant something other than or rather much more than "Germany." Carl didn't know this—he spent his days in Berlin in the basement of the Assel—but he could picture it and *in the letter* he saw it all very clearly: he connected the news bulletins he'd heard on the car radio with his knowledge of the area and the fanciful notions he harbored about his Thuringian countrymen; in his thoughts, he was becoming carried away by the demonstration and little by little, almost automatically, he ended up imagining a man who, without hesitating, climbed to the pulpit and shouted: "Brother miners, open your eyes, we're rich! The richest of all!"

The man didn't mean this spiritually, not in relation to God. He meant the uranium, the Thuringian uranium deposits. He demanded that SDAG Wismut be immediately expropriated from the Russians and the uranium be sold to the *highest bidder*, "from anywhere in the world, brothers!" There was some laughter, but it was no joke. "Colliery comradeship, not dictatorship!" the man shouted in the nave, and his cry echoed for a long time.

Without a doubt, Carl wrote to his parents, this man had worked for Wismut as a miner and judging by his age, he'd been working the mines for thirty or forty years. His voice had sounded strangely tinny, maybe his larynx or lungs were already being eaten away by cancer from the radiation, like so many fellow uranium miners. It was the same with Carl's grandfather, who had spent half his life underground. "What oil is for the Kuwaitis, uranium is for us!" the tin in the pulpit jangled over

137

the heads of the congregation. "Let's found the ore-duchy of Gera and Schlema, of Ronneburg and Seelingstädt with the miners' emblem in the crest!" That was the conclusion of his speech, concise and well thought-out; there was no more laughter now. The man took advantage of the brief silence to intone the song "Come, brother miners." A few old-timers, all of them Wismut miners, joined in, as did, little by little, everyone in the church, then the organ too, one thundering chorus and echo of the coming ore-duchy.

This was no utopia. It was a man with a proposal from the depths of his own ground, Carl wrote.

There wasn't a single representative of the opposition, nor any of the romantics from the grassroots action groups who could have offered a comparable initiative, just this man from the mountains, a miner and pit-brother, with his tinny voice that at first had shone down from the pulpit alone and isolated like a Davy lamp and then, at least for a few minutes, outshone everything else and in this way rekindled the euphoria of revolution one more time. No one but this miner was able, Carl wrote, to project a vision of brotherly comradeship, rich and free and tolerant, a Thuringian-Saxon ore-duchy, supported by the pride of its inhabitants.

Carl stopped writing. His wrist had warmed up and was loose. For a moment, he had forgotten that his story was invented; he'd let himself get carried away. It was the first time that writing had given him so much satisfaction and joy, and anxiety immediately set in: maybe he wasn't a poet at all, just a prosaist, a letter writer—a letter liar, to be precise.

WHITE WOLVES FROM OUTER SPACE

"A lot of buildings are here," the Shepherd said. He looked around the room with satisfaction and rose to give a short welcome speech.

Some of the emissaries acted like clan chiefs and were also identified as captains. Some had wound scarves around their heads and were done up like pirates, others wore heavy, steel-toed boots, overalls, and safety goggles around their necks. Their building's address was their title of nobility. That's how they introduced themselves and how they were addressed: "86 Kastanie said" or "What does 64 Kollwitz think?" and so on.

Before the start of the meeting, Carl had stood outside on the street like an usher and pointed out the entrance to the Assel.

"Is this where it is?"

"Yes, please watch your step, go down the stairs and turn left."

Skeptical looks were the least of the reactions. One of the captains asked at the top of his voice if "this hole" was the site of the new Mitte plenum, upon which the Shepherd banned the use of the word *plenum*. This word made him want to puke. His objection carried weight—it was spoken by no less than the captain of the first captured building in the East, Hoffi, the veteran captain, 20 Schönhauser, their admiral in a way. "And please, dear friends, fellow combatants and guerrilleros, it's better to call them *inhabited*, inhabited buildings, not squatted!"

Hoffi hated the usual vocabulary. He hated words like "info-shops" and "socio-cultural" and had so far been able to prohibit their use, at least among his own pack; "none of that treacle," the Shepherd had said, whatever he meant by that.

Actually, Carl still had work to do. This was the tail end of the masonry. He put a small partition wall in the back area of the Assel to make a small, separate room—"for the distribution," he said. "For tools and bricklaying materials," added Henry, who, still Carl's sidekick, often knew more about the pack's plans than Carl. Carl liked working with Henry. Together, they'd achieved something and earned each other's trust.

"A lot of buildings are here," the Shepherd repeated, "many of the early ones, but new buildings, too, I see . . ."

Because of the expected crush, Hoffi had summarily decided to use Fenske's cellar (the most spacious room in the catacombs) and had single-handedly built a long table out of sawhorses and planks. Except for the tiny hatch in the air shaft to the courtyard, there was no natural light in the space, so they set up construction lamps. Hoffi had not only ignored Dr. Fenske's ban, he'd also unceremoniously cleared away the mysterious (maybe sacred, maybe cursed) left boot collection and piled it against the walls.

Around a dozen emissaries had shown up. Almost every day, new addresses of "buildings taken into custody" were making the rounds. Dozens of them. Half the city, thought Carl.

"And it's much more than a response to demolition and vacancy," the Shepherd stressed, "it's the blaze of resistance." Hoffi loved fire metaphors. And he loved the jungle warrior Ernesto "Che" Guevara's foco theory, which called for the kindling of "hotspots," separate, scattered, smoldering nests of revolution, the preliminary stage of widespread conflagration.

The captains of the buildings on Kastanien Allee were accompanied by three delegates of the United Left, which had a particular interest in the aguerrillas and their organization. In addition, there was a third group that called itself the "Wydoks," most of whom belonged to 5 Schönhauser, a building that had been taken "into custody" only a few days after number 20. At the time, Hoffi the Shepherd had called for "unconditional solidarity of the aguerrillas with number 5," and since then the two groups were close. A couple of shady loners had taken seats at the Shepherd's table. Everyone was drinking beer, lots of beer.

Carl was the bricklayer, no question, but he was also someone who saw what work needed to be done, which is why it fell to him to take care of refills: it was the first time in his life serving as a waiter, as an orderly to be more exact, at least in a rough, oversimplified way that only involved hauling up a few fresh crates of beer.

For a while, the Wydoks made jokes about Fenske's boots and then finally declared that they were determined to run in the local election *as a party*. Radio P would be their own broadcasting station, "the first free radio station in the East," 106 megahertz on FM. They'd been thinking about having their own television station as well, also pirated. Their model was TV Stop in Christiania. It would be more accurate to say they talked about it; their own visionary discussed it, Little Frank (everyone called him that), head technician at Radio P, whose broadcasting team shifted constantly among the attics of Schönhauser and Oranienburger Strassen in order to criticize the "occupiers' swinish system" and to proclaim the "Free Republic of Utopia" in the ether. Carl had the sound of Little Frank (of his voice) in his ear; he'd often heard Little Frank on the radio in his Zhiguli. He was surprised at how short Little Frank actually was. His voice, in any case, grew large when he announced the aim of "Wydok's autonomous operation." "As long as the buildings are still the People's Property, take them over, because they belong to YOU," was his central message, though it was difficult to make out (in the static of the ether), embedded in music by Sandow, Tom Terror or Feeling B, along with tape recordings of younger, unknown bands, and interspersed with their pounding interval signal, Beethoven, the first notes of the Ninth Symphony followed by the motto "Wydok, this is Wydok speaking, the white wolves from outer space"—and so on.

"Our transmitter power is forty watts, range—five kilometers," Little Frank concluded his speech. Great applause in the cellar.

In the Shepherd's view, Radio P was "absolutely crucial," because it connected the inhabited buildings and could pass on warnings.

"This touches on our real concern," Hoffi announced. He stood up, spread his arms wide and proposed that this gathering in Fenske's cellar be followed by regular meetings, as a kind of advanced training—a "defense colloquium."

He followed this with an incoherent speech about life and work in the so-called underground. In the glare of the construction lamps, the cellar colloquium turned into a gathering of ghosts that expanded in countless shadows on the wall. A confederacy of ghosts, Carl thought when the Shepherd asked him to bring up another fresh crate of beer. When he returned, a man Hoffi had earlier addressed as Comandante rose to speak. Some of them had referred to him as "the demolition expert" and others knew the man as Krusowitsch or Kruso. After he arrived, the man who bore these many names had taken a seat on one of the tall salon chairs. The Shepherd had sat down on the other.

For two seconds, the Comandante gazed down at his open hands as if he needed to glean there one more time what had actually led him to this dim place. Although it was still winter and cold outside, he wore only a short, dark leather shirt. His arms were darkened with oil or soot. He wore his long black hair in a braid; he looked like a Native American. Like a chieftain without a tribe, Carl thought.

Before returning to his work (he still had plaster in the pan that had to be used), Carl heard the Comandante's recommendation:

"Anthropomorpha. That's the solution."

Dogs were used in war two thousand years before Christ, as is generally known, he explained, and to illustrate the point (or for what other purpose?), the Comandante slid a spiked collar across the table.

"Trench dogs, water dogs, messenger dogs, explosive detection dogs . . ."

He cleared his throat. He spoke very softly, partly into his open hands, which lent his words an air of wisdom and a prophetic character.

"Some of your buildings have set up guard duty; that's com-mendable. At 86 Kastanie, there's an anti-Nazi locker in the hall-way with halberds, shakos, and a compressed air horn for alarms. This is good, very good, nothing against it. Some buildings have bars on the windows and some, as far as I know, have posted signs in the room—*Fascist-Alarm Procedures*. It's all exemplary, but it's pointless."

He cleared his throat.

"It won't stand up to true violence and people with real weap-ons." Again, the Comandante lowered his gaze and read from the palms of his hands:

"In defending your buildings, border dogs are the solution. *Former* border dogs, to be precise, from the former border. With a proper bite, as far as Nazis are concerned."

He fell silent and looked around the room. Despite his air of calm and superiority, the Comandante gave Carl the impression of being damaged. It wasn't so much what he was suggesting, instead something in him seemed damaged—his soul, or how to put it?

"Anything else?" the Shepherd asked.

The Comandante pulled a book with the title *Police Dogs* and a pile of paper from his jute bag and began reading out loud.

"Berry von der Schweizerhütte, previously acquired by Lieutenant Colonel Muschwitz, veterinarian and dog purchaser for the National People's Army. Price point three hundred marks, paid with a money order to a breeder in Neubrandenburg."

One of the captains laughed, a small disturbance arose.

"The breed registry provides us the progenitors' names," the Comandante continued, unruffled. "Frei von Peenestrom, Fred von Falkenbruch, Ondra von Hildakloster, Cilla von Teufelskreis—and so on. The breed registry documents not only Berry's early years in Neubrandenburg, but also his demanding course of training in the Wilhelmshorst border dog kennels and from there to the Wall, here in Berlin. After the so-called Fall of the Wall, all traces of him are lost—which isn't surprising in the chaos of those days. Many of the dogs were transferred, stolen, relocated. This means there are dealers, trading centers. One of the most important is the German Shepherd Association, which runs an establishment with a large parking lot south of Potsdam, right on Highway 2. It recently changed its name to The Prussian Pub. In front, there's the rest stop bistro and in back are the kennels: a trading center for animals like Berry, fierce, in demand, and unspoiled."

His left eyelid drooped slightly and twitched.

"Berry, a Rotweiler from the anti-fascist defenses—if you know what I mean."

At that moment, Carl left Fenske's cellar; his plaster was set. Three or four more shifts and the roughest work would be done, construction in the Assel. Then he'd head home. He'd sleep a bit first and then write, hopefully.

PART IV

PART IV

COUNTRYMEN

"Father found"—that was the most important news after the start of the new year. Suddenly Carl's father had resurfaced. For obscure reasons, he had been swept from Büsum, a tiny village on the North Sea coast, back to the Giessen central transit camp, where the missing person announcement that Carl's mother, with Dr. Talib's help, had sent to all the interim camps, transit camps, and temporary shelters reached him. Walter had not managed very well up north, Inge wrote to Carl. He wasn't able to get a footing; there hadn't been any "opportunities."

Although everything Carl thought he knew about his parents had been called into question, this failure did not surprise him. His father was not the kind of person who sought connection, quite the opposite. He was someone who was happy being alone and who avoided meetings that were not part of his daily routine; someone who shied away from others as much as possible: how on earth, then, could it work out for him—as a refugee in a village on the North Sea? In the end it was a defeat and if there was any reason that Walter Bischoff had not made any serious attempt to locate his wife, then it was this: separately after Giessen.

In early February, Walter arrived at the Diez train station wearing his hunter's rucksack on his chest and his accordion on his back, like a wandering minstrel, a member of an orchestra scattered by the turmoil of the times. He came one train too early and so initially set out through the city alone, despite his baggage. He moved slowly; he was in no hurry. He wandered along the boulevard that was busy at this hour and suddenly saw his wife, Inge. He first recognized her by her gait, even from a distance, by the movement of her head, the way she stopped and gazed at the shop windows, coming ever closer, until he stood before her—"as if out of nowhere," Inge wrote to Carl, adding, "We're so happy."

A couple made for each other, Carl thought. The anomaly was over.

His mother now wrote weekly. Every week an installment of this story, so difficult for Carl to comprehend, which Mrs. Bethmann, the sparrow of Avignon in the Gera-Langenberg post office, reliably forwarded to him. There were these letters that testified to everything and in them there was also all that was unsaid, all that Carl had to imagine and fill in, based on her choice of words, on what she left out, on gaps and unevenness in Inge's handwriting. Ultimately, this was about his parents, whom he pictured going through *it all*, two once-familiar people on their way in a strange, new life.

In March, asylum in the Farmer's Tavern expired. A few of the residents had found work and lodgings, others had to move to transition housing in Osthofen. To the seventh cross, thought Carl.

Inge and Walter now lived with the Talibs, in the basement, in one of the children's bedrooms. The doctor's family had taken them in. There was a camp bed freshly made up with a duvet. Dr. and Mrs. Talib from Syria, four children between the ages of four and fourteen, and two fifty-year-old emigrants from the East, together under one roof. They ate together; they talked a lot. Dr. Talib treated Carl's father with respect. To him, Walter was the head of a small but widely scattered family, who had finally arrived after a long odyssey. "Something cast you out and now you are here, with us," Talib said.

Every Monday (and whatever the weather), Inge and Walter walked to Montabaur, to the central employment agency. That way they saved the bus fare. Later, they were told that refugees, emigrants, and evacuees were allowed to use public transportation free of charge. "But in any case, we like to walk," Inge wrote Carl, "and the landscape is really very pretty." Since leaving, they saved every cent, "for later, for the next step." Carl did not understand why, at this point (their old way of life destroyed without a new one being ready), their *next* step had to be kept a secret. What did they have planned *now*? Evidently something it was too early to reveal.

Carl was familiar with his parents' phase-it-in, tentative approach to life, but the violence (suddenness, recklessness) of their escape had almost overshadowed it (just as your ears are deafened immediately after an explosion and your hearing returns only haltingly, thought Carl, and the comparison seemed fitting). *Phase it in* was a favorite expression of his mother, eclipsed only by *operative*—it had seeped into daily usage from the vocabulary of her specialist language (not secretarial, but specialist): "We'll phase it in, Carl, and then be fully operative."

Carl had grown up with this language. To his mother, who came from the east Thuringian countryside, it had been the language of the city, of modernity and progress, elevated and aspirational. Commanding it indicated . . . Carl lost his train of thought. He fingered Inge's letter, the thin, slender sheets of paper with a delicate, pale yellow flower pattern along the bottom edge.

His parents had opened a bank account, in which they had already "scrimped and saved a modest sum." Inge used this expression, which reminded Carl of his grandmother's stories about the years right after the war. First you had to leave behind everything you owned just so you could start scrimping and saving what little was left? Did it really have to be that way? Was that the necessary condition?

His father repaired the wiring of the large menorah in the Talibs' entrance hall (the candelabra weighed almost twenty kilos) and adjusted the carburetor in Ahmed Talib's car. Since he was working on the car, he also bled the brakes and changed the oil. Walter was astounded that this 1986 Opel Omega A hadn't yet been serviced once—care and maintenance, Dr. Talib didn't have the slightest idea. They don't know much about it in Syria, Walter thought. Walter's favorite thing was lying under the car. A lot had simply been neglected in this Opel, Inge wrote Carl. Inge never passed up an opportunity to be proud of Walter, and of Carl too, naturally, as when "her men" spent an entire Sunday together "working" in the garage. Carl pictured in his mind—his father's commentary, his patience (with regard to the Zhiguli), and his whispering over the open hood with the motor running: he listened and spoke to the engine, he touched it, knocked gently on this or that spot, he was an engine-whisperer . . . Strange, but that's what we were, Carl thought, father and son in the sound of the engine, in the sound of certainty, the big Bischoff and the little Bischoff, tightly enclosed in the old life (absurdly, the thought of two people in aspic flitted through his head).

No doubt his father missed the garage, his own tools, the Zhiguli, and maybe even Carl. The garage was in Gera, in the east Thuringian Elster Valley. The Zhiguli was on Ryke Strasse in Berlin and behind the small back courtyard copse, Carl was squatting in a Berlin cellar apartment, the place he had chosen in order to transform his precarious mundane life into a purely poetic existence. Gold out of shit, thought Carl.

No, he didn't think that way. Because everything around him expressed the future. The sight of his three worn mattresses on the floor, bound together with rope, the broken black-and-white television at the head of his bed and the soot-covered sheets hanging at the window and the coal box near the oven: it may have all been shabby and squalid, but it was full of promise, all these decrepit things (and the half-dilapidated building) all expressed the future. Disintegration was promise, not death, just life, that was the paradox of the time.

Then, in early March, a telephone call from Gelnhausen. For Mr. Bischoff at the Talibs. Walter was invited to a job interview. An appointment had to be made immediately, as if there really was no more time to lose, even Saturday afternoon wouldn't be bad.

The company CTZ (Computer Technology Zollnay) was located on the outskirts of Gelnhausen, high above the town, in a large, white mansion straight out of the American South. It had not only the antique columns, but also a balcony supported on the shoulders of half-naked Amazons, elegantly bowed under the burden, gazing dully into the Kinzig valley.

Only years later did Walter admit his doubts and in doing so evoke an image of this Southern mansion: in the entryway, on the wide, softly creaking staircase with the soft, burgundy runner, he was suddenly seized, almost overwhelmed by a feeling of almost boundless inferiority. It was the first time in his life that he had experienced it in this way and out of the blue, the ugly old word massa came to mind. "In any event, our future looked black and then, for an instant, I saw myself as if I were a black person too, a dejected and graying one, over fifty, simply too old to be a useful slave." He admitted this was absurd and he felt uncomfortable that such a thought had even occurred to him, not to mention his talking about it, and that perhaps the cause of his reaction didn't come from that moment on the stairs, but rather from something that had happened to him in the weeks prior, a kind of transformation, a wearing away and thinning out of his self in the time he was alone, in the camp in Büsum on the North Sea coast . . .

First, they had been taken to accommodation right on the water, a large bunker on the drill ground of an infantry barracks.

Forty people, who had to be relocated after a few days because of an insect infestation. Not so bad, actually. From Walter's point of view—he had decided to be extremely patient ("Some difficulties simply cannot be avoided," was written in the green and orange colored copy of the *Guide for Migrants from the GDR* that each of them had been given in Giessen)—there had only been a few moths.

They marched along a kind of trail on a dyke, led by people from the company responsible for their care. It was seriously cold, but the path was beautiful at low and high tides with gleaming mudflats and a soundless sea. On the way, there were the usual jokes about the accordion case on his back.

They marched inland about five kilometers to a large gymnasium—freshly renovated and well prepared: the entire area was partitioned into small spaces with cupboards and cots, three or four Easterners in each. The hall filled quickly and, ultimately, there were forty or fifty of these cubbyholes lined up next to each other like rabbit hutches, divided by very narrow passageways in which there were always one or two people pacing nervously and brazenly staring at others' beds.

Walter's problem was the accordion because it didn't fit in his locker or under his camp bed—there simply wasn't room for it, so he kept it on the foot of his bed. At night, he stretched his legs over the case, to keep it safe. He could have slept like that, looking up at the basketball hoop over his head, but the hall was just too loud and too stuffy, even though a few of the windows were always open.

Disturbances broke out after just a few days; a woman in the next cubbyhole was attacked because her child sang half the night—now the girl screamed every night. At the harbor newsstand, Walter bought newspapers and read the job listings. Once a week, he took the bus to the employment agency. On the bus, there were others from the sports hall who were making an effort, but all told, it seemed pointless. "No one could tell us why we'd been shipped *there*, to the mudflats, or what we were supposed to do there." Nor was there anything about the area in the migrant guide. Everyone wanted to go to Hamburg or at least to Bremen. Word had it that in Bremerhaven, migrants were housed in hotel ships and in the former red-light district or even in empty apartments seized by the city.

When the weather permitted, Walter sat outside behind the hall and played his accordion. "Straight Jacket!" one of the attendants (or guards) called to him and raised his arm. He'd recognized the song. That was the nicest incident in his time on the coast, Walter said once. Only fifty meters away, there was a small waterway that the people from the company called the harbor stream. On the other side of the harbor stream, there was a kind of storehouse and a row of detached houses. When the light went on in the living rooms (before they drew the curtains and let down the shades), Walter could see the silhouettes of the locals, their evening gestures, self-assured. That's how it set in and then grew, secretly, day by day, that crippling feeling of being inferior, weak, and worthless.

There were two or three drinkers' cubbies, where they played cards or threw dice; the game was called Liar's Dice. Every night, the rattle of the dice—a trying sound. They used the blue plastic cups that every migrant was given as a toothbrush mug along with a few other things for their daily needs, basic cosmetics, in Inge's words. The game: two dice and the attempt to lie well (more precisely, to bluff). A one and a two were a *mex* and only mexes had to be revealed, otherwise you could lie: "Mex!" Mex meant victory, several minutes of yelling and a round of schnapps or beer. After ten or twenty rounds, it sometimes happened that one of the players couldn't find his way out of the hall and in his distress pissed between the beds. The stench was dreadful, so the company providing the housing banned alcohol and began inspecting the cubbies of the "East Swine" for bottles. After one employee was injured (hit on the head with a bottle), his colleagues refused to enter the refugee hall ("that pigsty").

"It's worse here than in the East," the players agreed, and it was their East German protest that produced a relaxation of the rules, at least for Christmas and New Year's Eve—with disastrous results. The hall was cleared a few days later. A hundred migrants were transferred by bus to Giessen, back to the central refugee transit camp.

The entrance to the CTZ offices was at the back of the mansion, but the staircase on which Walter suddenly saw himself as if a black person ("dejected and graying") led to the sunny side of the mansion, directly to a large room with a balcony and honey-yellow walls.

Zollnay, the head of CTZ, was standing behind his desk. He wore a wide-brimmed hat and a thin dustcoat that reached almost to his ankles. He was short and broad-shouldered with a round face. For a moment, he looked like he was ready for a duel but then he offered Walter his hand: he was the boss, there was no doubt.

To the left of his desk sat a man who was introduced as the managing director and to his right was a woman from the personnel department. The personnel department for the southern region had skipped over Walter's unfavorable origin (the East) and come across rare and, yes, valuable qualifications. A man from East Germany who knew five computer languages—what on earth?

"Our facility with all its standards here in the Imperial Palatinate . . ." Thus began Zollnay's recruitment speech.

Walter looked at the floor: gleaming, dark, wide-planked parquet flooring.

He was to start work immediately.

*

Something significant had happened again and Inge wrote Carl
that they knew exactly what they wanted and this was *the next
step* on their way.

Walter Bischoff was hired as a teacher. In CTZ terminology,
he was now a *trainer*. As a trainer, Walter taught computer programming languages with mysterious names like Pascal, C++, and
Cobol. He would be traveling from one large company to another
all over the West, up and down the country, the boss had said.

In comparable job postings in *Computer Week*, which Walter
had read in preparation for his interview with CTZ, the salary
was 7,000 deutschmarks a month. CTZ had offered him a starting salary of 5,000 deutschmarks and Walter had agreed immediately. It didn't seem proper to him to negotiate over such sums.
"His income is *enormous*," Inge wrote Carl, and Carl had to agree
that the amount was incredible. So, what everyone had always
suspected was true: the West was prosperity and gold.

In the end, the enormous salary didn't change their spar-
tan lifestyle in the slightest. Their thrift remained, and even
increased as they readily gave in to certain fears (homelessness,
hunger, general ruin) that hadn't played any role at all during
their "emigration." Perhaps these fears had been suspended
in favor of their utterly irrational decision. Carl was the only
one who started calculating (and hoping). Occasionally, the
exchange rate on the black market was ten to one. That meant
that his father was earning 50,000 East German marks a month.
A fraction of that would be enough, Carl thought, to cover
a few years in Berlin, repairs on the Zhiguli—maybe even to
buy a different used model. He'd seen some stunning Mazdas
with large, shiny hoods and surprisingly broad fronts . . . For a
moment, the thought of getting rid of the Zhiguli filled him with
shame—he knew he could never do it. As if I were getting rid of
my father, Carl thought.

*

Again, a new life began. Two weeks after the conversation in the White Villa (that was actually what it was called in town), the Bischoffs moved into a furnished apartment in the CTZ boss's private house. "Only my mother lives in the house now," Zollnay had said. For some reason he was insisting they move in and change their registration to the Garten Strasse address in Gelnhausen-Roth without delay. The phrase "net cold rent" sounded unpleasant. "We'd prefer the rent warm," Carl's father, who was unfamiliar with the term for the cost of rent not including utilities or maintenance charges, told his boss.

The apartment consisted of two small rooms on the attic floor and a dirty, glass-walled storage room, which was actually a sunroom left unfinished. Inge and Walter: they'd both noticed the rusted beams over the bedroom window. The entire house seemed incomplete. The balcony was ringed by a balustrade of still unplastered aerated concrete, covered with moss and an algae-like plant. It smelled musty but that didn't seem critical; after all, it was the first time in months that the Bischoffs could put aside their rucksacks for a while.

"It's a relief," Inge wrote to Carl. Unfortunately, their rooms were not a self-contained apartment, but Zollnay had said that something could surely be done at some point.

Each time they entered the building, the door to the apartment beneath them would open (as in an old comedy film) and the boss's mother would step out and, smiling, would stretch out her arms and say, "Countrymen, my dear countrymen!" That was the usual opening to her monologues about her son, the benefactor, who had connections in the highest circles (she mentioned "the chancellor") and as a result, everything would work out for them, for Inge and Walter. She was a strong, stocky person, with apron strings tied in front of her stomach.

The Bischoffs' apartment faced the road that connected Gelnhausen with the smaller towns in the direction of Hanau and Frankfurt. Their view onto the valley: the railway embankment and the Kinzig river, which curved at that point, adjacent to a marsh, then diffuse land up to the highway with its rumbling day and night, and sometimes a mountain would appear on the horizon. Was that the Spessart range?

From their balcony, Inge could read the town limit sign: "Lieblos 1 km." The towns in the area had such names: Lieblos (Loveless), Bösgesäss (Badrump), Altenhasslau (Oldhatemild), but there were also Linsengericht (Lentildish) and Meerholz (Seawood).

Inge, at any rate, was ready to warm up to the view and the field past the road. To the left there were a few gardens, in which small livestock was kept, "but with very careless and slipshod fencing." Once a loose chicken was run over. Inge wrote Carl a very detailed account with a level of compassion and grief that was completely out of proportion to what else was happening to his parents, to him (their son), and in the rest of the world. Carl's own explanation was that his mother, with her Thuringian background, was a friend to all chickens, broadly speaking, their godmother, as it were. He could picture it: his mother crossing the road and feeding the chickens with the remains of her breakfast, breadcrumbs and eggshells, to which chickens, as everyone knows, are nearly addicted. She would talk to them—"Countrymen, my dear countrymen!"—and the hens would peck and nod, nod and peck, non-stop. They expressed their agreement in the direct, excessive, silent-film type manner that only chickens are capable of, which made Inge giggle.

Mornings, Walter would walk to the Southern mansion along Herzbach Weg, three kilometers uphill. There, the trainers gathered in a large room with several desks to prepare their classes. He didn't have his own desk, but then no one did at CTZ. His route to the mansion passed a large American army base, the

Coleman Kaserne. Earlier, during the Second World War, it had been called the Herzbach Kaserne. When he passed it, Walter's eyes would sweep over the reddish-brown sandstone relief of Nibelung figures that protruded distinctly from the facade and, on some days, wanted to speak with him—about his future plans, future battles, about conquering the world.

Because it was the custom in Thuringia, Bischoff greeted the soldiers he saw, mostly near the main entrance. "An armored division," the boss's mother had said. The young GIs, who weren't used to anyone greeting them, looked at him, astonished.

"Hi, man!"

It was all incredible, but it happened. Walter didn't own a briefcase yet. He used his hunter's rucksack from Gera and he was the only one who arrived at the mansion on foot.

In April, after three weeks of preparation (the short man in the hat and dustcoat called it his "familiarization period"), Walter Bischoff drove a company Mercedes to Hamburg and taught his first class. The car was a black 1974 Mercedes 280E that required an additional bottle of motor oil every three hundred kilometers. Walter had bought himself a map and drawn in his route, first to the hotel. Outer Alster, Inner Alster, the center of Hamburg was a madness of one-way streets—all of them full of Western cars: for a second, that was Walter's impression. Although he was sitting in a Mercedes, he still had his Zhiguli point of view. His West was deeply rooted in the East, simply too deep, Walter thought, as he started another circle along the Alster.

The computer school was on the grounds of the international port and so Walter was let through several barriers, one after another. His forehead was covered with sweat and he was surprised. He could do *everything* here. He was CTZ now. The West opened up. But why? What for? Strange questions. He knew very well. "I'm an imposter from Gera"—that's how he felt. For about two kilometers, he drove slowly and carefully between towers of containers, in a strange car through a strange land. "It's just stress," he whispered to himself and stepped on the gas.

There were undoubtedly students on the course who could ask a few questions about Unix that Walter Bischoff couldn't answer. They let him know this; they tried to show him. "The most important thing is that no one figures out where you're from, actually,"—Karajan, the head trainer at CTZ, had said this to him. Karajan had shown Walter how the course material should be presented, what technology he could expect on site, and how it should be handled. The most laborious were the transparencies for the overhead projector. Each course was a jungle of transparencies. "An *Easterner*, Walter, you understand—a lot of them wouldn't put up with that, not at 1,000 marks a day tuition," Karajan had said.

Walter hardly slept that week. Nights, he would sit behind a few potted plants in the dimly lit hotel lobby, studying the latest technical publications. He read, took notes, and memorized the material he would teach the next day. He had bought his books at Staak & Beirich, a specialist bookstore in Frankfurt, which from then on he called "my bookshop." His bookshop had a single room with tall shelves, labyrinthine aisles, a corner where you could sit and read, and, in Walter's view, a heavenly selection. There, on Brauchbach Strasse, Walter also bought new accordion sheet music; it was the first time he had spent money only on himself (since arriving in the West).

In the breaks, Walter remained alone. He could more or less hide his Thuringian accent, aside from a certain coloring of the vowels that was *incurable*, as a speech therapist once put it while inspecting his vocal cords. Just in case, he had prepared a biography. Born in? He didn't know. Something would occur to him, if worse came to worst. Grew up in the Frankfurt area, that was surely enough—later in West Berlin. Why West Berlin? He didn't know. Maybe because it was in the East but was still the West.

Half the course. Half his life. On the Wednesday morning, Walter took a walk around the container port. It was probably forbidden. Someone was following him, but when he turned around, there was no one there, just the faintly undulating shadows of the container towers. It made him nervous, and so he got lost and was running late. In the end, he was about to start running when someone grabbed his shoulder.

"Where are you off to so fast?"

"I work here."

"Here?" The man had on worn metalworker coveralls. Maybe it was also a shabby uniform, container guard, if there was such a thing. He looked Walter in the eye, penetratingly, severe, with a trace of pity, perhaps.

"No, somewhere over there." Walter pointed in the direction he assumed the classroom was.

"My boy," the man said, "you have to go that way." He pointed in the opposite direction. The man was tall, muscular, and bald. He looked like Walter's father, when Walter was a child, in a village called Culmitzsch that had disappeared long ago. His father was long dead too. He had spent too much time underground, mining uranium.

"Look at that board over there, my boy. It's still good, isn't it? Take it with you, you can always use a board like that, sooner or later."

The board lay before one of the container towers.

It was a good board.

When Walter Bischoff came up to the school building, board in hand, a few of the course participants were standing outside, smoking. They watched him. He put the board in the trunk of the Mercedes and wiped his hands on a rag.

On Friday, when the course was finished, Walter wandered through the city. He avoided the shopping area and didn't go to a café. After a while he reached the fish market and continued along the Elbe beach. Although it was too cold for it, he sat on the sand. He watched the ships coming and going for a time. The West, the West—no other thought. Inge had suggested he visit the last of the remaining emigrant barracks on the America Quay, "but only if you still have the energy and time for it." She had read about them. Her ancestors had emigrated from Altenburger Land to St. Louis, Missouri. "It might be nice to see it," Inge had said, but Walter fell asleep on the beach. When he woke, it was dark and it was raining.

The windshield wipers only worked grudgingly. Dampness seeped into the car and the ventilator didn't work. He drove with one hand on the steering wheel and dried the windshield as best he could with a cloth handkerchief. He'd have to change the head gasket in the Mercedes before the next course. And maybe he could also do something about the fan. He thought of the board in the trunk. And he thought of his father. He was still very tired, but he had done it.

THE ONLY PATH

Every time he climbed out of the Assel, Carl felt numb. He fished his cigarettes out of his pants pocket and babbled nonsense to himself. Good nonsense, speaking it kept his life in balance. Besides, there was always something in it that he might be able to use later, some esoteric word or a little melody. Nothing more than that, but that's how it began; that was the starting point. He squinted in the light and plodded across the courtyard into the underbrush of Krausnick Park, where he sat down on a chunk of wall. He pulled out his notebook. There was a smell of spring.

The birches in the bomb crater had begun to bud. It made no difference that they were half-buried. Carl noticed a movement in the branches; it was Dodo, munching on the new twigs. The first buds were full and the Shepherd's strategic vocabulary was blooming, too. The military terms remained (the Assel as a shelter or U-boat) but the words "café" and "literature" were new. He'd read *Under Milk Wood* by Dylan Thomas. As always, they were meeting at Irina's before work, and the Shepherd was talking about it. At some point, he used the term *worker's café*. "The Assel is about labor and literature, that is, it's about a certain consciousness of it that is being lost these days. Labor and literature belong together. We want to maintain this awareness, especially in discussions—the Assel is open conversation, among workers, absolutely blunt, no taboos."

He also wanted to invite authors: "Not the usual names, of course. And because we're neither anti-life, nor anti-worker, drinks will be served, above all good, strong coffee, dark as night. And maybe a few other things, too. Wine, whiskey, nothing that contradicts literature. Giving the worker a home in this age means . . ."

The Shepherd talked about this point at length, looking Carl in the eye again and again. He had made Carl an ally. He'd seen his writing material, even in the days of Carl's fever, the books and the typewriter in the trunk of the Zhiguli, next to the tools and the meat. At the time, he had only been interested in the tools. Maybe Henry had said something as well, something about seven poems on a desk at the Acker Strasse Independent Bookstore Press (this—*Unabhängige Verlagsbuchhandlung Ackerstrasse*—is what was hidden behind their acronym, UVA).

Carl began to dream. From the Shepherd's talk about the café came glints of a small, sturdy countertop with the cold gleam of its synonym *bar*, and almost incidentally there arose the prospect of a small, regular income. This prospect was very important to Carl. In moments of anxiety, he would run through the possibilities that were open to him: mailmen and telegram messengers were often in demand. As were meat carriers, who lugged cold half-carcasses of pigs through the streets on their backs. They wore special white coats for this, with hoods, as if on an Arctic expedition, but really they only went from the slaughterhouse to the butchers or from one store to another, especially where the slaughtering was done without a license. Carl could see this right outside his window: ladders with the bodies of pigs split open in the courtyard behind the butcher's shop that faced Prenzlauer Allee. Coal carrier was also an option, maybe even gravedigger. They were always looking for gravediggers, as far as he knew. Carl was confident he could handle it physically. At sixteen, in his first year as apprentice, he had balanced seven-meter-long pieces of squared timber on his shoulder. Beyond a certain load, you started to hover. There was this inexplicable effect: the load turned into a rush, a kind of intoxication, at least in the case of squared timbers. With bags of cement, it was different. Cement only ever dragged you to the ground.

Although his life behind the small bomb crater copse at 27 Ryke Strasse may have appeared shabby and poor (the mattress raft on the cold floorboards with a defunct black-and-white television as a mooring), the word *poverty* hadn't previously occurred to him. And if it had: being a poor poet didn't seem a bad fit if you were a poet. All in all, he was on the right path, the only path. My existence is well justified, just not secure, Carl thought. Often, the opposite was the case, which was presumably harder to bear. If you asked yourself those kinds of questions, that is.

In Babylon on Rosa Luxemburg Platz, a retrospective was being shown that spring of films by the West German director Rainer Werner Fassbinder. An unknown land filled the screen with an actress named Irm Hermann, whose voice sounded in some scenes to be lacking almost any modulation and seemed to be imprisoned in her body. Her voice tunneled deep into Carl's aural memory. He could only remember one scene from the last film: a man standing in front of a supermarket who said, "There's got to be money there." The man didn't talk much. He wore bell-bottoms and a half-buttoned shirt with a wide collar and held a bottle of Ballantine's in his hand. His plan was to rob the supermarket.

Carl's plan was at first to keep driving as an unlicensed taxi even though he had practically no sense of direction and he found it difficult to talk with his fares. But the Zhiguli was his capital, after all, and, according to the constant refrain, capital must be put to work. This was the lesson everyone had to learn now. That the nearly twenty-year-old car with the orange roof would soon be worth nothing at all was something no one had said yet that spring. Carl only knew that it was his father's car, the warm, rolling centerpiece of their past and, strictly speaking, immortal.

Every two days, Carl drove in a few large circles, mostly in Mitte, on Moll Strasse, Pieck Strasse, and Unter den Linden, often in the evening after his shift in the Assel, which was in the process of becoming a worker's café but was far from ready to open and therefore couldn't be a source of income.

Berlin still felt foreign to him on those unlicensed taxi nights. He basically knew only one route through the city and so he tried to connect every new fare destination to it in some way or other. He arranged the few points that seemed familiar to him in a fancifully simplified picture of Berlin and refused to consider other possibilities, of which there must have been thousands (and in fact were). It was probably similar when he wrote—he didn't want a more intense relationship to the wasteland out there (to so-called reality or all that highlighted the triviality of his existence; he thought this for a long time). Moreover, he didn't like city maps. He mistrusted them and his eyes hurt as soon as he opened one of them; you could also say he couldn't cope with them very well. Folded into every city map was the odor of failure and futility.

In the Zhiguli, this often led to long conversations or discussions. Carl tried to cover up his ignorance and joked about what was stressful and nerve-racking. Enormous relief when his fares were able to guide him to their destination. When the trip went well, these customers often had a sense of accomplishment, of having gone through something that everyone should experience at least once (as the saying goes), and they tipped generously. Some said effusive goodbyes and hugged Carl or at least tried to—as if (after all this) they were at the beginning of an exceptional friendship. A white and orange unlicensed taxi erring blindly through Berlin's streets belonged, in an inexplicable but absolutely indispensable way, to the all-encompassing celebration of the times.

Almost every day, there were new openings in the Wall. Tours of the West were rare and naturally he didn't like crossing the border because then he would lose what little sense of direction he had and end up floundering in the city's outer districts.

Carl slowly drove out of the darkness of the East and crossed the old illuminated area of the death strip. No mines, no spring guns. He drove as if creeping forward on soft tires. Was it possible that they'd forgotten something somewhere? A particularly well-concealed wire, not indicated on any drawings, then the sudden detonation, the exploding Zhiguli . . .

He sometimes ended up in corners of the city he simply couldn't find his way out of, even when patient customers explained the route back. From Goten Strasse, Street of the Goths, to the city highway? It's very simple, young man. But Carl couldn't concentrate either on the directions to where they were going (there were simply too many conversations in the car for that and, yes, arguments once in a while) or on the directions back to the East, *back home* . . . First left, then right and so on,

Ostrogoths, Visigoths: his knowledge of history was no help here either. The area was harsh. A dark figure leaped in front of him on the road. Carl swerved; the right front wheel banged against the curb and a beer can hit the back of the car. Probably because of the Zhiguli, Carl thought, because he had entered the kingdom of the Goths in a Russian car.

In essence, Carl ignored the city. He wouldn't have been able to draw a map of the city's districts. He had only a vague idea of Mitte in the center and Nord above it. "Surely you have a map, young man," customers from a district called Steglitz had called from the back seat, an older, impatient couple who were not in a position to help. It was unclear why these old people took the risk of getting into his Zhiguli. That said, there were hardly any Western taxis in the East. And their pockets were likely filled with East German money that had to be spent. They badgered him until he had no choice but to stop and spread out his map of the city. The elderly couple stared incredulously at the pale yellow desert areas that covered the western part of the city on the East German map—on this map there was nowhere they could return to that night. The looked at each other and understood that they should never have crossed the border into the East. A lovely, elderly, frightened couple. They grabbed onto each other's hands, turned wan and yellow and slowly dissolved into the stuffy air above the Zhiguli's imitation leather seats . . .

THE SOFT RUSTLING OF PLASTIC FILM

Slowly and indecisively, Carl drove down Ryke Strasse. Number 13 was only one hundred meters away. A few days earlier, he had noticed the small, hand-painted sign: "ACUD Gallery—Secret Tip." Under "Secret Tip" was written "Finally!" and below that, a childlike drawing of a skull with big black eyes hanging upside down from the word "finally."

I'm the most secret tip of all, thought Carl. And should there be any artists in this area (he knew there were, he would have to meet them at some point), they wouldn't be waiting to be discovered, at least not the artists of Ryke Strasse; of this Carl was certain. The word "finally," in particular, seemed completely out of place on this crudely patched and mostly forgotten street that had long since entered a state of timelessness, connecting its inhabitants directly to eternity, which began somewhere down there, at its foggy, mist-shrouded end, where the two dissimilar guards stood day and night: the water tower and the television tower . . .

"And not everyone who requested admittance there survived it." With these words on his lips, Carl crossed the driveway. There were arrows drawn in chalk on the ground; a path through the bulky waste to the rear building. Lights were burning on the fourth floor. A few people sat on the stairs, smoking and selling beer. A girl shook the hair covering her face, blew it to the side, and looked at him but only to confirm that he didn't belong. No one said, "Finally!"

Later, Carl could barely remember any of the paintings in the exhibition. Large-scale formats. Red, black, abstract, and filled with despair. The male figures had penises as long and thick as their arms. "Whatever has three legs can stand," Carl's father had always said. It was a question of static equilibrium.

One hundred people in two rooms and no one was looking at the pictures on the walls. Carl lit a cigarette and sensed the endless superiority of each person in the room. He pictured the woman on the back stairs approaching him, nestling up to him and standing there next to him (with her hands on his stomach), with the utmost tenderness that he only ever witnessed in his dreams. All that could happen, any second now.

"Do you know the painter?" He'd addressed the woman standing next to him and pointed at one of the paintings.

"Of course," she said.

She didn't have a face or at least he couldn't see it. His gaze didn't penetrate. He only saw an oval spot covered with skin.

He didn't accept the disappointment and stayed for the better part of an hour.

Just before midnight, Henry the good painter came into the room and hugged Carl like an old friend. Henry held him close for two seconds, two precious seconds, which were enough to lure the painter of the large-scale pictures over. He greeted Henry first (without an embrace) and then Carl. His name was Wallrodt.

"The first free gallery in the East," Wallrodt said to Henry in a confiding tone, then started speaking about his work. He wore an Ernst Thälmann jacket covered with white, zebra-like stripes and a rusty wire butterfly pinned to the lapel.

Carl only noticed now that Wallrodt's paintings were done on large schoolroom maps. He recognized the "young African nation states" and the "Warsaw Pact countries." The map under the painting they were standing in front of was titled *The Industrial Conurbations of the Soviet Union.*

"Samara!" Carl called out (as if he had rediscovered a forgotten part of the world) and pointed at one of the conurbations showing through the paint.

"That's where the Zhiguli was built and here! Here is Zhiguli— actually it's a mountain range." Carl inadvertently grabbed at the picture and recoiled. Henry bent forward for a closer look at the spot—a gesture solely for Carl, conspicuous.

"Rilke, for example, was in Samara," Carl stammered, then fell silent.

Wallrodt looked at him attentively, as if he were waiting for something, a punch line, perhaps. He was even smiling. His friendly eyes rested on Carl before returning to Henry. I'm at the very bottom, Carl thought. And I don't even know where the ladder is.

"There are ruined places everywhere, whether here or in Ethiopia," Wallrodt explained. "What interests me is how we can take a stand in this shattered world." He was now speaking only to Henry.

"Is that why everyone here looks like they stepped out of Mad Max?" Henry asked and Wallrodt laughed as Carl edged his way slowly toward the door.

On his way downstairs, he noticed another chalk arrow, half-erased, pointing to an apartment on the third floor. From the hall, Carl could make out a table and a few other pieces of furniture draped with a thin, black plastic film that billowed with a soft rustle when he entered the room. The windows were also covered with plastic film. Candles were placed on the floor throughout the room. The walls were bare except for a small drawing, framed in gold like an icon, that drew Carl's gaze. It was the silhouette of a woman bowing before a naked man. As if following an old court custom, the woman knelt on one knee with her arms stretched out behind her and her head lowered, but just slightly, perhaps because she wanted to keep her eyes on the man's genitals or was kneeling only to see them.

"The drawing isn't finished, but . . ."

Racing heart, rustling film.

"Oh, excuse me, no, don't be alarmed. The light is broken, the whole electrical system here, nothing works."

Since he'd entered the room, the woman had sat motionless on one of the plastic-covered chairs but now she rose and, tentatively, approached him. Carl saw her smile, her high, gleaming forehead.

"Effi?"

The soft rustle of plastic film.

169

"Effi!"

The slender figure, her medium-length hair, under which her shoulders gleamed like silver epaulets. Some light from the hall fell on her face: it was Effi, there was no doubt. In his embarrassment, Carl stretched out his hand toward her.

"Effi, what . . . What are you doing here?"

"I'm Effi."

"I know, Effi, I . . . Did you get my letter . . . ?"

"Excuse me, but the door must stay closed during the performance."

With these words, she shut the door and returned to her chair.

The soft rustle of plastic film.

She hadn't taken his hand.

Carl had pictured it a hundred times but had never really believed they would see each other again, not even while writing his letter, that abrupt declaration of love, which more than anything was an expression of a sudden decision, a departure, that now lay months behind him.

"So, is this all part of your—*installation*?"

His question was naive and he immediately regretted it. He simply knew too little about art, he knew too few artists, as he'd feared.

Effi cleared her throat and picked up a note ready to hand near her chair. "Welcome to this room, wanderer. Behind you, the closed door to a long-forgotten room in a house that was abandoned years ago gives you one last chance to look at these things undisturbed. Things from the past. Your life. And me."

She didn't look at him. She looked absently into the room and put the note back on the floor.

"Ryke, the rich woman, welcomes you."

She said this slowly and clearly.

"We have time."

Carl examined the room, the window, the plastic covering everything. He could have fallen to his knees before Effi: here I am, take me . . .

After a while, he could do it: he could look at her, could observe Effi, without shame. He saw her broad, bony shoulders, her prominent collarbone, her pale face, and her wide, arched eyebrows with that never-tiring expression of alertness; he saw her fine, thin mouth with the small scar on her upper lip and her somehow shaggy hair. He saw the girl and he saw the woman he'd been in love with, since forever, Carl thought.

"We have time now."

She hadn't said it to him, just to the room.

After a while, something happened. The woman on the chair grew unfamiliar, she changed rapidly, with each breath. Carl now noticed traits of hers that must have escaped him back then. But that couldn't be it. He'd forgotten. Something about Effi that had struck him even then as hardened and damaged. Something had held me back, Carl thought. Now he remembered. More than shyness or timidity or the fear of being rejected. It hadn't lessened his desire, on the contrary. And now, there she sat, a puzzle.

Each movement was followed by the rustling of plastic film. It's the objects' breath, Carl thought, as if the building were sighing.

After half an eternity, the woman, who possibly was Effi, spoke to Carl. "What are you up to next?"

"And this—here?"

"It's just finished."

Carl led her through the small forest in front of the building. He briefly took her hand. She stopped, then stood very close to him. She was exactly his height. He'd forgotten that. Had she really always been this tall? She slipped a leg between his and looked into his eyes.

In his apartment, Effi (or the woman who must be Effi) became very quiet. She admitted she was hungry and Carl started fixing her something to eat. Because nothing better occurred to him in his confusion, he started to tell her how he had found his two-burner stove top, in which street he'd picked it up, how he'd finally scraped off the flaking rust from the burners and then "rubbed it well with butter." He pointed at this and that object (a plate, a knife). All these witnesses of his habitation now seemed peculiar to Carl and suddenly he had the feeling that he'd long ago found accommodation here, come aboard this road.

Because it sounded impressive and important, he also told Effi about the guerrillas (the aguerrillas) he'd *joined up with*, how they'd armed themselves with zinc-plated halberds, about their use of border dogs in battle, and all their plans. Effi sat on Carl's chair at the workbench, looking at him attentively, so he also told her about the Shepherd and the pack. Effi knew Henry as a painter. She'd "often heard" his name, which agitated Carl even more. He told her about selling pieces of the Wall and the worker's café (but not about stealing tools), he simplified the Shepherd's goals, emphasizing solidarity and brotherhood. "He's insane, but in a good way, you know?"

Effi nodded. She agreed with him. He saw the Christmas glow in her eyes and on her forehead that had a certain translucence. Everything about her exuded affection and warmth. She tilted her head slightly (as if it helped her hear him and see him better); she stroked the wood of the workbench while he spoke (the bench for work, Carl thought, she's stroking the work). He saw how slender her hand was; he saw her long, slender fingers and the way her fingertips caressed the grain of the wood. I've missed that, Carl thought.

"First Berlin, then Morocco. Big plans."

Blood rushed to Carl's cheeks—it was the first time Effi had referred to his letter, to one of the two poems he had sent along with his confession. She got it all, understood it all immediately, Carl thought.

"First Berlin, then Morocco," he repeated softly, "Capote, Williams, Bowles . . ."

"Matisse," Effi whispered and Carl now began to realize something, it dawned on him, something very simple, simple but vast and all-encompassing: he had never yet met anyone who believed in him, in his work, that is, and that's what he'd been missing. This realization was abrupt and undeniable, as if he'd suddenly found the name for a pain that had always been there. He explained to Effi that the building behind the small bomb crater copse was first and foremost a place to write, that he (probably) had ended up here precisely because it was a place to write. Yes, essentially, his writing itself had chosen this spot: "After a few days, I understood this, Effi."

"I have a child, Carl."

"What?"

"Freddy, he's four years old."

"And where? I mean, where is your child—I mean Freddy?"

"In Leipzig. We live in Leipzig, Freddy and I."

Freddy and Effi. She did not seem to want to talk more about it, at least not at that moment.

Fried potatoes with fried eggs (Inge's recipe with lots of caraway) and pickles on the side. Water pearled from the window and collected on the cupboard in a small puddle shaped like Lake Baikal. "Academy of Fine Arts": it sounded like music to Carl, it was the old Effi melody that Carl listened to enraptured. They recalled former friends, Effi laughed. It was easy and pleasant to talk to her, a discussion of the situation, out of which anything was possible, and so Carl also started telling her about Inge and Walter.

"Why not leave? But who has the courage? That's the real

question. You should be proud," Effi said softly and stroked the workbench. "I'd go if I could, away from all this."

That was Effi's view and although her answer no doubt had a dark, obscure side, Carl was grateful to her.

For some reason, his movements were often clumsy but he finally finished preparing the meal. Effi ate very little, as if she'd suddenly lost her appetite. After a while, she stood and went into the adjacent room. For a second, Carl saw her slender figure, the elegance of her movements. All evening long, he'd had to be careful not to stare at her and now he forced himself to keep eating and finally he even began clearing up when she called him.

"Cold feet!"

She was standing on the mattress-raft. She'd undressed but wasn't naked. She was wearing something on her skin that gleamed, some kind of fabric but not actually cloth, more of a filigree webbing with lace trimming and a plunging neckline. It's a kind of curtain, thought Carl, who had no idea. Because it was see-through, it was strangely not visible at first glance. Only on second look did he see the dark outline of her sex, marveling as at something one has imagined too often. It was Effi's first lesson. Carl knew what a *bodysuit* was, but he had never before seen anything comparable, something he'd naively imagined only prostitutes or clever princesses wore . . .

"Do you like it, Carl?"

She wasn't looking at him and for a moment her voice had sounded strange, like the voice of the woman in the room with plastic film.

"It's a present from my sister. She lives not far from here, by the way. I don't normally have underwear."

In his bare room, the sheen of the bodysuit had an extraterrestrial air. Effi was now an exotic being, shipwrecked on his raft. She stretched her hand out to him. He wanted to hug her, but Effi was quicker and took his head with both hands.

"I'm very tired, but you could lie next to me anyway, I mean, if you want to, Carl. Or will that be awkward?"

Effi lay right down on her stomach with her arms in front of her chest, which had an air of self-imposed captivity. She'd turned her head and tucked her chin to her shoulder; her eyes were closed and her face completely relaxed.

"Come now. Please."

Carl undressed and nestled up to her. He became hard. He felt the material of the bodysuit against his skin. At some point in the night, he felt a soft pressure that came from Effi, maybe still asleep. He penetrated her and she asked him not to move.

"Stay like that, alright?"

Carl kept still and then he felt it. Like a small hand that clasped him softly, let go, and clasped him again.

"Can you feel it?"

"Yes."

GRASS

Effi's mother had taken her own life—this was widely known in Gera-Langenberg. Effi was thirteen when it happened. "The child found her, all alone," was the story at the time. No one knew more than that. Nevertheless, stories spread in the area, nasty rumors and suspicions.

Carl didn't know anything either, of course not, since he'd never been together with her. He'd never been one of her close friends, nor part of her circle. Effi had always done things that were part of another world, to which Carl had no connection, perhaps because of his background (and despite the fact that he'd always longed to be a part of it). The only connection was a few hours of "art appreciation," a school subject in which he mostly experienced failure.

Carl had never forgotten their teacher Mrs. S.'s assignment to draw one of Albrecht Dürer's watercolors. It was called *The Large Piece of Turf*. *The Large Piece of Turf* depicted about a thousand blades of grass and a bit of earth. For a while, Carl fought against a feeling, for which he later found the word "humiliation" to be fitting, but he finally found a solution.

Initially, he found it very difficult to let his pencil *simply glide* over the paper, but eventually his wrist relaxed and he drew more and more quickly until it became a frenzy, of dashes, fine, long, short, fast strokes, crosshatching—in Carl's view it was the only way he could do justice in his own way to the endlessly detailed variety of *The Large Piece of Turf*. Carl remembered how secretly pleased he was with his drawing (proud, even, and full of expectation).

To grade the assignment, Mrs. S. went from one bench to the next. Occasionally she would pick up a sheet and look at it for a few seconds, but mostly she decided ad hoc.

"What is this supposed to be, Carl?"

She gave his grass a four. Carl could still feel the injury. A few days later, Mrs. S. had disappeared. From Yugoslavia to the West, in the trunk of a car, it was said. Carl could remember: it started with rumors, then came the flag assembly, during which the headmaster judged the "traitor" and her escape harshly (but in a tired voice). First, she gives me a four and then she disappears, Carl thought at the assembly. And that's how he remembered it: as a double mockery.

Carl didn't know what grade Effi's grass drawing had been given. You didn't hear much about other classes, but he did know that Effi painted *seriously*, she also acted on stage, and at thirteen had taken a course in magic—shortly after her mother's death. In eleventh grade, she'd played the lead role in a school production of *Effi Briest*, enthrallingly and with depth of feeling, according to the teachers.

Carl had admired her: Effi's body in clothes from some distant era and her voice in the semi-darkness of the dining hall, where the play was staged. The word "desire" hadn't yet surfaced but it was certain that Carl's longing had begun right there, in front of the hatches through which meals were served and which were now part of the stage.

He'd hated Instetten and the Major, too; both were miscast and terrible actors. Effi was not ashamed of her role, not in the least. "She can act anything, even the kissing," things like these were said, which Mrs. Schimpf, their German literature teacher, took in with some concern and incredulous astonishment. A few of the students couldn't stand it and made fun. In fact, they were the ones who, from then on, spoke only of *Effi*. Effi's real name was actually Ilonka. Ilonka Kalász, her father was Hungarian. At some point, her friends also started calling her Effi—or just Eff, which was meant affectionately.

"Effi sounds much too sweet for me," Ilonka had said to Carl, with her leg between his thighs, in the small forest in front of his apartment building.

"It's Fontane, after all," Carl had replied inanely.

"And Eff? What do you think of Eff?"

He pushed his papers aside, he smoked, he wanted to go outside again. He needed air now, air and movement. He crossed the small bomb crater copse to the other side of the road. From there you could keep both towers that guarded his street in view at once, even at night. On one hand, the television tower's flashing red light on the horizon as it gave signs from the heavens (when it wasn't shrouded in clouds or fog), and on the other, the lovely green Gatsby light on the stubby water tower. Good old watchman, Carl thought, lighthouse for poems, but he'd already stopped looking at it when he reached the corner of Sredzki Strasse and listened only to the noise of his footsteps.

He had twenty poems, maybe only ten that really counted. He had seven poems at a publisher—and now: Effi. Now he had Effi.

Effi in the plastic-film room.

Effi on the mattress-raft.

It was as if he'd already achieved something, as if he'd found the right direction. As of now (*from now on*, Carl thought), everything could be different.

"Eff, yes. Eff sounds good."

He walked down Ryke Strasse, toward the Ryke Retreat, and after just a few steps, his mouth opened, and the murmuring began. He couldn't really help it (he often didn't even notice). A few people came toward him and Carl turned his head to the side. He looked as if he were whispering to the ruined facades or as if he were deep in prayer, a long, meditative prayer in which certain words were repeated endlessly, completely unintelligibly, just breath and tongue in the echo chamber of his head, where step by step something was struck, or more precisely *struck up*.

A woman coming toward him laughed.

She thinks I'm not quite right in the head, Carl thought, I couldn't care less. He didn't care what any woman thought because now he had Effi—it was a triumph. He wanted to go back to his workbench and *create something*. Never again would he let himself be misled by any specter whatsoever. Never again would he kiss a fur cap.

A three-wheeled, lever-driven wheelchair stood in front of the Ryke Retreat. It gleamed in the light of the streetlamp like an extraterrestrial machine. A small puddle had collected on the scuffed seat. The vehicle had been there for several days and was slowly weathering. His father could have explained the mechanics. *The lever* had been one of his favorite topics, earlier, when I still knew my parents, Carl reflected, and then he didn't give it another thought. He thought instead of Effi and the drawing in the plastic-film room, just a few lines, a woman on one knee, her sumptuous clothes and her humble posture . . .

A point he himself wanted to reach: Effi was already much farther along on this path. And obviously she didn't speak about it. She wasn't very interested in whether people could find her exhibition. On the contrary, except for a few half-erased chalk arrows, Effi had rather hidden herself away in the ACUD, hidden herself from him, too, in a certain sense, but Carl's thoughts didn't progress far that evening, especially since it had seemed planned that *he* would find her, he and only he, after all, who else? Effi's touchstone must lie elsewhere. It was something higher, to which Carl also felt drawn, just as he was drawn to her, to her glowing form, to her body in the bodysuit, not flawless but perfect. All this mingled in his head to a fantastical expectation of happiness that could not be separated into its constituent elements.

THE MOTHER FLOOR

It was peculiar to park on the street and be the dark silhouette in a car, waiting for some stranger to come along and get in the car with the same casualness with which a crime begins. It's as if I were being written about in exactly this moment, Carl thought.

Short trips generally cost five marks; something people just knew. Not stating the amount was one of the rules and part of the elegance and generosity in this illegal realm. A brief dance performed in silence. This did not apply to longer trips, for which the fee had to be negotiated, as quickly as possible, something that became more difficult with each passing day.

Eventually the enthusiasm for disoriented illegal taxi rides ran out. The tide of goodwill ebbed and there was a sea change in the mood. Even the customers of unlicensed cabs wanted primarily to get quickly to where they were going. The clearer it became where the trip was headed (their small country's long journey into oblivion), the more pensive Carl's customers looked. They were considering their prospects and lately that had come to mean *money*. A taxi driving through the streets without any sense of direction was not something to celebrate (not anymore), but something that could easily be taken advantage of and misused, even though it rarely happened in the end.

On his taxi nights, Carl tried to park on streets where he could get Radio P. Their broadcasts were never longer than forty-five minutes, perhaps because the transmitter had to take cover and change locations. They mostly played music and occasionally Hoffi the Shepherd could be heard either alone or in conversation, an outcome of his collaboration with the Wydoks Media people. The Wydoks' operations dominated the station. Radio P announced the addresses of newly occupied buildings (their number was by now well over fifty) and mediated contacts. The "exchange" was broadcast daily, and it helped "allied buildings" barter urgently needed things in a kind of moneyless economy. There were status reports, interviews, and advice on how to deal with the city, the police, and the so-called owners. And there were nightly calls to "hammer on the roofs," an eerie thundering and drumming over the city that sometimes lasted until dawn.

On Radio P, Carl heard a band called Herbst in Peking— Autumn in Peking—for the first time and he immediately wrote the name in his notebook, one of the few entries made in those days. A record player was at the top of his wish list.

Because they'd held a minute of silence for the victims of Tiananmen Square, Herbst in Peking had been banned last summer, the Shepherd explained over the radio, and he compared the singer's voice to a stream of fresh lava flowing from Europe's underground, "at once glowing and dark."

Carl waited for the singer's name. He looked out into the street and had Effi in his mind's eye. He always had her in mind—Effi in her bodysuit, Effi on the mattress-raft. I'd do anything for her, Carl thought and at the same time he was afraid he'd drive away the miracle with such thoughts.

From the Shepherd's talks on Radio P, Carl learned more about the worker guerrillas in the Assel, sometimes also called the worker-and-farmer guerrillas, although there were no farmers on Oranienburger Strasse aside from Hoffi and his goat.

The singer's name was Rex—Rex Joswig, lava, the lava-man.

Carl savored his drives to Effi's like expeditions to a warmer climate, to a territory of imminent joy. He took Adlergestell. Henry claimed that going via West Berlin and the AVUS highway would be significantly shorter, but Adlergestell was the way Carl knew, the way he trusted, the way that gave him the freedom to dream as he rushed toward Leipzig.

Later, whenever he thought of Leipzig, a specific image came to mind as if caught in time. It was an image of a young mother, standing half-naked in front of the refrigerator, a child on her hip. She had one hand on the open refrigerator door. Her head was turned toward Carl and Effi, who were sitting at the table talking to each other, and the woman at the fridge used the word *condom*. Carl remembered the word and his feeling (inferiority, shame) that this mental snapshot preserved. While the woman continued talking, the refrigerator light lay on her baby's face, the cold light of the "Mother Floor."

The Mother Floor—in the world of student dorms, that was the official designation, and the women also used the term. The Mother Floor was a half-floor above the doorman, who had usually gone by the time Carl arrived in the evening.

Effi's room was at the end of the hallway. The easel to the left of the door and next to an oval paint-encrusted table. Her son Freddy slept on top in a bunk bed. Underneath were piles of folders, drawings, cardboard, paper. A window ran along the entire length of the room with a view of a sports field and, on the horizon, of the gleaming black skeleton of the gasworks and the stretch of wasteland that ended at the grounds of the Deutsche Bücherei—the DB, as the Leipzigers called the German Library.

Carl wanted Effi. He wanted to be with Effi, but not on the Mother Floor. He avoided the women and their chats in the hallway or the communal kitchen—a repulsive room painted a nicotine-yellow that almost completely swallowed the light from the fluorescent tubes. Two rows of cupboards, a couple of half-broken highchairs, on the wall a laminated list of the kitchen rules. Carl was convinced that the women must view him and all the other males who made their way to this floor as representatives of those shady losers who, for whatever reason, weren't able to live up to their roles as fathers.

Often, the young mothers on this overheated floor wore nothing more than large, faded T-shirts or roomy men's shirts, called "grandfather shirts" (a kind of pre-war article, recognizable by the high-quality material, the double seams, the good workmanship, and the shirttails that hung below the hip). These would be spotted with the dried remains of some kind of baby food or other and sometimes darkened by fresh islands of spurting milk. Flip-flops flapped on their feet. In any event, these women moved with great self-assurance and ease around the floor and also with the kind of nonchalance which signaled to Carl that a male looking at this (their) territory of child-rearing and care was no reason to hide anything. Many of them were hardly older than twenty. Effi was twenty-three, a student in her final year. "This here is real life"—this thought occurred to Carl and he wrote it in his notebook. Here was a beginner, trying to understand the rules as quickly as possible and, most of all, not to make a fool of himself.

He accompanied Effi on her errands and to the kindergarten. He helped with the laundry and went to the DB for a few hours every day to write:

zenakel, watzi und söns
always said it, poor kaspar, poor watzi,
like shadows through walls (creeping),
like mushrooms from the ground (peeking)

And so on, for pages. He had begun experimenting. His watzi-phase (that's what he called it) was another attempt to switch off his thoughts, at least while writing. But poor Kaspar still got through and Carl decided to read the Arp poem again.

Even on his last day on the Mother Floor (Carl couldn't help but think of a kind of lower deck when he heard the expression, sometimes of Greek mythology, too), he spent a few hours in the library. When he returned, his brown fake leather bag was filled with books. Freddy was already in bed and Effi lay next to him. Carl touched her shoulder, Effi raised the covers. He snuggled up to her and they made love, silently, slowly, almost without moving so as not to wake Freddy. Later they sat together in the kitchen a while, drinking coffee. The Mother Floor quieted down by early evening. There wasn't a single television, and no one listened to the radio. The only telephone was locked in the porter's lodge. Sometimes you could hear it ringing, for a long time, endlessly.

It was that evening that Effi decided to escape the Mother Floor.

"Could you help me do it, Carl?" She wanted to move to Berlin.

They talked it over half the night, until the coughing started. It was as if a bizarre mechanism were set in motion: first, a single dry attack, then a series of hesitant little coughs, followed by a second bout of coughing from the other end of the floor, and finally the entire chorus, a rattling and whistling from bronchial tubes, punctuated by hard, dull barking.

Although Effi's room was far from the kitchen, she could immediately recognize Freddy's cough. She hugged Carl and said goodbye. He would sleep in the so-called playroom, diagonally across from the kitchen. Carl pushed aside the toys that completely covered the rug and crawled into a teepee the children had built out of sheets and blankets. He'd taken *Opus Zero* by Hans Arp with him.

> kaspar kaspar kaspar / why have you forsaken us . . .
> have you turned into a star . . .

MILVA

There were a few evenings on which Carl was almost certain someone was following him. A blue Skoda would appear in different places and disappear again, a detail he only became aware of later. Too late.

He parked in a short, dark dead end near Jojo. He had often stood there, across from the club, or somewhere nearby, either on Tucholsky or Novalis Strasse, depending on his mood. He usually opted for Novalis: "Do you also take pleasure in us, dark night? What is it you hold under your mantle?"

The view of the street from the car. The parking lights were on, that was the sign. Sometimes people raised an arm when they stepped out from the club to the street and were still uncertain; then Carl would flash his headlights briefly, nonchalantly, like in a movie, and he immediately had the feeling he was part of a fictional world, in which anything could happen (absolutely anything). It was good cinema, only in his head. Sparked by a way of walking or talking. Sparked by the alienation he felt toward himself. Sparked by the deep desire for lawlessness that was in the air and smelled intoxicatingly of freedom, of spring and freedom, and hence the avidity in every breath, the gratitude for everything surrounding him that was collapsing, falling apart, an entire state, a power structure.

Until someone came (it never took very long), Carl was engrossed in his monologues. Usually they had nothing to do with whatever was happening at that moment, they were just sounds, words, verses from the murmurings. He dreamed, whispered, and scribbled the words *People's Chamber* in his notebook. The good old chamber and then the connection: the people and the chamber. The people in a chamber, why had it never occurred to him before? The expression had become invisible over the years, always there, every day, a thousandfold, but invisible. Only now, on the occasion of this—as it was called— free election, in which the people themselves had voted for a chamber, did it re-emerge. The people would now have their own chamber, for themselves, so they could finally be alone and free, Carl thought as the back door opened and fell shut, almost in the same second.

"Prenzlauer Allee."

Carl hadn't seen the man coming or heard any footsteps. He turned around. The man was young and well dressed. Carl couldn't make out more than that. The man sat right behind him, not on the right side as was usual. Carl turned onto Pieck Strasse.

"Haven't you ever been afraid?"

"Of what?"

"Of death."

"Of death?"

"Being murdered, bumped off. Have you ever thought of that, *colleague?*"

The man leaned forward as he talked and breathed on Carl's neck. Ever thought of that. No, never. It occurred to Carl that *colleague* didn't fit. He noticed that the man smelled good (freshly shaven). That the Zhiguli didn't have any headrests.

"Death in a taxi, never heard of it?"

"No. Why?"

Stop the car, open the door, and run.

Jam his elbow backward, right in the face, and run.

Yank the steering wheel and . . . Ever thought of that. A reproach with big, hungry eyes. Children in Africa, in Angola.

"You don't read the newspaper or what? You don't listen to the news and all that? No television—now left."

"No." I just see ghosts in the snow.

"And a warning, you didn't get a warning either? There's always a warning, colleague." He sounded concerned. He smelled really good. Freshly shaven. No headrests. Could kiss my neck. Brown bottle, brown smell. Deodorant jingle to "Summer in the City."

"No, I . . ."

"Nice car you have here. 1100 cc, right? Basically a Fiat, an Italian, but from Siberia."

"It belongs to my father."

"Oh." He snickered. "Well, where is your Pa-pa? Does he know that you're *poaching*, on someone else's turf? Better that he's not here now, right?"

Something yanked Carl's head back: "Brrr, brrr!"

Carl yelled and braked sharply.

"Works like a horse!" The man snickered again and loosened his grip on Carl's hair.

"And now we're going to ride to your place, colleague—giddyap!"

Carl turned and parked in the shadow of the water tower.

"Are. We. Already. There?"

With each word he yanked on Carl's hair.

"Does that mean yes?"

"Yes. Ow!"

"No."

"No?"

"No, horsey, giddyap!"

With Carl's hair, the man directed him up Ryke Strasse to the small bomb crater copse.

"Ah, now we're there! Should I tell you a joke, colleague? Yes? Do you know—do you know what's good about the fact that so many comrades from a once-honorable Ministry of Security are now sitting behind the wheels of our taxis? Yes? No? We only need to say a name and . . ."

He snickered again and almost forgot himself. His grip loosened.

He knows where I live, Carl thought. That was the joke.

"Now you're going to get out and walk slowly through the trees and then you'll just watch for a while."

After a few steps, he shouted, "Stop!" and made a gesture that Carl had never seen before, something between a victory sign and a revolver. Maybe it was just the number two, the second warning. Carl did not call for help and didn't escape into the building. He just stood there, rooted to the spot, a puppet of his fear, clinging to one of the elderberry shrubs. On the other side of the street, a man got out of a car—it was the blue Skoda. He crossed the street with no particular haste and handed the man who smelled good a large knife, a kind of machete, actually. Carl trembled. It looked like he was shaking the elderberry, as if he wanted to shake the copse awake at three in the morning.

The good-smelling man looked in Carl's direction, lifted the machete, and slashed the Zhiguli's tires with a few powerful thrusts. Each tire gave a short, almost astonished whistle, followed by a sad hiss. For a moment, the two men stood there uncertainly and looked at their work. The fragrant one waved at Carl again and got into the Skoda. The other had one more idea. He gathered a few of the small, loose cobblestones and hurled them at the back of the car. The rear window didn't clink, there was more a ripping sound, a sharp, violent tear. At the same time, a yell echoed behind Carl. Sonie stormed past him, roaring. He was brandishing the hooked rod, but the stone-thrower was already in the Skoda, and then it was over.

They squatted next to each other on the mattress-raft for a while. Sonie examined Carl's head and told him about Charlotte Knospe. Rhubarb had begun to sprout in Knospe's vegetable bed in front of the building and so the old woman let herself slide down to the courtyard at least once a day and then had Sonie or Carl carry her back upstairs. "She relies on us. But what happens if we're not here? What then?"

Carl's head was a giant wound. He passed his hand very gingerly through his hair and had small, bloody tufts between his fingers. He didn't know what to do with them and held them in his hand. The skin on his head burned and suddenly he began to shiver. Sonie made some tea. He bustled around in Carl's kitchen as if he knew what he was doing and suddenly Sonie, too, felt close to Carl.

"She often talks about her husband Otto. She calls her rhubarb Otto, have you heard that? Otto Knospe had been a chauffeur, had a lot to do with cars. You'd have liked him, Carl!" He was silent for a few seconds, that was the wrong turn. His zinc-plated halberd lay next to the raft. It looked worn and shone dully.

Before Sonie left, he gave Carl a tightly folded note.

"It was under your wiper."

The note said MILVA, nothing else. Written in black marker.

Carl said, "I got this once already—this message, I mean." He showed Sonie the note.

"This *message*?" Sonie asked.

"What do you mean?"

"MILVA!" Sonie replied.

"The singer?"

Sonie sighed. "It's a guild, a clan, Mister Zhiguli, more or less honorable. Mitte is *their* territory, has been since the early eighties, tolerated by the powers that be, bad and invincible."

"How did they know . . ."

"At this point, it doesn't matter, Carl. They have their rules and rivals are put out of commission. Some even use a taxi meter, the Botax 80. Illegal taxis with a meter, do you know what that means? That's like illegal and legit at the same time. Some say there are now four hundred of them. And then you show up in your Zhiguli with an orange roof and side stripes like the gay patrol."

Carl looked at the ground in silence. *Hooray, we're still alive,* weren't those lyrics from one of Milva's songs?

"Why here?"

"What?"

"Why did they let me drive home?"

"The taxi driver's honor code, probably. 'With us, everyone makes it home'—or something like that. The stupidest things always have to do with honor."

After Sonie left, Carl shuffled into the kitchen and rinsed the bloody hairs off his hand. Then he pressed his ear against the wall:

"Effi?"

He felt dizzy and had to sit down. The flute player over the workbench: so fine and unblemished. The Mediterranean. Longing, light. The shock wore off, millimeter by millimeter, and the insult began to take its shape: "Giddyap, horsey, giddyap!"

For a moment, Carl was close to tears. He stood up, wanting to go downstairs, but he couldn't walk. He would have to wait a while yet.

The smashed car alone on the street.

His father's car.

Endless maintenance and care.

Didn't last very long under your watch, Carl.

A shame.

Weak-kneed, he crept back to his raft and turned on the television. For a time, he stared at the drifting snow. Two faint ghosts appeared and were soon blown away. Maybe his parents. Then he fell asleep.

The Stassfurt's billowing white roar—like surf on his wound. Carl lay with his head against the television all night: hair stuck to the screen and someone hammered on the door.

They're coming, Carl thought. Four hundred.

The Shepherd immediately took Carl in his arms: goat, Carl thought and breathed deeply. Ever since his feverish nights in the Assel, it was the smell of resurrection.

"We'll finish them off, I promise you. Those taxi swine. They're traitors to the workers. This is what's going to happen now and everywhere—if we don't oppose it."

Carl's arms hung limply over the Shepherd's shoulders. He rubbed them hard several times, which did Carl good for a moment. And yes, the pack had brought goat milk in a leaky aluminum jug. "This will get you going again," Ragna murmured as she disappeared into Carl's kitchen with the jug. She's looking after me, she's always there, Carl thought. Henry and Arielle had also come, along with half of the pack and a few other people Carl didn't know. Dodo stood on the stairs, nibbling a moldy poster of fruit.

"Why in the world did you decide to do *that*, Carl?"

"Do what?"

"Drive a taxi. You, a bricklayer, a construction worker."

"There's got to be money there," Carl murmured and he suddenly remembered the name of the film: *Gods of the Plague*. He could see himself now, in the movie, laconic and determined to do the wrong thing.

"Your car key, Carl, we need your car key," the Shepherd said softly but insistently as if he had said it before, and he probably had.

"In the end, they were all shot," Carl whispered, but naturally no one knew what he meant.

An ancient tow truck was parked on the sidewalk, a converted Opel P4. A woman who was called Adele led the commando. She wore stained metalworker coveralls and was smoking. She spoke Russian with the men who were jacking up the Zhiguli. At the right moment, Adele shoved a pile of bricks under the car and the men changed the back tires. They formed a small, effective unit that made do with the simplest tools. As usual with Russians, Carl thought. In the end, the front of the Zhiguli hung from the back of the P4. The Shepherd negotiated with Adele. She stood next to him and Carl saw how tall she was, broad-shouldered, strong. He liked her from the very first moment. The Shepherd put something in her hand. She smiled and looked over at Carl.

"I'm coming too!" Carl yelled (almost in a panic) and took a quick step toward the tow truck.

"Nyet," Adele said.

"It's not necessary, Carl," the Shepherd murmured and held him by the collar, as you would to keep a child from running across the street.

"It's all arranged. You need to rest. Take a few days and then we'll talk it over. Maybe Henry will stop by, or Arielle."

The tow truck lumbered from the sidewalk onto the street. "Lada Karlshorst" was painted on the driver's cab.

They hugged Carl, one after another, finally even Ragna. Arielle, too, almost tenderly and despite the fact that she (as a neighbor) (the Lady of the Five Coals and Seven Poems) didn't actually have to say goodbye to him. Henry left cigarettes for him and promised to show him the sketches for UVA's "first fall list" on his next visit.

Dodo had discovered old Knospe's vegetable bed, but the Shepherd held him back. He pulled the animal behind him on a short rope. It didn't look crazy, not even strange, just relaxed and unobjectionable.

Carl understood that he had become part of a community and he watched them go for a while. They strolled down Ryke Strasse, toward the water tower. Hoffi, the Shepherd, went first. The dark sail of his poncho, his light, springy gait, the swing of his braid, left, right, left, all radiated certainty. That's what was still missing from Carl's own life.

PART V

INGE IN GELNHAUSEN

When Walter was on the road, Inge stayed behind alone in Gelnhausen. Even over some weekends, when one course was tacked on to the next, which did happen, two or three courses, one right after another. Cobol in Hamburg, Pascal in Paderborn, C++ in Düsseldorf, and so on. Inge missed Dr. Talib and the children. And, yes, she missed Diez, even Diez.

Sometimes Inge went to religious services in the Marienkirche, four kilometers on foot. She liked the benevolent face of the child in the altarpiece. "Mary's child, the way he looks at me, does me good," Inge wrote Carl. She didn't tell Walter anything about this, she hadn't been to church for decades.

Carl's mother had always liked writing letters and postcards, but since her departure, her emigration or whatever they called it, it was different. For one thing, Inge kept in touch with Carl (with him and *home*—the word had imperceptibly become filled with meaning), for another, in writing him, she was explaining the new world to herself—she recorded what happened and communicated it. It was an unfamiliar process for Carl and for Inge. It was unusual to write to one's own son about these things, about estrangement and the homesickness that had crept into her energetic emigrant heart and some days almost paralyzed her. "But we know exactly what we want, Carl"—the usual sentence when doubts rose.

The day before Walter's return from Paderborn, Inge wanted to get a few sprays of spring blossoms for the table. The weather had grown suddenly warm and lilacs were blooming here and there. Inge crossed the fields toward Kinzig and walked along the river for a stretch. There she encountered a man. He startled her—she had been lost in thought about their "longer journey," as she often put in her letters. The tall man headed straight for her and came very close. Inge was blinded by the sun. She held a few lilac branches in her hand and considered beating the man's face with them.

"You must think you're very bold."

"Why?" Inge asked.

"It's very foolish of you." The man sounded cold and mean. Inge held the branches in front of her chest like a shield.

"What else needs to happen, what is it going to take?" the man shouted, shaking his head angrily. Then he walked away without another word. Inge felt paralyzed and gasped for breath. This was the moment that fear first penetrated to her core: what if everything turned out to be pointless and wrong?

On the way back, she passed the chickens. "Countrymen, my dear countrymen . . ." Again, the chickens nodded in their direct, jerking way, which left no room for doubt. All hens are Thuringians, Carl's mother thought, all hens and me.

They were starting to settle in. At Manpower in Wächtersbach, Inge took a training course in office administration and learned how to use a computer program called Word. She enjoyed learning it and was proud to be using this new technology. "Like Walter," Inge wrote Carl, "though on a completely different level." Her final assignment was to write captions for pictures illustrating a fictional story. She wrote far too much. All of her captions were as long as little stories. Nonetheless, Manpower was satisfied even if it never led anywhere.

She joined the Barbarossa Gymnastics Group. With some astonishment, the women welcomed her into their midst. For them, Inge Bischoff came straight out of the wilderness, from a region they knew almost nothing about, though they had heard this or that over the years. One of the most frequent questions was whether they'd had enough to eat over there. When the trainer had to miss a day and asked Inge to fill in for her, the atmosphere in the locker room darkened. The bodies of the Barbarossa women clustered in front of the window and then separated before one of them conveyed their verdict: "We don't even know her." The speaker didn't say it directly to Inge, almost to herself, yet loud enough to be heard.

After class, the women walked each other home for safety's sake. They all knew about an *incident* with the American woman from the base, but they never talked about it. They marched together from one house to the next and watched until one door after the other was closed and locked. In the end, only Inge and old Ursula were left on the street.

Old Ursula was a beautiful woman—tall, thin, and sophisticated. She regularly went to the theater in Frankfurt and read Flaubert novels. Inge admired her. She called Ursula "a fine person" and "determined." When her loneliness became overwhelming, Inge would call Ursula (from a public phone in town) and they would talk for a while. Or Ursula would drive over in her Jeep, which she'd inherited from "a friend I used to have," a GI from the base she had been with for a long time, when he went back to the States. She told Inge about her past and Inge wanted to know *everything*, including Ursula's trips to America.

As darkness fell on the street, the women talked of their former lives: Ursula about her life in west Prussia near Gdansk and Inge about her life in east Thuringia in Gera. Inge Bischoff admitted to Ursula that she was homesick. She admitted that watching the American soldiers in the morning was her only joy, especially their rhythmic chanting. "We can always hear them from a distance, their footsteps and their songs." These comments would have been impossible in front of the Barbarossa women, that much Inge had understood. Black men with strong, gleaming upper arms. Every morning, a few minutes after six, the Americans ran right past Inge's balcony on the cycle path alongside the road. Then she would wave, and the Americans would shout something and "were delighted," as Inge recounted it. She was convinced the soldiers then sang a little louder, just for her. Most of them were black, even the women in the ranks, "some quite fat, but very natural, *so natural*," in Inge's words. "A few months ago, we still had Russians outside our window." This wasn't actually true since the Russians never passed in front of her balcony in Thuringia and were hardly ever seen anywhere. What Inge had seen on the bus and every day on her way to the bakery cooperative were the windows of the officers' quarters in Gera-Tinz, their lower panes covered with newspaper.

"They don't even have curtains," the passengers on the bus from Langenberg to Tinz would remark.

The windowpanes taped over with pages from *Neues Deutschland*—it was one of the images from Carl's childhood that kept surfacing in his mind. He had pictured their lives behind the newspaper in great detail, brief scenes, mostly in the kitchen: a man with heavy hands, sitting at the table, his hair imprinted with a line from his peaked cap, and so on. No one really knew much about the Russians in Tinz. They kept to themselves, but Carl could see them and still pictured them whenever he thought of newspapers and, as a result, a sense of trust had developed, a sense of friendship even, purely imaginary.

The Americans returned to their base along the railway embankment. Inge never missed a chance to watch them, feeling a puzzling sense of longing. "It's always the same people in the lead and the same in the rear, but they stay together, in lockstep, trotting and singing, singing and trotting, like in the movies," is how Inge described it to Carl. The Americans were a world unto themselves, and they radiated a great calm, "a deep reassurance," Inge wrote, whatever she may have meant by that. All in all, it was "a beautiful experience" that did her good, here in Gelnhausen. "That does us good," Inge would also say to Ursula.

Wise Ursula had replied that foreigners always recognized each other and always had.

"One outcast recognizes another," Inge whispered and they both had to giggle, but softly because it had grown late and dark. Old Ursula waited until her new friend from the East had disappeared behind her door and then walked home alone—slowly, unafraid, tall and proud as she was. Later, Ursula again made a case for Inge Bischoff in the Barbarossa group, but Inge was no longer interested. "Not for any money in the world will I lead them," concluded her letter to Carl on 18 May 1990.

From the beginning there had been a few peculiar things about Walter's job at CTZ, the way he was paid, for example. Around the beginning of every month (the exact day was never predictable), Carl's parents found an envelope on the staircase that led to their apartment. The envelope contained a cashier's check, a small piece of colored paper for 5,000 deutschmarks, with a blue border and black lettering; it was basically just a note like a fuel voucher torn from a pad. Since Walter had never seen his boss's car in front of the house or on the street, he assumed the old woman took care of these payments. Maybe *she's* the boss, the real owner, he thought. Maybe she comes upstairs at night (as mentioned, there was no door between the floors), stands at our bedside, mulling over whether I'm the right trainer for Hamburg or Düsseldorf with an overnight stay in the Rheinstern Hotel . . .

It was this method that gave Walter pause: as if he were being paid for some service that did not allow for further questions (or direct contact), which is why his salary was not simply handed over in the White Villa. The boss wants it done without having to look at me, Walter assumed, and decided to let the matter rest even though there was something offensive about an envelope on the staircase.

Then Walter remembered his boss's comments as he handed Walter the keys. They'd sounded appeasing on the surface but held a clear warning: "Under certain circumstances, my mother can be difficult. When that happens, it's best if you and your wife would please just stay upstairs in your apartment as quietly and for *as long* as possible." At the time, Walter Bischoff hadn't asked for clarification, in fact, he hadn't really heard it. After their weeks in Büsum, Giessen, and Diez, the prospect of a position that came with an apartment of their own was simply overwhelming and nothing other than good.

You could hear the Barbarossa women suck in their breath when they learned where Inge and Walter were living. They all knew or had heard something but didn't want to say anything specific, which piqued Inge Bischoff, who had a deeply rooted sense that people should do the right thing. Inge decided to make an effort. She patiently listened to Mrs. Zollnay's monologues when the old woman, as if drawn by invisible ropes into the stone entrance hall, lifted her arms: "Ah, Mrs. Bischoff, you know . . ." Once Inge brought her a quarter of a freshly baked apple cake: "Just a small token . . ." She'd often been thoughtful like this in Gera and it was a continuation of an old, neighborly custom, a bit of her previous life. After all, she could be a kind spirit here, too, on Garten Strasse in Gelnhausen-Roth.

The old woman was delighted. She pushed her stomach forward under her apron and stroked it in quick circles. Then she took the plate out of Inge's hand, draped her arm over Inge's shoulders, and asked her what she thought the outcome of the next election in the Bundestag would be. "It will be very important for us, especially for my son, of course, but also for you, Mrs. Bischoff. We must fully support the chancellor, isn't that right?" Inge Bischoff nodded mutely and slipped quietly back upstairs.

Walter Bischoff's sole focus was his work. He taught his courses, before long in Lübeck, Nuremberg, and Stuttgart, too, and often in the Hamburg container port. In the meantime, he'd made a habit of wandering between the towers of containers during the breaks ("Where've you been off to, roving again, you old rover?"—roving, that good old Thuringian word). The port security knew him by now and Walter no longer got lost. Nothing was more relaxing than a walk among the containers in the port. He turned at this or that corner, walked up to this or that giant steel crate and studied, half-distracted and dreaming, the destinations on the waybills behind the small grilled windows. He wondered where he would like to be shipped to, if it came to that. He knew perfectly well where. He knew what their dream was.

He never returned without a piece of wood or half of a brick, he stuck to that. Paderborn proved a good source of lost screws and nails, Stuttgart for ropes, cords, sometimes even a nice piece of wire. Before loading all these things that could come in handy someday (as his father had taught him) into the trunk of the Mercedes (in which a small collection had soon come together), he cleaned them, at least cursorily. At some point he would have to build a small shed for them at the house in Garten Strasse; he'd have to talk to the boss about it. Or the boss's mother.

Like the baking and the "neighborliness," afternoon coffee time also derived from their earlier, abandoned life. Just that everything was an hour later than in Gera, because Walter, when he wasn't traveling (which was rare enough), didn't return from the White Villa until five in the afternoon.

On that day in June, yes, it was already June, sunny and warm, Inge was brewing coffee and setting the table near the window with a view of the meadows and fields along the Kinzig river. The sharp smell of the chemicals that were spread on the fresh vegetables wafted into the house. A hot-air balloon rose from the airfield.

Inge spread out the tablecloth that the Talib family had given them as a goodbye present. "We'd like to give you something that will remind you of us," Mrs. Talib had said. The tablecloth was very large, heavy, and richly embroidered. It had been intended for a family-sized dining table. Inge had to fold the cloth several times, leaving visible only an indecipherable section of the embroidery that depicted the exodus from Egypt.

Everything was ready and she sat down at the table. "We lit a candle for you. We also have a present. We'll send it," Inge wrote to Carl. It was 8 June, Carl's birthday. Inge stroked the tablecloth. She tried to remain calm. Just stay calm, Inge. She stood up and looked outside. A chicken crossed the road and nodded at her.

BLACK TEETH

Summer began with a raising of the flag. In Fenske's cellar, the Shepherd unrolled the fine cloth: black silk on which a scarlet "A" had been sewn. "This is our 'A,'" the Shepherd said. "It recalls our difficult beginning, our *Anfang*; it recalls the dignity of work, of *Arbeit*; and it recalls the *aguerrillas*. It is a threefold 'A.'"

"'A' as in *Assel*," Henry whispered behind Carl. Then they followed the Shepherd upstairs, the flag draped around his shoulders like a musketeer. They crossed the drying loft, passing a small broadcasting station that Little Frank had created by hanging blankets and sheets. Without a word, the Radio P technician pulled a steel ladder out from behind the chimney and set it in one of the skylights.

Half of the pack and a few captains were gathered on the roof. The sun was shining, the weather was warm, and the view was intoxicating. Down Oranienburger to Tacheles, over to Friedrich Strasse. Facing them was the park and Museum Island, surrounding them were the brownfields and ruins of the inner courtyards with their dilapidated sheds and outbuildings, the tiny human figures, the streetcars, and the broad crowns of the trees: all of this lay at their feet, all the strange power and glory of the big city wafted up to Carl and left him speechless.

Hoffi the Shepherd pointed in this direction and in that, to indicate houses that had just been "taken into custody." In fact, they had persuaded the city's district councils and their housing offices to adopt the formulation of "taking into custody" and more than that: the apparently thoroughly unsettled state officials were even prepared to issue "certificates" that this or that building had been claimed "for the purpose of future habitation" and "secured against trespass and unlawful entry." "Our permit," the Shepherd had said and laid the document on the counter. It was actually just a notice of no more than eight lines, stamped, dated, and signed.

The Shepherd solemnly handed the flag to Henry, who, in a death-defying climb onto the roof, attached it to the nearest antenna. Carl admired Henry. Someone with that much courage could also be an artist, that much was obvious. The Shepherd had prepared a short talk, very little of which could be understood because the wind blowing over the roofs tore the words right out of his mouth and scattered them arbitrarily over Berlin. It's a benediction, Carl thought without knowing exactly what that meant.

He had joined the pack, but only ran along like a pup, trailing them, his head lowered, lost in thought and poetry. Often he wasn't thinking at all—just ruminating on words that held short, magical melodies, around which everything in his world revolved. A world in which nothing was more important than the imminent poem.

The poem either comes or it doesn't, one of the older poets had said (Carl had forgotten which one). It sounded wise, but it wasn't reassuring.

Working in the Assel had given Carl a foothold for the time being. Now he had to be sure that it didn't demand too much of him. Just as there were days reserved for the Assel, there had to be days reserved for writing, during which he could forget everything going on "outside," in the Oranienburger cellar or in the rest of the Shepherd's realm, in so-called reality. He needed these hours at his workbench, to sink into a few words that held the poem he could hear but couldn't yet write.

Carl knew he would never be as proud a creature as Ragna or Henry (or even Kleist in his own way). As a bricklayer, he'd given his all. He had earned Hoffi's respect and Irina's affection when she came down to the cellar with food, coffee, and her warmth. The Shepherd had never tried to enlist him in the pack's raids. He had assigned Carl *other tasks*, a kind of barracks duty—the rearguard, Carl thought. I'm only good for the rearguard. Even his parents had recognized that.

The Shepherd's poncho: looming dark and large in the backlight. Carl followed his gestures and tried to grasp the territory he was sketching out—Berlin! Saint Francis on the roof of his city . . . Who had spread his wings. Who at any moment could take flight and sail into a glorious future.

Carl thought of Effi—a warm feeling. Effi would come and then. Then everything would work out. He looked over at Ragna, who was standing on the other side of the flag, calmly looking out into the distance. "Dragged out of the gutter by his dick"— Carl had not come up with the image. That's not how he thought about himself and Ragna, not at all; it was just this raunchy, hirsute saying that squatted, smirking, in his mind.

*

After his illegal taxi debacle, Carl had found an envelope with 200 marks in his mailbox, a few crumpled, worn bills that smelled of tool theft and flogged pieces of wall. Among them was a 100 mark bill with Karl Marx's head. Someone had drawn a heart around "Karl" with a ballpoint pen, a detail that Carl immediately forgot. A few days later, Hoffi had officially offered him his "new employment" in service of the Assel, "in the name of everyone here, I'd like to stress," the Shepherd had told him. He meant the pack, who had gathered, as usual, for their weekend breakfast at Irina's.

"Carl is a bricklayer, a good bricklayer, who, when necessary, eats stones and cement."

The Shepherd had never been present when Carl tasted the mortar, but he knew about such things; nothing escapes him, Carl thought. Tasting the mortar was an ancient practice that Carl had observed among his oldest and most experienced colleagues on construction sites—of course the old bricklayers had never swallowed the cement; they'd only stuck a fingertip in the mortar box and put it in their mouths. They tasted it and spat it back out in order to determine exactly the mixture's consistency and "oiliness" (as they called it)—but their teeth suffered from this practice over the years, which was evident when they laughed (and the old ones laughed often). It was the laughter that inevitably revealed it: their brittle, black teeth, corroded from the acidity of the calcium carbonate.

"Put differently: Carl will be the first worker to be given permanent shelter in the Assel during these stormy times and this is a good—I mean, *exactly the right beginning*. To our worker's café!" He raised his coffee cup.

Carl worked three days a week, afternoons or evenings. Initially, he alternated with Henry, who always came straight from his studio with paint on his hands. They earned six marks an hour, thirty marks a day, which Irina paid them from a special cashbox.

There had been customers from the beginning, even without an official opening. Most were people from the pack's circle, generally residents of the houses taken into custody. They sat on the beer crates or other seats they carried to the cellar themselves, wobbly chairs, a half-rotten lounge chair, any discarded furniture found in back courtyards.

Now and again a student wandered into the Assel—a university psychology department was located in the next building. The building immediately adjacent to theirs had been destroyed in the war, all that was left was a brownfield with a path connecting Oranienburger Strasse with Krausnick Strasse. A few pale apprentices of the fine arts came from the studio buildings in Monbijou Park, right across from the Assel. Not far away was a small, open-air children's swimming pool—the season had just begun—and occasionally someone would cross the street from the pool and buy a cheap bottle of Berliner Pilsner in the Assel.

Beer was always on hand from the start—the Shepherd proved generous on this point as well, requesting payment only as "voluntary" donations "for our cause."

Only the working class was missing. For whatever reason, workers did not come to the cellar, which, after all, had been set up primarily for them. "It's the old divide, expanded historically." Carl, who could only agree with Hoffi on this point, felt this divide—deep within like a badly healed wound.

The Shepherd decided on the spot to talk to workers on the street. Carl stood on tiptoe, watching him through the Assel's cellar window: the poncho-clad Shepherd, with his braided beard and flailing arms. Before him stood a few men in reflective vests gathered around a hydraulic lift, their white helmets pushed back onto the napes of their necks. These were workers in the high-voltage brigade, who had been renovating the overhead power lines for the tram. Carl could see their reserve. He knew what they were thinking and how deeply rooted their distrust was—or did he no longer know?

Surprisingly, they did come. "This is Carl," the Shepherd said, "a worker, like you." Carl nodded to them and saw the mockery in their eyes. Still, it wasn't contempt. Maybe it was even uncertainty that they were masking. Everyone is vulnerable, everyone is seeking their place in these new times, Carl thought. They drank beer and remained silent, showing their respect. They examined the bare cellar spaces and scrutinized Hoffi who explained the Assel to them (the U-boat, the shelter, the worker's café) and then he segued to the threatened elimination of the tramcars, which would entail the elimination of the overhead power lines, the high-voltage wires, and the tracks, and would also entail the elimination of public transportation, and this ultimately, logically and inevitably, would entail the loss of jobs for the high-voltage brigades: "Or has any of you seen a tramcar, in the West, I mean?" the Shepherd asked, faintly triumphant.

"What will be left? That's the question for today. Just a few abandoned tracks, nothing more."

The workers shook their heads. They drank, smoked, and changed the topic. Then they drank faster, cracked jokes, laughed, and eventually began yelling at each other, in that hearty, good-natured way that was only possible among workers. On the television show *Want to Bet . . . ?* they'd seen Kim Wilde in her skin-tight pants (*absolutely everything* was visible), then the conversation turned to cars.

"How's the Datch?"

"The Datch is fine."

Carl realized they were talking about a Dacia, a kind of Romanian Renault, if there could be such a thing. He thought of the smashed Zhiguli somewhere in Karlshorst with the Russians. His father's car, his and my car, Carl thought. He picked up another crate of beer and heard the warm murmur, grateful work murmur—isn't this what he actually longed for? To be acknowledged by *normal life*?

Carl gathered the empty bottles and carried them into one of the back cellars that they had begun using for storage. When he returned, the workers were getting ready to leave—Hoffi said goodbye to each one with a handshake. Carl saw their end-of-the-workday faces, their sparkling eyes. He envied them their awareness of their status, some determination from time immemorial that admitted no doubt in their character. It was not the class consciousness frequently invoked over the past few decades—it was something that lay much deeper. "Origins and traditions," Carl whispered as he lugged a few crates the workers had sat on back to Fenske's cellar. "Workers have certain reserves of inner convictions that are like irrefutable lore," Carl had once read in a treatise on the status of the worker written by a working-class writer who had raised the question of "why one should become a worker."

A rush of shame over Carl's new position at the Assel slowed his steps momentarily; looked at more closely, he had simply sunk over the years from a skilled worker to a student and from a student to a waiter (vendor of beer bottles), unskilled, a laborer, or even less than that. But it was the right way (it had to be the right one), because it would lead, in a time of transition, of patient transformation, to his writing.

After the visit from the high-voltage brigade, the Assel was "furnished." It was, without a doubt, a consequence of their "proposals," "the critique of the working class at the worker's café," which the Shepherd was ready to adopt without reservation and impart with enthusiasm: their goal now was a "cozier atmosphere." They also added a selection of simple dishes and a greater choice of drinks. In the space of a few days, the pack collected usable furniture from the condemned houses in the neighboring streets and schlepped it through the wilderness of Krausnick Park into the courtyard behind the building, where Irina washed it down.

Carl saw the tables and chairs drying in the sun, in an odd and peaceful group. No two pieces were alike, but they could all be used and some vague promise radiated from these mute witnesses of existences that had met their demise long before.

Two men, who lived at the end of the road in Tacheles, the reinforced concrete ruins of a former department store, which had recently renamed itself as the "Art House," welded heavy drill rods to a section of steel tread plate to make a kind of counter. Carl knew these men. They'd been among the Assel's first customers. Day and night they wore welding goggles and metalworker coveralls. Their faces were covered with soot, their hands gray and scabbed. "They embody the connection between art and the hardest labor," the Shepherd had said. For some reason the Tacheles welders were crazy about Dodo. They asked after the goat every time and requested goat milk. Dodo, often wandering around alone, liked it when they curried her, and enjoyed the attention.

Carl, in the meantime, had mastered milking the animal. The Shepherd had taught him how; it was, in a sense, part of the bartender's job. The udder cannot be full, and you cannot grab the teat (of which there are only two, not four as on cows) in your fist: two to three fingers are enough.

To be milked, the goat stood on a large feed crate in the stall (as if onto a stage, Dodo liked to jump up on the crate). That made it easier. After some difficulties at the beginning, Carl mastered the art and Dodo got used to him. She no longer bleated, or if she did, then contentedly. Goats can do that: bleat contentedly. Dodo often followed him like a dog for a while after milking. This wasn't surprising. After all, it was Carl who brought her fodder and regularly mixed in some of the fresh straw that the Shepherd brought in the GAZ and unloaded into a section of the shed in large, tightly bundled bales.

One day, the welders from the Tacheles brought the goat a pair of welding goggles as a present. In the welding goggles, Dodo looked like an early aviator; her bristly, white goatee also recalled the pioneers of the time in their flying crates—for Carl, this was the defining image of those days, which passed quietly and almost monotonously, in quiet euphoria, if such a thing exists.

"They smell the border, obviously," the Shepherd shouted over the engine noise of the GAZ. The welders had used chain link fencing to turn the open back of the jeep into a makeshift cage.

"And then they want to go back. They get homesick for the death strip, if you like, the way a lifer longs for his prison cell— these border dogs, Carl, they're animals that behave like humans, you know what I mean?"

Carl sat in the passenger seat. With the noise, he could only understand the Shepherd sporadically. To prevent further damage, Hoffi had begun collecting the dogs that were still in the buildings.

"Absolutely unbelievable that he hadn't thought of it," the Shepherd roared, unable to calm down. His rage was directed at the Comandante, whose border dog strategy had failed and even worse: more than a few of the dogs had escaped from the buildings they were supposed to protect. Alone or in small, renegade packs, they were now roaming the city. During the day, they were seen in the park at the Brandenburg gate and after dark they spread out in the streets. In Tiergarten Park, it was said, a small pack had grabbed half-cooked meat from a Turkish family's grill, and in Gormann Strasse, the animals supposedly surrounded an eighty-year-old pensioner, and bit through her net shopping bag.

"The Wolves Are Here!" screamed a headline in the *Berliner Zeitung* and so the Shepherd began to worry in earnest. He feared "investigations" that would endanger everything—"us, everything!" He had trusted the Comandante, who had disappeared several days earlier. "He's probably already abroad, procuring weapons," the Shepherd shouted in the engine noise and erupted into sudden laughter. He shook his head and stepped on the gas.

"Dog catcher, we need a dog catcher," Carl yelled. It sounded helpless, but the idea immediately reassured the Shepherd.

"I'm sure the newspapers are exaggerating as usual," the Shepherd shouted and brushed the blowing hair from his face. Someone had washed the GAZ. It gleamed and the patches of rust in the army green were now dark islands. They slowed and were driving at the pace of a parade. The Shepherd scrutinized the buildings lining the street right and left, occasionally asking Carl to write an address in his notebook. He's surveying his realm, Carl thought.

A flag with skull and crossbones hung from the back of the jeep. Each time they stopped to examine a building more closely or load one of the abandoned dogs, the Shepherd straightened the flag. Maybe he'd rather be a pirate, Carl thought.

30 Tucholsky Strasse, 206 Linien Strasse, 5 Kleine Hamburger, 169 Acker Strasse, these were the addresses. They drove past the Eimer underground club on Rosenthaler Strasse in a building taken over by musicians from various bands, then they passed two "inhabited buildings" on Kastanien Allee (the street of the good poems) and stopped at Café Westphal, which had once been the outlet store for a liquor factory. They had a drink and the Shepherd talked with a man named Chris, who was unloading a decommissioned VW police van. He knew that Chris was an old acquaintance of the Comandante's "from his previous life in the north, on the coast, a former colleague, as

it were," the Shepherd explained as they climbed back into the Russian jeep.

Hoffi dropped Carl off at 20 Schönhauser Allee, he wasn't done yet. Carl watched him go. The border dogs in the cage barked, all of them German shepherds. Eastern dogs have a shorter build, was one of the Comandante's tenets. In addition, they have stronger pigmentation, that is, they're often darker and gray. Western dogs, on the other hand, have a noticeably sloping topline. "They're less compact. Which one is healthier will be evident before the bloodlines get mixed again," the Comandante had said, and it was only part of his peculiar speech.

The skull on the flag flying from the GAZ wore an eyepatch, Carl hadn't noticed it before.

"Whatever you need, Zhiguliman," Ragna murmured. Without looking carefully at what she was doing, she grabbed tools here and there from the shelves and placed them on her distribution tray for Carl. Among them was a drill with a cranking handle: "Generally, there's no electricity in the stairwells."

On the wall between the shelves hung a photograph of a group of men in front of a metalworking shop. Each held a tool in front of his chest as if it were the real proof of his identity. A huge pair of pliers, a sledgehammer, a grease gun, and so on. *León 1911, Melchor Martínez Workshop* was written on the bottom of the picture.

"That's Buenaventura Durruti as an apprentice, isn't it great?"

"Who's Durruti?"

Ragna smiled. "The one in the middle of the top row."

She hadn't understood his question. Evidently Ragna couldn't imagine that he wouldn't know who Buenaventura Durruti was. Carl stared at the photograph. Durruti was a tall, gloomy man with a fixed gaze and a beret. Someone Ragna revered. A man she would love.

"First a workshop, then the entire country, right, Carl?"

She approached and touched the glass over the photograph.

At a door far down one of the adjacent cellar corridors, Ragna explained a few more things which could prove important for what he was planning.

You could tell the door's lock had been repeatedly pried open and crudely repaired. Ragna called it the practice door. Carl learned that some doors were best pried open from the bottom and some from the side. "Sometimes you just need to caress them a bit, some are like that, Carl." She looked into his eyes. There were various locks that required different methods. She talked about them and about what to do if someone threatened to report him or called the police. She mentioned the "General Ban on Incomers' Residency in Berlin," a very old, almost forgotten law. In fact, no one could say whether or not it still applied. In this case, it was probably the same as with most laws—they were still in effect, but *not seriously*. Their meaning had been forfeited.

Ragna's deep, hoarse voice and her small, squarish hands. But Carl wasn't thinking of *that*, he was trying to concentrate. Ragna's earnestness helped him focus; there was something reassuring about her and she reminded Carl distantly of his childhood and adolescence, of Sundays in the garage with his father: adjusting the carburetor, bleeding brakes, applying Elaskon to prevent rust—it was their old, well-ordered life, which had seemed permanent, a life in which you acquired the skills needed to understand, care for and, if necessary, repair the few (valuable) things you owned.

Taking over an apartment was a serious but manageable task and forcing open a door was the proper answer—to what? To the situation and its demands. "We can no longer wait endlessly until some face or other shows up," the Shepherd had said.

Ragna entered each tool in a distribution log and had Carl sign for them.

"When you're done, just bring them back."

Even now, in June, she wore her fur cap and her boots. She was the gamekeeper. Custodian of the tools and all the abandoned buildings they could help save, thought Carl.

CARL'S THOUGHTS

"I'm Bad Santa, bringer of doom," Carl whispered to himself as he trudged down Dimitroff Strasse. On his back, he was carrying a sack full of tools and several door locks he had acquired from the Castorf hardware store on Pappel Allee (Castorf was considered the specialist for building and apartment occupiers' needs).

"Effi in Berlin" was the name of the fairy tale that was supposed to come true, no, not a fairy tale, a novel full of happiness and optimism. Carl's apartment on Ryke Strasse was too small for the fairy tale, and in any case, Effi had a place of her own in mind. Having her own apartment was her dream. Very tentatively, she'd asked Carl if he could help her, if he knew "how it was done." At the same time, she'd mentioned a certain area, a preferred street on which two of her artist friends lived. It was the Richard Sorge Strasse in the Friedrichshain district.

It was a run-down neighborhood that seemed particularly foreign to Carl and quite *strict*. He couldn't come up with another word for it. Even the way to Friedrichshain seemed dismal. Yet in the rear buildings throughout the district there were dens in which you could hide away, and from there, well hidden, you could wrest your own share from the new world: gray, brick-lined dens full of promise just waiting to be taken possession of, perfectly suited for it—you just had to be able to recognize them, it came down to the right choice. Window frames without paint were good. The dirtiest possible windowpanes were good but still no guarantee. You can't rush things or rely only on a hunch, Ragna had told him. The first condition: the den (definitely) had to be uninhabited. There was no point breaking into one of these seemingly empty apartments if someone was sleeping there. Or if it was inhabited by people who happened to be out shopping. Second condition: basic utilities. Apartments without water, for example, were unusable. There had to be a stove for heating, a cooker was also welcome.

Carl carefully climbed the spacious, dimly lit staircases in the front buildings and searched the facades of the rear buildings for untended windows. The crumbling linoleum, the smell of floor polish. At first, it did him good to listen to his footsteps and their faint echo in the stairwell. Then it felt good to pause for a while on a landing, to be quiet and remain still. It did him good to let the world outside roar and be completely clear inside, without a single thought, just hallway, stairs, light. Just a brief flash in one of the tiny panes of leaded glass arranged around the large windowpane. Dream-deep the small, cobalt blue window with the engraved star.

It was nice to look from there through the often narrow, rather shaft-like courtyards into a presumably empty apartment—the outline of an open door, scraps of curtains left behind. Carl saw Effi's life there and he also saw his own life. He saw them together in this room, at work; he saw the table where the cigarettes lay, where the wine bottle stood, where they periodically poured a glass, just so, as everyone wanted, as much as they were in the mood for, the table where they met at times, touched each other, slept together and then went back to work, and so on, all night long . . . He saw scenes of great warmth and togetherness, more than love, if that were even possible, he saw friendship, sex, work. They were companions and together, they would do it: they would be artists.

215

For whatever reason, Carl especially liked the unplastered houses with the exposed, brown masonry of hard, fired bricks. The walls were the best fit for his idea of a new start together—bare, fired bricks could protect both writing and drawing (or painting), the open, honest brickwork, its rawness and warmth along with the word *tenement* that, given its meaning, at first seemed repugnant but then, in another way, through the rhythm and sound of *tenement*, the way *tenement* creeps into your ear, became alluring again simply as a word (in doing so, it pretended it was nothing other than rhythm and sound) and what it turned into in the process, a boat on the dreamed sea of this city, a boat that wanted to be at home here and nowhere else, that could anchor here with the banished glow under the sail of its compliant heart . . . , wrote Carl. He'd pulled his notebook from his pocket and was writing—he was writing!

As if in a frenzy, he occupied three apartments one after the other in four hours: 25 Sorge Strasse, rear building right, third floor next to Seidel; 65 Sorge Strasse, third floor, previous tenant Görth; 66 Sorge Strasse, side wing. It was a hunting expedition, a campaign, a battle (with blood on his hands at the end), and it was a victory. The heady rush of squatting and of love was enough to suppress his fear and push aside his doubts. After all, he was not a criminal, a professional burglar, or a thief. What he was doing was necessary and just. There were only fleeting reappearances of the unease that accompanied him constantly in those days in all his undertakings as the question of whether what he was doing was appropriate for someone who wrote poems; ultimately: was he a poet? Banging doors, endless doubts. *We* can do it, Carl thought and braced himself against the door and, also, with all his strength against the actual, unmistakable squalor of these buildings, against his own squalor, lost as he was in this city.

Breaking into an apartment wasn't particularly difficult. A blow to the door, holding your breath, listening, then another blow and listening again—thundering silence. Now and then there was a noise but no one came into the stairwell. Until he stopped being careful and focused only on finishing the job quickly, on accomplishing the mission.

But why on earth did it have to be *three* apartments? First: to show Effi what he was capable of, that she wasn't wrong to believe in him and have confidence in him. She would come and have the choice of three apartments. They would sit in the Café Westphal and he would lay out on the table for Effi no fewer than three keys. Good Castorf keys to good Castorf locks. She'd walk through the apartments and in one or in all three, she'd sleep with him, right there, immediately . . . These weren't really Carl's thoughts, just short circuits, hazy reflections flashing through his brain, juvenile stuff—so then, second: three apartments— simply to have a choice. And third: three apartments to be sure that at least one of them would be a match, especially given the expected conflicts with the authorities. It would not be child's play; even though the state officials were easily weakened, cowed, and duped, you had to count on resistance and obstacles.

66 Sorge Strasse: the third and last apartment. Right after Carl had inserted his crowbar and tentatively thrown his weight against the door (to test its resistance), a neighbor stepped into the stairwell. In these months of upheaval and awakening, the ability to skip, or rather, dismiss time-consuming formalities had become widespread. What Carl was doing there with his bright red crowbar was obvious and unmistakable; there was no need for questions or explanations. In a soft voice, Mr. Frieling (that was the name on the door plate) asked *what exactly* Carl had planned. Mr. Frieling was a tall, handsome man, a pensioner, probably a widower. He wore a rather scruffy corduroy vest. He made refined gestures and had a slight lisp.

"For my wife and child," Carl said almost truthfully and added the appropriate script: studies, pregnancy, Mother Floor, "she needs an apartment now, that is, her own place."

"Mother Floor," Frieling said in a nasal tone and shook his head. Then he offered Carl the use of his tools. With Frieling watching, Carl found it difficult to use the brute but necessary force. He was more cautious, less criminal, and for a while he dealt with the door but to no end. Frieling talked. He kept trying to calculate exactly how long the apartment had been vacant. He obviously knew how important this detail would be in a dispute with the authorities. "So then, Mrs. Gröber died last year—in February. It's a real shame that she didn't live to see it all . . ."

Carl asked Frieling for a glass of water (a scene out of a film) and when the old man was gone, he made short shrift of the door. There was an ear-splitting bang and the sesame opened; the noise echoed in the stairwell like a gunshot, like an explosion. Unfortunately, far too much of the wood splintered out of the door frame. Carl refastened the largest pieces provisionally with small nails—he had everything with him and was proud about that. Frieling didn't seem to notice the disaster—or he chose to ignore it. Carl drank the water, thanked him, and started replacing the lock.

Frieling was impressed that Carl cleaned the windows right after he had broken in. Somehow it made Frieling happy, almost boisterous. "You can do the same at my place!" he called across the courtyard. Then he waved shyly and gave Carl a thumbs-up, a gesture that evidently wasn't very familiar to him but one he'd decided could be made at that moment. He could not know that cleaning the window was a precautionary measure, an outer sign, a mark for all the other squatters stalking through the city. They were easily recognizable by the way their eyes swept over the building facades, by their concentrated ambling (they ambled, but with concentration). Freshly washed windows were more important than the lock in the door or the new paper sign on the door, *Ilonka Kalász*, written as neatly as possible. Effi's name.

GIANT WINGS

Hoffi had noticed Carl's hesitation and waved him over. When the Shepherd sat on the hairdressing chair, he was about as tall as Carl standing.

"Over by Adele, those are Russians, *friendly* Russians, understand? Pour them some more milk, please."

He hadn't made any effort to speak softly and for a moment Fenske's cellar fell silent. The Comandante, who had taken his seat on the second salon chair, rose and began to speak. The crown of his head almost touched the ceiling and so he stood, leaning forward slightly, in fighting stance. He was, as always, dressed in black; the short sleeves of his shirt looked as if they'd been gnawed at by hungry animals; the skin on his strong arms looked unnatural—like leather, Carl thought, in any case, not human.

"Failure is grounded in these buildings . . ."

Carl, whose role was limited to bringing fresh goat milk and a few bottles of beer to the table, was surprised by the changes in the Fenske group. Adele from "Lada Karlshorst", who looked at him with warmth, was the only one he had immediately recognized among the new faces. Carl decided to ask about the Zhiguli later. Next to Adele sat a burly, nearly bald man, who stood up and offered Carl his hand.

"Titov, Vassily."

"This is Daddy Vassily," Adele said very softly.

The Russian nodded and gave Carl's hand a brief, firm shake as if they were sealing some agreement.

219

"General of the Sixth Rifle Brigade in Wuhlheide, in Köpenick," Adele whispered, lowering her eyes, and Carl briefly wondered if he had misunderstood her. It was just too loud at the table and not a time for conversation.

The fraction of the united leftists had not returned to the cellar and a few of the captains were missing. The Wydoks had already been at the table for an hour, mostly to celebrate their victory: "2,890 votes! The Free Republic of Utopia lives!" In the local elections their "autonomous action" had received an incredible 0.1 percent. They showed their banners and were proud of Radio P. Just before the election, Emil Schnell, the Minister of Post and Telecommunications, had personally asked them to free up the frequency. "He asked, get it? The Minister of Post! He calls us up and begs for his frequency! We immediately put the call on broadcast." They all laughed but only briefly; the dog fiasco weighed heavily on them.

The Comandante talked for a while about the poor conditions the valuable animals were being kept in, the bad food and care.

"I'm going to speak broadly: border dogs are very sensitive creatures. Their pedigree is noble and their history anti-fascist, essentially for generations. This means that nowhere in this world, *nowhere* I say, will we find a living creature better prepared for our fight. Nowhere will we find a four-legged animal better able to protect our buildings from skinheads and fascist gangs. I'm not talking about a protective barrier, no, it's *in their nature.* That is, if you *really want it,* if you yourselves are ready for it, if it's *part of you.*" He paused. "If you don't want to just drink and fuck around."

Two of the captains (or proxy captains, 15 Duncker and 86 Kastanie—basically it was never clear who exactly was sent to represent the buildings taken into custody) jumped up and started swearing at the Comandante. The leathery-skinned man lowered his eyes. He waited like an adult remaining calm when children are squabbling. Then he continued speaking. He declared his willingness to help with further rounding-up of the dogs, with "bringing them home," as he put it in passing. And he calculated the balance that would have to be paid to the dog handlers. Again and very slowly, as if he expected each of his words to be written down, he named the seller's address: "German Shepherd Association, The Prussian Pub, Michendorfer Chaussee. There, just outside of Potsdam, in the rear extensions and kennels, is where the handlers are domiciled. That's their trading center. You can smell the cages from the restaurant counter."

It soon became clear that payment was the point on which spirits were divided, as they say (or used to say). Three hundred and fifty marks for Berry von der Schweizerhütte alone. 86 Kastanie jumped up (again, this time knocking his chair over) and announced that his building could no longer accept this speculative cellar forum *as a plenum*. "We also reject the term aguerrillas. Where is your working class, anyway?" He looked at the Russians who were staring at him silently and were completely rigid. The Shepherd drew Carl over to him.

"The Comandante's father is a general in the KGB, did you know that?" This time his whisper was very soft, barely audible. "I'm sure they all know this." He gestured toward the Russians. "Only that one doesn't," he nodded at the Kastanie man, who felt encouraged.

"We've always been proud of buildings like 20 Schönhauser," the Kastanie representative beat his fist on his chest. "The first free building in the East. The first of the early buildings. But since then, people have started selling its freedom. User contracts, subsidies, job creation schemes—dough from the police state! Bread from the swine-senate! And now? Now we're supposed to pay a dog tax to a nut job who calls himself Comandante, Kruso, Cockroach or whatever—a dog tax for

Kazakhstan! Kazakhstan!" His voice cracked, then he left the table and marched outside without another word. Two of the other captains hurried after him.

"I'm sorry, very sorry," the Shepherd roared, "if you don't understand this opportunity! And your *plenum*—shove it up your asses, you ass-faces. We're not in the central committee here! We're here with those who do things instead of always just talking! This is the East, not Kreuzberg! It's a worker state. Here, the cops are on our side! But you'll never get that! Because you don't understand what's really going on. Because you're completely Westernized, you decadent Western occupiers, you—"

Carl touched the Shepherd's shoulder. He gave a start and fell silent but then started coughing as if he had swallowed something (the most significant part, probably, about solidarity, a good life for each and every person). He coughed and gasped for breath. "Those rats, occupiers . . ." Dodo trotted into the cellar and straight up to Hoffi. She laid her head in the Shepherd's lap (as if she were a dog). The goat wore the welding goggles from the Tacheles around her neck like a rare piece of jewelry.

Unfazed, the Comandante broached the actual topic of the colloquium: a better, "militarily precise" defense of the buildings, yes, also in view of possible attacks by the police, especially by their evacuation commandos, but he downplayed the point. He was ready, he stressed, to fundamentally agree with the senior captain on the subject of "partnering with the organs of state," nonetheless, they had to be armed. Standing slightly bent with his neck extended, like an animal ready to fight, the Comandante gazed down at Hoffi, who looked like he had been propelled backward into his chair, then he looked at the door.

A young man who looked familiar to Carl walked in. Maybe it was just that they looked a little alike. The man held a stack of paper in front of his chest. The Comandante nodded at him and drew a semicircle with his hand and Carl's doppelgänger

(doppelgänger was an exaggeration, but the similarity was clear) handed out the sheets of paper. Most were sketches, pale and hard to make out, of rolls of barbed wire and chevaux-de-frise for stairways. A roll of wire netting for window barricades. Boards of nails in the cellar light wells. Their structure along with explanations in a schoolboyish scrawl.

"On densely nailed boards, for example, the foot does not sink onto the nails fast enough or even at all. Such boards are ineffectual"—the Comandante was stressing "ineffectual" when Carl left the cellar.

The Comandante's adjutant stood at the bar. He looked exhausted.

"Good sketches," Carl said.

"Not mine, just copies. From the *Handbook for Squatting Action*. Kruso expanded and developed it more in the direction of action, if you know what I mean. He invented the battle rods, by the way."

"Ah, those rods with . . ."

"With the strange hooks, yes."

It's Edgar, thought Carl—now he knew. Edgar Bendler from Gera-Langenberg was the Comandante's adjutant. Absolutely impossible, he thought, but it was, without a doubt, little Ed. At school, he was in the grade below him. On Charlottenburg Weg, Ed had lived in the apartment building across from theirs. From his bedroom, Carl could see into the Bendlers' apartment: kitchen to the right, bedroom to the left, the curtains were kept mostly closed. The last time Carl had seen Ed was in Halle, but he hadn't said hello. Bendler had presumably studied in Halle, but maybe not. And now, here he was, standing at the bar in the Assel. Strange enough if you considered the circumstances. Maybe he's following me, Carl thought, which was absurd. Surely it was all just coincidence. All and nothing. But that someone *from there*, from the same street (my home street, thought Carl), had made it all the way here, to this underground spot . . . For a moment, Carl saw his life from the outside, not for long, but very clearly. Things happened. You had no influence on them. Your so-called own life; it was a completely unlikely story, spooky, in fact.

"What'll you have?"

"I recognized you right away in there, Carl. You didn't recognize me, did you?"

"I did. Well, not right away . . ."

"We spent a lot of time together, back then, in training."

"Yeah." Carl didn't remember.

"And now you're acting like we don't know each other."

Carl was silent. He knelt down and pulled two bottles of beer from a crate under the bar.

"Carl Bischoff. First in football, then in track and field. Middle distance—you trained like a madman, but there was no point."

"Why?"

"The 800 meter circuit around the Hausberg, remember? Again and again, endlessly. And then you fell in love with my cousin."

"With your cousin?"

Carl looked at the window. Darkness was falling slowly on Oranienburger Strasse. He'd forgotten all of it. He had trained with Edgar Bendler. Sixteen years old. But he was only in love with Effi.

"You went to dance class with her. In the Youth and Sports Club."

"She looked like you, right?"

Now Edgar smiled. "Maybe."

"And you played football too, leftback, defense, right? And then we switched to running, track and field, we trained an awful lot . . ."

"Five times a week, Carl. Even when you took dance classes, we still trained, always in the evening, on the Hausberg in the forest. 'Business as usual,' you always said."

Carl slid Edgar a bottle across the steel tread plate.

"Do you remember the cinders, Carl, the slag? When they resurfaced the track?"

Carl shoved his right hand in his trouser pocket. It was a reflex, a gesture that expressed defensiveness stronger than he'd planned.

"Even though we washed the cut off right away, in the stream, it didn't heal. Everyone knew that the slag was uranium waste material. Didn't bother anyone at the time. The stream and the sports fields are gone, did you know that?"

"No, I—I haven't been there in ages."

"Go on, show me, Carl."

Edgar smiled at him. It was just Ed, little Ed, whom he had trained with a long time ago, almost every evening in some previous life.

Carl pulled his hand out of his pocket and slowly laid it on the counter. The steel tread was cool against the back of his hand. A small, dark half-moon shimmered under his skin where the wound had been. A small, dark moon of cinder embedded in the white ball of his hand.

"Is the Comandante your friend, Ed?"

"Kruso?"

"Yeah, the Comandante."

"We live together. Out in Wilhelmshorst, to the southwest, in the old officers' HQ. I think that's why, that's why they call him that—Comandante. The building belongs to the Red Army. We can stay because Kruso's father . . ."

"I know."

Edgar looked questioningly at Carl, but Carl just smiled. Maybe he liked Ed. Back then they'd been close. Five evenings a week.

"We know each other from Hiddensee. A lot of people from there drifted to Berlin, across the sea, like a shifting sand dune. They settle into the buildings here and start cafés. The Westphal, the Rat Pub, the Wydoks' bar on Schönhauser—all island people with a lot of experience, especially in gastronomy. Freedom finds its disciples, always and everywhere, if you know what I mean."

Carl's hand still lay on the counter, as if he'd forgotten it there. It looked naked and vulnerable, like a turtle with its shell torn off. Ed touched it very lightly. He stroked it with two fingers. Tenderly.

"Radioactive. Maybe it's good for you, Carl, right? A bit of dirt from home under your skin. Slag in your writing hand. Or have you stopped writing?"

"Do you remember Effi, Ed?"

Before Carl left the Assel, he straightened up Fenske's cellar. The boots remained; the Shepherd felt it was important even though no one believed any longer that Dr. Fenske might come downstairs to his cellar again someday. He'd become "quite incapacitated" according to Irina.

The Comandante's sketches were pinned up on the wall, right on a map of Greater Berlin. Carl wondered for a moment where the pins had come from. He imagined the Comandante pulling a small sewing kit from his trouser pockets (a gray, woolen packet) and placing it on the table. This sewing kit made him unassailable. It was this last missing detail which showed everyone that the realm he ruled was impregnable. He opened his sewing kit, various pins and needles, thick black yarn, spools of thread—the captains, the Russians, the Shepherd, and the Wydoks guys, all of them silent and attentive.

The drawings were captioned like chapters in a novel: "Battle in the Staircase," "The Battle Rod," "The Tools," "Nails and

Spikes," "Retreat," and so on. Carl's eyes wandered from page to page:

"Active defense is best fought from the upper floors. This position offers the greatest protection from attacking police officers. Throwing:
  stones
  full bottles
  shopping bags filled with water
  paint bombs
  Molotov cocktails
  old cathode-ray tubes (great splinter effect)
will prevent the attacking policemen from invading the building.
Comrades, be sparing with the projectile material!
Only throw when you're sure you'll hit the target.
In this phase of the battle, you can also launch unmounted window casements. If you throw them horizontally, they whirl through the air. Since you can't predict their trajectory, they have an enormously disorienting effect on the attacking police."

Like "giant wings," Carl thought. That was Baudelaire. Suddenly the image of the window casements whirling down to earth was painful. For a long time, Carl hadn't understood the poem about the albatross. Or truth be told: the simile left him disgruntled. He was as ungainly as the bird, but still terrible. He was no albatross and would never be one. He also wasn't one of the mariners who tormented the bird; he hated them. Carl wasn't a poet, and he wasn't a bricklayer. He just worked in an underground bar in a building that had to be protected with tumbling wings: "If you throw them horizontally, they whirl through the air." Defending the house would result in its destruction.

He walked from Oranienburger back to Ryke Strasse. It was after midnight. He took a long detour through the park, across the river and once around Museum Island. He relished the

227

tranquility, the sound of his footsteps in the center of the city. What was a building? A large, petrified ship you could talk to. There were too many things he clung to. As a bricklayer, he had built buildings. A building was full of things that had to be protected. I am attached to them, Carl thought, that was the truth. He loved things. He conspired with them and liked to be alone in their company. Matter is more magical than life. Who was it who said that?

MY APARTMENT

Two weeks later, Effi came to Berlin. They met on Bersarin Platz. Effi was agitated, almost frantic, she *shone*. Her eyes glowed, as did her high forehead that had something noble, aristocratic, but also something childlike about it. Either she talked very quickly in fits and starts or she said nothing and just nodded. Somehow, they managed to have a conversation. Everything about her emanated anticipation and gratitude. She laughed about Carl's tool bag, which he had brought along just in case. She felt the rough canvas and he had to list all his tools for her. Effi didn't know what a *Bello* was ("Bellow, Saul Bellow?") and Carl explained the purpose and use of a mid-sized sledgehammer. She respected the trades and their related skills. The fact that Carl was a bricklayer counted more than the seven poems on a desk of the UVA, which he had unwisely told her about. But she had no contempt or disregard for his writing and the prospects Carl associated with it, at least that's how he saw it.

"With a simple hammer, you often can't accomplish much." That was something his master bricklayer liked to say. Once in a while, Carl would say it, repeat it automatically in self-defense. He thought of the Roman numerals their teachers (Master Bocklich and Master Ebert) had notched into each one of their tools in preparation for the apprenticeship. They were thirteen apprentices; each one had his own tools and his own number. For three years, Carl was number XII. The XII was written on his helmet in blue nitrocellulose lacquer. Sometimes they said to each other, "Hey, Seven," or "Eight, come here for a minute." At first it was mostly a joke but then it became a habit and they started calling each other by their numbers outside of the construction sites as well. There was something significant and even cultish about it, in a good way.

Effi looked at him. She had given her notice on the Mother Floor. Together they tried to organize her next steps, the period after she moved to Sorge Strasse: first, the registration for water and electricity, then the residency registration office, then the property management's office—or better in reverse? They both spoke rather confusedly. Our future, Carl thought. All that would come now.

On Sorge Strasse, Effi became very quiet. When they left number 66, the last of the three apartments, she staggered for a few steps, then leaned against the wall of the building. Even then she looked elegant. Her slender body, slightly curved, her knees bent a little. "I'm sorry, I feel dizzy." Carl stood behind her and didn't know what to do.

They sat in silence for a few seconds on the curb of Sorge Strasse, which was beginning to remind them of the worry, the *Sorge*, in its name.

"I only have today. I have to move out in a week. Then we need a place to stay, Freddy and I."

"I understand . . ."

"No."

"What do you mean, no?"

"You don't understand." She took hold of Carl's arm and pulled on it as if it were a switch. Her face was very pale and her tone almost formal. She thanked him again and then said it.

229

"Two rooms, I need at least two rooms. My child needs a place for his things, and I need somewhere to sleep—and when I want to work at night . . . These just won't work. We need *two rooms*, understand?"

Her "understand" sounded desperate. At the same time, the effort it cost her to confront Carl with her reality was unmistakable.

It was a disaster. He hadn't thought, he'd only dreamed. He'd dreamed of a den instead of thinking about the *rooms*, the spaces that were necessary. He'd occupied three dens and dreamed their new life into them.

He had dreamed away the child.

Poof.

Suddenly, his campaign through Sorge Strasse was nothing but vanity, madness, and, yes, an expression of insufficient love.

"I haven't eaten anything yet today," Effi said and stood up. They walked toward Dimitroff Strasse in silence. Carl's tools rattled with every step: you failed, Number Twelve. Get lost, Number Twelve.

In a bakery on Dimitroff Strasse, they ate sandwiches and drank coffee. At some point Effi brought up an exhibition in the Martin Gropius building that she wanted to see. Carl told her about a short film festival in the French cultural center on Unter den Linden and mentioned a Pink Floyd concert the following month. "On 21 July, on Potsdamer Platz," Effi murmured. There was something magical about saying addresses in the West, knowing you could go there at any time.

Without wasting any words, they roamed the surrounding streets, scanning the facades. In a corner building on Ebeling Strasse, on the third floor, Carl inserted his crowbar, this time in front of Effi's eyes.

It was a front-facing apartment that appeared to be vacant. A corner apartment with dirty, empty windows on both sides, so at least three rooms, if not four. Almost too good to be true, so Carl rang the doorbells of the adjacent apartments to inquire, but no one answered. There was green linoleum on the staircase and the walls were freshly painted, not a good sign, actually.

A copper nameplate above the doorbell read *E. Lange* engraved in cursive script. Carl's crowbar between the two leaves of the large front door. He went about it technically and made it look a little harder than it was. The door gave way immediately, almost without a sound. Only a fine crack in the wood over the lock, nothing more.

The apartment was completely furnished, but felt uninhabited, abandoned. Stagnant air and a sweetish-sour smell. There were curtains on the windows they hadn't seen from below.

"There's been no one here for ages."

"Hungarian refugees," Effi whispered.

"Or dead."

Effi looked at the floor.

"I mean, apartments of dead people often stay like this for years, untouched. Where we lived in Gera-Untermhaus there were entire streets . . ." Carl's explanation wasn't making any difference, so he stopped talking.

Effi had tears in her eyes.

"It would be really wonderful here. It would be *so good.*"

She walked slowly from room to room and spread her arms wide. She went into the kitchen and opened the lower cabinets. Dishes, pots and pans, everything there. Carl went into the bedroom. A double bed, only one side used, the cover half drawn back. One second and he had shaken the dent from a head out of the pillow. It was a reflex. Effi stood behind him.

They were exhausted and it would have been impossible not to sit on the bed to rest at least for a moment. It was pure exhaustion, which gave them permission.

When they woke, it was night. The bedroom light worked. On a single hook next to the door hung a few aprons and next to it was a key rack. Carl found a key that fit the front door lock— another easy victory. He slipped out of the house and bought wine from a kiosk in a small, run-down park on the opposite side of Dimitroff Strasse. He was tense and in high spirits. He hadn't failed. He was the man with the tools. When he returned, the apartment was dark and Effi was standing behind the door. She just looked at him, her eyes wide, nothing else. She'd found a jar of pears in the cupboard under the window. They drank wine and ate the pears. Then they went back to bed. A streetlamp shone directly into the room.

In the morning, Effi washed the glasses. She left her things on the kitchen table. Effi's apartment, Carl thought. Big enough for *everyone*. He locked the door and handed her the key. She put it in her pocket and put a hand on his cheek. A good moment. On the way downstairs, they rang at another door.

"Erna from upstairs, you mean. She hasn't been there for a long time. They came and took her away in the middle of the night."

Mrs. Pennmann from the first floor scrutinized Carl and seemed to be considering.

"She's in a home now."

"You mean—for good?"

Mrs. Pennmann raised her head.

"We're family," Effi whispered. "We wanted to visit her . . ."

"Ah. That's who you are."

A crooked, paved path, then the old people's home with the gable facing the street. It was behind the Kosmos cinema on Karl Marx Allee, a "beautiful new building," as Mrs. Pennmann put it. Carl wrote her name in his notebook. If necessary, they could name this tenant as a witness to prove vacancy. Which surely wouldn't be necessary, Carl was convinced. In the end, Mrs. Lange would understand everything, but for that, she has to see us, Carl thought, we just have to go see her and describe our difficult situation, openly and honestly.

It was hard to say what happened next. The smell of old age and illness. The woman at reception and her doubtful look. Effi's effusive sincerity. "Yes, we absolutely need to speak with Mrs. Lange, it's about her apartment . . ."—the affectionate tone, the deceit. Then, minutes later, the sight of the tiny old woman padding hesitantly down the long, bright corridor that was lined with windows on one side and stone-gray doors on the other. Her dressing gown covered with pink, stylized roses and quilted in a rhomboid pattern, stained, with sleeves rolled up. Sticking out, a small, soaring, almost transparent hand with which she touched the windowsill at intervals as if to reassure herself that it was still there. She would brush the sill lightly with her fingertips in an elegant, almost dancing gesture and over it all, her doubting, expectant face. That was how she walked toward them. This image would haunt Carl for a long time: when was the last time anyone had asked after her? Maybe there were children, or maybe there was no one left. Just us, Carl thought, with the key to her apartment in his pocket.

"My apartment? What about my apartment?"

Her thin, white hair hovered about her head like a small, silver cloud, shiny and dandruffy. She could be puffed away, her whole, tiny being could be puffed away.

"My apartment?"

Her voice trembled and now the small cloud trembled too.

"But it's *my* apartment."

Mrs. Lange slowly retreated step by step. Carl saw that she wanted to say something else, but she didn't have enough breath. Finally, she waved her hand in the air as if chasing away an insect, "Go away, go . . ."

16 WÖRTHER

A large, yellowed foam-rubber mattress lay next to the stove and in front of it stood an empty bottle of Bacardi. There was also a half-empty can of moldy ravioli, from which (upright, in a circle) about twenty cigarette butts protruded. Stonehenge, thought Carl. A dark green crocheted blanket went with the mattress and Freddy lay under it, invisible, covered up to the shock of his platinum blond hair.

"You can lie low here for a while," the man in the front building had said. His name was Franz and he had shoulder-length hair, which he brushed behind his ears as he talked, a gesture that felt familiar to Carl, an eloquent gesture, which he himself never made, despite his own shoulder-length hair. The gesture was that of a blues musician on stage announcing a song or of women explaining something with such earnestness and concentration that they didn't notice the movement of their hands in their hair.

Lie low for a while.

Carl pictured the people who lay low here. The foam-rubber mattress was lined with dark, blurred edges. For Carl it was the secret map of a largely uncharted territory for whose discovery he, Effi and Freddy had been chosen.

"The entire floor belongs to the Shepherd."

"It *belongs* to him?"

"He reserved it. In case of emergency, as it were."

There were four apartments on the floor. Three one-room dens and this one, which was suitable, with a hallway, kitchen and a so-called "Berlin room," through which you reach another, smaller room. Freddy's room, Carl thought, everyone needs their own room, it doesn't work otherwise (in life).

"The previous tenants emigrated, eight or ten years ago already. Someone ripped out the cooker at some point, but we'll find you one, no problem. How do you know the Shepherd? From the guerrillas?"

He wore white gym shoes and a Levi's jacket and jeans. Nothing indicated that he belonged to the pack. The Good Empire has sympathizers in all social classes, Carl thought.

"Yes, but we don't really belong—I mean, not really to *that*," Carl stammered.

"We'd always hoped that someone with a child would move in here. Our little one can play with Freddy. If you need anything, let us know. We're in the front building on the top floor."

"What do you do?" Carl asked and blushed. It had just slipped out of him, a dubious attempt to offer a bit of solidarity.

"Radio engineer. In the Star Radio factory. And you?"

Effi at the window. The crown of the chestnut tree with its faded flowers in the courtyard.

"A good place for your easel," Carl said after (gingerly) putting a hand on her shoulder. Effi nodded.

"In that cellar—were those your friends?"

"Yes, I work there. It's the Assel."

To the right of the door that opened onto the Berlin room stood a small fridge that actually worked. It was empty. On the wall above hung a pencil sketch—streets, intersections, names, and a dotted line that crossed the outlines of the adjacent buildings: the Café Westphal, the Zinnober-Laden Theater, and a few other addresses of allied buildings that were often mentioned in Assel colloquiums. The good Shepherd, Carl thought. After the disaster in the nursing home, the Assel had been their last resort.

In the Assel, they'd also met Nora, Effi's sister, who'd brought Freddy. She was thin and pale with large, bright cheeks and dark rims around her eyes. Half of the pack quickly gathered around the child, who did not seem fazed by the hubbub. There wasn't a single one of them who did not want to hold Freddy at least once and yes, the child was actually real.

Henry, who was filling in for Carl at the bar, poured them all cherry juice. Irina served the reheated leftovers from their lunch. All of a sudden, there was talk of "Carl's girlfriend," even of "Carl's family." Effi looked helplessly at Carl, but she couldn't do anything about it. Nonetheless, she apologized with a look of pure goodness and gratitude, after which Carl was prepared to do anything. Hoffi arrived and spoke first with Effi's sister, probably because she was so tall and beautiful and because she looked severe with her prominent, high cheekbones and her hair tightly drawn back. Nora explained the situation to the Shepherd.

Everyone made suggestions until the Shepherd called Franz— using a radio telephone. "His latest acquisition," Henry whispered. The telephone had a suitcase-sized case with an antenna that stood on the floor behind the bar; the device the Shepherd spoke into was larger than a briquette.

Hoffi liked Freddy. He gathered him into his arms and together they went to the stall in back, "to say hello to Dodo." The Assel, the shelter, the U-boat, only now did Carl appreciate the simple, deeper meaning of all the obscure talk.

Nora's boyfriend Ralf was waiting out on the street in a black VW Passat. "16 Wörther" was written on the note; Carl realized that the address was only a few hundred meters from his apartment on Ryke Strasse. Everything is coincidence—and isn't. And at some point, it will all be good, Carl thought.

Ralf was *elegant*, a man graying at the temples, maybe ten, maybe twenty years older than Carl. He drove very fast and talked about the wretched roads, the Passat, the monetary union, and about what needed to be done—for Effi and Carl. His brown suede jacket looked soft and expensive. It was the jacket of a winner. Carl admired the car and ignored Ralf's question about his checking account. He didn't understand what Ralf meant.

"Ralf is with Woolworth," Nora explained, "he's in charge of the entire East."

Two days later, Ralf stood at Carl's door and pressed a small bundle of bills into his hand. "We turn four grand of East marks into four grand of West marks. You and me—that's what's called monetary union, my friend."

And Carl would earn one thousand. One thousand West marks—an unbelievable amount. Carl's empty account was suddenly a blessing. Ralf did a quick tour of the apartment and dropped a few tips. Everything was easy, everything was doable, Ralf knew what to do—or what he would do, if he were Carl. Carl felt dirty in Ralf's presence, or at least like a loser, like someone who would never accomplish anything. Ralf stopped in front of the oven and read the page with Carl's latest poem that hung from the hook.

"'The ships quietly entered the city,' I like that, Carl. Keep it up, I'd say. And don't forget to make a deposit!"

He slapped Carl on the back and as if in a reflex, Carl stretched his hand out and touched it: Ralf's winner's jacket, the soft, precious leather of the West.

LITTLE FRENCHY

The next morning, Carl found a wad of paper in the entryway under the mail slot. He uncrumpled it and found his car key. On the sheet of paper was a single sentence: "You earned it, Zhiguliman." Underneath was a large "A." A like Adele, Carl thought. Adele, *Arbeiter*, Assel, the invincible A.

The Zhiguli gleamed in front of the house: repaired and washed. Precious.

That evening, Effi and Carl went to the Franz Club, on the corner of Schönhauser. Effi's dance was an elegant march across the room. Carl tried for a few steps, but he couldn't follow her without looking ridiculous. He didn't have the movements; his hips froze and his arms grew still. It looked like he was just trotting after her, like a rhythmically nodding dog.

Carl watched Effi: the way she marched toward the stage, leaning forward slightly, arms bent, hands in fists with her head thrust forward, as if she were discovering, step by step, a new, unknown land—all this with an expression of unreserved joy that went straight to his heart.

At the edge of the room, Carl trudged in place for a short while under the window of the Franz Club, where live bands he knew from before played now and again: the unrivaled Angelika Weiz, Pascal von Wroblewsky, who'd played with Dizzy Gillespie, Fusion, Bajazzo, Engerling . . . He shook his long hair, the way they used to (to the blues) and started to sway his torso back and forth. All in all, he felt good. He had been with Effi the entire time, first when she moved in, then in the property management's offices, where the Shepherd's name paved the way: "Mr. Hoffmann sent you, right?" That Hoffi was also known as "Mr." was another surprise for Carl: the Good Empire was spreading in circles, ever larger circles. Signals-Franz from the front building had "removed" a cooker somewhere and in the rubbish bins of some rear courtyard on Dimitroff Strasse they found part of a shower unit that actually worked after Franz and Carl painstakingly assembled it.

Freddy got the first shower. He screamed as if on a spit but was completely overjoyed. Freddy admired Carl and wanted to *work with him.* He held Carl's hammer and pounded nails into a board. He raised the hammer and opened his eyes wide, only to squeeze them shut at the decisive moment. After three weeks, he called Carl "Papa."

"Carl," Carl said, "I'm Carl."
"I know what your name is."

For her exam, Effi had a series of etchings planned. The woman with the courtly bow, the image from her first night in the ACUD, was one of them—Carl was rapturous. He thought he could write poems to Effi's etchings and maybe they could have a joint book, self-published in a run of ten or twenty copies—he talked about it, he felt called to be ambitious in her name. More exactly: he felt ambitious for both of them, for Effi and himself, it was now all one.

Effi looked at him calmly and attentively. She nodded and explained what it would take. Carl's view was that it couldn't be very difficult to build a printing press himself, "out of an old laundry mangle with a hand crank."

"But the rollers have to be aligned," Effi objected, "the rollers are often the problem."

Carl thought of the poems he'd write now. He could already picture them, neatly typed.

Effi stroked his arm and Carl took her hand. He felt the desire to put his prick in her small, cool hand but then something in her was almost immediately extinguished. She stood up and said that she had no idea how *all that* could possibly be managed. Her voice was hard, toneless, without any pleading. Carl was taken aback—and promised her he would do it.

This was the beginning of their best time together. With the thousand marks that his empty bank account brought him, Carl wanted to go to Paris—with Effi, in the Zhiguli. Effi's response was, "How could anyone refuse an invitation like that?" or something in that vague, generalizing vein from somewhere far above him in the darkness of the Berlin room. She was holding his wrists tightly and pressing them deep into the foam-rubber mattress. At the same time, she pushed his legs apart with her feet.

"I thought you wanted to go to Morocco, Mr. Bischoff?"

"That will be our next trip."

"And the south of France, what about that?"

"That, too. Before Morocco. We'll drive to the Languedoc, through the villages along the coast."

"And the money?"

"What about it?"

Effi tightened her grip and Carl started to talk.

The old dream of the Mediterranean, living on the land, a sunlit stone house. He could tell her everything; in this moment, he trusted her. Effi started moving and Carl's voice grew softer, almost inaudible.

"Name three French authors!"

Carl whispered the names: "Blanchot, Bachelard, Duras."

Effi responded to each name with a small thrust of her hips. "And more?"

"Bataille, Balzac, Lautréamont . . ." Carl returned the pressure: "Baudelaire, Mallarmé . . ." Effi repeated the names. She imitated Carl's faulty pronunciation and laughed.

"Keep going, keep going, little Frenchy, or is that it already?"

Effi stopped at the entrance to the residency office. She wore a long, thin summer dress with spaghetti straps. Carl could see her chest rise and sink.

"Maybe the police already know everything. Maybe they have completely different information."

"What *information*?"

"About your friend. The Shepherd, Hoffi, that's his name, right? I mean the one who has seized entire floors and buildings."

"He doesn't *seize* them. And he doesn't do it for himself. Otherwise, we wouldn't be here, Effi."

"Do you think *they* care about that?"

The address was Pappel Allee, the building on the corner of Pappel and Dimitroff. It had a row of large shop windows on the ground floor and behind them was a fabric store. A windowless staircase led up to the office on the third floor. The walls were painted brown, and the steps were badly lit—stairs for ghosts, Carl thought.

With its heavily secured doors and windows, the room where Effi had to present her identity papers looked like the anteroom to a large prison. After they checked in (a sign behind the glass partition: "Please speak loudly and clearly!"), they were sent down a windowless corridor to the waiting room facing Dimitroff Strasse. What was unusual about this corridor was that it bent—a tunnel around the corner without any side exits.

Effi trembled with fear. Carl led her to the window so that she could look outside (into freedom) a bit and see people leading their daily lives. A streetcar (which wouldn't exist for long, according to the Shepherd), rumbled placidly out of Kastanien Allee onto Pappel Allee. Carl could feel the dull thud of the tracks under his feet and up to his heart. His gaze wandered over the tracks of the subway and back to his first days in Berlin.

The kindergarten that Effi had found for Freddy was around the corner on Schönhauser Allee. "How old is he then, the little rascal?" and "Fine, no problem": no one had asked for papers. A name and the sight of the freshly combed Freddy were enough.

Two hours later, Effi was legal. Her ID read 16 Wörther Strasse, Berlin 1055. Effi was a Berliner. She'd done it. Now she could *go home*. They walked down the windowless hallway, around the corner, down the ghostly stairs and then, out on the street, Effi hugged Carl and didn't let him go for a long time: "Carl! Dammit, Carl!"

Once a week, Freddy stayed with Nora. They didn't have a set day, so Effi had to plan around Nora and her schedule at the Palast Hotel, where she worked in the piano bar. The bar was round and very small. It resembled an island in the vast top deck of an enormous cruise ship. The piano played all night, invisible, somewhere in the background.

"There are very quiet guys who barely smile. If you smile back, it makes them happy," Nora explained. "Some will talk to you and ask directly. That's OK. You say you work here, but *not like that*. You give them a number and then come those who do take care of that; there are always a few ladies in the house. And then there are the Rumpelstiltskins, those annoying gnomes, who flick their cash over the counter. They crumple fifty- or one hundred-mark bills into little wads and try to hit me. I trample their money the entire evening. It's their balls, you know? It turns them on." She rolled her eyes and made a strange, tilting motion with her hand that Carl wasn't familiar with.

Aside from businessmen and tourists, the Palast Hotel piano bar had a small (very small) group of regulars, the playwright Heiner Müller, for example. "He puffs away on a fat stogy and talks very softly. 'Black Label'—he doesn't say anything else the entire night long. I could mention you to him, Carl, you know? I mean, you write. I could show him some of your work, what do you think? Maybe then he'd talk to me?"

RARE BLUE

"Left, I said *left!*" Effi had screamed at him, and Carl had cursed but it didn't matter. They were screaming and laughing at the same time. Effi laughed with her mouth opened wide, her head tilted backward, gasping for air, baring her teeth. Effi laughed like an animal, and the Zhiguli ran better than ever. The Russians in Karlshorst had done something to the engine.

There were only one-way streets, a thicket of one-way streets and a thousand Frenchmen in Renaults, who honked and waved enthusiastically when they saw the boxy car from the Volga. Traveling like God, Carl thought, traveling with Effi, and Effi, with the map open on her lap, suddenly serious, her brow wrinkling, concentrating intently, responsible, her beauty was almost unbearable: "Left, left!"

The waiters on Place du Trocadéro displayed their arrogance and the tiny receipts under the espresso cups were a strange custom. They fell on the ground, were blown away, and suddenly you felt ill, not equal to the new world. The small, round, brass-edged tables on cast-iron legs were soothing. They sat outside, in front of the café, at their backs the sunroom and the broad, curved counter with mirrored columns, behind which the waiters disappeared. How much would you need to have this *forever*? A thousand a month? More?

Their euphoric conversations and walks through the city: sun, warmth, half-closed shutters and fantasies about the lives hidden behind them. The heavy doors of the town houses with golden knobs the size of a child's head. Everything was gold and every passageway was an opportunity to press up against each other. Carl and Effi stood at the balustrade of the Pont Neuf, on one of the semicircular balconies above the bridge's piers. Effi looked down at the river and said, "Too bad." Too bad that she now, at this moment, would like to *do it*. Carl felt her hand. Like a penitent, Effi knelt on the stone bench. A boat came up the river and slid silently under the bridge. It didn't matter at all if anyone saw what Effi was doing. It was more than shameless, more than desire, more than anything in her life until then. They were celebrating the freedom they had unexpectedly been granted. Paris was the first proof of it; Paris was truth: always unreachable, and suddenly, there they were, on the Pont Neuf.

Contrary to Carl's expectations, Effi hardly wanted to see any art. She preferred going for walks. Only Rodin was important to her and the Musée Fragonard, an anatomical chamber of horrors ("interesting specimens," she said), where they spent a lot of time, sketching. She stood in front of shelves with jars filled with what looked like preserved flesh, flesh in a yellowish liquid.

Carl wanted to see Marie Curie's laboratory in the Institut du Radium in the Latin Quarter. He wanted to see the shed in which radium had been discovered (*isolated* was the proper word for it). He asked Effi if she knew that Marie Curie invented the word radioactive. And the term radiotherapy: "For a substance that transmits something, a message that penetrates everything—you, me, everything, without limit."

"Yes, please," Effi whispered, holding Carl close.

At the street entrance, Carl could already feel it, a feeling of being at home, so he plunged in. "Everything is radiating," Carl whispered, "even her logbooks, the paper, the ink, every word is radiating. They should only be read with protective clothing."

"And that appeals to you, doesn't it? I mean, you'd like your poems to be like that, right, Carl?"

Suddenly, all the goodness of this world was at home in the Curie Museum. Five severely pruned trees in the courtyard and the roar of a large air conditioner. A few people in white smocks passed by, perhaps on their way from the cafeteria. Research was still being done on this campus. Only the radium shed had been removed. A sign said as much—since then, everything had been "decontaminated." Carl smiled. He daydreamed. He saw the slagheaps of Culmitzsch and Ronneburg, the fields, the home frequency. He could absorb it through the crown of his head and stream it out from his solar plexus. His aura expanded.

A beggar sat outside the door. Carl gave her some money and she thanked him: "Thank you, je kiffe for you."

He and Effi didn't go to the Louvre, they just walked past it. They went into a bookstore, where Carl opened a few of the books, stroked the pages, and then carefully replaced them on the shelf. In an artist supply store, Effi bought a "rare blue." Carl weighed the tiny tube in his hand and wanted to know more about it—how Effi would use the paint, which picture it was for, and so on. Effi dodged the questions; she didn't want to talk about it. So Carl talked. More generally, about this or that, he sought her agreement, but Effi remained silent. After a few minutes, he found every one of his words repulsive. And yet, he'd felt nothing but enthusiasm and anticipation, like a child who knows the biggest presents are yet to come.

"Our secret is held in this paint, Carl," Effi said, but not until after midnight when she stowed the small tube in the glove compartment. He saw her face, illuminated by the bluish light of the jewelry store he had parked in front of for the night. They'd brought sleeping bags and had a nice surface to stretch out on in the car; Carl had stuffed a towel into the space between the front seats. Effi looked at him, her blue face watching Carl with interest. The expression on her face said something like, "Yes, that's how it is in a car," evidently from experience. Carl closed his eyes.

The next morning, Effi's shoes were gone. Tired and absent-minded, she'd slipped them off and set them outside the car, very neatly, next to each other. They hadn't been drunk, they'd just gone to sleep—as if Paris were their bedroom and the Zhiguli their bed. Effi went to breakfast barefoot and laughed about the mishap. That was the best moment. Maybe in my entire life, thought Carl.

They lingered over breakfast and then went looking for an exhibition of works by Joan Miró in the lobby of some grand hotel. Carl had heard that Miró had treated some of his paintings with a regular blowtorch. "The deep connection between tools and works is always forgotten," he declared. Effi saw only paint and shapes. When they returned, the Zhiguli's rear lights were smashed. A man was leaning against the jewelry store; he was smiling. A vegetable market with stands and tents had been set up on the boulevard's median strip.

"You're probably not allowed to park on the sidewalk," Carl murmured.

"Though it's wide enough," Effi said and, "I guess Paris isn't Berlin." She wanted to cheer him up but couldn't find the right words.

Carl wanted to bring something home from Paris too and spontaneously bought a Chinese calligraphy set and an instruction manual even though, apart from a few words, he did not understand French. He could still learn it, why not? The goat-hair paintbrush was in a small bamboo tube. The kit also contained a slate inkstone with a small hollow. Carl was fascinated by the gold lettering on the inkstick made of soot and animal glue, which had to be rubbed in the hollow of the slate stone and mixed with water until it formed a good, liquid black. Effi did not say anything about it until the drive home, just outside of Berlin, when she asked Carl, "What do you want it for?"

"To write," Carl said. "I want to write."

He felt a desire to explain in more detail, but he knew he shouldn't talk so much about these kinds of things anymore. He didn't want to be *that guy*, whatever that meant: the theorist, the non-artist—the one who talks too much. The result was a slight cramp in his heart.

"Soot and water to write: there's nothing better, Effi," Carl would have liked to say, along with a few other things.

This time he drove into the city from the West, the Dreilinden border crossing, an enormous terrain. They went straight through one of the lanes, past steel gray barriers, no one was interested in them or the Zhiguli. The Berlin bear, the heraldic animal on the median strip raised its paw in greeting. It looked clumsy, pudgy, and awkward. For a major city, it was actually too small; only the raised paw seemed oddly large, as if something else must be stuck in it—and yes, in fact, as Carl now saw clearly, it was holding a weapon.

Effi and Carl had crossed the West twice—a thousand kilometers as if it were nothing, even without taillights. Not once did Carl think of his parents—that they must be there somewhere, maybe nearby, close to the Hessian highway. As if they had disappeared forever, gone underground in an unknown country.

Spanische Allee, Argentinische Allee, these wonderful names and the view of the radio tower on the horizon: it was pure promise. Carl swore to himself that he would now take life very seriously. Work on the poems. The book—his distant goal. A book of his own! He just needed to be disciplined, to work, to write, then everything was possible. A bit less Assel, maybe. And at some point, he'd have to pass twenty, you need more than twenty poems. He thought of possible magazines. It was worth trying. Or anthologies, a few applications, maybe, a literary stipend from the Berlin government. Two thousand marks a month—a sum so large, he hardly dared say it out loud.

They discussed all this, Carl and Effi in the Zhiguli, and everything to come. And Effi agreed with him, she encouraged him, and she spoke about herself too, which was rare. About the stress from her final project and the printing press Carl had promised her. She already knew where it would go in her room. Paris was behind them and Berlin before them. They kept touching each other, spoke earnestly, with serious expressions, and Effi kissed Carl.

THE WORKSHOP

Before leaving Leipzig, Effi had thrown out her old easel. "Too bulky and already half-broken," was her reason. Carl recognized in it a sacred object that should not be left behind. He tightened it up with his screwdriver and fastened a reading board (as he called it) onto the upper third, a place for an open book or the current poem. After some back and forth, he set up the converted easel to the right of the stove. It was important for him to encounter what he'd written in this way. Now he could pace around his apartment, more or less distracted, talking to himself, dreaming, until his glance happened to fall on the poem: unintentionally, in passing, so to speak, it was much easier to see what needed to be changed.

Another possibility was just standing in front of the easel and staring at the page, but without reading it, at least for a while. Carl was allowed to pick up the paper, touch it, even lick or smell it (sniffing the script). Then, at some point, he would read it aloud and listen—only to the tone! And whenever Carl had been away from it for long enough beforehand, he could hear very clearly what was *out of tune* in the poem.

Even if the result of this process was merely another, very similar version, after Paris Carl kept working doggedly and with discipline as he had resolved. So-called reality and its abundance ("the most exciting times of our lives," as everyone was claiming)—it would never have occurred to him to write about it, not even in a journal, never mind that he clearly wasn't in any state to keep a proper journal (with regular entries). The main question was whether or not the next line would work. The next line and its sound preoccupied Carl, not the demise of the country outside his window. If the poem didn't succeed, then life wouldn't either.

Early evenings, Carl would walk down Ryke Strasse on his way to Effi. He looked forward to the route, which now had a different meaning than in previous months. The security of the small bomb crater copse, the silver-gray sheen of the cobblestones under his feet, the lights of the two dissimilar towers at the end of the street. He crossed the street and turned off it with a last glance at the water tower, the guardian of his monologues.

"Someone's waiting for you in the back room."

Freddy had insisted that he be allowed to stay up until Carl arrived. Effi hugged Carl in the hallway, holding him tight for a moment. The chaos in the kitchen, the children's clothing, the smell of a mother's den: all this gave him a sense of security and inner peace. He stretched out on the bed next to Freddy and told him a story that opened with "There once was a small dragon," but then meandered to things that had just happened. "Just like me!" Freddy exclaimed and could hardly believe it, while Carl continued the story impassively. After a while the boy caught on and listened only for the passages in which he and his life appeared. Soon he was interrupting Carl and explaining what had *really* happened.

"But it's a story, Freddy, understand?"

"No."

"Some of the story is like your life, maybe even exactly the same, that happens, but other parts of the story are different."

"So who is it then? A different boy?"

"Yes, another boy."

"Do I know him?"

"I don't know. Maybe."

"Where does he live?"

"Up here." Carl tapped a finger on his forehead and Freddy looked at him incredulously.

"In your head? Show me!"

Freddy grabbed Carl's hair and tried to look into his right ear. Because there wasn't much to see, Freddy stuck his finger in Carl's ear.

"Freddy! If you scare the boy, then that's it for the story."

Effi was cleaning the front room (which she used as her studio and bedroom) and Carl secretly hoped she could hear the story too. He, himself, in the back room with the freshly showered boy in a cloud of mentholated chest rub and soap and her in the front room at work—wasn't this the beginning of much more?

As soon as Carl re-emerged, Effi dropped onto the mattress (now covered with a bedsheet) for "a quick rest" and ended up sleeping for an hour or two. While she slept, Carl washed the dishes—he liked washing up; it was a kind of meditation. Afterwards he made himself a coffee and worked at the kitchen table. He spread out a few of Effi's sketches that were preliminary studies for her final project next to his own sheet of paper and started writing about them. For her exam, a theoretical component was also required—a kind of concept statement. "I have absolutely no idea how it's done," Effi said, "or what the point is." In that moment, Effi had been both helpless and scornful, an expression Carl had not seen on her face before. He'd immediately offered a few suggestions and it soon was clear that he could help her. At the same time, Carl wanted to show Effi how good and substantial her work was, despite all her doubts.

He quoted Gerhard Altenbourg ("A line can do everything.") and referred to Klee's Tunisian drawings. Still, Carl wasn't sure what kind of conclusion it would lead to. Essentially, it was about the ambiguity of very simple contours. He quoted Jean Arp: "Maybe I'm the child of a dot." It was wonderful because it suited particularly well the childlike simplicity that made Effi's drafts so touching. Carl would have liked to bring Giacometti in too, even though he wasn't relevant. Carl was fascinated by Giacometti's way of working, the way he used his entire studio with scratches and chalk drawings on the walls, the way his work (its manic force and despair) drew everything into its wake and in the end, with an inexplicable but absolute necessity, the sculptures of thin, walking men emerged, leaning forward, taking large steps . . . That's how it should be, thought Carl.

Everything was easier to write than poems. In addition, Carl realized that commissioned work did him good, an assignment, concrete, with a beginning and an end. He wondered if he could apply this method to writing poems, if this would enable him one day to break the magic number twenty with the raw power of a concrete deadline.

Around ten or eleven, Effi got up and stumbled half-naked into the stairway. She wasn't wearing her gleaming bodysuit, just a shirt. He heard the toilet flush, and she came into the kitchen, deathly pale and feet dragging. She placed a cool hand on the back of Carl's neck and looked at what he had written.

"You have beautiful handwriting, Carlo."

She brushed the page with her fingertips, feeling the writing. Carl pushed his chair back from the table and pulled her onto his lap. She was still half-asleep and didn't resist. Their slow back and forth in the kitchen window. Afterwards, Effi made herself a big mug of coffee and returned to her studio. It was the time when Carl inevitably became tired.

Under the large window in the Berlin room were two trestles supporting a few boards (actually the sides of an old linen cupboard): Effi's work space. She registered that Carl had followed her, but it made no difference to what followed. She simply sat there. It was as if she were able to block out Carl's presence (and to forget, to erase him). Maybe she was looking at her reflection in the window or at the other lights across the courtyard and how the wind in the chestnut trees moved the leaves and blurred the light. This could go on for an hour or more, but sooner or later, she would come to again and start unwrapping the copper plates that were covered in soft, dark cloth. A few times she picked up one of her large needles, made a certain motion in the air and put it aside again.

Carl closed the door to Freddy's room, which had to be left open a crack when the boy was falling asleep, and he lay down on the bed. Not because he wanted to sleep, but because there was no other reasonable place in the room. He shoved the pillows under his back and watched Effi practice a line. Then he turned his back to her to give her the possibility of taking up the needle and setting it back down as often as was necessary for sketches in the air. He wrote a few lines in his notebook, about Effi, actually, even though he knew that you have to be alone for that—a real journal required it. He leafed through the art books next to the bed. The covers were stained and covered with circles of red wine. He read all the underlined passages and covertly the notes between the pages as well. Fundamentally, Carl hardly knew more about his partner on that evening in Wörther Strasse than he had back in school, when he'd admired the legend Effi from a distance: Effi, whose real name was Ilonka, whose father was from Hungary and whose mother had committed suicide. And now, here he was in Effi's bed, and his hand smelled of her.

Although there was hardly any furniture, Carl found the apartment cozy: a plain set of shelves, a clothes rail, the mini-fridge near the bed, which Effi used as a nightstand. The drying rack next to the stove. In the middle of the room was a round rug that Effi had brought from Leipzig. It was strewn with toys: building blocks and cowboys. All in all, the room had become more of a workshop and that was the best thing about it. Carl realized that he had always been searching for exactly this place. One of Effi's pictures hung on the wall opposite the bed: it showed a woman whose dark torso grew from the surface of a table. The table and the woman had the same ornaments. The transition was seamless.

Carl stretched and closed his eyes. It was after midnight. Effi's face in the cone of light from her work lamp, that Effi-concentration on her forehead. He had noted the word: drypoint. He heard the rustling of the chestnut in the courtyard and sometime later, already half-asleep, he heard the needle (or whatever it was) very clearly and nearby, and then ever farther away. It was Sunday, and the tool-landscape in his father's garage drifted past, its familiar glow. He saw Master Bocklich and Master Ebert, notching their apprentices' flat chisels with the roman numerals I through XIII with a hacksaw. And he saw Ragna standing in front of Durruti for a while, until the man with the tool stepped out of the photo and asked her to touch him, which she did.

WORKING LADIES

"They came right away," the Shepherd said and nodded across the bar at the women. "They're workers, Carl. And their work, God knows, is not easy. They chose the Assel—instinctively. Because they know they're safe here. And I'm sure they also saw our flag with the invincible A. And look—over there."

The Shepherd beamed and looked at Carl expectantly. "The men from the high-voltage brigade are back on board. They're beginning to understand, too, bit by bit . . ."

Carl thanked him for the car, repairing the Zhiguli meant a lot to him. "Thank Adele and the Russians when they're our guests here in the future," Hoffi replied. He kept talking about the usual subjects in a way that was hard to understand but very appealing.

Outside, night was falling, and the Assel was filling up. Until then, Oranienburger Strasse gave the impression of being off the beaten track, quiet, almost dead, like the side streets on the edge of a small city, through which a streetcar occasionally rumbled to keep the area from falling into an eternal sleep. That was over by early July. The women, according to Henry, had started working the night of the monetary union. Since then, they would sit in the Assel, at a round table right in front of the bar, drinking cocoa, which could now be ordered and was prepared in a few seconds in a Panasonic microwave under the counter—the appliance was a sensation. And still more had changed in Carl's absence: there were now several kinds of whiskey and vodka, a magically shimmering throng of bottles that blinded the eyes. Other drinks were available, too, even banana juice.

A cluster of guests crowded the bar. Carl did his best but there were too many. He was nervous and clumsy. Not just the high-voltage guys, but also Carl and everyone else in the cellar tried not to stare at the women constantly. And yet, at first the working ladies were hardly distinguishable from the other guests. They hadn't starting painting masks of makeup on their faces and their legs hadn't yet turned into sleek, shiny plastic limbs. No one could have said with certainty which of them were *working* and which weren't. Adding to the confusion was the fact that some of the women, whom Irina called "our girls," were even sitting in the Assel before noon as if it were the only place they had far and wide (which, indeed, it was).

The Shepherd just stood there, smiling. Now and again, he would pick up the brick-sized receiver of his radio telephone and have short conversations. He looked very satisfied during these calls, like the commander of a burgeoning empire. "Hans is on his way," the Shepherd told Carl as if he'd just reached a difficult decision. Then he put the brick back on the case and disappeared through the back door into the courtyard "to milk Dodo."

"The table of tarts wants cocoa: one, two, three, that's a job for me-e-e," Hans hummed to himself and heated the milk. At the same time, he opened a few beers, wiped down the counter and put the glasses out. He was dexterous and his movements looked elegant—he was the ideal bartender and together they could manage. Hans was the stage manager at the Komische Oper, Henry had told Carl. His age was hard to guess and not just because of his shaved head and round face. He was thin, wiry, and wore brown leather pants (which he always had on) and a jean jacket with metal buttons. Hans, it was said, already had an *artistic career* behind him—first as a singer and then in the theater. He hadn't studied in these fields at all, he was a natural. He had started as a washroom attendant in the Karl-Marx-Stadt district theater and eavesdropped on the auditions, hidden in the third row. That was his education. His earlier years as a hewer in a uranium mine (Hans had talked about them once at one of their Irina-breakfasts) were far behind him. Nevertheless, Carl could feel that radiation from home when he was next to Hans—and this reassured him: with Hans, he could manage everything, even if he looked like a fool trying to serve the new drinks. Hans the hewer just laughed and, laughing, on they worked in the flow. From Hans, Carl learned what he needed to know. He was Hans's apprentice at the bar.

"What's going on here, Hans, where have they all come from?"

"You mean the tarts? Or the Russians?"

He stepped closer to Carl, perhaps only because it was too loud.

"This area was always *pure pleasure*. Only for the past few decades did things look a little different."

"But why the Assel?"

"Because of the worker-guerrillas," Hans replied with a serious expression. Then he burst into laughter and Carl had to laugh too, but more because of Hans, who choked and started coughing. He pointed at the cigar box they used as the cash box. "Real money, Carl, you know? With us, the new times are coming—and that changes the situation."

The new coins were heavy in the hand. They felt *real* and, yes, valuable. "I'm not going to spend my nice Western money on that," old Knospe had said, and sent Carl to buy four loaves of bread the day before the monetary union.

"And Hoffi?"

"Let's just say: he sees things in his own particular way. He took them straight into his heart, good Samaritan that he is. At first, they only came to use the toilet. They stood there in their horrible leggings and politely asked permission. Now they're our *working ladies*. And where it will lead, we don't know." Hans sounded both conspiratorial and peeved. "At some point completely different kinds of people will turn up, that's certain, and they won't ask politely, not politely at all."

Carl would have liked to think about this more deeply, but the bar demanded his full attention. He learned to look up only when he'd completed the previous orders. Looking up once meant four or five new orders right in his face, bam-bam-bam (like sustained fire), beer or schnapps, and if he was unlucky, also a flatbread, which Hans called the "Assel kebab." The Assel kebabs (served cold) had ham, corn, and a greasy lettuce leaf. They were prepared behind the counter on a tiny corner of a shelf. The corn came from ten-liter cans that stood on the floor next to the radio telephone. There was a ladle, but it was more practical to grab a handful of corn—the correct portion for the kebab—straight from the can. The ham came pressed into sausages the size of an upper arm and shrink-wrapped; it had to be diced first. A milky secretion that looked like brake fluid spurted out of the meat when it was cut.

"Hoffi, I believe, has read a bit too much. Too heavy on the role of meaning if you understand what I mean. And the whole thing with looking after the workers, I find it . . ."

"First: we must learn to be free," Carl blurted out. He cleared his throat (where did this rage come from?), but then he had to finish: "Freedom, how to be free, is the first thing we need to learn, and to learn it as fast as possible. Otherwise, revolutions will always change into their opposite—that's what Hoffi said on Radio P."

"Freedom, freedom—no one wants to know, Carlo. Too afraid, my friend. Afraid of freedom, loathe it, even. Take it from someone who was at the very bottom, in the mine, underground, and for long enough. You're tired, shattered, but you have work, your daily life, a garden, and a few rabbits you can slaughter for Christmas—revolution? Fine, the fat cats have to go, let them believe in revolution, but deep in your heart you want everything to stay the same."

"Hoffi knows more about it than all of us," Carl countered cautiously. "And he has ideas."

"Oh. Yes, of course. And you're one of his favorites, right? Kleist is completely jealous."

Carl fell silent. He was finished with the ham and concentrated on the flatbread. He had spoken with his head lowered and he now forced himself not to look up. He didn't like the way Hans spoke about the Shepherd.

"Hoffi sees the Assel as a pontoon between the Cold War and communalism, do you see that, Carl?"

Carl's knife was stuck in the bread. Hans took it out of Carl's hands and slowly pulled the blade out, millimeter by millimeter. He inspected the cutting edge and held it in front of Carl's eyes.

"I think you misunderstand me, colleague. This here," Hans waved the knife in a large arc over the heads of the people standing at the bar, "is the best thing that could happen to us, to all of us, *compris*, guerrillero? After all, we're all in transit. This pontoon, U-boat, ark or what have you, is just a little shaky. And the shark, it has teeth, you know."

Around fifty people were watching as Hans took hold of Carl's collar with his fingers and slowly wiped the large knife clean on it.

"The blade has to be nice and dry. Ham slime sticks like glue."

It was after midnight when one of the working ladies wanted to slip by behind Carl. Carl grabbed her—a reflex. Hans had gone, and there were only a few guests left. She screamed as if Carl had touched her with a hot iron. "Don't touch me, you jerk!"

Carl shrank back and the woman passed behind the bar, which was taboo for guests, and disappeared through the passage to the courtyard. Carl followed her and noticed for the first time: on the right side of the passage, which he had only roughly plastered, there now hung a board with a row of hooks. A few of the women had scratched their names next to the hooks. It was reminiscent of a school cloakroom. Kati, Elke, Janin—if those were the schoolgirls' names, these must be their gym bags. The woman grabbed the bag on the Kati-hook and started to change. Her badly dyed blond hair stuck out in all directions; she was wearing a lavender windbreaker, which she now took off along with the rest of her clothes, not paying the slightest attention to Carl.

Carl trudged back to the bar and began cleaning the counter. So, the passage to the back courtyard was now a women's changing room, the working ladies' base camp—no one had filled him in on this detail.

"I can't work out who's crazy and who's not," admitted Irina, who had recently started helping serve and had decided to keep the door to the cellar open *for anyone and everyone*, despite the rush.

"No rules here, no damn laws."

That was her attitude and Carl understood why Hoffi called her "little sister." Without a doubt Irina admired the Shepherd, but she did not talk as much about the "workers" or "worker guerrillas." The Assel should also be open to wastrels and the down-and-out ("the artists of the street"); for Irina, everyone was "of equal worth." A few of these equally worthy individuals did not come in before three in the morning. "Hot drinks are free at that hour," Irina said. She would pour coffee and listen to their stories. She knew all their names: Philosophical Willi, the Nightingale of Ramersdorf, the Handcart Pole (who dragged a wooden handcart with a model of the Statue of Liberty behind him, sold stolen newspapers and gave away flowers picked from the park across the street) and a man named World Peace, who always carried around a guitar case with a stringless guitar. He played and sang ballads all night long. World Peace and Philosophical Willi were friends. Willi (also called Smiling Willi) was elegantly shabby. He wore a light, finely checked jacket and trousers that were too large, and had a moustache. Before speaking, Willi always smiled. The smile was his prologue and then it was impossible not to listen to him. He playfully drew long arcs from the Pre-Socratics through Schleiermacher to the pharmacist on Schönhauser Allee, for whom he cherished an eternal (and unrequited) love.

A few days later, when the pack was gathered at their weekend breakfast, the Shepherd unceremoniously declared his little sister Irina the general manager and Hans her deputy. "Someone who knows what's what," whispered Ragna, who was sitting next to Carl, scraping the flesh out of her avocado. Hoffi's understanding of the day's requirements didn't prevent him from talking about the strategic significance of the Berlin underworld. There was no longer any talk of the border dog fiasco, although there were still a few incidents. The first order of business was now digging a tunnel right from the Fenske cellar to the Charité's hospital bunker.

"As soon as the Assel calms down, we'll get to work on *that*. Good carpenters and bricklayers will be in demand again."

He looked at Carl, who smiled in embarrassment. It wasn't clear to Carl what the Shepherd wanted with a hospital bunker. He was briefly unsettled by the escalation in Hoffi's fantasies of resistance. It reminded Carl of the moments of fright he felt when an emergency was announced in a combat alert. That sudden fear of a nuclear strike felt by Soldier Bischoff in the distant past. Good thing we lost, Carl thought. And just in time—if there is such a thing as losing just in time.

The following night, a man in a brown National People's Army tracksuit stepped up to the bar. He wanted "just one beer" and then to pick his wife "up from work." He didn't look like a pimp. Besides, the women all had "normal jobs" as well, according to Irina.

"Kindergarten teachers, for example. There are quite a few kindergarten teachers among them."

"Kindergarten teachers?"

"They're trying something new. Rita, for example, across from here."

On the other side of Oranienburger Strasse, on a small rise on the edge of the park, was the kindergarten building. Carl had seen the children. In good weather, they played outside, some pressed their faces against the rusty wire fence and shouted at the guys in the Western cars driving past every day, constantly.

FOUR OF SEVEN

". . . we request your permission at short notice to publish the following poems . . ." Carl stood motionless in front of his easel, then read the sentence a second time. Four of seven, he thought. Four of the seven made it. And three of them completely unchanged (uninjured). The Acker Strasse Independent Bookstore Press suggested a change only to the Morocco poem with the soldier in the U-boat at the roots of Africa—"for reasons of space," as they put it. The poem was decidedly long and they therefore suggested that Carl consider publishing only an excerpt. Which was not uncommon.

Carl Bischoff was requested.

Suggestions were made to the author.

He experienced a great shift.

Carl stared at the page. The letterhead was precious. First "Acker Strasse," second "Independent," third "Bookstore," fourth "Press"—four titles of nobility in a single line. He was no longer alone in the world. They had contacted him. Continents were shifting.

In the proofs for an anthology of young German authors ("writing by a new generation"), Carl read four irrefutable poems. Everything about them was right. No new version would be necessary: Carl recognized that now, even though his heart was in his throat. These poems were *free*. And because of this, they almost seemed a little strange to him.

He put the kettle on and brewed some coffee. He went to his workbench and started writing. He was filled with a sense of calm. Before this it wasn't clear that they were actually finished, Carl thought. That was the strangest thing about it.

He stood up and pressed his ear to the wall. The wall was ice-cold in the middle of summer, and something was rustling softly behind the wallpaper, as if something were trying to get out. Maybe just out of my head, Carl thought and reached for the letter.

"I know," Arielle shouted, "I know!" She expressed her joy without reservation (and without blinking). For a moment, Carl felt like a child showing good grades, but it didn't matter. In the end, he owed it all to Arielle. And to Henry, who had passed the poems on, and to Ragna, who had brought him to this building, and to Hoffi, who'd arranged his lodging, and to the pack, which had taken him in back then, in his fever, behind the movie screen. In the right place, Carl thought, aboard this street.

"Henry told me," Arielle chirped and plucked the letter from Carl's hand. His neighbor, as so often, was wearing only a kind of baggy shirt, a nightgown maybe, or something that looked just like one.

"He's very happy for you, Carlo. Buried himself in his studio again, the good painter has."

She scanned the letter from the publishing house and tapped on it: "Did you see? They want a photograph of you. Sonie can do that."

"Sonie?"

"Sonie's a photographer, you knew that, right?"

She bent down and pulled a box out from under the shoe cabinet. She rapidly pulled out a few pictures, that showed her, if Carl wasn't dreaming, naked.

"Not those! Sorry." She wasn't particularly embarrassed. "But these here. Pretty good, right?"

She laid out the photographs next to each other on the floor: Ryke Strasse in the snow, Ryke in fog, Sara's shop, Knospe's garden beds and her vegetables, the building and the small copse, the old water pump on the corner of Sredzki Strasse, the synagogue, their courtyard, the water tower, and so on.

Carl had underestimated Sonie. As he had Arielle. He didn't know much, nothing, actually, and the world was a mystery.

He walked through the bomb crater copse, crossed the street and then looked back at the building. Only the fourth floor was visible above the trees; the lights of the lower floors shone through the leafy branches. Carl saw the light in the stairwell and the lights in the stairwell toilets that were always lit and he saw Sonie's silhouette when it briefly appeared at the window.

It was strange to stand there, staring at his own building. It felt almost like something forbidden, or at least unwelcome. It was an offense, a statement of mistrust. This made the building seem unfamiliar and he felt himself unfamiliar, and after a while, it became hard to believe he really lived there. And if he didn't stop soon, it would become almost impossible to go back, he'd have to tear himself away and go his own way (as they say) to quickly forget that sense of strangeness that with any exact, deeply attentive observation inevitably gains the upper hand—the strangeness between everything and oneself. It's really difficult to see the things you're looking at, Carl thought. But everyone knew that. Everyone who had ever summoned the will to do so.

Strolling down Ryke Strasse did him good. For some reason, Carl remembered an argument between Ralf and Nora, which he'd observed unnoticed. He'd been on his way to Effi's. At first, he'd only seen Nora. She was coming toward him on the other side of the street, with long, rapid steps, her head raised and evidently very angry. It was raining and her hair was wet. Then Carl noticed the car following her. It stayed close behind her, but then accelerated and drove alongside her. It was Ralf in the Passat. What Carl had (secretly) admired was the way Ralf matter-of-factly claimed the street for himself and his complete disregard for the rest of the traffic. With one hand on the steering wheel, his torso leaning across the passenger seat, he spoke with Nora (or talked at her) through the open window. Even now, in this situation that was surely unpleasant for him (Nora rushed ahead without the slightest pause), Ralf struck Carl as a winner. How could this be? And could it be that Carl even envied him?

PART VI

THE NEXT STEP

"My dear Carl, I often think of you and sometimes wonder—are you really managing alright?"

Thin paper and blue ink. The handwriting on the back shimmered through and rebelled against the writing on the front of the page. The return address was very neatly written (meticulously, Inge would have said), with a large W for West before the postal code. Stamps with an image of the postal bank in Frankfurt. Next to the postmark, a promotional franking: "13–15 October 1990: Jester Market, Gelnhausen: The Largest Folk Festival in the Kinzig Valley." Underneath was a small figure, probably the titular rascal. He wore knee breeches, a traditional jacket, and an odd (Indian) cap on his head. He was squinting and holding his head at a slight angle.

"Why haven't we heard a word from you?"

"Are you really managing alright?"

The questions made Carl feel good. In them, he recognized his mother from before. His parents had always been concerned for him and had created an extensive set of rules to protect him. In Carl's memory, these rules made a particular sound, a soft hum or buzz. It was the constant thrum of worry, the undertone of his childhood, which did not fall silent even on the sunniest days.

The rules impressed Carl, they kept him in check. Only very gradually, little by little, did he become aware of how stereotypical they were and a heresy crept in: that outside those rules, that is if he could skillfully circumvent them, anything and everything must be possible.

Carl became reckless. He lost any sense of danger, of threatening situations, ultimately the sense of his own mortality. He fell out of a tree and landed in the hospital. He got into fights, always with the wrong people. At thirteen, during the summer vacation, which Carl preferred to spend on his grandparents' farm, he jumped off the high roof of a barn (just because) and rammed his knee into his face. A penny-sized piece of bone broke off his eye socket. For the eye doctors it was a rare case and therefore *interesting*. They looked for the bone penny but simply couldn't find it; it had slipped off somewhere, paid in. Carl sat on a chair in the center of the examination room and the doctors felt his skull again and again, day after day.

"Does this hurt? And this?"

His parents had often visited him in the hospital. They gave him a small transistor radio, with which he could listen to the commentaries from the First Division matches. They sat at his bedside, fear still written on their faces, and Carl found their reaction excessive.

One problem was the large, shiny goose-egg on his right eye, a suspicious swelling that would not go down. Carl felt no pain at all. He felt perfectly healthy, he only had this goose-egg on his head and was mourning—the lost summer.

Carl spent six weeks in the eye clinic. Summer vacation ran riot outside, and he was stuck in the hospital. He shuffled down the hospital corridors in his striped pajamas and one day, at the end of the third or fourth week, Carl discovered the door in the vestibule that led directly to the cellar. He'd assumed he would be called back, but no one was paying attention to him. The stairs were unusually broad and elegantly curved. Some light came in through the shafts outside the cellar windows. There were sinks and bathtubs everywhere, the tiles on the walls were cracked and discolored, the pipes rusty.

In the largest room, three cast-iron bathtubs were lined up against the wall, like the wagons of a short, underground train.

The engine was a large boiler with a black stovepipe. Carl marveled at the vehicle and held his breath—something was moving in the middle tub. He stepped closer and saw it: two large, darkly gleaming fish glided nervously back and forth. Of course, they'd noticed him earlier. It was an unreal sight. Carl stood there for a time, motionless. Someone kept fish down here in the eye clinic's washrooms and bathrooms. A faint thundering came from above, a dull vibration. The water in the tubs also trembled—maybe a hospital bed on the way to the OR. Otherwise, all was quiet, and all was quiet inside Carl, too. He saw their eyes; the fish were definitely looking at him. Their broad mouths and the small growths underneath; they have beards, Carl thought, and they're ancient.

He laid his cheek on the edge of the tub and cooled the goose-egg above his eye. Then he stretched out his hand, very slowly, and laid it carefully on the bottom of the tub. The water reached up to his elbow. It was ice-cold. The fish had to pass his arm and sometimes they brushed against it, very lightly. It was this touch—there was no word for it. To this day Carl couldn't say if he had been utterly happy or utterly unhappy back then, in the basement of the eye clinic. In his childhood.

At CTZ, Walter Bischoff very quickly rose to become one of the company's indispensable trainers. He now taught courses in Zurich and Vienna. "But for now, no farther," Inge wrote to Carl as if their next goal were waiting somewhere in the distance. And, indeed, she informed Carl that soon, once his father had learned "the métier" well enough, he could begin "auditioning" for other, larger firms.

"International firms, Carl, *transatlantic . . .*"

Transatlantic was not part of his mother's vocabulary, but Carl liked the word. It contained large ships, pirates, and Christopher Columbus on his *Santa Maria.*

In the beginning, Inge had stayed in Gelnhausen alone with only the old woman downstairs, always ready to stretch out her long, bony arm toward her. "It's a witch's house," she wrote Carl, and in the end it became a reason to accompany Walter on his trips.

In Zurich they stayed in a little hotel on the Limmatquai, just a few meters from the Limmat river and its olive-green water. It was no luxury hotel, but venerable, with a pale Jugendstil fresco on the facade. Their room was tiny. A dark, narrow hallway led to a rear exit on the Seilergraben. Right next to their room, a cable car rose out of a simple house to the upper city, something that seemed strange and, yes, made-up. The cable car emerged from the second floor of the building: "The gondola comes right out of the balcony," Inge wrote to Carl, "almost like in a fairy tale." She was also enchanted by the square plates at breakfast.

That was the situation. The small, decrepit country of their origins still existed with quite a few people who hadn't left (Carl, for example), whereas Inge and Walter were now in the Hotel Limmathof in Zurich, Switzerland, and what's more: Walter Bischoff *worked there*—hard to imagine but apparently true.

On the very first day, Inge hiked around Lake Zurich. She had the hunter's rucksack on her back, "with my basic equipment," as she called it: the green rain cape, her aluminum bread tin with two double slices, an apple, and a water bottle. Inge with the hunter's rucksack—that was now the first image that came to Carl's mind when he thought of his mother. The practical way she handled being abroad, as a wanderer.

On the second day, Inge roamed around the train station, on the lookout. She decided on a small group of women. The women boarded the train and Inge followed them. She waited out in the corridor for a while, listening to them. She only understood a few isolated words, but the *way* the women spoke to each other (and the language itself) sounded trustworthy. So she entered the compartment, introduced herself and asked if they might allow her to join them.

"Forever?" Swiss merriment.

"I've seldom felt so welcome," Inge wrote in her very long letter from Switzerland. And it was probably for this reason that she told Carl the full names of the four women who were all from Opfikon: Rita Brugger, Yvonne Farner, Annelie Kühn, and Helga Wegemann.

As he read, Carl spoke the names out loud. They did not seem made-up. It all happened—in reality. The only thing that seemed implausible was that the woman on the way to Rütli was his mother.

Inge Bischoff made her way. It was admirable, but there was also something driven about it, like her impetuous, almost furious departure from Gera. Fundamentally extreme, thought Carl. Still, being underway in foreign parts was obviously good for this woman who was his mother. It calmed her. A restlessness that previously must have been sealed up deep inside her had been freed and found a beat, then was transformed, if not into serenity, at least, step by step, into a tolerable form of existence. Until then everything had seemed "dammed up," as his mother had put it back then in Gera, before her departure, her emigration, as she called it. This didn't explain much. For Carl, it was a puzzle that extended from Giessen, Rheine, and Diez to Gelnhausen.

And now to Switzerland: the Rütli train, the Rütli meadow, the Rütli Oath. And Wilhelm Tell, a freedom fighter. An anarchist, even. A man like Durruti (Carl had looked him up). A man, in any case, who was *on their side*—that's how it felt to his mother and in other respects it was a good day, still warm in the evening so that they could all sit outside, in front of the pub, the four women from Opfikon and Inge Bischoff from Gera.

"Oh, nature here . . ." Something Carl had almost forgotten in the upheaval: his parents loved mountains. But even what his mother wrote about them in her letter didn't sound like they were an enjoyment or a diversion. She was "doing" it all, as if she were on a march. She was underway and had to keep going.

As with earlier letters, this letter gave Carl the feeling his parents were on an expedition. Maybe they had a specific goal, but the route was uncertain. They still had to find it depending on the conditions they faced, all the contingencies that were unpredictable and caused them trouble, made them take detours and make compromises. In any case, things were not as simple as Carl's mother always tried to present them in her letters with her constant refrain of "the next steps"—a mantra intoned in order to reassure him and perhaps herself as well. Maybe my parents have gone insane, Carl thought. "What on earth were you thinking?" his mother had asked him when he was still a frighteningly reckless child, ready to jump out of a tree or off a barn roof.

On her last day in Switzerland, Inge climbed up the Zürichberg to visit James Joyce's grave. It was her way to set herself a firm goal every day. In a flyer listing local attractions, she saw a photographer of the writer: the caption read, "The author of *Ulysses*." Inge hadn't read any of his works, but she thought of Dr. Talib, for whom James Joyce was "one of the great wanderers." What had Talib said about him? Inge couldn't remember. She'd been preoccupied by other things.

Because someone was sitting at the grave, Inge first took a short stroll. The cemetery was next to a zoo; she heard the cries of the birds in the aviaries. She viewed the gravestones and the dates—every age was represented and there were names from around the world: a man named Keller-Staub married a French baroness. Inge strolled and listened to the animals outside the cemetery. It was a rare moment of internal peace when the calm she longed for set in.

The man sitting at the grave was still there. Inge approached and saw that it was Joyce himself, now she recognized him. Turned slightly away, the author of *Ulysses* seemed to be looking at the forest behind the graves. Inge laid a small bouquet of dandelion flowers on the grave (on behalf of and as a gesture of thanks to Dr. Talib). Joyce didn't notice because he was staring at the fir trees or, as Inge came to believe, was lost in thought.

Inge rested for a moment on a small stone bench across from the grave on the other side of the path.

"At first, it startled me," Inge wrote to Carl. "Imagine, a man sitting beside his own grave. Who wants to do that? Yes, it's just a model of him, in bronze probably, but so completely natural, life-sized with a cigarillo in his hand—I'm sure that if Joyce had a dog, it would be lying there somewhere too. Only his eyes weren't visible. His gaze seemed suffocated behind his glasses, really ailing, I mean, if Joyce actually had bad eyes, then I understand why he's sitting like that, facing away with his ear turned toward the grave: he can't see what's going on in front of him, but he's listening the whole time."

It was Inge Bischoff, his mother, who thought such things— and wrote them. Carl still hadn't gotten used to it. Part of this was surely also in the nature of letters. A letter is a collection of sentences containing thoughts that would otherwise (without the letter) have disappeared without a trace. A letter was an invitation to disclose something about oneself, a temptation to divulge. In one moment Carl felt a vague pride in his mother and in the next he envied her, and somewhere in his incomplete thoughts about her, a question formed: why wasn't he the one who was sitting on the small stone bench in Switzerland and why hadn't he also set out into the world? But that's you, a second, equally unfinished thought murmured.

On her way up the Zürichberg, Inge stopped at the display window of a dance school. The dancers' shadows shimmered through the half-closed blinds. It was a strange, probably Swiss mix—salsa with samba and rock and roll. Her feet began to move. Inge took a few distracted steps on the sidewalk. An invitation to join the dance, "Chumm, mach mit, s'Tanze isch en Hit," was written in Swiss-German on the studio window.

On their last evening in Switzerland, Inge and Walter lay in bed, telling each other about their days. "Reviewing the day," was Inge's term for it. It had become one of their regular habits during the courses. Inge had bought a few things and prepared a light dinner: on each bedside table was a plate with open-faced sandwiches and a sliced apple. Walter had set down the accordion on the suitcase rack opposite the bed. "Did you practice?"

Dr. Zwingli from Oracle Schweiz was extremely pleased with Walter's teaching. Right at the start, he had asked the German trainer about his background and Walter immediately told the truth.

"I think it's easier for citizens of small countries to relate. A different kind of understanding, almost a feeling of solidarity," Walter said to Inge and took a bite of his sandwich.

"In a country even smaller than your own, you're less afraid of getting lost," Inge replied and snuggled close to Walter. "It's as if you already know your way around a bit."

Behind the wall, the cable car rumbled into the building. It was the last one of the evening.

Then Inge recounted her day: the Fluntern cemetery, the Alps, Joyce at Joyce's grave (Walter's reaction to everything connected with Inge's admiration for Dr. Talib was rather reserved) and the Sonja dance school.

"What were you looking for there?"

"A crash course," was Inge's pointed answer.

"In what?"

"Rock and roll."

"But you can rock and roll."

274

"Swiss rock and roll."

"Go on, dance."

"Now I'm too tired."

"Just a few steps!"

"The room's too small."

"Come on!" Walter's hands on her hips—a scream; giggling, Inge jumped to her feet, took a few steps forward and back and made a fantastic swoop with a bow. Walter laughed.

"What?"

"That's Swiss rock and roll?" Walter grabbed Inge and they danced, smoothly, without music, just panting and Walter's breathless voice:

"Roll, roll, roll everybody."

WHICH ANIMAL ARE YOU?

They had *different rhythms* (as they say), but Carl didn't want to let it show. Staying out all night dancing sometimes was now part of celebrating life, at least it was for Effi and all the others who looked like they knew what the new freedom was and went dancing some nights. Only Carl became tired. He had the daily rhythms of a construction worker in his blood. He woke early and always started his day with breakfast. He needed his roll with cheese, mixed fruit jam, and coffee. These things were inscribed in him, perhaps inherited. As a young woman his mother had gone to the stalls every day at four in the morning to milk the cows and feed the pigs. Carl thought of his mother; it was a warm feeling, a feeling of home, the opposite of going out to the Franz Club.

Effi danced in front of the stage. A few people with beer bottles leaned against it and stared at her, looking unpleasantly Berlin-ish. Effi's mischievous vivacity, her tucked-in elbows and her small, cheerful movements when she danced. "Cheerful"

275

was one of her favorite expressions. Nothing was better than "cheerful." Someone who was cheerful had mastered life and knew what mattered. What Carl needed to understand here was that "cheerful" ranked miles above his brooding attempts to creep his way into a poetic existence through the antechamber of poetry. It would never work as long as Carl didn't understand the main thing: how to be cheerful.

Actually, I'm just tired, Carl thought.

As soon as he lost sight of Effi, he became anxious and felt abandoned, which was rather strange—a thought that made him even more confused. He started to hate the club and the guys next to him, screaming into each other's ears. There were things that they now, in this very moment when you couldn't hear yourself think, urgently needed to tell each other. Their faces shone as if they'd just won some great victory. But I have Effi, thought Carl. I'm happier than everyone else in this room, that much is clear.

Effi was now dancing in his direction. Carl fought his way toward her, rather bearishly, with no rhythm at all. He stomped up to her flat-footedly and touched her shoulder.

"What would you like?"

"Anything!"

She beamed at him. Her forehead had that childlike glow.

Carl stood at the bar for a long time and when the bartender finally came to him, he ordered double of everything. He could sip his drinks alone if Effi was still dancing, still had to dance because she was so *happy* (and cheerful), but then, suddenly, her hand was on his arm.

"Who are they for?"

They found space in the lobby facing the street. The lovely row of their cool, gleaming glasses on the window seat. It was absurd, actually, but Carl was proud that he had taken action, gotten something to drink for both of them. The lobby was too

loud for a conversation. Effi drank quickly. She counted the glasses
("Six glasses!"). Beer dribbled down Carl's chin, Effi laughed and
so it was party time. Effi's laughter: she covered her face with her
hands, took a step backward, bent to the side—she had tears in
her eyes. Like her dancing, something about her laughter made
Carl look suddenly old and awkward, which was entirely due to
him. Carl regretted that he couldn't become a part of her laughter.
Like her dancing, Effi's laughter was completely self-contained, it
belonged to her and embodied something he could only marvel
at. Yes, he marveled at Effi and thought: I am not the man for this
woman, not worthy of her. He had to drink faster. Four poems in
an anthology, that's it, thought Carl. But then Effi's hand lay on
his arm again. Her arching eyebrows and a look like a promise,
large enough for both of them: I know what's happening here with
the two of us, and I know who you are, Carl Bischoff.

The way home restored him, the coolness on his eyes. Effi had
played handball as a child. She sprinted for a few steps, slung
an imaginary ball into a net and laughed. She had been born in
Greiz. The poet Reiner Kunze had lived on her street, just two
doors down.

The best thing Kunze ever did were his Skácel translations, Carl
replied, or something along those lines (his ears were ringing). He
didn't say: I love those poems, which would have conveyed the
simple truth most clearly. He didn't say: I love you, Effi from Greiz.

"I once wrote out Kunze's *Letter with Blue Seal* by hand, the
entire book. It belonged to my second cousin, who was in my
class. We sat next to each other for three years without knowing
we were related. Only at the graduation dance, when our fami-
lies stood across from each other in the room . . . Her name was
Antje, Antje Seifert. I haven't seen her since." Carl pointed at
his nose and suddenly felt the loss. "She had our family's nose,
the so-called *Culmitzsch nose*, Antje, I mean." Carl stumbled, he
was drunk. And tired.

277

Effi lowered her head and looked at the sidewalk. In the distance, a shot—then another shot. It's like New Year's, Carl thought. An image of the Pope thanking God for German unity flashed before his eyes; he'd seen it in the news.

"Which animal are you, Carl?"

"Which animal?"

"What would you say? What do you think?"

It was an unpleasant question. Carl thought of lions, zebras, cormorants. Mentally, he made his way through the zoo, zigzagging from cage to cage. He found it hard to walk straight.

"I don't know. No idea."

"A dog. I think a dog."

Effi had stopped. Carl plodded on, staggering a little, a sorry sight.

"Carlo, heel."

Her *heel* hadn't sounded like a command, more like a short, addicted moan. Effi spread her arms wide.

"Carlo."

When Carl stood before her, she placed her hands firmly on his cheeks and pulled him toward her. "You know what you do best, Carlo?"

"Bark?"

"Lick."

AUTUMN

autumn is calm & custom. autumn
is rake, wood, is mild
coolness on the eyes &
random goosebumps, is also
the good old battle-feeling, faint, furtive, skull-silent
the sketches mature . . .

Carl's raft of mattresses docked and he slowly surfaced from sleep. The toilet off the stairwell was too far in the mornings, somewhere on the way to Novosibirsk. In the kitchen, he didn't have any sheets covering the window and each time he wondered if he was being watched from the building opposite, naked on his shabby little stool. He thought of Effi. Effi in her bodysuit. Effi in Paris. Effi had freed him. No more inhibitions, no false shame. His pigeon chest in the mirror, the view outside, the crumbling facade, the beautiful, golden stream of his urine in the sink. Ice-cold feet and even colder tiles—this was autumn.

For breakfast he had two rolls with honey that had hardened and had to be scraped out of the jar in thin, curling leaves. He drank instant coffee—a new product that Carl welcomed because it left no grounds. Or had instant coffee already been available in the East? Sometimes things were fuzzy—before and after. Strange how a compass direction could express everything, an entire history. In the East. In the West. North and South seemed relatively meaningless. He liked the word Nestlé—a small nest, Carl thought, even though it was surely a proper name. Carl read the label: Nestlé Germany. Now Carl was from Germany, too— he tried to feel this. It was unfamiliar. He found the company logo, a small drawing, a nest from which two fledglings stretched out their beaks. A mother bird sat right in front of them, ready to feed them. Or she was just coaxing them, explaining something or telling them a story, Carl thought. The label was very interesting: the little nest company originated in Switzerland. "How nice," whispered a quiet voice that was at home deep inside Carl and still bleary with sleep, "how nice." Because he was thinking of his mother? Of Joyce's grave? The grave was also a small nest, the last little nest as it were.

Clearly, working on the poems had changed how he thought. This was surely good and only occasionally confusing. The crudest connections seemed to draw themselves, stupid things, short circuits, valuable insanities, all of which he had to write down immediately. Carl hated anecdotal poems, the small, predictable stories, especially their smugness, the silky, hollow knowledge of good sons-in-law. A good poem had to be a cascade, a glittering stream in the magical light that it, itself, constantly creates.

At half past seven, Carl set off for Oranienburger Strasse. The first leaves had fallen in the small copse in front of the house, covering the ditch between the trees, which the last long rain had washed clean. Old Knospe's garden bed was freshly dug up. The evening before, he had heard her outside on the rope, the long leaps of her featherweight body down the staircase, a sound that was neither loud nor soft, as if someone were killing flies with a flyswatter, Carl thought.

He enjoyed the short trip through the city. He took a path along Acker Strasse, past the bookstore press, *my* press, thought Carl. Under his sweater, he wore a white shirt from the second-hand shop on Potsdamer Platz. He'd recently begun shopping there, clothing priced by the kilo. And he wore his father's garage shoes, black and narrow, but comfortable. "Those were my wedding shoes, my boy," his father had once told him. "Highest quality." Once Carl had applied shoe cream and polished them, they were as good as new.

No one had asked him to dress like a waiter, but the Assel was changing, too. Only Fenske's cellar remained untouched. The Shepherd had insisted on it, as he'd insisted on keeping the "women's dressing room." Hans called it the "tarts' cloakroom." Fenske's cellar and the women's dressing room were Hoffi's stipulations, which (after some back and forth) left the way clear for tearing out the provisional structure of welded rods and installing a "suitable bar counter," as Hans put it, "with a keg cooler and beer tap." Also included was a counter sideboard with enough room for glasses, bottles, and a cash box.

Hans and Irina now did the talking at the pack's meetings. They had something that Hoffi the Shepherd mostly lacked—a gastronomical eye, or how else to describe it? The next significant step was connecting another (narrow) vaulted room in the cellar to serve as a kitchen. That would make preparing the Assel kebabs (for example) much easier. This was something that Carl, who usually refrained from joining the debates, applauded enthusiastically. He was no cook; his head was filled with poems.

The expansion stemmed from Irina's talent for solicitous persuasion. With all her neighborly warmth and helpfulness, she had been able to make exchanging the space in the cellar for a storage room in the side wing palatable to the retired pastor, Hielscher. The room was next to Dodo's stall, in the dry, front part of the ramshackle garden shed. The pastor liked the goat. Sometimes he called out something to Dodo across the court-yard when she was trotting back and forth through the floors of the empty side wing. Then she would look at him for a long time out of one of the broken windows with a questioning look. "They're talking to each other," Irina claimed. Maybe that was the clincher. She regularly brought Hielscher a jug of the richest goat milk, which the pastor refined into cheese (using his secret recipe). On the day of the kitchen expansion, Hielscher brought a tray of cheese triangles down to the Assel, where half of the pack had gathered.

"Please help yourselves, help yourselves! You young people don't know—"

He smiled uncertainly, gasped for breath and waved his hand in the air to strike out what he'd just said. He suddenly pressed the tray of cheese into Henry's chest.

"Here, young man, take this, please."

The old man turned abruptly and shuffled out the door and back upstairs. Embarrassed, Henry passed the tray to Hoffi, whose eyes, for some reason, were suddenly brimming with tears.

"A starting point of this, how should I put it, cross-generational solidarity..."

Carl immediately understood. The old man's encouragement was balm for the warrior soul. In those days, things were developing differently than Hoffi had imagined and at a breakneck pace.

"If we now have a kitchen..."

The Shepherd trailed off and tenderly stroked Dodo's hide. The goat looked up and became very still.

This was the moment. Something happened that, later, no one was quite sure if they'd really witnessed it or not: Dodo slowly started to rise, centimeter by centimeter. At first, the Shepherd kept stroking her, then let go. Everyone stared at the goat. The animal was hovering, high enough off the floor to look directly into Hoffi's eyes, first at him and then at each person in the cellar. Her scrutinizing gaze. Pupils like arrow slits.

The Shepherd hooked his rod onto Dodo's collar and spun the animal in the air. Once, twice. It looked elegant. Then he left the Assel, pulling the goat behind him. She still flew a good distance above the ground and scrambled her hooves in the air slightly.

"You've seen it, now you've seen it," the Shepherd murmured. "What wouldn't be possible if..."

Carl reached for the cheese. It was real and tasted of goat.

Two days later, Irina brought news of old Hielscher's death to the cellar. The Shepherd suggested they all go to the funeral. A funeral service was held in the Sophienkirche, where Hielscher had been the pastor for decades. Afterwards, coffee and amaretto were served in the Assel, which the Shepherd had summarily closed for the day. He recited Hermann Hesse's "Stages" and spoke of a "pause for breath." It was time to stop and come to their senses: "What were our goals?"

There was, however, too much agitation among the mourning pack for this question to be considered seriously. Irina took advantage of the opportunity ("When are we ever all gathered together?") to start a shift log. A large notebook with a hand-drawn chart for day shifts and night shifts: "A double shift system to handle the daily rush."

As she assigned the shifts, it quickly became clear that the pack alone could not cover them all. And not everyone welcomed the work. The majority of the pack hated tourists, others preferred to be guests, to have a drink and enjoy the freedom and the evenings. Ragna explained that it wasn't in her nature *to serve* someone, but if it were an emergency, she was prepared to do it. What Henry wanted most of all was to get back to his studio, which left Carl adrift for a moment.

"We won't be selling the Wall much longer," the Shepherd pointed out. The pack also had to suspend their forays for the time being, except for smaller opportunities here and there. "As long as the investigation about the dogs continues, we have to be careful," the Shepherd murmured to the mourning pack, "especially now. As you know, another law applies now. The new sacred cow is private property." He raised his voice again: "Our future is the tool. We can use it ourselves or lend it to an unemployed worker, to brigades that are making themselves independent, to cooperatives, to associations. Our tool archive is well stocked, for a long time, I'd say. We can make a hundred buildings livable with them, half of Berlin!"

"In the inhabited buildings, there are too few who know how," Ragna countered. "Too many good-for-nothings, students, free-loaders, all those guys with two left hands. Too few tradesmen, Hoffi—as always."

Ragna sounded tender when she called the Shepherd by his nickname. She pushed her cap to the back of her head and for a moment she looked like a frightened child in a carnival costume.

"They're good enough for the Assel," Irina decided and tapped her pencil on the shift log. "There's always a couple of them loitering here every day. Whether they're in front of the counter or behind it . . ."

"That's how it is, Irina, that's exactly how it is." Hans, who had only been smiling to himself until then, nodded thoughtfully.

Since Hans had quit his job as stage manager at the Komisches Oper, the Assel had become his stage. Now and then he pitched in but often he just stood at the bar, talking with guests or "the girls." He wanted to know everything about them: what they earned and for what and how they would manage in winter, outside in the cold without taking off their clothes, and so on. He treated them to cocoa made with Nesquik, about which he made a pun, but the women didn't laugh. Now and then, they gave him some detail, but never much information. "You know how they're able to simulate penetration?"

Carl didn't know. He saw something gray creeping across the floor. It was the last woodlouse, beyond any doubt. He had let the creature go last time, almost a year ago. Henry had used the cement bags for charcoal drawings, and he had smoothed the damp walls, with their own juices.

The insect wore the plaster like armor. What a burden, Carl thought.

THE BOOK

The "long-awaited UVA anthology" was a collection of mostly unknown names apart from "Matthias" BAADER Holst and Jörg Schieke, two real poets. Carl held the book in his hand. A slim paperback, cheap paper, and surprisingly large photographs—a full page for each portrait. Appearing in a book with Schieke and Holst consoled Carl. The photograph was a blow below the belt: did he really still have that adolescent fluff on his face?

I knew it, but I no longer *saw* it, Carl thought. Or forgot it, just forgot as the years went by. What was up with someone who forgot what he looked like? Who looked obliviously in the mirror? "I needed someone to tell me—I needed someone," Carl whispered. Effi.

Carl tried to see himself through Effi's eyes: his long, unruly, only half-combed hair, his leather jacket, cigarette in hand, the soft, serious cheeks (lonely in some way, but not suffering), the dirt under his fingernails, probably from digging out the coal and then: that moustache, the countable number of adolescent hairs that made everything (absolutely everything) about him ridiculous. How could Effi Kalász be with someone who looked like *this*?

At the very least, Sonie should have told him ("You need a shave" or "Maybe you should shave," something along those lines), but he'd only taken photographs, with light, without, standing, sitting, in the hall, in the kitchen, and in front of a picture in his "studio," an enlarged scene from Hieronymus Bosch's *Last Judgment*—for whatever reason. He sees me as part of its martyrdom, thought Carl. "Carl Bischoff, with moustache, before the *Last Judgment*" was the photograph that the publishing house chose.

Carl tore himself away from these thoughts and paced around his room. He placed the book on his easel and calmed himself down. He leafed through a few pages and read the poems by Schieke and Holst. Holst had died in an accident on the night of the monetary union; he was run over by a streetcar at the end of Oranienburger Strasse, just a few hundred meters from the Assel. Carl went to see the spot later; it was simply unbelievable. Schieke worked in Bar Number Five in the Wydok people's building, usually with a French guy named Jimmy, who, it was said, knew Robert Smith of The Cure personally. Now and then Schieke also came to the Assel. He would sit at the bar and drink red wine. He was tall, looked somehow Native American, didn't smoke, and radiated a gentle superiority. Schieke had contact with the "scene," and sometimes would talk about it. This and that, always sketchily, but that's how Carl learned that many of their readings had taken place in a back building on Ryke Strasse, right next to the small bomb crater copse. That's Ryke Strasse, thought Carl, but I'm blind to it. Schieke, who had written splendid poems like "Large Letters of a Difficult Student" and "Seaman's Spasms," preferred to talk about football matches. Carl hadn't kept up for a while. All he had now was the radio in his Zhiguli. His television was only a docking station. Carl realized how isolated (no, how *busy*) he'd been in the past months. Just to say something, he finally replied that he had spent half his childhood in defense for Traktor Langenberg FC before switching to track and field and running middle distance, "a complete waste." Without thinking, Carl had used Edgar Bendler's words. His old training partner, little Ed from back home, had not reappeared.

Schieke still played. He was the sweeper for THC Franziskaner FC, who played every Sunday in the city league. The team had named themselves after a pub on Oranien Platz where they gathered before and after their games; their practice pitch was the lawn in front of the Reichstag.

"Come by sometime. We can always use another fullback," Schieke had said. Schieke, the author of poems like "Calm Blood" and "After him, the Deluge." Since then, Carl had thought about soccer shoes. And socks. And shin guards. And a hair band, maybe, in THC's colors: black and orange. THC stood for tetrahydrocannabinol and was a thinly disguised allusion to the club's openness and diversity, but Carl learned this only much later during his first and only game.

LARGE FORMAT

Effi painted, Carl wrote and together they would succeed. "Art and sex are accomplices": who said that? Everyone. They went together.

"You shaved!" Effi stroked her finger along Carl's upper lip. She caressed him.

He had brought her the book. He had hesitated at first because it was ugly and the title was embarrassing, but especially because of the photograph.

"*The Joys of Escape, the Thirst for Beer?*"

"That's the title."

Effi took the book from his hand and glanced at the dedication. She smiled faintly and opened it, stroking the pages (without reading them). Then she hugged Carl.

Carl felt rescued. In the kitchen he started talking gravely and euphorically. He described the gallerists who showed up at the bar in the Assel night after night. An exhibition of Henry's "animals" was already planned, large format horses, goats, all those gentle, melancholy creatures that sprang from Henry's imagination. Hans, who had also begun painting again (exclusively penguins), had suggested making the Assel a gallery—one thing led to another in those nights, things came in a rush, one on top of another, an invitation to join in.

"If not now, when?" Carl asked softly and laid his hand on Effi's. A show in the Assel cellar, as a first step, then one thing would lead to another. When he didn't have to think about himself alone, Carl had strength he otherwise lacked. Having Effi at his side made him strong. More exactly: with Effi, Carl could summon courage.

And Effi? A reflection of appreciation on her face. The less said the better was her way in these matters. She let Carl take charge but didn't defer to him, if such a thing is possible in life.

*

The important thing was for Effi to start making progress too. In the inexhaustible and seemingly enchanted tradesmen's court-yards of the Scheunenviertel neighborhood, left untouched for decades, Carl had found a laundry mangle. Henry helped him convert it into a rotogravure press. Transporting the cast-iron base frame to Wörther Strasse was *a feat* (as Carl's mother would have put it). The Shepherd helped with the GAZ. Together, Henry, Carl, and the Shepherd heaved the several hundredweight-heavy contraption up three flights of stairs. Panting, Hoffi looked down into the courtyard and declared that this apartment still had enormous strategic importance. Effi was shocked.

"Only in case of emergency," the Shepherd placated her. In the end, the aguerrillas were happy that "people like Effi and Freddy" had found a home here.

Two days later, Effi was ready for a first test print. The laun-dry mangle stood at the foot of her bed—working and sleeping, that's how it should be, thought Carl. He watched Effi complete her preparations with fascination and reverence. She had tied on an apron and a headband held back her hair. She rubbed one of the copper plates with a viscous, tar-like substance, using a small, round, thick piece of felt (on closer examination, he saw it was a tampon). Then she wiped the plate clean again, first with a rag, then with her bare hand. She was deep in concentration but looked up once and smiled at Carl.

Unfortunately, the press failed. The mangle (or the thing Carl had enthusiastically called "our press"—he loved this old household device that was probably a hundred years old) did not work. It all looked good from a technical point of view, especially Carl's addition of a kind of slide that made it possible to move the plates horizontally toward the rollers and the large, beauti-fully curved steel struts and the freshly oiled base—but none of it worked. The mangle did not have enough pressure for a clean (even) print and by the second attempt, it was already creaking.

"It's the rollers," Effi said very softly.

"Maybe if we adjust them . . ."

With determination (and helplessly), Carl screwed the rollers a bit tighter. His wrench slipped out of his hand and sailed across the floor. Effi just stood there, deflated.

"This crap is no use."

She meant the work, the etchings, the copper plates.

"I have to pick up Freddy."

Her voice was flat. There was no note of reproach, it was merely as if all of a sudden everything had become pointless and useless. The old appliance, the prints, Carl's presence and, essentially, hers too. And it was as if, ultimately, nothing else could be expected.

I LOVE YOU

"Dodo, my girl." The Shepherd's entire body was trembling. He lay on his back in the straw with his eyes closed and breathing rapidly.

"He didn't want to go to the hospital," the Comandante repeated to everyone who joined them in the stall. The space was already overcrowded.

"Dodo, Dodo, the entire drive, he kept repeating it."

Carl could see that the Comandante was unsure about his decision (the stall instead of the hospital). The Shepherd's shirt was torn, and his arms were scratched but not bleeding. When Dodo licked his wounds with her rough tongue, his eyelids fluttered.

Dodo did not leave the Shepherd's side. Carl knelt down and started milking the goat (as best he could). Irina poured the milk into a cup and tried to pour some into Hoffi's mouth.

"I think he's asleep," Carl murmured. "Maybe it would be better if we left him in peace."

His voice trembled. In the stall, Carl felt responsible. Dodo only allowed Hoffi and Carl to milk her. Irina handed the cup to Carl, who drank it absentmindedly.

"What on earth—" In despair, Irina grabbed the Comandante's arm. He immediately yanked it away from her and took a step back.

The last light of the day hung in the stall window. The Shepherd's trembling made a constant but faint rustling in the straw, like that of mice.

The Comandante cleared his throat and tried to look over all those assembled in the stall. "A few weeks ago, Hoffi, I mean the Shepherd, your leader, had announced that he and the aguerrillas would not be taking part in these battles and certainly not in the war over Mainzer Strasse."

"That's right," Irina answered. Her voice sounded strained. "Those are *your* troops. We see no reason for them. Why should we fight for some buildings squatted by people from the West. They aren't our people, never were. They just laugh at us." She was near tears.

The Comandante lowered his voice: "In the middle of the fight, he suddenly appeared on one of the roofs opposite. Like a fata morgana. He spread his arms out and flapped his poncho like wings. He didn't fight, he just yelled, he kept yelling. As if he wanted to call attention to himself and that probably was his strategy. He walked around up there like a god but completely unprotected."

"What did he yell?"

"At some point we noticed what was going on. A few meters farther back, there was Kleist, hidden by a chimney. They'd started to encircle him and were slowly getting closer. He stood there like he was going to jump, with the tips of his toes already in the air, I'd say. The madman wanted to jump with a Molotov in his hand, like a living bomb. Militarily it's nonsense because—"

"Forget that," Irina snarled, "go on!"

"You have no idea. As I was saying, it was the wrong strategy. Kleist must have cracked. He screamed, 'I love you!'"

"What?"

"'I love you.' Several times, very clearly, at which point the Shepherd began to beat his wings. Then everything happened very fast. Hoffi flew toward him like a dervish. Everyone ran, but the Shepherd got there first. I'm sure about that. In the end, there were only cops on the roof, everywhere, Kleist pinned between them, screaming like he'd been skewered. Hoffi saved his life, that much is certain. He probably didn't even realize it, the little idiot."

"And Hoffi?"

"Naturally we ran off, I mean—disengaged. We tried the street, cops and battles everywhere. We found him on a shed roof in the courtyard, half-caved in. Rotten wood, old tar paper, and so on, well chosen, I'd say. He was wedged in. He hung in the air, upside down and laughing. I swear, he was laughing when we got there and we removed him surgically, very carefully and he laughed the entire time. At some point, he got tired. On the way home, I had to keep explaining to him, again and again, everything that happened, as if he forgot everything right away each time. That Kleist was safe, that justice had prevailed, solidarity and so on, everything that Hoffi wants to hear. And each time that I asked, 'Hoffi, did they push you off the roof?', he'd answer, 'No, no, I flew.' Then he became even more tired, his eyes were closing, and he started trembling. In the end, he just wanted Dodo. 'Home to Dodo, to Dodo in the straw.'" His voice dropped again: "With the right weapons, that would *never* have happened."

For a moment, there was silence. The only sounds were those of Dodo chewing and the Shepherd's trembling in the straw. Irina shook her head as if exhausted, her hands on her temples.

"He's sleeping now. He's getting some rest," Henry said.

He nodded at them. Carl touched Ragna on the shoulder and they stepped out into the courtyard.

"It's already pitch dark," Carl said. He wanted to say more, but the giver of tools was crying, so he took her in his arms. They'd known each other almost a year. Tools and light oil, Ragna's smell. The woman I feel closest to, Carl thought. The woman I can understand. The right woman, he thought, if *that* was what the decision was based on.

Hans poured beer. At this hour there were few guests. Of the girls, there was only Rita, crouching in the hall in front of her wardrobe, getting ready for the evening. Carl had a shift, according to the notebook. But something about it was wrong; it was all trivial now. Hans pushed a soaked note across the counter, an order from Fenske's cellar, Carl's beat. He spilled the vodka and then a wet beer glass slipped out of his hand. He saw the Shepherd in the straw and his trembling spread to Carl's hands like an echo. Hans rummaged in the shelf under the cash register and handed him a cookie. Hans raised his finger in warning: "One is enough." Carl didn't need any hash. He'd decided that long before, but when Hans wasn't looking, Carl reached into the shelf a second time. Then he poured out two Ballantine's.

"For the bar, tonight." Although Carl had learned in the meantime that there were better whiskeys, he had stuck with Ballantine's. It was an expression of his loyalty and constancy (in this case to Fassbinder and, in essence, to Irm Hermanns' voice):

"To Hoffi, Carl!"

"To Hoffi."

Carl prepared a small flatbread with ham and returned to the stall. The Shepherd and Dodo—they were asleep. Irina had set up an oil heater. There was that comforting blend of artificial and animal warmth: Carl breathed in deeply and stretched out in the straw next to Dodo. He briefly closed his eyes and pictured Hoffi next to him in the Zhiguli. He saw the jam jar of milk next to his mattress. Hoffi didn't move. The trembling had stopped.

Adele was sitting in Fenske's cellar with Vassily and a few other Russians, sturdy, young comrades with buzz cuts. Either from Adele's garage or Vassily's unit, no one knew exactly. Carl considered the fact that a Russian general in civvies would show up in a place like the Assel to be a symptom of the final collapse of the old order—even if he were Adele's father and maybe only wanted to protect her, Carl thought. She called him "Daddy," but so did the other Russians.

Vassily immediately asked if he needed help and greeted Carl like an old friend. Adele gave him a sympathetic look. The Russians evidently knew about Hoffi. Carl Bischoff was their favorite bartender and they treated him well. Every time they came, they'd ask Carl about the Zhiguli and always praised his Russian, even though (despite nine years of classes) it was embarrassingly fragmentary. On this evening, Carl would have liked to sit down with them for a glass, but he had to get back to the counter. He was a little unsteady on his feet, lacking the energy with which he usually pounded out his rounds of the bar, a pace that lent his work rhythm and structure.

Holding a defense colloquium on this evening (after all that had happened, thought Carl) would be completely inappropriate. On the opposite side of the table, where the Comandante sat, lay their training weapon with the magazine next to it ("placed at their disposal" by the Russians). They'd been practicing with it for a few weeks. Carl noticed that something copper-colored gleamed in the magazine. Careless Russians, thought Carl, but nothing more, he had other worries. In a low voice, the

Comandante began speaking of revenge and of the need for better weapons in battle, but got no response. Without Hoffi at the table, he had no support in the cellar. In any case, not enough of the captains had shown up. Carl recognized two people from August Strasse and a man from Linien Strasse. A few seats between them and the Russians remained empty. Linien Man's comment that the Assel was a "tart hole" that could no longer be considered a *plenum* was too loud to be ignored. Still, the "storming of Mainzer" had to be worked through in the name of the victims. To which one of the August people announced that he was only there as an "observer." "And for the milk, of course!"

They snickered.

"No more milk today." Carl had put away his tray and wanted to leave the cellar.

"But, but, guerrillero, surely you can find an udder in this . . ."

"Tart hole?"

"As you like, guerrillero. And we do our own milking, right?" Linien Man stood up and made a pumping gesture. Then he walked slowly toward the door, emphasizing every step like a cowboy in a saloon.

"So where is she, your fucking goat?"

"I'll put a plenum in your head." Carl had no idea where that came from: he cocked the Kalashnikov.

The magazine was locked in place, fully loaded, like in a film. With a man named Carl Bischoff, played by Carl, who looked angry and dangerous.

"Apologize now."

"What?"

"Apologize!"

Linien Man was white as a sheet. Carl tried to find a way out of the scene but couldn't. He couldn't shoot the man, could he?

"Apologize! Right now!"

"I apologize."

"What for?"

"For . . ."

"For stupidly insulting the Assel, the goat, and the Shepherd."

"I apologize for that."

"Say it."

"I apologize for stupidly insulting the Assel, the . . ."

". . . the goat, and the Shepherd."

". . . the goat, and the Shepherd."

"And now in one sentence."

At that moment Carl knew. It was like a burning, glaring hole in the bubble that surrounded him and now he only had to concentrate.

"I am sorry . . . *please* . . . for stupidly . . . insulting the goat . . . and . . . *please*—" Linien Man began sobbing; he had lost control and fell to his knees.

It was a very distant way out and only for that reason did it appear so small. By now Daddy Vassily stood to Carl's right and Adele to his left.

"That's not your weapon, Carl," the Comandante whispered. Carl clearly heard the deep respect in his voice. Maybe they would just knock him down and then he could go home. He could lie down in the back, in the stall with the Shepherd, bleed a little, cry a little, and then calm down.

"It's not your weapon either," countered the man played by Carl. His anger had cooled significantly. "This is the weapon that Vassily had put at the colloquium's disposal for practice. And I'm just practicing."

Now the way was open. Carl deliberately turned toward Vassily and said: "Want to bet that I can disassemble and reassemble this baby," he stroked the barrel of the gun with his right hand, "in twenty-five seconds? Blindfolded." This baby—he really had spoken like in a film, even though he had turned back into Carl Bischoff, a bartender at the Assel.

"I bet you can't," said Adele, who had immediately understood. This, in turn, gave Carl the opportunity to place the baby on the table slowly, carefully—cut.

There was a smell of urine. Linien Man with the plenum in his head had peed his pants. The Russians took him outside and came back into the cellar. Their faces were strained but none began hitting Carl. Adele handed Vassily a handkerchief and he blindfolded Carl.

Darkness. Good old darkness.

Carl breathed the darkness in and grew calm.

Twenty-five seconds. Carl had made a name for himself with his speed in Pioneer Battalion 6 of the National People's Army in Merseburg. His hands simply had a good (tender) relationship with small, perfect things and their perfect interplay—smooth, cool, lightly oiled. A delicate, almost sexual action under his fingertips that put a weapon together, though its being a weapon was not important in the moment. Because he was fast (fast and skillful), Carl was in the group, led by Lieutenant Colonel Buderus, who could compete with the Russians. The regiment of the brothers-in-arms was housed on the edge of town. At these "peace meetings," the winner was awarded SL (short leave from Friday to Sunday), in exceptional cases even LSL (long short leave from Thursday to Sunday). For a simple private, who could only leave the barracks twice in six months, there was nothing better. The Russians never got to go home.

Carl groped for the gun and lined it up. He tested the distance between his body and the table. Twenty-five seconds. Why had he suddenly felt such intense hatred? Not only for Kleist, for whom Hoffi had *flown*. Why hadn't anyone said anything about that? And where were they now, Kleist and his love? Why had everyone remained silent? It was as if the pack had gone mute with the Shepherd's fall and its language had died out.

Vassily's order: Slavic, familiar.

You don't forget how, Carl thought, not in this life.

Spring, rod, pistons, cylinder.

For Carl, every movement was defiance—and grief. Even if everything was happening too fast for unpracticed eyes.

LURKING SKIN

Carl took care of Freddy for a few days. He had the morning to work, then he picked the boy up from kindergarten in the afternoon. In slow motion, they ambled to the bakery on Wörther Strasse and ate "pudding pretzels," the knotted kind of Danish that this baker called a "Viennese Eight." They got along famously. The child gave Carl a sense of security, made him feel grown-up, like a real part of this world. Carl worked better when he knew that he would do something with Freddy later; he used his time well.

Furthermore, it was good to be out of the Assel for a while. He worked three days a week, roughly every other day. After the currency union, his pay was six marks an hour along with the tips that the bartenders shared with the kitchen staff. A ten-hour shift brought Carl about eighty marks—an amount that seemed appropriate to him, especially because it was paid right away.

There was something in the relationship to Freddy that bound Carl to Effi. He wouldn't have gone so far as to use the word "family." Something kept him from thinking along those lines— timidity, immaturity, shyness perhaps. He didn't seem ready. In the hours with Freddy, the child he once was appeared and sometimes he felt very close to that boy. At Freddy's side, Carl relished Effi's motherliness, as Freddy's companion (this man disguised as a child), he had a certain claim to it. Carl didn't think this way. He didn't know much about it, but he could feel the effects on him. Admittedly, Effi's maternal aura was erratic, flickering, and there were days when it was completely extin-guished. Then some kind of trapdoor came down and everything tumbled into the void.

"She's your muse, Carl, not your mother."

Such thoughts.

After four days, Effi came back to Wörther Strasse with her large, worn portfolio under her arm. Carl saw the white exhaustion on her forehead, which gleamed in the dimly lit stairwell. A tired smile, the battle was won, she'd done it. She talked very softly, as if she were hoarse. She rhapsodized about the studio. Freddy had already fallen asleep.

"Steel rollers as thick as your arm," was the first thing Effi wanted to tell him about. "Bredlow himself rarely uses them. He takes his things to the Graetz Printers on August Strasse. He has them print them. He offered to take me with him one day—isn't that great, Carl?"

Four times *he*.

"Antique" and "a nice old piece" was what Franz from the front building had called Carl's laundry mangle. It now stood right next to Effi's bed, a hundredweight-heavy memorial of his failure, ordering him to keep his mouth shut as long as Effi was gushing about Bredlow and her work with Bredlow's press. Why that required her to stay for four days somewhere in Pankow is something Carl did not ask. Why not? Because something pivotal was unclear: Effi and Carl. Were they actually *together*, a couple (as it used to be called)—or not?

Carl wanted to make some coffee, but Effi reached for him, a hand on his crotch. Effi kept the hand there as she stood and started doing something with her other hand on the back of his neck and between his shoulder blades; she worked on him like on one of her sculptures. She hadn't asked about Freddy yet.

*

Franz had invited them to his parents' farm in a village south of the city for the weekend. The elderly couple's kitchen, the bench, the stove—it was all very simple and familiar. The onion pattern on the dishes was the same as in Gera. The dishes were still there in the cupboard, waiting, in stacks, Carl thought. All the abandoned things and their disappointed whispering. They were no longer part of a home, what an insult, yet also a puzzle they had to agree on. There were always a few insolent cups who insisted it was all *just temporary.*

After the meal, the old people washed the dishes. The young went outside to survey the farm: studios, workshops, maybe even a small hotel—Franz had plans. It was a square farmyard, the roofs were freshly tiled and the spaciousness of the empty stalls lent them an almost festive air. Carl admired the cross vaults and the row of supports in the cowshed: he knelt down and touched one of the stone feeding troughs.

"My mother often took me to the stalls with her. I would stand in one of the hay cribs between the animals. I was one or two years old. One time the crib fell over and . . ."

"You, as a bricklayer," Franz began and asked Carl a question about the salt in the walls. Freddy ignored Carl, as if they hadn't eaten pudding pretzels together for four days. Effi was silent.

After coffee, the two of them walked along the village green and she said it.

"Everything that I've done up to now is garbage."

Carl was shocked. Then he talked wildly about the "good days recently," their life in Berlin, which was just getting going, her work with prints and "where that could lead."

"You could—do *anything* with it."

"No, I can't."

"You could show your work in the Assel."

"In a cellar? Without light?" It was the disdain in her voice, the contempt.

A hundred meters further on, the village ended: a bus stop, a turning loop around the fire pond, next to which stood an electricity substation, tall and slender like a tower, with a pointed tile roof and a steel door. Behind it, the fields began.

"I had very good teachers. But what I've done is garbage." Effi's face in profile and something in it that Carl hadn't seen before. Something that barely tolerated him and his eagerness. Or actually no longer tolerated it at all.

"It's my own fault."

She was talking now about some teacher who had always been completely on her side. She defended herself. An onslaught from the darkness. An attack on her life.

"What do you mean by fault?"

They stood in front of the transformer station. The dull hum of the electricity and the little yellow sign with a lightning bolt and skull and crossbones: "Warning! Danger!" For a moment, Carl wondered if the buzzing was inside him, in his skull, the sound of disappointment.

"Earlier, when my mother would take me with her to the city, we always passed a house like this, in the bus." Effi didn't look at Carl as she spoke. She looked at the door of the transformer station. "Once I asked her who lived there, in that small, pointy house without windows, and she laughed and said, someday—"

"Carlo!" Freddy came storming up to them and threw himself into Carl's arms; the boy had rediscovered him.

"Someday we'll go in and see."

When Carl came to Wörther Strasse from the Assel in the early evening, he met a tall, angular man on the staircase, a blond giant with shoulder-length hair who was the spitting image of Freddy, his adult version, so to speak. Carl didn't think about it for a minute. He'd earned a lot that afternoon and had drunk too much; a faint movement played around his lips, he was murmuring a few words, refining what he wanted to tell Effi about Dodo, who had flown again. A time of miracles, Hans had said.

Giant-Freddy wore a half-unbuttoned Hawaiian shirt with large flowers under a jacket (too thin for late November) and held an open bottle of red wine in his hand. It was Bull's Blood, which was still sold by the bottle, the cheapest wine far and wide. He beamed at Carl and paused, as if he wanted to say something, but then kept going downstairs.

"Papa lives here now," Freddy shouted at the top of his voice and threw himself at Carl. For a fraction of a second, Carl saw himself stepping aside and letting the blond kid sail past him into the void. The boy impetuously pressed his soft, chalk-white cheek to Carl's face. He seemed very happy. Out of the corner of his eye, Carl saw that Effi wanted to say something, but Freddy was faster.

"My papa's name is Rico, did you know? Why didn't you know? Mama, Carl doesn't know Rico's name. I want to be a music player, too, like Papa."

"They're called musicians," Effi murmured.

"Is Papa putting me to bed—or Carl?"

It took a while for Freddy to calm down. He talked without stopping, then fell asleep in the middle of a sentence.

Effi had washed the dishes and cleaned the kitchen, which she otherwise never did in the evening. The small, square kitchen table between the cooker and the washing machine. *The Joys of Escape* anthology on the breadbox, as if left over, a relic from times long past, full of happiness and promise.

"Rico's not moving in. He has the apartment opposite."

"Opposite? That's the Shepherd's apartment, the whole floor . . ."

"Not anymore."

Carl learned that the reservation had been lifted. Hans had released the floor. The Shepherd's empire was disintegrating.

"He had been looking for a place for a long time."

"For a long time?" Carl was drunk but not an idiot. "And then he *found* one here?"

"What was I supposed to do? I can't forbid him. I can't . . ." Effi's voice was harsh and helpless.

"Are they all going to come now? I mean all of them. From before, right here to Wörther Strasse, third floor?"

Carl was talking nonsense and it probably wasn't fair. He didn't know what to say. He had to concentrate but was just too tired. He pictured himself in a short film, standing up and leaving. Up Ryke Strasse to the small bomb crater copse, in coldest November. I should have left *right away*, Carl thought and realized he had less strength for it than he'd thought, maybe less than ever before. "Then just go right ahead, with Mr. Hawaiian Shirt," Carl would have said in the film.

Because he was hungry, Effi started to make him some sandwiches. Very slowly and conscientiously, in a kind of hypnosis. Effi was trembling slightly. She saw that he'd noticed, and Carl saw her look, and they were close again.

"Cheese or liverwurst?"

He stared at her beautiful, slender hands with the knife and bread and forgot what he was going to say. His skin was taut; it was a lurking, lecherous skin. Like a junky, thought Carl. A dependence, the full extent of which only became visible in that moment.

Effi talked about Nora, her sister in the piano bar. She'd finally talked to Heiner Müller and the laconic drinker had scribbled a small text for her on a napkin, "just a few lines." Effi stood up and rummaged through a small stack of papers in her kitchen cupboard. The sight of her hands. Carl hung on to the table tightly and read the napkin: "In every real man / is hidden a child / that wants to die."

"Why did he write this for her? Odd, isn't it?" Effi asked, shaking her head.

Woolworths had promoted Ralf. "To general representative," said Effi, who knew as little as Carl what that meant. Carl imagined the black Passat on the highway, pulling away from everyone.

Around two in the morning, the entrance door in the front building slammed and steps crossed the courtyard and climbed to their floor. Actually, it was not one of the nights when Carl usually stayed over. There was quiet for a while, aside from the endless noise of the city, then soft guitar music. Effi slept. Mr. Hawaiian Shirt sang, not particularly loud, but loud enough that they could hear. "The child saved me," Effi had said once, that was all. She never talked about her past. There was a ban that must have had to do with her mother's death, that much Carl had come to understand. When Freddy was born, Effi was nineteen. Carl had often tried to imagine it: what did he look like? The one who had managed to conquer this unapproachable, enchanting, and kissing creature named Ilonka Kalász? The answer was Rico. Rico Schmidt.

CARL'S DREAM

". . . and no one knows where the journey leads," Hans said.

He looked elegant. He stood very straight, his hand on the tap and his chest thrust forward like a singer just before a solo. To check the foam, he held the glass almost perpendicular to the tap.

"And then we come into play, if you know what I mean."

Hans took a gulp and wiped his mouth. He wore his brown leather pants and an army-green pullover with a zipper. Although he frequently mentioned Hoffi's reference to a U-boat in his speeches, what he was saying now seemed much less bleak. His eyes shone. He had a piercing gaze and seemed to be friends with everyone, with Irina, with the prostitutes (the girls, the women,

the working ladies), and essentially also with Carl, whom he'd
taught the basic one-plus-one of running a bar.

"It's completely naive to think the Russians will simply with-
draw." He was lisping even though he wasn't drunk or only
barely.

"What an insult, imagine. Losing the big war in the end after
all. The fascists as victors. Half a million good fighters go home,
just like that? Who can believe that, Carl? All I say is: Daddy
Vassily!"

He alluded to "contacts" and said he had "spoken with people."
At the end of an impressively logical chain of arguments, Hans
revealed what was obvious to him ("and to anyone with eyes"):
Vassily was part of a Russian covert operation whose mission was to leave behind a beachhead of "supporters" after the
Russian troops withdrew—"an underground, sympathizers, what
do I know, well educated, acting in solidarity, loyal. A kind of
guerrilla army, just like ours, Carl, only spread out over the
entire country, you know what I mean? And what do you think
the operation is called?"

"?"

"Dosvidanya? Ring a bell?"

Hans looked at Carl with eyes that were suddenly very bright,
that almost looked white, as if he were blind or dazzled. His
voice was calm, his delivery thoughtful. It was one of those
remarkable moments when Hans spoke the plain truth, getting
wind of something far into the future.

"These troops, bang in the middle of the country, Carl. And
what we *see* here is their very first step: the recruitment phase.
People like Hoffi, some from the pack, maybe you, Carl—you
drive a Zhiguli, you like Adele, she installs new rear lights for
you for free, wham bam, just like that, maybe they slip you money
now and again under the door, no idea. In any case, Vassily has
taken a liking to you and only wants you to serve him—I don't get

it . . . Not to mention that Comandante Kazakh Kruso, the man has too many names. Why do you think they sit around in his colloquiums every week? Why do they bring him weapons—for *training* in urban warfare? An AK-47? To defend the inhabited buildings? They don't give a shit. Have the Germans won after all? That's what they're asking. Vassily's troops—they're the dark red in the Red Army. The deep, dark red of their fatherland."

As long as Carl was dreaming, it seemed perfectly clear that it was the truth.

THE ROSE OF JERICHO

Expansive and lisping, Hans took over the Shepherd's role. He supervised the storeroom and recorded daily consumption. Food and drinks were now bought in a supermarket called Metro, somewhere far away, almost outside the city limits, in any case no longer in the old corner Konsum shop on Tucholsky Strasse. He also drove the GAZ but without the death's head flag.

During the day, tourists came to photograph the dilapidated, colorful facades with the scrap-metal sculptures out front and the large puppets that hung from nooses out the windows and swayed languidly in the wind. The people in the ruins the Shepherd had declared to be inhabited houses were now a *scene.*

The "ambiguous customers" in Fenske's cellar bothered Hans, but he understood "the historically conditioned nature of this back room" (in his words). Besides, Irina pointed out, all discussions were pointless as long as old Fenske was unwilling to relinquish his cellar.

Hans tried to make the best of it and started trading with the Russians: heavy Soviet winter coats, bayonets, fur hats, even entire uniforms with medals, basically everything that could be delivered from the depots and storage rooms of the withdrawing Red Army—valuable goods that he sold to customers from the West (mostly tourists).

After a trial phase, he was even offered an armored personnel carrier and a MiG 21. "At scrap prices, but in top shape," as Hans put it. Both were sold immediately, apparently to patrons of modern art who were springing up everywhere. An association that called itself the Mutoid Waste Company planned on reconstructing Stonehenge with tanks (in the middle of Potsdamer Platz), but the Russians were asking fifty marks a tonne for each tank, which was tempting, but add it all up (twenty to thirty tanks were needed) and Mutoid Waste couldn't afford the price. The jet fighter, in fact, stood behind the Tacheles not much later. The Tacheles welders, who still regularly showed up in the Assel (mostly because of Dodo), both swore that the MiG *landed* there "one night." The armored personnel carrier found its way into the fleet of vehicles belonging to a man by the name of Motte, who had a motor pool and rental agency for large antique vehicles "at reasonable prices" in an empty lot on Mulack Strasse. Everyone in the neighborhood knew the Ikarus bus that Motte drove to go shopping. One day, Carl noticed an IFA W50 with balloon tires. "Two hundred," Motte said, "special price for friends," but Carl just wanted to sit in the driver's cab for a bit, light the glow plugs, let the motor run and dream—just the noise and the smell. The armored personnel carrier served for a while in the battle against the neo-Nazis—the best weaponry that the Comandante was ever able to get.

In return, the Russians demanded a permanent right to hospitality in Fenske's cellar for them "and their friends" and a repeat of Carl's Kalashnikov performance. "As cultural program, so to speak," Hans explained putting his arm suddenly (and a bit too forcefully) around Carl's shoulders. "It's their greatest desire, a simple desire, Carlo, nothing more than that! German—Soviet friendship, that's us now. And if not us, who, please tell me that, Carlo!"

Hans had said "please."

Carl opened the Assel at eight in the morning. He opened the windows and doors to disperse the night's sour air. Then he turned on the coffee machine, which needed time to warm up. Carl put his notebook on the refrigerator in the kitchen and covered it with a sweater a guest had forgotten. (Things were often left behind, some rather nice.) He liked to have his notebook nearby. He kept it ready but didn't want anyone asking about it. Then he brewed some tea for the Shepherd and prepared a small breakfast, a slice of bread, butter, a bit of cheese, Hoffi didn't ask for more and often left some of it uneaten, which then became Dodo's and occasionally Dodo got everything.

Carl used the morning milking to tell Hoffi what was going on in the front of the Assel. "Dodo and Carlo," the Shepherd chuckled, propped half-upright in the straw watching Carl. When Hoffi chuckled, half of his face was completely immobile. Carl did not mention his Kalashnikov performance. For that story he invented a worker who had recently started coming to the Assel every morning for breakfast. "He's from the brigade, one of the high-voltage guys," Carl said. "A worker who serves others, then talks with them, discussing all their problems—no different than you'd always imagined, Hoffi, that's how things are now." The Shepherd nodded but said nothing. Now and then he turned his head and looked out the window. Talking was hard for him. Only during the milking did he say a word or two, like "firmer with the grip" or "good girl, Dodo."

After Hoffi fell asleep, Carl asked him, "Why 'I love you'? And what was Kleist doing on the roof?"

Hoffi looked contented. He slept a lot. All impatience and severity, if he'd ever had any, were gone. Certainly, it was a burden for Carl that aside from Hoffi, who could hardly move, Dodo would only let him and lately Irina (at least) near her udder. Then again, Carl felt bound to Hoffi the Shepherd in a way that he hadn't been conscious of before. He'd always stayed on the margins so as not to lose sight of what was most important (his writing). It was as if Carl had just become part of the pack.

Carl skimmed the names in the shift log: Domke, Kreide, Riedel, Filzer, Uffel, de Haan, and so on, twenty or thirty new names, including a man apparently called Ling Ling. No one knows if these are their real names, Carl thought, but there were some good people among them, younger than Carl, people who wanted to start inventing themselves. Or were just looking for a port, for somewhere to land, to lie low, at least for a while. Naturally flotsam also washed up, fortune seekers, posers, predators, and runaways, spongers and drifters of the so-called new era.

Meanwhile, Irina had set a fixed date for assigning the waiter and kitchen staff shifts. Hans advised her, especially with regard to everything concerned with the choice of new personnel (that's what he called them: *personnel*). In this case, too, for Irina "everyone was equal and equally worthy," a principle that Hans could only modify occasionally (and only in particular cases).

"No one has ever asked what the pay is here," Hans said, and Carl hadn't ever witnessed anyone asking either. It seemed that being part of the movement was more important to them, being in it and of it somehow, not outside in any case.

Among the new ones there was a small group that liked to retreat to the kitchen and the storeroom, to be as undisturbed as possible. These creatures, so afraid of light, had found their refuge in the Assel. And there was a second, larger group that did not fear the light of the cellar and changed everything.

There were:

Kerschek and his so-called "Kerschek afternoons," their games of chess. Each customer brought his own set. As Kerschek went from one table to another, he served, made his next move, and whenever possible insulted his opponent. His greasy hair was pulled back in a ponytail and his playing style was belligerent. "I may not look like a genius, but." That was Kerschek, and his clientele grew with a constant stream of new challengers who absolutely wanted to play him and be insulted by him.

There were:

Little Taboo and her big brother Chris from the next building, who had sought shelter in the Assel one rainy afternoon and then never left. Little Taboo was only fifteen. Irina knew that the siblings came from "difficult circumstances" and as a precaution had declared the girl taboo. Her brother Chris played the trumpet and had musician friends, and not just any musicians. He knew Polish and Hungarian bands that exploded the cellar with their music. He knew Kevin Coyne! With Little Frank's help, Chris installed a gig-grade speaker over the bar and there was no question—it was easier to work dancing. This led to a change in the shift log: the waiters and kitchen staff grouped according to their musical preferences. There were Doors nights, nights with Lou Reed, Nick Cave, U2, Pink Floyd or Genesis (*Selling England by the Pound*), and a permanent favorite, Element of Crime.

There were:

Four women named Susie. The old, maternal Susie, who wanted to kill herself or emigrate to Cuba but then settled on renovating an attic flat in the Bötzow district. The pretty Susie who was later together with Henry. The philosophical Susie from Bonn, who lived two buildings down. And the black Susie with her deep, gravelly voice, who came from the Ruhr Valley and wanted to be a restaurateur. She was the only new one who was interested in *earlier times*, in the first days of the Assel and what it used to be like. She drove a VW Scirocco, spoke French, and was doing a traineeship at the Bode Museum. Also, she had a dog. Because Carl particularly liked this Susie, he showed her the hole in the wall of Fenske's cellar; it was hidden behind a few loosely arrayed boards. Hoffi's last grand project: the tunnel to the Charité bunker.

"The Charité has a bunker?" she asked with her husky voice, grabbing Carl's arm to keep from being swallowed up by the hole.

There was:

Martha, the psychiatric nurse who was looking for *something different* and did her work with a firm hand.

There was:

Andy, who wore a fedora for three years, a present from a priest in Boston.

There was:

Tina, with large, dark-rimmed eyes, with whom everyone fell in love.

And there was:

The Brazilian who was only called Brazil and lived at Irina's for a while. Brazil organized the piano. When he worked, there was tango dancing, even though there wasn't enough room.

There was:

The tall, good man they called Godewind. Godewind from Hiddensee, who spent winters in Berlin and at the first warmth of spring returned to his island.

There was:

Filzer. One day, as a sales rep for ready-made soups and cleaning products, Filzer stumbled down the stairs of the Assel. On his first shift as cook, Filzer introduced three new soups: Japanese I, Japanese II, and Japanese III. They had very thin noodles, freeze-dried with chicken, beef, or shrimp. First you pulled the tab from the plastic container and a small, white dust cloud rose (like when an ancient tomb is opened). Then you poured boiling water on the contents and the unbelievable happened: what looked gray and dead before suddenly blossomed. It was a kind of resurrection, a Rose of Jericho that steamed and smelled enticing—Carl had never seen anything like it. As a final step, there was nothing to do but carefully pour the Japanese rose into a white café-au-lait bowl that had (if possible) been rinsed out. The thin-sided bowls, almost translucent in the light of the counter, were used for everything, also for salad and potato soup. The rose could unfurl completely only in this bowl. Because they were too hot at first, Carl often carried them out on a small, round cutting board with a fresh slice of flatbread—the soup smelled beguilingly good.

The smell reminded Carl of his childhood, of the Saturday noodle soups at twelve thirty, of the small, sticky, dark bottle of Maggi that made tiny gurgling noises when shaken over the soup—and of the Maggi itself, which he couldn't get enough of. Maybe your parents have to be far enough away before everything returns as desire, Carl thought.

When Carl arrived in the evening, Rico was sitting in Effi's kitchen, and why not since he was Freddy's father and lived next door. Carl had promised Effi that he would find her a wardrobe, whereupon Rico offered (unasked) to help carry the wardrobe upstairs. In the same breath, Rico announced that he was very happy not to need anything like that, he wouldn't know what to do with it anyway since he didn't own much more than what he wore on his body, and so on, the whole hermit philosophy, half-monk, half-Thoreau.

A wardrobe would be "good firewood at best," Rico said and Effi looked at the floor in distress.

Freddy's goodnight story: should Rico take over? Or should Carl keep telling it? Or both together, Carl and Rico in a duet? The Little Dragon with guitar and song? Rico did have an astoundingly good voice, if a little schmaltzy, as could be heard from next door (if Carl was any judge). Until then, Rico hadn't done anything with Freddy. Maybe that will come as a *next step*, as my mother would say, thought Carl.

They would already be asleep, but then would hear him singing at night in the courtyard. Carl was not deceived: the song was for Effi. Rico was drunk and playing the troubadour.

PART VII

PART VII

WE ENTERED A HOUSE IN BAD SODEN

Inge and Walter's next step was to terminate their Gelnhausen lodgings. What Carl's parents were now looking for was *nothing too large* and above all *nothing permanent*, as if they wouldn't (or couldn't) seriously settle down anywhere again. Compared to their earlier existence—thirty years in the same town, fifty years in the same hilly east Thuringian region—their new life seemed a kind of nomadism and fittingly, their search for new accommodation was not done very systematically.

"We entered a house in Bad Soden," Carl's mother wrote. It sounded like the opening of a novel. A bright, gleaming stone staircase led them downstairs. There were only two conditions attached to the large basement apartment: first, no alterations, and second, lawn care. There was a large cast-iron bed under a window that was just beneath the ceiling and looked onto a large, freshly mown, gradually ascending meadow behind the house. Even standing on her tiptoes, Inge could see nothing but grass, as if she'd shrunk or were looking out of her own grave. The grass had an underwater irrigation system that could be controlled from the bedroom (right from the grave, Inge thought). It (the lawn) had to be kept "always fresh and green," the man from Bad Soden explained. Maybe they sensed that we're slaves, Walter said later—one of Walter's so-called jokes, as Inge would say, and the end of the novel.

They worked their way through the addresses. Furnished apartments were rare in the Main-Kinzig-Kreis district—three or four ads a week, which Inge circled with a ballpoint pen. They used the 280E. Where the car was parked on the street, there were no longer any oil drips. Walter had also repaired the fan. In his free time, he lay under the Mercedes. Or he walked along the Kinzig with his accordion and played for the river. "He's either tinkering with the car or with his rhythm," Inge wrote Carl, "which does him good."

Mosborn, Rossbach, and Bad Orb—furnished lodgings generally required garden work or pet care, occasionally also care of an elderly or ill person. One of their last stops was on the second floor of a newly constructed building in Bad Orb. The man lived alone with his three large, fawn-colored mastiffs: "My animals are completely free here." It sounded tolerant and liberal. The man's forearms were freshly bandaged, and he wore a peaked cap of worn, gray leather. What was most memorable was the dogs' wild scratching and whining outside the door while the owner showed Inge and Walter their "new home," waving his thickly bandaged arms around: the built-in kitchen and the light-brown tiled stone floor with *radiant heating*—a technology that was new to Inge and Walter. The bus stop just opposite also seemed an advantage.

In the end, they decided on a small attic apartment in a place called Meerholz, a few kilometers to the south, across the Kinzig River, on the other side of the valley. The house was in a drab housing development with chain-link fencing and a paved turning loop; it was a brick building. In the front garden were two amphorae that looked antique. There was an enormous flower calyx over the mailboxes—so large that you could put the mail in it, too. Inge briefly imagined a plant that gulped down Carl's letters, which she waited for so eagerly every day.

Strictly speaking, it was just a room with a sink at the end of a long, windowless hallway. At the head of the staircase was the toilet, which they shared with a young man who was renting the room next to theirs. They never saw him face-to-face, only his dark outline in the hallway, diffuse and blurry in the half-light. The young man was "very considerate," as Carl's mother put it. The only noise that came from his room was a soft ticking, like that of a large clock. When he used the toilet, the ticking came from there as if he, himself, were the clock.

The Floeth family lived on the ground floor—the landlords were friends with old Ursula from Gelnhausen, "a really lovely coincidence," Inge wrote Carl. "Our being from the East is the reason they let us have the room. Can you imagine, Carl?" Whenever possible, Inge assessed things positively: we did this right. The week went well. Those were pleasant days. We accomplished a great deal then. In that case we really did everything right. And so on.

One disadvantage was that there was no bathroom in the garret. "If you'd like to take a bath, you are welcome to come downstairs," Mrs. Floeth had said on the day they moved in. Mr. Floeth was retired. Mrs. Floeth still worked as an X-ray technician. She was a large, warm-hearted woman with her hair pinned up who reminded Walter of a Bavarian actress. *Bagdad Café* was the title of the movie that Carl's father had seen in the dining hall of the transit camp on the North Sea. Back then, feeling forlorn on the North Sea, he'd fallen in love with this woman, with her kindness, and especially with her courage and vitality. Her name was Marianne Sägebrecht, or Jasmine, actually, the woman in the film was named Jasmine, but Walter had recognized that the kindness and courage were Marianne Sägebrecht's.

A few years earlier, the Floeth children had lived upstairs. There was no television, only a radio, which didn't bother the Bischoffs—breakfast with the radio, "that's our luxury," is how Inge put it. It didn't sound like an elevated standard of living (which would have been a goal—and an explanation), on the contrary: things from earlier surfaced in their thoughts and played a role in what happened to them: "Our first radio, Carl, do you remember? The Star 111 with the golden speaker screen?"

Was that the actual direction of their wanderings? Back in time, back into homelessness? In order to recollect who they'd been and what they'd wanted back then? *Before my birth*, thought Carl. He found this thought oddly touching: his parents without him, before parenthood. He phrased it like this (and only for himself): Star 111 is something that was right and good in their old, previous life. A memory on the road. A guiding star for the journey.

At the end of October, after courses in Hamburg and Paderborn, Walter Bischoff returned to the White Villa for a week. Every afternoon, Inge met him there after work, a four-kilometer walk. On Friday, she set out earlier than usual; she'd allowed time for errands. As always, she passed the Coleman Kaserne, where the entrance gate was unexpectedly standing open. With her short, determined steps and almost without hesitation, Inge entered the compound: "It just drew me in."

The base seemed abandoned. Only a small troop of soldiers was marching behind the barracks, a dark, supple outline, moving off slowly. The site was vast. In the middle of the courtyard was a pond, encircled with shrubbery. A dock emerged from a strip of reeds. A GI stood on the shore, half in the reeds; his bearing was at once fluid, dreamy, and military. He was looking at the dock and at the small boat that was tied to it. A light wind rose, and the hull of the boat knocked gently against the dock. The soldier just stood there, without moving, like in a painting, but then, as if the soldier had actually only been waiting for Inge, he walked directly to her. "May I help you, ma'am?"—Inge understood that much, none of what followed. Russian would have been easier. The GI handed Inge a leaflet and began speaking to her in a broken German that sounded lovely, almost intimate.

Because Inge still hadn't said a single word, the soldier took the leaflet from her again and pointed at this and that: tank course, *football*, barbecue. He offered to accompany Inge, but where? Inge Bischoff was now confused and explained what she actually had planned. The GI smiled wisely and pointed at a larger building behind the pond; he touched his fingertips of his flatly extended hand to the bill of his cap and walked off.

The store with groceries was next to the officers' casino. It all seemed very plain, a few shelves, baskets, and freezers, but all the products were American as far as Inge could tell. She was too nervous to look more closely. And was she really the only white person in the store? And was that the reason they were watching her? Inge's head began to throb, every movement became complicated: a white woman from the East. On an army base of the United States of America. Inge was suddenly aware of the impossibility of the situation, the absolute impossibility, and her heart stopped. She stared at a ketchup advertisement she couldn't read and leaned her hand on a piece of frozen meat— the cold ran up her arm like an electric shock and the ground swayed beneath her feet: so this is how it ends, Inge thought, *here* between the shelves, this is where they catch you, here you finally fall to your knees, ready to confess to everything . . .

"Yes, yes," Inge cried, "I ventured too far, just *too far!*"

When Inge came to, someone was pressing an ice-cold bottle of Coca-Cola against her neck; she was sitting in the casino. Maybe it was just a normal café. It looked completely normal, American-normal, with artificial-leather benches and tables screwed in place. She was surrounded by women in uniform with yellow chevrons on their arms. She nodded at them and that was what Inge always recounted later: "Something in their faces immediately communicated itself." She couldn't describe it more precisely. Not just friendliness, "also *a need*," as Inge put it, that was immediately very familiar to her, completely familiar.

"It was the friendliness of those who have to live in a foreign country, of those who aren't at home. Those who are ready to offer the warmth that they miss," Inge wrote Carl.

Inge recognized one of the women right away—from early morning training. For Inge it was a reunion, unexpected. She was Winona, her daughter Kathleen. Winona laughed and showed her large teeth. She didn't remember the woman on the balcony. She looked Native American, dark complexioned, black eyebrows. Inge drank her Coke, almost greedily, her dizzy spell (panic, collapse, or whatever it was) had made her thirsty. Winona smoked a Pall Mall and talked. The waitstaff brought food and so it was time for the first real hamburger in Inge's life—Inge Bischoff, fifty years and one month old. Winona called her *Eenguh.*

Outside by the pond, the leaflet-GI immediately marched up to her; he kissed Winona and took the little one in his arms. "This is Johnny," Winona said and offered Inge her pack of Pall Malls.

When Inge left the base, music sounded from the loudspeakers—as if the party were starting just then.

For Walter and Inge to stay on Garten Strasse was his mother's only wish, the boss had told them. Shortly before they were to move out in early November, a door was built at the top of the stairs, which closed off the Bischoffs' floor—like their own apartment. In addition, a telephone line was installed for separate connection, a fine, thin cable, nearly invisible. Until then, the only telephone in the building was in old Zollnay's living room on a small cabinet under the window. That had never bothered Carl's parents much. They were used to living without a telephone and, compared to the situation in Gera with Mrs. Schuler and her canine harbinger of misfortune, there wasn't much difference. They'd only knocked two or three times at the old woman's door to make a phone call and even then only because it was necessary to reach someone in the White Villa quickly.

The renovations did not change the Bischoffs' plan to move out; there was a stronger force driving them. But having their own door and their own telephone behind it gave Inge some breathing space in which she began to formulate a new and marvelous thought: she could talk on the telephone—with Carl. Just three days later Carl held her letter in his hands. Inge thought of the telephone booth in the Gera-Langenberg post office, run by Sybille Bethmann, her old friend from her exercise group.

ANDROGYNOUS

"To come to the most pressing matter first . . ." It was as if Carl's writing hand were paralyzed. As soon as he straightened the paper on the workbench and held the pen between his fingers, he felt the stiffness in his wrist—all of a sudden, everything in him balked. He faltered in the middle of a word and regressed to a kind of childish scrawl. He recalled tent sites and vacation camping grounds and the duty "to make contact at least once a week." Failing to get in touch would cause others to worry, or make them twice as worried as they already were. It would be ungrateful. It was actually hard to believe how completely his writing hand failed in those moments far from home. Every word had to be coerced. Even the mere length of a word! Those marks that seemed forcibly connected—small curve, large curve, dash, and backslash—his wrist felt wooden, as did his brain when he tried to formulate a sentence in his thoughts but failed because he had gone completely witless, stupid, vapid, he'd plummeted into ignorance—or, in other words: he had become so far removed (in no time at all!) from all the talent and analytical skills that were necessary in order to become once again, there, at home, his parents' child (the schoolchild, too) and fulfill the related tasks and duties . . .

The beginning had always seemed easy: you affixed the spit-moistened stamps exactly in the marked box. Sometimes there was a word like "stamp" or "affix stamp here," which sounded encouraging: the card would be stamped, made ready for the mailing route, without a doubt a proper initial step, although with its own pitfalls: the fact that the stamp had now been used brought additional pressure.

Carl often wanted to begin with the address because it seemed easiest, and yet he realized that he absolutely could not remember it. The name, yes, but the house number and the postal code simply eluded his grasp even though he tried very hard to recall them. Evidently, he had even forgotten where he was at home— and was he still that same child if he couldn't remember? On the one hand, there was something strangely seductive, almost rebellious about this condition of self-forgetfulness at the end of vacation. On the other hand, behind it yawned an immeasurable sense of desolation, as if he were now utterly alien and alone in the world.

For a few seconds, Carl was gripped by the question of whether Inge and Walter were just as far removed, so far that they (essentially) were also no longer the (his) parents . . .

He stood up and went to the sink. His lying face in the mirror. He bent over the sink and splashed his face with water. The coolness on his eyes was pleasant. He now saw the room—the kitchen, the workbench that was his writing space. He saw the letters and envelopes: a small, sloppy pile. The sketches on the wall that he had labeled almost a year ago as "The Way of My Parents." A few of the places plotted in pencil were faded or too cursorily marked, not neatly enough. Write neatly and clearly, thought Carl. He sat back down and wrote.

First the tale of a "really good offer for a position in hospitality." Then the tale of a plan to continue his studies—in Berlin. He'd have to catch up on some language courses, Latin was required now and a special certificate for English. In addition, he had brought along his masonry tools so he could always earn something—"and, yes, I'm actually no longer in Gera," Carl wrote. "I have a small apartment in Berlin in a very quiet area, nothing special, but not a bad building. I imagine you're surprised and . . ."

Lots of good actions. And only one failure—he'd abandoned his post. The rearguard. Something demanded that he turn this fact into a well-considered, forward-looking decision. Anything else would be meaningless and just an additional source of worry, Carl thought, even though Inge and Walter were the ones to be worried about.

This embellished résumé had a strange effect: a few things no longer seemed impossible. In any case, Carl counted as a *student* again, to have access to the many advantages of a student ID. He was registered in the German Literature Department, which had its offices on the Museum Island, not far from the Assel. He hadn't set foot in the building (a structure as black as a reef and covered with bullet holes), but every night after work, he passed it on his walk home and sometimes stuck his index finger in one of the holes—just to feel a dream he could not forget.

In this dream, Effi had been a snail. Sitting in the hollow of one of those bullet holes, she had said, "I'm androgynous." Touching Effi in the hole (her moist, slimy body) meant triggering a kind of miracle: then a bell rang deep in the building and the German Literature Department opened and freed the way for their joint happiness. In the dream, it hadn't been clear exactly which hole the snail (Effi) was in and Carl tried a new one each time he passed.

Drenched in sweat, Carl started awake. His raft lay crosswise, it was night. He remained still for a time then stretched his arm out on the floor (as an anchor in the current) until it was ice-cold. After a while he got up, went into the kitchen, and reread his letter.

What he'd written reminded Carl of the notes of apology from his childhood, penned in the light of a tiny pocket lamp (in bed, under the covers) and furtively placed late at night on the shoe cabinet in the hall, where his mother, the first to pass it in the morning, would find it. Among the extensive note communications that their small family had established, the *shoe cabinet note* was one of the last means (in cases of larger infractions) of reducing the size of the expected punishment—confinement to his room or, even worse, loss of television privileges, and in extreme cases, both. The notes always ended the same way and, because of his poor spelling, always had the same mistake:

"I want to *improove* myself."

Letter in hand, Carl returned to the bedroom. He opened the stove door and burned the paper. The following morning, he went to the post office on Kollwitz Platz and sent a telegram listing his Berlin address. Then he treated himself to a pudding pretzel, strolled home and wrote down what (actually) had happened to him. In broad outlines at first.

FROM THE SEA

"They suggested that you go up against one of them. They want to make it a contest," Hans said, framing it as a request. He eyed Carl with a mixture of respect and unease.

"They're threatening to *bust up* the Assel, whatever that's supposed to mean."

The Russians offered a hundred marks a match as a starting fee. Daddy Vassily *privately* offered an extra fifty marks for each new record. Four marks a second, Carl calculated, plus the bonus. Fewer shifts, more time to write. It only made sense if he were able to be more relaxed about it. I almost shot a man, thought Carl. His stupid, old military service catching up with him out of the blue, an ancient pattern. His heart was still beating in his throat on his way home that night and for days he couldn't slip back into that precious sphere of absentmindedness and tiredness in which the words revealed themselves to him the way he needed them—raw, untouched by thought.

One way would be not to take it so seriously, to see it more as a game, and it shouldn't turn into anything else in any case, which, on the one hand, is why he could turn down the offer. On the other, Carl felt responsible—not just for the Assel and the pack that took him in, but also for the Shepherd in the stall and not least for Dodo. It was the feeling of being friends, being part of something greater, and the feeling that it was now time to be there for them.

As so often, Carl entered Fenske's cellar, this time not as a waiter, however, but as "a poet who has served," as Daddy Vassily generously announced him. Carl was happy to do it. A poet—with Russians, that was not something to be ashamed of, on the contrary, it was a title of honor that required humility and earned love.

A red banner covered the table, on which the weapon lay next to a blindfold and even a small bottle of gun oil. Everything was prepared. One of the two salon chairs had become Vassily's usual seat (where all the chiefs had sat, thought Carl).

"*Tri, dwa, odin . . .*"

Vassily counted down, as if for the launch of a Soyuz rocket, and clapped his hands. Now Wednesday was Kalashnikov Day.

And Fenske's cellar was filling up again. The places left empty after the building captains withdrew were soon filled by Vassily's *friends*: soldiers in civilian clothing (according to the rumor), the Mazda dealer from next door who bought used Ladas on behalf of the Russians, two Irish construction workers, various people "from the scene," as Hans put it, and sometimes also the guys who acted as "the girls' protectors." All in all, a complicated group, who wanted to "discuss a few things" or just be entertained and who drank goat milk with vodka. Dodo's milk had long become legendary, a magic potion, if you hadn't sampled it, you weren't with it that autumn. Because Dodo never produced more than four liters of milk a day, they only served small portions, which made the drinks all the more precious.

New competitors showed up who were better than Carl, but he also got faster. He now had a practice weapon (with a folding stock, his own *Kashi*, as he sometimes called it). The Russians had wrapped it in a blanket and hidden it in the tunnel to the hospital bunker. After a few weeks, Carl took it home because it was much easier. In his apartment, he could practice undisturbed.

When he examined the gun closely, a few woodlice fled from the blanket over his workbench. In a flash, Carl grabbed a glass and crushed them all, one after the other. Their slate-gray shells shone, and they felt strange: like the prickly vibration of an extremely fine mechanism between his fingertips; but also like greasy meat. Greasy, ivory-colored meat. After a few seconds, the clever creatures had rolled themselves up into large globules. "They breathe through gills," Ragna had said. "They come from the sea."

"Tell me a little something—about the sea," Carl whispered and had to chuckle. Then he put his ear to the glass and listened.

*

There were days without Freddy when Carl slept at Effi's. Her gloominess (or whatever he was supposed to call it) required him to be strong. On one side, a vague presentiment of failure, and on the other, intention and discipline. Mornings, he sat in the kitchen and wrote. He listened for Effi to wake, usually around noon. Until then, he tried to get as much done as he could. He was freezing. He would turn on all the burners on the cooker and they glowed like lava; the smell of their heat was raw and reminded him of the air in factories. They never really warmed up the room.

When Effi started to stir, he put on water for coffee. He set the cups on the icebox next to the bed then crawled into bed and snuggled up to her. In a certain sense, it was a reward; she let him do it. She lay on her side, one hand under her cheek and with the other she sought Carl, hardly moving. Sometimes she also said, "Don't move," or "Wait," and when he then felt the velvety waves, it only lasted a few seconds. "You there?" She was proud that it worked that way, without Carl having to do anything.

Over coffee, they made plans. The days when Freddy stayed at Nora's were rare and precious. Carl would have stayed, but Effi wanted to be alone. "I so rarely get to be alone, you know."

In the evening, they go to the cinema: once again, Krzysztof Kieślowski's A Short Film About Love, Effi's favorite film. The beautiful Magda and the young Tomek. In Magda, Effi sees the ideal of an independent woman, level-headed, content, a woman who comes home in the evening to be on her own and to paint. Or to meet lovers. In addition, there's the boy, a voyeur, who spies on her, who admires and desires her—through a telescope.

"But they're not actually a couple. She mocks him, he nearly kills himself and only that arouses her interest," Carl says.

But when were people together? The good, old-fashioned word for it, or was it not used anymore?

In Babylon Mitte, French films from the seventies are shown. They see *Themroc* with Michel Piccoli, in which a police officer is cooked and eaten, and *The Last Tango in Paris*, with the chewing gum scene at the end that Carl likes so much. He's rapturous and wants to talk about it with Effi, but she remains silent. In everything that makes an impression on her, Effi sees first and foremost nature, instinct, the animalistic, something that art is made from, something that you recognize or not, that you know about or not, that you either belong to or not—not anything that can be talked about. The chewing gum, well, fine. Talking about the chewing gum that the dying Marlon Brando sticks under the balcony railing before he drops dead probably means being on the other side, in the realm of thought and theory, not in the realm of art. Carl asks himself why he brought up the chewing gum.

Only later did he realize why: it was pure euphoria. He'd reacted to the movie like a child (which he often did), in this case like a child completely taken with a film about sex (to put it simply), and maybe that was where the contradiction lay. The chewing gum scene stood for everything and also *for that*, without it being necessary to mention *that*. The chewing gum scene stood for the butter scene and yes, certainly, Carl was prudish and also his feelings were hurt. Effi had caught him out even though he agreed with her about nature, he was on her side (the side of art), but now he was compelled to maintain his position, compelled to speak nonsense; she was pushing him away, to the other side and not for the first time.

And yes: he felt it in his groin when he sat next to Effi while Marlon Brando (48) rubbed butter over the doll-like Maria Schneider's (19) asshole. Should he try it with Effi? And was her remark perhaps meant as a hint in that direction? And were all these thoughts not proof that Effi was right?

EFFI

Effi reaches for Carl's hand. She looks at his watch, then at his arm and then up his arm to his neck (the way an animal looks over its prey).

On the evenings she does drypoint, Effi listens to sitar music. "Twenty strings, Carl, imagine." Her contempt for her own work and for success, which (as Carl sees it) requires only a few small changes, mere technicalities, underscores her position. Meanwhile Carl is just a former builder who doesn't have an artistic bone in his body.

Effi reads little, but reverently. Her books are wrapped in newspaper. They lie on the breadbox in the kitchen or on the bed. When she talks about them (which rarely happens), her voice becomes low—and serious. Even if a book is short, she takes a long time to read it. She prefers older works, her selection is peculiar: she reads *Adolphe* by Benjamin Constant, *The Layman on Wisdom and the Mind* by Nicholas of Cusa, and she was especially taken with Balzac's *The Wild Ass's Skin*. "Do you think there's anything really new in literature?" She is not interested in reading the new French authors Carl tries to impress her with. What Carl tells her about them is enough.

Now and again, Carl thinks of a moment in Paris: they're standing on the bank of the Seine, looking over at the bright, sunlit buildings across the river.

Carl points to one of them: "What would you say if I'd bought that building—for us? If that were our house?"

Effi: "Then you would really have surprised me for once."

*

Effi gave Carl a small calendar that opened like an accordion and is kept closed—and this is the key feature—by a magnet in the border. It's a strange and, in any case, impractical calendar. The kind of calendar that is clearly a useless gift. Only once they're back in Ryke Strasse does Carl open it wide enough so that all the weeks and months are unfolded. Only then does he notice: over every week, lightly written in pencil, is "Effi," fifty-two times.

Effi loves music that is "cheerful." "That sounds cheerful," she says about a short, fast blues track on Carl's favorite cassette, "I find it very gutsy." About the rest of the tape they're listening to in the car, driving on the highway with a cassette player on the back seat that needs four new batteries every three hours (Carl has a whole bag of batteries in the trunk), Effi doesn't say a thing, not a word for ninety minutes. "He was at Kerouac's grave, on his tour," Carl tells her (meaning the singer on his favorite cassette tape). "He was playing in a warm-up band for Frank Zappa, unbelievable, right?" Why is he saying this? Why is he defending his music? Why does he always get defensive with Effi?

"Cheerful" has the verve that Carl lacks.

Effi used to look like a hippie girl. That's over. She now prefers to wear stylish clothing as if she doesn't actually value it much. Elegant and scruffy at the same time, if that's possible.

For a time, Effi creates "small things." Watercolor on parchment, framed with elderberry twigs that she collects in the bomb crater copse. The watercolor, no larger than the base of a bottle and as light as air, is sewn into the elderberry twig frame with black thread that she also uses to fasten the twigs together. Carl marvels at the construction. It is easily destroyed, crushed, between thumb and forefinger . . . Carl doesn't know why this occurs to him, it's just a thought. Covering the paint is a web of very fine lines, maybe of ink. As usual, Effi says nothing about them. Only when Carl asks does she say: "It's kid's stuff."

She gives Carl a small carving. A kind of underwater creature with a few tentacles and a cleft fin. A sentence is etched into the creature's stomach: "I AM A NICE ANIMAL! DON'T HURT ME."

Effi has changed. Her eyes glow. She says a few offensive things and uses clichéd expressions Carl has never heard from her and then: "I know everything about you. Don't forget it." And: "That's why I'm here, so you can also experience it." (She means life *as it really is*.) And a bit later: "I'm not good for you." It sounds like a rejection of Carl *as an artist*. As if she'd given up on him.

Effi had done some baking, she calls: "*Leutschers*, cake!" *Leutschers* is Thuringian. "As children we always said *Leutschers* instead of *Leute*—for our people."

A crude thought: Carl wants to cash in Effi's value, to take advantage of it. He has a right to it; he has earned a right to part-nership, the ugly word, but it fits more exactly than other words: because it encompasses both business and affection without revealing anything about the balance of the two. As if it were possible, for example, to pursue love with elements of business (in a businesslike way) or run a business with elements of love (lovingly). But Carl has never thought that way.

Effi is grateful. Nothing is self-evident to her. She treats Carl with respect (the word is too sober but catches the essential part of it), although she senses it: how much Carl needs her. Then the other Effi: unapproachable, reserved. And her sudden outbreaks of scorn, her disparagement of *everything*, which frighten Carl. Something he is not equal to. The tired "hello" at the door, the half-kiss. Carl is hurt, he takes it all personally and at the same time tries not to show it. Lying in wait for signs of love.

Effi and Rico? Rico is not only the original of Freddy, he is also a representative of *cheerfulness*. He acts as if he's living a life of his own, but he doesn't really have anything to do. He hangs around, plays the guitar or stands behind his door, listening for the opportunity to run into Effi "by chance."

Living next door to Rico means: guitar and singing or a soft but audible whistling—the Rico-sound is always present now. And Rico actually does play in a band; *he* has nature, the groove, rhythm in his blood.

Did Effi know that Rico would come? And if so, since when? Did they plan it together? No, that is absurd. It's absurd to think this way. The question is: does Carl have to defend the fortress and show the flag?

Soft whistling at night.

We're no longer alone, Carl thinks, and won't ever be again.

IN SLIPPERS

Carl's parents were silent. Their answer to his confession was: no letter, no telegram. Carl tried to call them in Gelnhausen several times from the post office on Kollwitz Platz. Each time there was only the old woman on the receiver and each time she merely crowed two words: "Too late, too late."

Yes, I left the place I'd agreed to stay in, Carl thought, but after all no one could expect him to stay there *forever*, as the rearguard in Gera . . . He started to worry. He leafed through Inge's letters; maybe he'd overlooked something, a hint, a clue.

But no, there was nothing aside from her repeated mentions of their "next step" and her claims that they knew what they wanted, and so on. He arranged the letters into a chronological pile. His mother's handwriting: familiar. The addresses: foreign. Foreign like the stations on a day trip: Lahn Strasse, Rhein Strasse, Berg Strasse, Herzbach Weg, Garten Strasse, and now a street called "In Börner," whatever that was supposed to mean. "In Börner in the Meerholz neighborhood," Carl whispered and wrote the name meaning sea-wood in his notebook: Meerholz.

Maybe they had always had this dream, thought Carl—an adventurous life with hiking boots on their feet and light packs (aside from the accordion case). There were things that spoke against this: for all their adventurousness, Carl recognized in his parents a not-untypical rigidity; in any case this was not sheer euphoria. There was something stiff, something exaggerated to their determination that bordered on desperation. "I am determined to take all this a bit more calmly," Inge had written him just a few weeks earlier and her next sentence turned it upside down: "I'm sure that if you were close by, Carl, it would be easier for us!"

What was the point, Carl wondered, why this forceful break? Maybe it was a kind of self-conquest? A forceful wrestling with age and weariness that inevitably creeps into the body and mind at fifty, the fear of death? Is that what was driving them? And wasn't it absurd to think about your own parents this way? Whom you love and miss and haven't sent any sign to for weeks now?

Although Carl was earning quite well with the proceeds of his Kalashnikov number (or whatever he might call it), he was smart and careful enough to sign up for one or two evenings a week at the counter or in the kitchen. From the shift assignments Carl learned that his status in the Assel had changed; almost all the new staff, with whom he essentially had no connection, wanted to work with him, even the chess monster Kerschek, but in the end Ragna's name was always next to his in the shift log, as if they were a couple.

Because we're friends, Carl thought, two tool people. And a fur cap kiss, but that was long past. And Carl no longer thought of Ragna's hands (not necessarily, anyway), and when he did then it was because of the nearly unbearable odor that the working ladies brought into the cellar, a smell that surrounded them, an aura, both sweet and sour, if that was possible; they overcharged the atmosphere ("perfume and sperm," according to Hans). The guests around their table started drinking faster; Carl saw the thirst in their eyes, their lust; he saw their stiff backs and the way their breathing became too deep.

It wasn't only the Assel that had changed, Ragna had too. She no longer wore any fur or cap. Her black hair was smooth and shone in the half-light. She no longer looked like a creature from ancient and early history. On her bar shifts she wore what Hans called "her little black dress." Anyone standing at the bar could watch her powerful arms at work, her snow-white skin. Only her hobnailed ankle boots recalled the old Ragna from the revolutionary tool archive—and her way of walking, which was more a kind of marching. "She molted, but she's still the same animal," Hans summed it up.

Working the bar, Carl never asked what anyone would like, he didn't ask "What'll it be?" or some similar nonsense. He only asked, "You've decided"—without a question mark. Are you the waiter? No. This here is just a man going from table to table, making notes, scrawling on a pad with a pen. In fact, he had to write *everything* down, every single beer, large or small. Carl didn't have the bandwidth, as if his brain were already completely occupied (inhabited, Hoffi would have said) by the noise of the Assel and its submarine tour through the night, a mind-boggling amount of detail that blocked out everything else.

Closing time was a battle. Initial attempts were made around three, accompanied by a flood of orders and stubborn exchanges. Meaningful conversations set in. The last and very last rounds were rung, invitations offered. Generous invitations, compliments, declarations of love, somewhat later came a burst of hatred and tears and always the same story: the attempt at the very last minute to start a great friendship, namely with the waiter, the last person still around in this world. After him, all that was left was night, death, eternal loneliness, and so on.

There were assaults, scuffles. Guests who didn't want to pay. Guests who gave away their money. One guest who climbed back into the bar through the window over the working ladies' table ("tart table," Hans said), stepping through the glass and slicing his leg open from top to bottom, blood everywhere . . . Sometimes, though, things were different. It happened very rarely, but it did happen: suddenly you took a shine to the final customer, for whatever reason. Maybe just because she looked sad. Because she was beautiful *and* sad. You locked up the Assel, turned off the lights except for one candle, way at the back on the very last table. "And that's fine, Carl," Ragna said, "more than fine."

Two half-naked working ladies who hadn't been picked up yet were standing in the passage, changing. Carl tidied up the storeroom and carried the cardboard from the empty juice and schnapps boxes past them into the courtyard. It was tight in the passage and the women (these were no longer the kindergarten teachers from the early days) made a few comments, but nothing that could make Carl lose his composure. On the way back, he caught a sharp elbow in the ribs, in the dim light he saw the face: no skin, just crumbling makeup, cracks and aged indifference— death in slippers flashed through Carl's mind. "Like death in slippers," was what his father always said when someone looked really ill. The expression sounded harsh, but his father's voice was always soft, sympathetic actually, when he said it. What fascinated Carl were the slippers—death wearing slippers made Carl associate a specific way of walking with it: if you hear shuffling, then it's death. So lift your feet, boy. Sit up straight. Don't make a face like that—these were the first measures taken against death, only now did Carl understand. Were parents always right?

I want to improove myself.

The woman wasn't smiling. She would have liked to knock him down, Carl was sure of it.

"Did you do the cardboard already?" Ragna called down to him as she measured off the Assel with her hammering steps, clearing up the last glasses.

The universe arched over the courtyard: sucks your brain out, right through your eyes, Carl thought. A small light was lit in the stall and Dodo's goat smell wafted over to him. "Doing the cardboard" was the most disliked task at closing. When Carl tried to flatten the rebellious boxes (first with his hands, then with his feet), he staggered, flailing his arms in the dark and coughing, and was suddenly overcome with the feeling of being completely isolated, as if he'd drifted off. The sky was too high, too clear, the fresh night air was like ice in his face and it sliced into his lungs. After ten hours in the U-boat (the tightly packed bodies and the strange greed with which they sucked in the spent air of everyone's breath, full of tobacco smoke, sweat, and bodily smells, and then breathed it back out, on and on, from mouth to mouth, until everyone in their trance was intimately connected and like each other), Carl no longer had the strength to face the world outside. "And we were woodlice in the Assel / and our breathing was a rattling / as if through gills in and out," Carl blabbered in the direction of Krausnick Park and crept back into the cellar.

"Mulackritze or Sophien Club?" Ragna asked. Carl couldn't hear her, but he read her lips. His head was pounding, from inside, as if raw. It was the dull echo of the music still beating behind his temples. The metallic blue carnival garlands of the used-car dealer flashed right into his brain. Their path through the polished Mazda front bumpers, across the wasteland to August Strasse. The Car of the Week, enveloped by the murmur of silence. The Christmas deal. Payment in installments with strings of lights. Carl tried to force his eyelids up over his smoke-inflamed eyeballs and succeeded; for a while, he stumbled blindly through the darkness at Ragna's side, streaked with tears—Ragna looked at him.

"I have really sensitive eyes."

"Completely normal," Ragna replied. Carl sensed that she saw something in him but didn't know what. Just that it was good.

The Sophien Club on Sophien Strasse was the port for the last drink of the night, the after-work spot for bar staff. Here the most urgent stories were told, stories filled with warnings and special intel about the wild lands—spreading ever deeper into the darkest, most remote back courtyards—of pubs, dives, and living rooms with pop-up bars.

Standing next to Ragna, Carl was bathed in an atmosphere of warming attention. There were always a few people who tried to talk to Ragna or just to stand near enough to listen to her rough, penetrating voice.

A woman who kept her mouth very close to Ragna's cheek after pushing Carl aside told her about Ici on August Strasse, "a black hole" that didn't pay her more than four marks an hour. Carl listened to the story or didn't listen. He drank wine. He was pleasantly tired and relished being the man at Ragna's side. Now and again, Ici's founder was referred to as the king of the neighborhood—no one knew why. Maybe because he looked like an aged Jesus, a Jesus without the crucifixion (if that's possible), but maybe only because he spoke French and always looked like he was constantly thinking of the word Montmartre. The king and his wife presided from an antique sofa near the bar and drank white wine all day long. The taproom was very narrow and decorated with terrible pictures arrayed in "Petersburg hanging," as the queen emphasized. She had painted most of them herself, it was said, and whoever was not prepared to show her work *visible* respect, whether through close observation or an artistically minded pose, had a bad hand of cards in Ici. "They constantly summon me to the sofa and whisper comments to me—which people they like, which ones I'm supposed to serve first, and so on. All day long," said the woman with her mouth near Ragna's cheek, so close that in the fervor of her story, her lips could (and did) give Ragna brief, accidental kisses, which didn't seem to bother Ragna, quite the contrary.

In the nightly circles of the free waiters, cooks, and bartenders, Carl understood that the Shepherd's ideas had been so peculiar and so big that they could only be misunderstood. Here in the Sophien Club, they all talked about "Hoffi" (as if they were his friends) and repeated statements the Shepherd was reputed to have made, more or less. As they did, their eyes shone as if an ancient, secret longing that could never be completely grasped was being put into words: the all-encompassing fellowship and community, concern for others out on the streets or wherever, the extension of the good to all, that brotherhood to which one had once been completely open, completely and utterly.

"When they were still grateful for the onset of freedom," the Shepherd had said. "When they didn't yet know what it means."

After his withdrawal into the stall (and into silence), the Shepherd's prestige had expanded into the fabulous. Hoffi had become a legend, but Hans also had a more-than-respectable reputation; justifiably so, thought Carl: Hans was a man who cultivated friendships and knew how to use them, a man who radiated something intoxicating, like a blessing, and—this was his latest coup—had begun to build a "mobile gallery" that used uninhabited buildings for studios and exhibitions. Hans was the man of the hour, the actual king.

When Carl turned onto Ryke Strasse early one morning, it began to snow. Daylight would not come for a long while yet and the tiny flakes gleamed like insects made of ice in the light of the streetlamps. A man was at work in front of the house. He wore a brown fedora and coveralls (like the ones Carl's father wore). His movements were amateurish and jittery.

The man had broken up the surface of the sidewalk and created a narrow trench that extended all the way to the small bomb crater copse. He must have started very early or even the day before.

"Do you live here?" the man asked.

Carl didn't know what the right answer was. He felt the snow tickling his face. It was his second winter on Ryke Strasse.

"You live here, but don't pay any rent, is that right?" The man jammed his spade into the half-frozen earth.

"This trench is for a cable," the man added. "The electricity will be cut off for a while in a few days."

"When?" Carl asked, trying to keep his voice steady. The cobblestones on the street had grown a thin coat of snow.

"In the next few days."

The man looked at him. He was much older than Carl had assumed from a distance. He wore old-fashioned glasses with black frames, work glasses perhaps, what was remarkable about them were the blinds against light coming from the side. These were definitely not aviator glasses but, just as with the welding goggles given to Dodo, they underscored the pilot-like aspects of his existence and its solitary and daring qualities. And yes, the man looked determined, almost enraged. At the same time, he looked as if he were struggling against something he suspected was much too large for him.

SARA'S MAGASIN

Mornings, the boy crept into Effi's bed, snuggled up to her and went back to sleep for a bit. After a while, he would cautiously shake Carl.

The door to the toilet had to be left slightly ajar, not closed, and Carl wasn't allowed to leave because Freddy was afraid of the stairwell. Not a sound from Rico across the hall. Even his silence seemed artificial. It was a contrived silence. Carl tried to picture Rico. Did this man (this hermit who renounced everything) even have a mattress, or did he sleep on the floor?

Outside the building, Freddy automatically took Carl's hand and Carl felt that he had a father's heart. There were a few things that the two of them did together: driving in the Zhiguli along Bernauer Strasse to the grocery store, for example, with Freddy sitting up front. "Did you sit in the front again?" Effi would ask because she knew he liked that best. While Carl shopped, Freddy stayed in the Zhiguli, kneeling on the seat and gripping the steering wheel. He drove fantastic car races and won: "Zhiguli is better than Ferri! Did you know that?"

"Ferrari, Freddy, it's called a Ferrari."

On the way to kindergarten, they passed the Franz Club. The windows at bar height looked onto a small front garden, to which Carl felt immediately drawn. He couldn't explain it, the trampled, mangy plot of earth made him sad but also evoked a childish longing: Could you live there? Build a shack between those scanty bushes and use it to hide from the city?

The passageway to the kindergarten (Warning! Entrance in courtyard!) was not far from the place where the subway surfaced from the depths and continued on as an elevated train, two floors above the ground. Each time, Freddy demanded that they stop there and wait until one train emerged from underground and another disappeared into it. It was cold. The February wind blew in their faces, but Freddy kept a straight face. He was a serious child with serious wishes. In kindergarten there was a boy named Robert to whom Freddy had become attached. Carl remembered Freddy's first day—the silent horror in the child's face, but then it was as if someone had explained that there was no getting around kindergarten.

"Where is the train going?"

"Vineta," Carl replied.

First the dull thumping of the rails from underground and then the train emerged with its wide-set deep-sea eyes, in which a barely distinguishable flame of life burned: seeing whales could not be more uplifting. It had to do with their awkward magnitude and the antediluvian rattling of their dirty, lumbering carriages—a sound that sparked Carl's old confidence, his belief that they would make it *in Berlin*.

Before returning to his apartment, he walked to the water tower once more and circled the island with the watchmen and the roaring under the paving stones. Morning walks did him good. He listened to the sound of his steps (there was no wiser, deeper sound) and his mouth opened . . . These were not sentences, only words, and not even words at that, just a grumbling in his skull in answer to the whirling spirals of the bullet holes, to the sidewalk's granite flagstones with their chipped corners and the gray, grilled ventilation shafts of gas heaters that protruded wildly and brutishly from the ravaged facades like the snouts of futuristic animals—this street's desolation, thought Carl, and its mysteries, which grew as he passed, the Soap & Tobacco, the Water Tower Guestrooms, the officers' HQ, the Lohmann House, the Ryke Retreat, and, on the corner of Sredzki Strasse, Sara's Magasin, a ruin which had been a coffin depot, of which only the ground floor remained. The tail of the "g" of "Sarg," the word for coffin, had crumbled away, leaving an "a", and the "z" was missing in "Magazin," for storehouse, but Carl didn't see it that way. He'd never read it differently and had always repeated softly to himself as he passed: "Sara's Magasin, Sara's Magasin . . ."

In the meantime, the new cable trench had been extended all the way to the building. Carl made a detour through the cellar, to bring coal upstairs to old Knospe. On the wall above the mailboxes, someone had written WRUBEL — CAPITALIST PIG. Indeed, all the tenants had received a letter from a community of heirs, signed by a man named Wrubel. The rent for Carl's apartment would soon be raised from 31.80 to a round 50 deutschmarks.

"But you don't have a contract," Sonie had said in a toneless voice. "They come here from who knows where and want to cash in."

Old Knospe was waiting outside her door.

"Oh Carl, how good of you." She looked nervously past him down the stairwell. "The dead are returning, Carl. They pop up in the spring and in the summer, they bloom like crazy."

"Which dead, Mrs. Knospe?"

"The ones from before." She gestured toward the front building. "They come up from below and ruin the beds." She reached for the pail. "Take care, my boy. Take good care!"

It was ice-cold in Carl's apartment but at least he had the oil radiator. He lit the heater and a few candles as well, then put water on to boil. He paced once around the room and listened. The capitalists and the dead—on the same day, thought Carl. As if they were in the same troop.

He had the raft, the Stassfurt, the easel, and a small shelf on the wall, not more than a board fastened with nails and rope, which held his books. It all looked good. The board hung evenly (to a bricklayer's eye) and he imagined the first book of his own on it. He could see it. A drawing by Effi on the cover.

Carl began leafing through his notes from the past few days, there was always the chance he might find (suddenly, unexpectedly) something he could use, a bit of gold dust, an alluring outline, why not. Then he stood up, paced for a while and murmured words to himself; he was distracted and couldn't speak. He stood in front of the easel for a while, staring at the page he had written on. Faint music from the courtyard, Arielle's voice from next door. He returned to the kitchen, poured boiling water into the cup with his coffee. He reached for the screwdriver that lay next to the cooking plate (he gripped it firmly, it was from the Zhiguli's tool kit) and beat it lightly against the palm of his hand. Then he paced with the screwdriver in hand, and it was immediately more effective: he could walk and talk much better with the rhythmic beats. Words now emerged differently from his diffuse murmurings, a bit more vulnerable and frightened, perhaps, but also fresher and livelier, if you can say that about words (you can). He hardly raised his hand and only tapped the beat very softly, on rare occasions a bit harder, with passages that had already been driving him to despair, endless meditations over "a" or "u". It wasn't just for the rhythm, the tapping kept his language *awake*, it helped him stay focused. "Walking, talking, and soft taps with a large screwdriver—that was this morning's discovery," Carl wrote that night in his journal (which was more of a work notebook).

Around noon, he left the apartment. It must have happened just before or else he had overlooked it: in the bomb crater copse, the ground had sunk along the new cable trench. A few birch roots hung loose in the air and beneath them the arch of a vault was visible. It must have been the cellar of the old front building. A sooty whiff of decay and ancient sorrow hung in the air.

It felt strange to him, to turn left for the bakery and not right for Effi's. She was probably still in bed, in the warm den of her sleep. To go deeper and deeper, thought Carl—everything else seemed unimportant in comparison. On the other hand, it was good for him to simply look quickly in that direction and then set off in the opposite (his own) direction. "Because I'm not dependent, not addicted," Carl murmured, a lie he had to fall back on now and again, ever since Paris.

He stood with his back to the counter and ate his pudding pretzel. There was no table, just a high board right next to the shop window. A few people who came into the bakery knew Carl now. He knew what they would order, but *how* they'd order astonished him every time. It was the Berlin tone in their voices, their self-evident sense of themselves in this world on this day.

The balls of his hand no longer tingled. A small scrap of skin hung loose. Carl carefully bit it off and tasted something pleasantly sweet and machine-like. Licking wounds, thought Carl. His notebook, which he always carried with him, lay open before him. It was all wooden, insufficient. Nonetheless, it was good to murmur these words and to be alone with them. The most important thing was to stay calm. Which was difficult, very difficult. He could pronounce the vowels softly—that way he stayed in contact. That way he could hear what he was longing for. There was an invisible wall that separated him from the world, which would allow him to leave everything behind, all the misery of his inadequacy.

In the afternoon, Carl worked on his essay about Effi. At some point it had become clear to him that the name didn't fit: Effi. The "i" bothered him, especially its cutesy girlishness—who was called Effi these days? *Effi Briest*, a school play and how everything turned out—could that be told? Surely not. There was no kiss in Fontane, Carl had read the play again—and yet that is exactly how Ilonka became Effi. Carl's attempts to turn Effi back into Ilonka, Ilonka Kalász, that enchanting creature he'd admired from a distance for years, also failed. Effilonka? Filonka, Faloska—Valeska, Valeska?

Valé?

Changing the name—was that a betrayal?

Or just literature?

Night was falling when Carl suddenly felt very tired and had to lie down, at least for a moment. The raft was freezing. He pulled the sleeping bag up to his chin, undid his pants and reached for his dick, which was pleasantly warm.

There were several kinds of wind in the courtyard and Carl could differentiate them by the movement of the curtains at his window. Sometimes they mimicked small waves and sometimes they just billowed into the room like large potbellies of men with breathing difficulties.

Carl closed his eyes. Why did it have to be this way? And where did it come from? He didn't know. There was no explanation.

In his dream, Carl saw old Knospe flying down the stairs. She was holding Sonie's battle rod. She flew into battle and the Shepherd's poncho billowed around her narrow, bony shoulders.

THE STORY ABOUT THE BOARD

Two pages filled on both sides with wild, intertwining lines: that was Inge's letter. It was a shaky, yes, panic-stricken letter and at first glance Carl could glean only one thing with certainty from it: his father was unemployed. And one more thing: Carl's confession, his telegram, that fact that he was not in Gera (and hadn't been for a long time), but had moved to Berlin, did not make much of a difference.

His mother repeatedly interrupted herself, but Carl gradually understood what must have happened. "Ungrateful and without a shred of decency," is how the boss had characterized their move out of the apartment in Gelnhausen. "Despite his and his mother's obligingness, despite the addition of a door and telephone of their own . . ." According to him, Walter and Inge had just sailed into a finished nest from somewhere in the East, "without having accomplished anything on their own." They needed to learn what it means *to work*, the boss told them with a crazed look, Inge wrote to Carl.

But that wasn't enough for him. After they moved out the boss started spreading stories about them that were now making the rounds inside the company: for weeks his elderly mother hadn't gotten a wink of sleep and probably would have died if he hadn't given the Bischoffs their marching orders. The constant accordion-playing, wild music, stomping or jumping around like Indians every night, they almost brought the house crashing down. Not to mention that Walter couldn't play for shit . . .

For whatever reason, Zollnay's secretary had retold the story in great detail. Whereupon, without hesitation, Walter had marched into the boss's office and quit. He left the 280E at the White Villa and walked home in the middle of the day. Walter didn't teach the contracted courses in the following weeks (Munich and Hamburg). And if Carl understood his mother's report correctly, he had called the boss a slave driver and a bold-faced liar, who—as if this was at all important—didn't have the slightest idea what good accordion music was. At that, the head of CTZ threatened him with complete annihilation through compensation claims. Even in Inge's letter, in her wild abridgement of the events, it sounded as if the final point about the accordion (actually, the criticism of Walter's playing) had been the decisive factor.

Driven by the thirst for revenge (no one had ever called him a slave driver), the boss continued his slander, which was simply idiotic and baseless, but then something else happened: two days after Walter quit, the head of CTZ found a load of wood, nails, wire, and screws in the trunk of his Mercedes 280E. Walter had kept delaying and then, in the heat of battle, he missed his chance to secure his collection.

The points of view could not have been more different: for
Walter, the contents of the trunk offered him a chance (once
again) to earn his father's praise, a man long dead, of course,
but who was nevertheless always present and had accompanied
Walter (in this way) on his lonely travels in a foreign land. For
the head of CTZ, on the contrary, the contents were *rubbish*—as
they would have been for almost anyone, not only for those in
and around Frankfurt. For the boss, the contents were welcome
rubbish; the final proof that his former trainer was a slob and a
ragpicker. And probably insane.

He took photographs of his trunk, had the pictures blown
up and pinned them to the board with the trainers' working
schedules in the stairwell of the White Villa. Walter and the
trunk of the Mercedes became a topic of conversation, as he
had hoped. The staff smoked and talked about him, voiced
their assumptions and recalled the coveralls Walter Bischoff
had often worn. The boss had once come across him like that,
stretched out on his back under the Mercedes, very busy and
uncommunicative. It was all very strange, the boss said, and
here a new thought flashed through his mind. It was an extreme
but well-founded suspicion. He now asked himself—himself
and everyone he met—if "the material in the trunk" didn't look
exactly like that? Why else would you have the rusty iron, the old
metal? In short: had the trainer Walter Bischoff perhaps been
planning a bomb, a dirty bomb, an attack on—who knows? In
any case, as a trainer at CTZ, Bischoff had gotten access to the
head offices of the largest companies in the West. And anyhow:
a specialist from the East, with those qualifications? A computer specialist from Gera? Gera? Is there even such a place?
And so on.

For days now, Carl had been eating his breakfast in the
stall before milking Dodo. First breakfast, then milking. The

Shepherd (or what remained of him, a brownish man, just skin and bones, Carl's mother would have said) rolled around in his nest a bit then stuck his head out of the straw, like a large bird.

"Are you worried?"

"The entire letter, the shaky writing that looks like it's unraveling."

The Shepherd looked at him fixedly. A hollow-cheeked creature with large eyes who listened. A rumor was circulating that Hoffi, after his fall (or because of his fall), had acquired an even deeper wisdom. Often he said nothing for days and when he did, as now, he spoke only very slowly and softly:

"There's your father, Carl. And there's the boss. At first, the boss behaved like any normal employer. The rest was all icing on the cake. Renting an attic apartment that was hard to find tenants for, without a door or telephone. A job center that paid the first wages. The so-called training period in which your father already filled the coffers, which is why . . ." The Shepherd sighed and took a deep breath. "The cashier's checks on the steps are also completely normal. And a good guarantee that a claim would never be lodged, my friend. So then. Don't worry. That leaves the issue with the car trunk. That's more difficult, Carl, and very personal. Maybe material for a poem. *O mother of my mother and Her Lordship* . . ." The Shepherd sighed again.

"Walter is your father, who, as you see, also had a father. A father who only praised Walter once in his entire life. That's what you told me, remember? So then. The only praise—for a wooden board. A board that Walter, his son, had found somewhere in the village. And carried home. 'That's a good board, my boy,' your father's father said. 'You can always use a board that like that, sooner or later.' Think about that, Carl."

The Shepherd looked Carl in the eye and slowly retreated into the straw.

Carl couldn't remember ever having told the story about the board. Maybe in his fever back then, in the very first days? Or when he was in shock after the taxi attack?

"Your parents, Carl, they are, as it were, crosswise in the landscape. It's like with a goat on a cliff." He fondled Dodo and closed his eyes. "The goat doesn't fall in the end, right?"

Carl hadn't heard the Shepherd speak coherently for a long time. This was the last time.

DRAW & WARD

When Carl finally finished the poem he'd been working on for a year (basically since Effi's arrival in Berlin, he'd written down the first lines in the stairwell, back then on Sorge Strasse), the warmer days set in.

He recited it out loud to himself. Something was different than usual. The poem hit a point that he hadn't been aware of before. As if it hadn't been written by him and that was the best thing about it.

The sheet on his easel, the typewriter's impeccable writing—he needed to move around, and he knocked on Arielle's door. He'd have preferred to bellow right through the wall: "Come, come, dammit, and read this right now!"

"Would you like—a coffee?"

"Are you going to be published somewhere again?"

They agreed to meet that evening. They planned to go together to the Krähe and meet Effi there.

Carl paced around his room a few times, whispering the lines. He was ready, he had it. The ships slowly sailed into the courtyard to pick him up. No, no—he had to be careful, but yes, yes, he had it, and it was greater and smarter than he was.

He had titled it "draw & ward". *Draw* read backward gave

ward and that's exactly what happened in the poem: "the wind pushed the avenues back into the flow meter of their dreams, the ships quietly entered the city," and so on. Good material. He opened the window. The air smelled of spring. Effi was surely still asleep.

To Carl's surprise, Arielle appeared accompanied by Henry, and Henry had brought "a good friend from Leipzig." That's how Henry put it, his face full of the joy of a surprise. Carl, who was not at all used to visitors, didn't notice his expression. He awkwardly invited them into his kitchen and offered them a glass of red wine and only then did he get it: Henry's good friend from Leipzig, whom he affectionately called the "Highlander" (it must have been a nickname), was Thomas Kunst. The great Kunst, who had written poems like "Viennese Blood" and "The Appointing of Youth to Sleep" and whose first volume of poetry would be out that spring. Carl was sure that Kunst was going to be one of the luminaries of their time, or no: he already was one. And this very person was smiling at him. He wore a red sash and had closely cut hair with a thin braid on one side. His slim build, the large size of the back of his head, probably full of verse, Carl thought.

"The Highlander has a daughter in Berlin," Henry explained. "When he's here, he sleeps at my place, in the studio—he likes to spend the night in the studio."

"So do I," Carl wanted to say, but that would have been ridiculous.

Kunst walked around Carl's room. He touched the hinges at the top of the easel and praised their construction. Naturally, he had immediately understood that he was in the center, the holy place. Then he read the poem "draw & ward", taking a long time. Carl returned to the kitchen and refilled their glasses, his hands trembling. Arielle stayed with Kunst, Carl heard their voices.

"You never told me about Thomas Kunst."

"You don't tell me anything either, Carl. Effi's show in the Assel, you should have left that to me, I know people who . . ." Henry stopped talking when Kunst came into the kitchen.

"Finally, some alcohol!" the Highlander shouted and reached past Carl for his glass.

"So."

Carl stared at Kunst who suddenly looked dead serious.

"It's hell, my friend."

He cleared his throat.

"Don't get me wrong, Carl, it's the best thing I've read in a long time—envy, my friend, envy! I'm turning green, right here at my temples."

He tapped his head and emptied his glass in one gulp. All of a sudden, "draw & ward" had a launch, with a party.

"How did you come up with it, Carl?" Arielle asked and closed her eyes. As always when Arielle asked a question, her curiosity was pure, without arrogance or deviousness, which allowed for an honest answer.

"It was the sound of absence," Carl answered without hesitating. "For that, you need specific shoes, a hard, flat sole but with a heel. And you need a large empty space, of stone, with an echo. Unter den Linden, for example, in the staircase of the old national library. I went there often, just to walk. Especially on the staircase, but also in the halls with the old, pre-war catalogues. Actually, there was nothing for me to do there, but it's nice just to look at the old writing on the cards. I do that for a while and then keep walking with those echoing steps. Afterwards, I go to the reading room and order something that can only be read under supervision. Something valuable that you have to wear white gloves to read. Huge folios with ancient anatomical prints, for example, that's how I discovered Vesalius, the 1555 second edition of his *Fabrica* in the typography of Claude Garamond. I kept ordering it, reserved it, then extended the reserve, and

351

when I arrived, there it was, at the desk, waiting for me and after a while I couldn't imagine having to live without this old book . . ." Carl abruptly fell silent—what he was saying sounded over-excited.

"Steps that reforest the heartbeat," the Highlander hummed into the glass he held up to his mouth as if it were a microphone—he was quoting the poem! A warm current flooded Carl's heart, a childish pride, and he started talking about things in his head that were still very unfinished, but important and urgent. He had come upon Balzac's *Theory of Walking* and Benjamin's *Arcades Project*. He talked about them, stammered, blushed, and fell silent again. Again, the Highlander came to his aid:

"The sound of footsteps is for us. Walking, footsteps—not ambling or creeping, not the flaneur, that cheap figure, just footsteps, the streets, the spaces, and their noise—it all lives inside us with its sound. The present moment and its sound at perception's ground zero, that, Carl Bischoff, is what your poem speaks to me about."

Carl didn't know what to answer. Henry raised his glass: "There you have it Carl, that's it. To you, old bricklayer!"

The Krähe was overcrowded (as always). Effi waved at Carl. She was standing at one of the back tables. It wasn't actually a wave, she just raised her arm, it looked dismissive. They hadn't seen each other for a few days for various reasons but mostly to "give each other some space," as Effi called it. When Carl introduced the Highlander, Effi smiled.

"A poet from the throne of the National Library," Henry said, and Carl understood why Kunst was so familiar with the sound of ancient libraries. He worked in the reading room.

"Then we've surely seen each other before," Effi replied, stiffening. "I used to go there often." She seemed completely entranced by her former proximity to the DB.

The Highlander stared at her, as if dazzled. It was a kind of hypnosis, a special ability of Effi's, maybe from her time as illusionist. Effi and I are together, Carl wanted to say but instead offered to get drinks. "Now we can celebrate," he said in a low voice to the group, but especially to Effi who obviously could not have known about "draw & ward". No one reacted. Effi didn't either, it was just too loud in the Krähe.

For the past few weeks (as if there had been an agreement), in the bars in the so-called scene they only drank wheat beer and only smoked Gauloises. Carl carried the large, ice-cold glasses of wheat beer to their table. Only he and Effi drank wine.

Effi.

The Highlander held his face in the warm stream of her smile and why shouldn't he? He would have a book in the spring. He was the only real poet at this table.

Carl drank too quickly. Henry spoke with Arielle and Arielle kissed Henry. The Highlander leaned toward Effi and said something into her ear. Effi laughed and now Carl wanted to leave. He stood up, but only went to the toilet, which no one seemed to notice.

"To 'draw & ward,'" the Highlander called out when Carl returned.

Carl nodded and tried to smile but the celebration was over. Effi looked at him inquiringly: "Is it a secret?"

"Secret," Carl repeated tonelessly and raised his glass, but it was already empty. He knew he was making himself look ridiculous, so he stood up "to get some fresh air," that's all he could manage to say.

He knew the woman behind the bar (Katja). He'd met her a few times at the waiters' nightly meetings in the Sophien Club. Katja wore a fur coat and was a little insane, but she was good-natured and warm-hearted. Those large brown eyes, when he would stop back in the Krähe after midnight for a last glass before bed. She knew his favorite spot at the bar was behind the coffee machine. As soon as he appeared there, she would slide the bowl of crackers to him. Why wasn't it Katja, why Effi?

Katja let him use her tray for the next round. Carl's body automatically slipped into a waiter's stance—at once unyielding and smooth.

"A master in action!" Arielle called to him.

"Our waiter," Effi said.

They clinked glasses. The occasion was forgotten. Without wasting time, Carl emptied his glass. He talked with Henry and Henry laid a hand on his arm. Effi was absorbed with the Highlander and the Highlander with Effi. He's fucking her with words, thought Carl, or had a thought in that direction. Effi now sat upright, her back stiff, as if an electric current were running through her. She has the most beautiful ass in the world, the drunk man in Carl's head offered as an observation.

"He asked for your picture to be put up," Carl said to Henry. They were talking about the Shepherd.

"I know," Henry answered. "And now he's receiving guests in the stall. They want his advice. For them, Hoffi is a kind of oracle. An oracle from the straw."

"The story about his fall has got around. No one was there, but everyone knows something about it. They claim Hoffi can fly, they claim that that's the only reason he survived the fall and that he hardly eats anything anymore and that he talks with Dodo . . ."

While Carl was trying to talk over the drunk man in his head (who was constantly making piggish suggestions), something happened. First his chest cramped and constricted. Then his throat, he could hardly breathe, and the music got louder. *This is a weeping song.* Carl's hand gripped the empty wine glass under the table.

Poor glass, it fought back.

Then it was too late. A small, inaudible crack. Pain like an axe up to the top of his skull. He relaxed. He had to look out for his pants. Have to look out for my pants, thought Carl. Henry stood up very slowly, as if in slow motion, probably so as not to scare Carl. His distraught face. The deep wrinkle between his eyes, all his earnestness. Good painter, Carl thought. He loved Henry and his flying animals.

First, they saw only blood, a lot of blood. Henry pulled Carl's chair back from the table. The extended hand that wouldn't let go of the glass. The fingers still gripped, which was completely unnecessary. Must be a cramp, thought Carl. The dark pant leg, soaked with blood.

"Shit, Carl, oh shit!" Effi shouted.

Carl stretched his hand toward her, as if to appease her, but there was still too much glass between his fingers for that, especially the large shard in the ball of his hand and there, that, yes, his thumb hung down as if hinged.

The Highlander laughed. Carl saw that he couldn't do otherwise, he was laughing out of fear. "Desire's drive grows, desire's drive and its silence," Kunst quoted Carl's poem.

"Draw and ward," Carl replied and showed him his hand full of shards. He was drunk and the lights in the bar shimmered in the shards. A good, calming heaviness flowed through him as if he were slowly being filled with lead. It's a kind of unhappiness, thought Carl. Around them, people stood up from their tables. Someone had turned off the music. *This is a weeping song.* The blood flowed out of Carl unhindered and the puddle on the floor grew. Doesn't have to be my problem, thought Carl, and he tilted his head back. He was exhausted. Paintings appeared on the ceiling and on the walls. They were Effi's paintings and Carl's poems were written between them. Good poems he didn't know yet with lines as long as birthday garlands. He had finally done it.

SISTER EFFI

His curtains were closed, his door ajar. Now and then, Arielle checked on Carl. Once she brought him soup in a small pot that drifted next to his raft for a while. Carl imagined Effi's footsteps on the stairs. She had to come sometime.

He wasn't a rigorous thinker when it came to Effi, everything seemed washed over and blurred by the current of his desire. His desire filled the space, kept it running—whatever it was. Faster, harder, then slowly again with his tongue. Or just before going, because he wanted it that way. Freddy's in his room, calling for Mama, but she does him, fast, slightly irritated, it's too much, he wants it too often, always actually.

His aching hand.

Just a few stitches.

A doctor his father's age sewed up his thumb. "Grabbed the glass wrong." The doctor asked Carl what his profession was and Carl had said bricklayer: that was the low point, the utter defeat, a bricklayer's hand without corns, without calluses, without traces of dirt under his nails. That's a writer's hand, Doctor, isn't it obvious? "It's just the shock, young man," the doctor said when Carl started trembling.

The mild spring air on his eyes, so gentle it could make you go blind. Carl plodded down Ryke, he reeled, his steps without any echo, he was missing the rhythm, the clarity: why were they together and were they *together*? No. He thought this only for an instant, it wasn't a complete thought, just something that flashes up from the bottom of a stream and disappears again.

Arielle had explained to Carl that he was the one who should apologize. Carl didn't need to understand why. He just wanted to see Effi and for that, any pretext would do. *I want to improove myself.*

"How's your hand?" She didn't look at him, only at the bandage.

"I did something wrong."

"Yes, you did."

"It was thoughtless of me, I mean."

"Freddy's waiting for me."

"I mean. Us, earlier. Back then, on disco nights, in the villages. We used to do that now and then. You just have to hold the glass differently, not with your thumb against the rim, you have to . . ."

Deep down, Carl knew that it was wrong to explain it to Effi this way, but he couldn't help it. He was still brimming with jealousy. And right now he could have used some warmth, a hand on his cheek. He had almost sliced off his own thumb. A finger for a poem, thought Carl—not too high a price if the poem was really good. And what also occurred to him just then went like this: "Glasses in the East were just different, Effi, not as thin and splintering."

Effi looked away, absently. Past him. At Rico's door across the hall.

"Before, Carl. All that east Thuringian shit. That's why I'm here. I'm not standing around anymore with guys who put out their cigarettes on each other's hands instead of dancing."

"That was about something else."

He'd started wrong. The hurt was a swamp. Next door, Rico started playing guitar.

"Really? What exactly was it about again?"

"You only did that to your very best friend."

"Right."

"Don't be sarcastic, Effi."

"Carl, I'm—we'll see each other later, later, right?"

Rico had started singing. Effi's door closed, slowly and almost without a sound, like a favorite book that had been read for the last time.

*

After his Kalashnikov screw-up in the Assel, the incident with the glass was his second relapse into rituals from the distant past (or whatever he was supposed to call it). "Not just you, Effi," Carl thought and closed his eyes. He lay on his back, his injured hand above his head. He curled up slightly on his raft and began to let himself drift. This is a weeping song. The riverbank, the hills, they slid past. His gaze northward: on the horizon appeared his home village with the large barns on the eastern perimeter, the three oaks commemorating peace, and the slate-roofed church tower. And there were his parents, coming across the fields from the village. It seemed they had good weather for their excursion. Carl's mother was pulling a wagon behind her and in it sat Carl, the child. It was only two kilometers from town to the autobahn. Carl had a cushion behind his back and on his lap the Star 111, their portable radio. On the back of the dark brown wooden case there was a flap that had to be opened from time to time to insert two new lantern batteries. Changing the batteries was a sacred ritual that Carl had observed a few times, completely spellbound by the sight of the many small steps that were required, and which his father worked through conscientiously.

They set up camp between two young birch trees near the autobahn bridge: the thermos, the picnic basket, the Star 111. They discussed each car that drove past. The main events were cars from the West, on a good afternoon there could be three, four, sometimes even five Western cars. Carl's father often sat a bit apart and closer to the autobahn. Child Carl saw that he held a small, tightly packed wad of cotton wool, which he held to his ear when a car approached, sometimes only briefly, sometimes for longer. "Papa's listening to the engines," his mother had said. Indeed, his father was able to identify *all* the models by their sound (without looking). Carl's parents longed for a car of their own and often discussed it. Mostly they talked about a

Zhiguli—with chrome fenders, chrome hubcaps, and the body snow-white like the birch trees along the autobahn.

It was dark when Carl awoke. He lit the candle on the Stassfurt and dozed a bit. Then he crept out of bed and went to the kitchen to get the AK47 from its usual place under the workbench. He took the gun to bed and slowly disassembled it. He would miss a few weeks, but the competition in Fenske's cellar could go on just as well without him.

"And it doesn't have to stay this way forever," Carl whispered.

The small stock felt pleasantly cool in his damaged hand, like a consolation. The wound wasn't actually all that large. I'm not mortally wounded, Carl thought and pressed the buttstock to his heart. Then he stood up and paced around the room. The mumbling started. He gently tapped the stock on his good hand. That ordered his words and calmed him at the same time. The stock was even better than the screwdriver. Speaking aloud and with soft beats, his gaze fell on the poem "draw & ward," and when he turned around at the window, Effi was in the doorway.

"Effi!" Carl clutched the stock as he said her name.

"The door was open and . . ."

"Oh, yeah. Arielle left it open. She checks on me from time to time."

"That's good."

"Yes, very good."

"What are you doing with that?" She pointed to the parts of the Kalashnikov on the floor next to the raft.

"It's the Kashi, my practice gun . . ."

Carl started to explain, and it became clear to him how much he had kept to himself, but kept to himself was saying too much: Effi had never been particularly interested in the Assel, quite the reverse. She didn't like the place or the pack.

"I just mean—what brings someone to do that kind of work, in that cellar, with the tarts down there?" Effi had asked.

"What do you mean?"

"I mean, there must be other reasons."

It was odd, but she had said it, Effi, who always deferred to life as it was and never showed ill will.

Carl talked: Fenske's cellar and the Russians, the Shepherd in the straw and his flying goat. His eyes fell on the nice, smooth stock in his hand, so he also told Effi about that. Methods he'd discovered for himself and his writing and then used. Without noticing, he beat the stock rhythmically as he spoke and marched a little on the spot.

He saw it in Effi's eyes: it all sounded crazier than it was. Not just abnormal, but alarming. Effi's face grew pale, full of sympathy, and Carl lost all strength.

"I'm not crazy, Effi, you know that, right?"

He hurried into the kitchen to open a bottle of Chianti, but he couldn't manage it. The corkscrew slipped from his hand. Only a few stitches, the wound ached, but he wasn't crazy. For everything there is a reason. The search for the transition, the fight for a poetic existence, a struggle that wasn't poetic. Each according to his needs, thought Carl. The last future was over but the motto still fit. Hoffi would have agreed. Carl missed him.

And now Carl really missed him.

Effi took the bottle from Carl's hands. Sometimes it was simply difficult with the cork: drops of Chianti splattered the wall. Effi wanted to wipe them off, but Carl took her in his arms.

"I love you, Effi."

He let her go and handed her a glass.

"And you see, I didn't crush it, not one little bit. I know how to handle them."

"To you, Carl, *and to your complete recovery.*"

A sentence from the echo chambers of hopelessness. Carl rewound it.

Really erase it? Yes.

Effi stood up and started getting undressed. Carl had trouble with his bandage. Effi smiled at him good-naturedly.

"Let me do it, wait. Now you're my patient, Carl Bischoff."

The nurse just wanted to go to the bathroom quickly first, barefoot, in her shirt.

Carl waited. The easel and its shadow swaying in the candle-light. The wind in the courtyard and the potbellies in front of the window. The red wine sprinkled on the wall—it was all good. Only Nurse Effi didn't come back, not after two minutes and not after five. Now that they'd found a way to be *together* again, it would be stupid to run after her to the toilet.

Ten minutes.

She's naked, Carl thought, where could she have gone? He stood up and in the hallway he heard her calling. A soft, cautious call, meant only for him, Carl, and no one else in this world.

He ran down the steps and yanked at the toilet door. Then Carl saw the lock. It had slipped down—the so-called outer lock. Effi was sitting on the toilet, her arms in front of her chest. She was shivering all over, shivering and giggling at the same time. Her lips were chalk-white.

"Effi!"

Effi in Carl's arms. Her body was ice-cold, and she couldn't stop giggling. It was a hiccupping, gulping giggle that wasn't particularly close to laughter.

"That was the lock that Sonie," Carl whispered and now Effi was actually sobbing, "that was the lock that Sonie installed on all the toilets," Effi was clinging to his neck and sobbing, "so the wind wouldn't open the doors in winter and the draft—" she couldn't stop sobbing, "and to keep the water from freezing, but—" he held her close and Effi sobbed and trembled the entire time.

"Effi, Effi."

PART VIII

INGE B.'S FOUR JOBS

At six in the morning, it was still cold under the roof in the garret. Outside the house, they could hear the hammering of the diesel car Mrs. Floeth drove to work in the hospital. Walter called her Jasmin, just to himself, Jasmin, who was actually Marianne. *Out of Gera.*

After the scandal in CTZ, Walter often withdrew. He liked to be alone, and he played the accordion for hours. His technique improved. On the side (no, it was, in fact, the main thing), he applied to various firms and had "job interviews of an inform-ative character," as Inge put it. In everything else that hap-pened, Walter did not take an especially active part and he often seemed happy simply to have escaped from the White Villa. *Goodbye, White Villa*—he had set the phrase to a little melody and hummed it softly to himself.

Since their emigration, his father had been living a double life, at least that's how Carl felt. A life that seemed to sway between computers and the accordion, a technical world and a musical one. What the West also revealed about Walter: that his father was a hybrid being, a rare transitional species between two eras, half-past, half-future. On the one hand, repairing engines and fans along with trunks full of scrap, on the other, uncommon languages like Pascal and Cobol, and the newest books on them at Staak & Beirich in Frankfurt. A boy from the countryside who had started an apprenticeship as a weaver at thirteen (his mother worked in the same factory) and later studied textile machine engineering. "We threshold creatures," whispered Carl, who in that moment started to realize that he, himself, belonged to that species.

It was also evident that with their departure, Inge and Walter had entered a time zone in which the behaviors and skills from their background (in a largely mechanical era, which, in this new, Western zone—that's what Carl called it—seemed already over and half-forgotten) could lead to misunderstanding, as had happened with the boss, who presumably no longer believed (or never had believed in his life) that you could repair a car yourself or that a good board lying in a ditch might prove useful one day.

Be that as it may: after a short phase of confusion, it was Carl's mother who took matters into her own hands. The new situation revived her willingness to fight. In a letter that arrived just a few days after her panicked missive, her writing was firm and clear again. For the first time, Carl learned a bit more—their common goal, his mother wrote, was a specific sum: fifty thousand marks. As to what they needed it for, she would tell him *soon*. It's a kind of game show, thought Carl, in which the contestant is given clues.

At first, Inge studied the job advertisements in the *Gelnhäuser Tageblatt*, then she borrowed a bicycle from old Ursula and rode from one address to the next in the rain and the cold: first, a building supplier on the edge of Gelnhausen (once again it was about a position for a forklift operator—all over Germany, they're looking for forklift operators, Inge thought); second, a wood mill in Roth; and third, a trucking business with a transport fleet on the highway, not far from Meerholz. No one was unfriendly to the woman on the bicycle, but from their expressions Inge could see that it was hopeless. It was something in their eyes, a certain resistance, in the way they spoke, too, that gentle Hessian German with softened endings slid past her into the void. Of course, she could be mistaken, since she had come to experience each empty street and every shutter rolled down at night as a rejection.

For two weeks, she delivered the *Langenselbolder Anzeiger*—she filled in for a Polish paperboy who had caught chicken pox. At five in the morning, she picked up the bundle of newspapers at the Joska printers and did her rounds. Even in bad weather, it was nice to walk through the sleeping streets and the exercise was good for her. The Endlich bistro, which opened at six, took two copies. At the end of her round, she drank a black coffee there. Outside it was still dark. On the wall of the breakfast room hung a framed poster of Bonnie and Clyde, who had run off and were finally shot down. Inge didn't know more than that about them, she'd hardly seen any movies. When she was young, she was in the barn or out in the fields—and on weekends she went dancing. Walter had told her about certain films. During his weaver apprenticeship, the cinema had been on the way to the factory. *Bonjour Kathrin* with Caterina Valente, for example, which the movie house in Berga had surprisingly included in its program. Walter had seen *Blackboard Jungle* in West Berlin. For *Round the Clock*, he had crossed the border three times; he had told her about it so often that Inge could talk about it with him—as if they'd gone to the cinema together.

On the last day of her stint delivering newspapers, Inge stepped into a telephone booth on Gelnhausen's old market square and called a few of the numbers in the job listings. These were private addresses; the openings were for domestic help and house cleaning. Because she was a German speaker and, yes, actually even a German citizen (although from the East), she got a job right away.

The job at the Mohr house on Lärchenweg is Inge's first address, twice a week. She walks the five kilometers from Meerholz to the Mohrs' in Gelnhausen on foot. The first time she wears the winter jacket from the clothing depot in Diez. First the stretch through the valley, across the Kinzig and the train tracks, then through the city and up the mountain. Half of the city is built on the mountain and the Mohrs' house is one of those in the forest near the top. The hunter's rucksack is on her back, with her work clothes and a cheap deodorant. In the side pocket, an apple and a lunch box with slices of bread. In the long, ivy-covered cement wall on which the house is built, like a fortress on a cliff, Inge finds the entrance.

The house has two stories, the top one open to the roof beams—there are hardly any walls and no doors. Two wooden spiral staircases are the largest and most important elements in the space. It almost looks like people here live on the stairs or at least around them.

"I felt comfortable with Mrs. Mohr from the very beginning," Inge wrote Carl, "even on the telephone, as if we'd known each other for a long time."

Inge is often in the house alone. She likes to step out of the kitchen onto the glassed-in terrace—just this one step and then the view of the entire Kinzig valley. She enjoys the sunlight, the warmth, and the work is easy for her; she breathes more freely and feels better here. She has never dreamed of such a house, only of a built-in kitchen. While she implements the cleaning plan she drew up, Mrs. Mohr goes to the nursing home and takes care of her mother. Mrs. Mohr and Inge feel kinship with each other and, yes, the two even look alike: their bobbed, medium-blond hair, their short, athletic stature with powerful legs; both are fifty years old. Mrs. Mohr confides in Inge: first the divorce, now her mother's illness.

They start making each other small presents. For the second Advent Sunday, Inge (the former inventor of cake recipes) brought her home-baked croissants and for the third Advent Sunday, the Bischoffs are invited for coffee. It's the first invitation they've received to a house in the West. Why had they come here, to the Kinzig valley, Mrs. Mohr once asked, and Inge's reply was economical: they were following an old dream.

The path up to Lärchenweg is covered with ice and Inge's heart is filled with a festive feeling. Mrs. Mohr is very friendly. She brings out the precious Christmas decorations that her mother had once saved in their flight from Bohemia. ("Something so fragile, the entire time, isn't it unbelievable?") She unpacks them piece by piece, like an old secret: blue balls, stars and a tiny glass trumpet—she blows into it. Then Walter, who manages to play a short melody. Mrs. Mohr's eyes fill with tears, just like that. "Always at Christmas time, just before going to sleep, I was allowed to blow into the glass trumpet one more time. My mother took the trumpet from the tree especially, then hung it back on the branch right after . . ."

"The evening did us both good," Inge writes in her Christmas card to Carl. In the new year, Mrs. Mohr's mother dies in the nursing home; Inge is no longer needed and the job ends.

The job with the Beerweins: Mrs. Beerwein in Selbold is Inge's second address. The wall next to the entrance is made of glass tiles, through which colorful light falls into the hallway. Even before Inge has rung the doorbell, Mrs. Beerwein is standing in the doorway and leads her into the house. It's not a grand home, but it is large. And it's surrounded by other houses that lie in the neighborhood like dead, unreal blocks with flat roofs and a square footprint. Mrs. Beerwein is very thin in her black sweatpants. At first glance she looks athletic, like an old high jumper, but then Inge sees her walk, her stiff knee and slight limp. While Mrs. Beerwein talks, Inge looks at her tanned, freshly moisturized face. Earlier, in Gera, I wouldn't have had the energy for something like that, Inge thinks. But Gera lies far behind her now, aside from the fear that catches her sometimes like a flash of lightning and reduces her to tears: no, she doesn't have any doubts, it's just the shock of homesickness.

Mrs. Beerwein is not sure if the new cleaning woman has been listening or not. She brushes her hand across her forehead (as if she were wiping away the rest of her lotion), she opens her mouth to firm her cheeks and stretches her head forward. For a moment she looks like a fish in sweatpants sticking its mouth above the surface of a poisoned pond.

Because the house is built into a slope, the entrance from the street opens onto the second floor. The floor below, half-buried in the earth, is set up as an apartment. A large room with heavy, dark furniture, bouquets of artificial flowers, and a leather couch with an exercise bike and a weight bench behind it; it all looks unused. Inge recognizes the vague silhouette of an iron grill outside the window. It's cool on the lower floor, the couch emits a sour smell, and Mrs. Beerwein opens the door to a back room, underground. Until now, she's hardly paused in her explanations.

Shoes, the room is filled with shoes—organized by colors and styles, on shelves up to the ceiling, maybe four hundred, maybe five hundred pairs. It's a fantastic and unsettling sight.

"Some people keep birds, I invested my money in shoes."

It was a confession that she needed to make before showing Inge the rest of the house. Mrs. Beerwein now seems somewhat nervous and embarrassed. In the neon light, the aging former high jumper looks even older and almost like a mummy; a mummy leading Inge through her sepulcher: four hundred pairs of shoes for walking in the beyond, in heaven, Inge thinks. That said, she finds the comparison a pleasant one—an aviary for shoes. Inevitably she thinks of Dr. Talib from Diez, who had held her old, worn hiking boots (for several minutes) in his hands. Once again, she feels embarrassed. She's not Snow White and

Dr. Talib is no prince, but now she recognizes something in the memory that she would rather not pursue any farther.

The lady of the house softly rattles (as if to call Inge to attention) a mid-sized ladder to the right of the door. Its metal hooks clatter against the rod that lines the room at head-height, almost as if along shelves in a large library.

"You'll need this for the top shelves, Mrs. Bischoff. Once a week is enough. There's a special cloth for it and . . ."

The shoes are her size, Inge noticed this right away. On the telephone, Mrs. Beerwein had asked for her shoe size.

"Please forgive any intrusion, young lady . . ."

It was odd, without a doubt, but the voice on the end of the line sounded trustworthy and what difference could it make?

After the aviary, Mrs. Beerwein doesn't have the energy to show Inge the rest of the house, but that isn't necessary, and it won't be in the future either because Inge works independently. Carefulness and autonomy are forms of resistance. Her diligence is resistance too. The conscientiousness that surrounds Inge protects her and makes her unassailable. The dignity of her work. Her propulsive, unflagging strength is enough for two during these days.

Inge comes once a week (always Wednesday) and proposes what should be done. Organizing the work herself makes her happy. Sometimes the windows are the focus, sometimes the kitchen, and always the birds. Inge arranges it so that she starts on the top floor and always finishes with the shoe closet. The basement is gloomy and, in a way that is hard to describe, *squalid*. For Inge, it's a good place. A place where she can be on her own, away from everything happening overhead (above ground). She turns on the neon light, closes the door and breathes in the smell of factory-fresh leather. It is completely quiet. With the wool cloth, she dusts the leather tops; very gently, she strokes

371

the birds. Occasionally she takes one off the shelf. She holds it on her outstretched palm and brings it close to her face: hello Rossi, greetings Manolo . . . She relaxes down here. The place is unfamiliar enough for that. There is a sense of security that is only possible in strange places.

The first time, Inge had counted: 434 pairs, unused. As Talib had said, Fate has recognized me as a wanderer, Inge thinks. Now it is showing me this here—as a test. How little you know me, old Fate. How well you knew me, Talib.

After twenty minutes, Inge re-emerges from the aviary; she goes to the leather couch, where she had put her pants, her sweater, and her rucksack. The dark cabinets on the wall are filled with binders; their spines are covered with year dates and strange abbreviations.

Upstairs there is coffee. They sit at the kitchen table. The lady of the house is wearing fresh makeup. She smokes, but only in short, frequent drags, exhausted and nervous, more as if she were sucking on a pacifier than a cigarette. She lifts the coffee cup to her lips and sets it back down. From time to time she sips yellow lemonade from a plastic bottle that she keeps on the floor near her chair; it's half schnapps, thinks Inge. They talk about the housework in the coming week, Mrs. Beerwein has crossed her ruined legs. She wears a black Adidas training jacket and a pink scarf on her head, as if *she* were the cleaning woman. Of her new hairdo (while Inge was cleaning, the hairdresser had come to the house), only her freshly dyed hairline is visible. Inge tells her that next time she'd like to "tackle" the glass blocks near the front door. The lady of the house is grateful: "Do you have any idea what it would cost, Mrs. Bischoff, if I were to book a company to clean them?"

This is one of the things that Inge does not understand, since Mr. Beerwein runs his own cleaning company, Beerwein & Co. Mrs. Beerwein clears her throat and reaches under the table.

She solemnly places a new pair of shoes next to her coffee cup.
They're red and slim, with a high French heel.

For a moment, silence reigns, a kind of devotion.

"Aren't they just—gorgeous?"

What is Inge meant to say?

"Very elegant, Mrs. Beerwein."

"Dear Inge, may I possibly ask you a favor?"

"What sort of favor, Mrs. Beerwein?"

"Would you be so kind as to slip them on, just for a few steps?
And perhaps with this skirt?" She reaches behind her back and
holds a skirt out to Inge. She has prepared everything. And
given herself some liquid courage. Her hands tremble as if the
skirt were very heavy.

From that afternoon on, modeling shoes was a set part of the
Beerwein job. Little by little, Inge shed her inhibitions. After
all, it was only a matter of a few steps (from the living room into
the kitchen and back) and with time she made it into something
of her own, she simply couldn't resist—these shoes on her feet
brought back that old ballroom feeling, the rhythm of her youth.
She began to turn now and again, to tap dance, to sway her hips
and Mrs. Beerwein clapped her hands enthusiastically and then
there was no stopping Inge: rock 'n' roll. Not only the basic six-
step but also the eight-step, with hops and jumps, accompanied
by the clicking and banging of the expensive shoes, like shots
on the parquet. Mrs. Beerwein shrieked with delight, "Dance,
Ingchen, dance!" and as fast as she could manage with her ruined
knees, she tottered to the record player and found the right music.

"You're in such good shape, Ingchen, in *such good* shape!"

"It's just the exercise, Mrs. Beerwein!"

"Call me Petra, my Ingchen!"

On her last Beerwein day (she didn't know it would be her
last), Inge wore a pair of dark blue patent leather shoes in which

it was hard to walk even with healthy legs. As she rounded the table at which Mrs. Beerwein was sitting (as if absent-mindedly, with her eyes half-closed), the doorbell rang.

"Ah, Inge, could you please see who it is," Mrs. Beerwein said.

It was a young man in a lightweight, beige coat from the Hanau tax office, as he informed her. He looked friendly. As he talked, he rocked back and forth on his heels (impatiently like a child). With both hands, he held a briefcase to his stomach.

"One moment please," Inge said and started to turn.

"And if I might ask, in what . . . capacity are you here, Mrs . . . ?"

"Bischoff, Inge Bischoff."

He was looking at her blue patent leather shoes.

"Frau Bischoff?"

There were many (good) (unimpeachable) possible answers. "I'm a friend of the house," for example, or "I'm just visiting to stroke the birds," or "I just come to dance once a week." But Inge said: "I work here."

And that was it for the Beerwein job.

The Joska job. The owner of the Langenselbold printers, for whom she had already worked once, if only for a few days, is Inge's third address. For Inge, this is the closing of a circle, but the owner, who constantly sways his head back and forth (as if everything is grounds for skepticism) does not remember.

"I delivered the *Anzeiger*."

"Is that right?"

Now Inge's task is the garden—the area around the house and the courtyard between the street and the printer plant, which consists of a jumble of low buildings and a covered loading ramp. The house is on the other side of the property and is completely enclosed in greenery. It has a terrace surrounded by pine trees, between which a few flower beds devastated by the winter are waiting for Inge's diligent hands. The grounds resemble a cemetery more than a garden and the surrounding pine trees remind Inge of James Joyce's grave. As with his grave, there is a wire fence behind the trees and beyond it, scrubland. You can hear the autobahn.

Joska's garden tools are as worn and inadequate as the man himself is elegant—with his dark, always precisely parted hair, tortoiseshell glasses, and suit jacket. Inge often works with her bare hands. She kneels in the dirt, scrabbling in it and breathing in the smell of the earth. We don't need much more, Inge thinks, and I'm strong. She digs and calculates for the hundredth time the expenses they will have to cover.

When Inge is in the garden bed, Mr. Joska pushes his wife to the window facing the terrace. Maybe she asked him to. "My wife is handicapped," Joska had said at the job interview. (Inge does not have a job, strictly speaking; there is no contract, only work.) Inge looks up and sees Mrs. Joska at the window. Sometimes the woman in the wheelchair opens her mouth, as if she wants to say something to Inge (and maybe she is speaking to her). Inge gives a quick wave and turns back to her work. Everyone can see how hardworking she is, even the handicapped woman behind the windowpane.

Mr. Joska is satisfied with Inge and starts to give her additional tasks: errands, shopping, trips to the post office and even to the bank. He offers her (in thanks and as a "small token of appreciation") a box of Mon Chéri chocolates from Ferrero. "Have yourself a treat, Mrs. Bischoff." He has just turned sixty-five. He shows Inge photographs of his retirement celebration. There are lots of photographs. A new manager has taken over the printing plant—"completely incompetent, unfortunately." And so on. Now and again, a sentence escapes him that Inge prefers to ignore. She wants to earn money.

Mrs. Joska cannot speak, she can only whistle a little. She makes faces and whistles. Sometimes the whistling becomes a word. Then, very slowly, with effort, another word, incomprehensible. She looks at her husband all the while, never at Inge. She looks at him and eventually gives a laugh. (At what?) It's an embarrassed, ashamed laughter. She can't help it, Inge thinks, but she's ashamed of her whistling.

Meanwhile, Inge has become a girl Friday. Although, as always, she works independently, the owner of the printing plant calls her into his office every workday for a report (his term). There, they go through the list of the tasks she has completed. Soon Inge is also helping with meals. Mrs. Joska is, as always, well dressed and her medium-blond hair seems newly styled. The owner of the printing plant ties a napkin around his wife's neck and feeds her. Inge feels out of place—it is simply too intimate. She believes that Mrs. Joska feels the same way; she can tell by a twitching in the woman's face. Joska starts showing Inge how the meals are prepared: the right temperature, the cooking range and its particularities, the medications. As they leave, in the hallway, another joke, this one obscene: "Well, Mrs. Bischoff, we could give it a try!" He makes the fitting gesture. "Couldn't we?"

The secretary at the printing plant tells Inge that Joska only married into the family and came "from somewhere in the East," probably Poland. After he donated the old presses to wherever it was, a whole series appeared in the *Anzeiger*: "Helping people is my way . . ." and so on. "He really played that to the hilt," the woman in the office whispers, then puts a finger to her lips.

After a few days, Inge is put in charge of Mrs. Joska's care, in addition to the garden work. It's actually not possible to do both, but a "no" is out of the question at the moment, especially after the loss of the Mohr job and the unfortunate end at Mrs. Beerwein's—whom Inge truly misses, something even she is surprised by. Inge thinks: I met the good ones already. Dr. Talib and his family, old Ursula from Gelnhausen, not forgetting Johnny and Winona, and, yes, Mrs. Floeth, Walter's new love, but no threat there.

What Inge writes Carl these days sounds like this: "Walter is looking for a position so now I'm the one making the contributions. I've earned a nice amount, Carl, it won't take much longer."

They've calculated it at the breakfast table with the radio in their Meerholz garret. What Inge misses is her view of the GIs' morning training and the Thuringian chickens in the valley. But the first panic, the fear of not making it, has subsided. Walter practices the most complicated passages of "Straight Jacket" (the accordion solo) and their room is filled with his instrument's roar, which penetrates everything and makes it shake—simply too much for any landlord, so Walter often leaves the house with the accordion case on his back.

His favorite spot is the bus stop below their housing development. It is covered, enormous, and abandoned—there's no timetable and hardly any traffic on the street. It's spring, but still cold, which doesn't bother Walter. He brings coffee and a blanket with him. The moments when he can just sit there and not think of anything, not pay attention or do anything at all, are the best ones in his life: the view from the bus shelter onto the opposite side of the street, empty except for a grassy slope, the warmth of the coffee in his mouth and then in his stomach, the pleasant weight of the accordion on his thigh . . .

They're traveling together, but Walter is on a different kind of journey. Like a planet, he has his own orbit, as Hoffi, the oracle, might have said, thinks Carl. The score lies open on the bench next to Walter, sometimes he glances at it, but he has it all in his head and has had for decades.

On the days he travels, the accordion stays in its case. Walter is preparing. In recent weeks he has been in touch with large companies like IBM, UNISYS, International Computers, and so on. This time he is traveling to Cologne, to EMI Electrola, a corporate group with many branches ("transatlantic"), that had invited him for an interview once before, just after he started working at CTZ. Walter did not go to Cologne then, he didn't even answer because the offer made by CTZ seemed so superb. Now EMI has contacted him again.

Inge sets out Walter's clothing and the night before, she washes his hair in their room's sink: "Come, Walter, I'll do your hair." Days earlier, Walter had inquired about train connections at the station; the times are neatly noted in his small UNISYS diary, a remnant from his time with CTZ. Inge massages his head, humming something; it's a tender moment, full of security, her song is pure fantasy. Sometimes it sounds like Schubert's "Der König in Thule," sometimes like Elvis's "In the Ghetto."

For weeks CTZ played dead, only to send Walter a completely useless reference a few days before Christmas. Not a reference, exactly, more of a hate letter. On the one hand, there is this reference, on the other, Walter's excellent qualifications—a programmer who can do anything, and who has four computer languages and practical experience with all the large computing machines. As a result, they invite him anyway.

"And this time I have a good feeling," Inge says, but she often says this. Again Walter feels the gentle firmness of her fingertips behind his ears, then she rinses the foam from his hair, which has turned gray this past year. It suits Walter, Inge finds.

After a few days, Mrs. Joska accepted that now Inge would be cooking for—and feeding—her. "Inge from Gera," as Mr. Joska calls her in a "Heidi, your world is the mountains" kind of sing-song across the printing plant's courtyard: "Inge from Gera, where are you?"

Inge makes a great effort. She washes the vegetables and counts the pills. She wants to do everything right and to do it well. She raises the spoon to Mrs. Joska's mouth, who fights with her tongue. Between bites, she whistles a little and Inge, in her eagerness, whistles back. Mrs. Joska laughs and sprays the rest of her mush over the table.

After eating, Mrs. Joska is laid on the sleeping sofa in the living room. Laid means: Inge pushes the wheelchair to the sofa, then the procedure begins. Lifting, propping, turning, and roll-ing. Weight transfer and "the proper use of leverage" is how the plant director demonstrated it. Inge already has some practice, but then what never should happen does: the wheel lock opens and the wheelchair hurtles mockingly backward into the room. It is out of reach and Mrs. Joska is hanging from Inge's neck: too heavy. Inge has to try without the wheelchair for support. She will try to fall so that Mrs. Joska will land half on her, half on the edge of the sofa.

"I'm going to let myself drop, Mrs. Joska."

Mrs. Joska is breathing heavily.

"Now!"

THE ENTIRE TIME

Ralf had disappeared, and it had been raining for days. Over Easter, Effi's sister in the Palast Hotel piano bar had met a Mexican from La Paz and (after a week that changed everything) had left Ralf, the champion of history. Ralf had disappeared, and since then it had been raining.

When someone leaves a man like Ralf, there has to be a reason, Carl thought. Ralf's jealousy maybe (it had gotten out of hand, Nora often complained) or maybe sex or some Aztec magic.

There had been no trace of him for days at Woolworth either, according to the woman from the company on the phone. She cleared her throat and finally mentioned that Mr. Schuster (Ralf) had recently had a small string of car accidents. On several occasions, the Eastern representative (as she called him) had come off the road. "Once a tree, once a wall." Her colleague had been uninjured, fortunately. But they'd been worried about him for a long time, seriously worried, and a clarifying conversation had been planned, which would also address the question of whether the extensive tour through the new Woolworth regions (extending, after all, up to Sassnitz, including Pasewalk, Stralsund, all those places up north no one knew anything about before) was a manageable workload and not too demanding. Since then, their colleague had been missing.

Carl remembered that Ralf had once told him (or, rather, had *explained to him* at the conclusion of a short lecture on the peculiarities of his position and the highway driving it entailed) that the Passat accelerates so quickly that some birds, for example, can't even fly out of the way in time. Ralf had been fascinated by the physics of it—the mass of the Passat and the distance divided by the elapsed time equals velocity, the conqueror's speed. It was a warm, lazy day with sun on Carl's face, which, as so often, he couldn't enjoy because some half-baked verse was tormenting him, as was his inchoate life.

They had sat on the grass behind the Käthe Kollwitz statue, Carl and Effi, the shabby artist couple, their relationship strained for weeks, and, next to them, Ralf and Nora, the dream couple with much better prospects. What Carl found especially depressing was his realization that Effi felt the same. He was pale and a feeling of isolation was going right to his core, through his skin, through his eyes, and it pushed aside without resistance everything that was at home in him. To talk about himself, about poems and the absolute, about his dream of another life, was completely unthinkable now. (Ashamed of what? That he was a poet, supposing he actually was? Or that he wasn't one? And so wasn't anything at all? Just empty and stupid?)

Ralf had taken off his jacket. As always, he was neatly dressed and radiated his superiority. Carl noticed that Ralf was wearing cufflinks, which he actually liked, maybe because it reminded him of his father in the early seventies. *Meticulous*, Carl's mother would have said. The representative for the entire East adjusted his cufflinks and started in: company weekend with behavioral training and skydiving. Management training sessions. The ladders of success and their rungs—he indicated them with quick, rising movements of his hand. More resolve and courage in life . . . And so on. Although this world seemed alien and essentially loathsome to Carl, he was impressed and, yes, felt insecure: would *all that* be unavoidable? A crippling thought. And how much time would he have until then? One year? Two years? He didn't even own a jacket.

"I don't even own a jacket," Carl said.

"I'll lend you one," Ralf said, smiling at him. "That's the first step."

That evening, he brought Carl the jacket, neatly folded in a plastic Woolworth bag. He wore his soft, brown suede jacket. He just stopped by, was fatherly, meant well. The jacket's collar (the lapels, Ralf said) was strikingly large, with tips that pointed upwards—like on a clown suit, thought Carl. It wasn't out of politeness or embarrassment that he accepted the jacket. It was something else, something inexplicable, there were no words for it. Fear, maybe, thought Carl, and then: yes, fear. He could admit it.

Since Ralf had disappeared, Nora slept at Effi's. Now and then the Mexican Nora called Chucho also came and gently asked how things stood. They had registered a missing person claim for Ralf at the police station. They'd gone to see Ralf's previous wife (two children) and checked out his favorite places (a few West Berlin cafés, the aquarium in the zoo, Peacock Island). Sometimes Nora wept. Several times a day, the sisters went to Schliemann Strasse to see if Ralf had returned to his apartment (their apartment). On the fourth day, something strange happened: tissues were scattered all over the apartment, on the floor, on the sofa, even in the bathtub, crumpled and freshly damp—with tears, flashed through Nora's mind, endless tears.

"He must have been here just before we arrived," whispered Chucho, who had accompanied them that day and was always ready to help any way he could.

"Maybe we'll find him, somewhere here in the neighborhood."

They quickly set out, full of hope. No more than two minutes had passed since they'd entered the side wing of the building at 3 Schliemann Strasse. They hurried downstairs, they would find Ralf, we're going to find him, thought Nora, thought Effi and maybe Chucho thought so, too, in Spanish, and when they pushed open the door, when they left the building again, Ralf lay dead in the courtyard.

Dead in front of the door.

At their feet.

It took her some time to grasp it all, Nora told Carl: "He was up there *the entire time*. On the roof for four days, in the pouring rain. Without food, even at night, four days just sky and rain. And he saw us, you understand, Carl, the entire time, from up there. Crossing the courtyard. And when the door closed behind us, I mean . . . He saw us! Effi and me. The entire time, in the pouring rain, even at night. He knew that we never stayed in the apartment long. And then he saw Chucho, and that . . . That tipped the scales. He saw that the three of us had come this time. He saw Chucho and you know how he was. And he was surely very tired, exhausted from four days up on the roof. And then he jumped, Carl. He *waited* for us. Do you understand?"

The exact sequence was important for Nora and she repeated it all one more time: from the first to the third day. Then the fourth day. The tissues on the floor, the wet tissues scattered all over the apartment, like a trail, just for her. Full of raindrops or tears.

She tried to come to terms with it, to stay on her feet. The wet tissues, that was the point. And then the shattered man, lying in his vengeful blood.

Nora remained remarkably composed (as they say), in contrast to Effi who lay on her bed, deathly pale, staring at the ceiling. Carl sat on the edge of her foam-rubber mattress and caressed her. Her cheeks were cold, and Carl was alarmed. She hadn't looked at him once.

As if it had been *her lover*, thought Carl. But he was sitting right there, he hadn't jumped and was taking care of her. And as inappropriate as the thought was at the moment, it had been surfacing everywhere, the childish question: who was *more* there for the other? And gives love, but doesn't receive it, thought Carl, and so on. Nora put her hand on Carl's shoulder and together they left the room. Effi's sister was tall, thin, and you could tell she had once been athletic.

She made tea and looked for "Effi's pills" about which Carl knew nothing. Pills?

"She probably isn't taking them anymore," Nora murmured and once again Carl admired Effi's sister for her—how should he put it—competence? Composure? It's important to keep your composure in life, Carl thought. He saw Nora stepping over crumpled banknotes to prepare a fresh Black Label. A glass that seems fuller when she serves it. *In every real man . . .*

"Effi is calming down again."

"What's wrong with her? And which pills?"

"She's calming down. She can't talk now, Carl. She just needs quiet. We'll let her sleep and then you can try again."

Carl looked out the window. The rustling of the rain (it was still raining) and the rustling of the chestnut tree in the courtyard, which had begun to sprout its sticky buds and give off a sweetish scent. Maybe the sweet smell was also coming from the garbage, from the trash cans under the tree, four square bins with their lids always half-open like hungry mouths. The garbage just opens its jaws, but the chestnut tree rustles, Carl thought. It's locked in here, like we are.

"But I'm out of the worst of the mess," the chestnut rustled, "made it to the fifth floor already . . ."

"This is *serious*, Carl," Nora tilted her head toward the living room.

"Of course, I understand, I . . ."

"No, I mean Effi." She looked him in the eye. "Effi and me, strictly speaking. But especially Effi. It has to do with our mother."

"How did she do—I mean, how did she die?"

Nora shook her head.

"There, on Schliemann Strasse, something happened to Effi. We had to carry her home, Chucho and I, she couldn't move. And her face."

Again, Nora shook her head.

"I think she didn't even see Ralf, she only saw Mama."

Nora stopped talking and looked at the floor.

"Where were you, actually, Carl?"

"Effi and I, we decided to give each other some space for a few days. We do that now and then. It's important to Effi. And if Effi says a week, then it's a week, no matter what happens. And after, we do something nice together."

"Something nice?"

"We take some time, go for a drive, with Freddy, to the Bötzsee or further north, to the Baltic Sea, in the Zhiguli."

"And? Is it time for something nice?" Effi stood in the kitchen doorway, in panties and an undershirt. Nora jumped up and Effi landed in her arms. They stood like that for a while, turning, very slowly, in a circle, as if dancing. Two sisters and death.

*

The first time Carl wore Ralf's jacket it was to the memorial service. It was too large for him and had the clownish lapels, but Carl didn't care. He wore it for Ralf.

Almost thirty people had come, including Ralf's first wife and their two flaxen-haired children. In his earlier life, Ralf Schuster had been the concierge in the Palast Hotel in Berlin, the eulogy revealed. Nora had never told him, or had she? Maybe Effi mentioned it and I just forgot that Ralf had been Nora's boss or one of her bosses, thought Carl. A few of his former colleagues had also come. Two sallow characters in thin, crumpled leather jackets whom no one knew sat in the last row. From Woolworth there was only a floral arrangement, small and shabby.

Carl took care of Freddy for a few days and walked him to kindergarten. The cool air and the morning walk cleared his head, it got him started and the day began with that good feeling of having an indisputable right to be on this earth. Outside the building, Freddy took his hand as always and later, when they stopped to watch the whales, he didn't let go.

On one of Carl's writing mornings on Ryke Strasse, a frantic clattering outside his door yanked him from his thoughts.

"The dead, they're coming!"

Old lady Knospe flew downstairs on her rope and Carl followed her. The crack in the ground in the bomb crater copse was now one meter wide and part of the cellar vault had collapsed: from the depths came a soft, panicked whimper.

"It's our friend," Sonie wheezed, poking his battle rod into the darkness. It was Wrubel, Alfred Wrubel. The cable trench digger was their new landlord, Carl only realized it at that moment. He grabbed the rod, then Carl's hand and together Carl and Sonie pulled the man up to the light. His face was ashen, and he could not walk for the pain. His work clothes gave off such a breathtaking stench that Carl almost vomited.

"Did you see them? You saw them, didn't you?" Old Knospe suddenly sounded very calm, even affectionate. She laid her small, wrinkled hand on the new landlord's chest, who just looked at the old woman incredulously and nodded: "Yes."

OLD ACQUAINTANCES

It was one of their weekend pleasures to walk together from Meerholz to the old center of Gelnhausen and buy fresh rolls, bread, croissants, and now and then also a piece of cake. Like vagrant accomplices, they sat next to each other in front of the bakery in the small, paved market square, drinking coffee at the base of a bust honoring Philipp Reis.

"Maybe Cologne isn't even necessary anymore," Walter said. "Maybe EMI isn't either. Soon we'll have the money and . . ." he took a sip and Inge smiled because she was proud of that. "You're the breadwinner now," Walter had said.

"Philipp Reis—inventor of the telephone," was written on the statue's pedestal and of course Walter knew about it: "1860. 'On the Propagation of Musical Notes to Any Desired Distance' was the title of his lecture. No one was particularly interested at the time."

"Maybe that's why we still don't have a telephone?"

It was nice when Inge laughed. It was a reward—for everything.

"Eighteen hundred and?"

"Reis was the son of the master baker here," Walter pointed at the bakery with the remains of his croissant, "and his own son was named Karl."

"You're making that up!"

Walter shrugged.

"When do we tell Carl?"

"As soon as we're sure, Inge."

*

On the way back to Meerholz, they crossed the meadows in the Kinzig valley and passed the airfield. The dirt road was already full of cars—license plates from Frankfurt, Mainz, even Munich. On the edge of the airstrip there was a low shed, against which leaned the tower, a hut on stilts clad in transparent PVC that resembled the blind of a hunter who feared bad weather. Next to the entrance to the bleachers (three rows of benches and a few plastic chairs) stood a US Army *Apache* surrounded by children. An American soldier sat in the cockpit.

"That's Johnny, Johnny is back from the war!" Inge shouted and could hardly contain herself. Where was Winona?

Corkscrews, loops, and nosedives—there was a carnival atmosphere. But it was nice to look into the sky even when there was nothing going on up there. "We too, Inge, we're going to fly," murmured Walter, inaudible under the roar of the planes circling over their heads. He suddenly felt proud of their power and elegance in a way that only a dévoté of engines could. Yes, he missed the Zhiguli. And yes, also his landscape of tools. The dim depths of his garage in Gera, the good old den. Soon they would truly leave it behind and now he felt the loss. He was almost in his mid-fifties, and he'd never flown. Doesn't matter, thought Walter. There was the spring sunshine on his face, the hand shielding his eyes. And the movement of his lips, as if he were whispering something to the heavens, as if he were speaking to someone up there.

When Inge looks back at Walter, Winona suddenly appears behind her and laughs.

"Unexpectedly again, Eenguh!"

They hug like old acquaintances.

It takes a while until the Americans have understood that Inge and Walter have come on foot. "No car," Walter stammers.

Before the air show is over, they drive in Johnny's car to Virginia State, an American bar in Bad Orb. It's a 1973 burgundy Buick Grand Sport with a white roof and very little room in the back seat. "Room for the dog," Johnny says and laughs. Walter admires the Buick that sways over the dirt road like a ship. Johnny turns on the radio, AFN, Chuck Berry—it's a dream, Inge thinks. Whatever begins like this is always a dream.

They listen to music and Johnny has a bottle in the door pocket. He drinks, then Winona drinks, too, and then Walter and Inge also drink. They drive around and are young. Inge talks with a simple, faulty syntax that she thinks is easier to understand. She's also talking very loud, so Walter lays his hand on her thigh, but Inge doesn't calm down. She's happy.

Walter looks around. It's the first time since the Bischoffs emigrated that they're eating out with another couple. Strange, sitting here amid all the GIs, Walter thinks.

They talk about anything and everything. Walter asks Johnny about the Apache.

"Miles!" Johnny calls and two tables away, a man stands up, joins them and talks about the Apache. The man calmly answers every question. He wears metal-rimmed glasses and has an ironic smile. After a while, he goes back to his table.

"That was Parker," Johnny says, "we were together in Iraq. He'd already flown that baby in Panama." Johnny interrupts himself and looks at Walter. "You're not spies, right?"

"KGB," Walter says curtly. "But we're on a completely different assignment now."

Winona looks up and Inge turns a little pale, then they all laugh. It was a typical Walter joke. And it has been a long time since Inge has heard one of Walter's jokes.

"The first time I met an American was in the early seventies . . ." Walter hesitates, because he knows that's not right but then he continues: "In Düsseldorf, at IBM. The East had bought their technology for its data centers and needed people who knew how it worked, 1971 . . ."

Walter speaks—as if liberated. All of a sudden there is a lot to say, and they travel back in time: Winona was ten years old then, Johnny fifteen. "My father had a farm," Johnny says, "in Iowa, on the Mississippi." They don't know the big cities. They've only been to New York once and to Sioux City a few times. The fields, the cattle, milking in the morning—that's all very familiar to Inge and they talk about it.

"We had lots of questions, but they were also interested in us, in our own stories," Inge later writes to Carl. "That was—how should I put it—new. It was like with Dr. Talib. Our story was just our story, nothing that anyone could immediately say was good or bad. Not living where you were born is nothing unusual for Johnny and Winona. Where you actually come from, why you're no longer there—they're ambushes, like in war, Johnny said. Isn't that interesting, Carl? In the afternoon, we walked back to Meerholz as if inspired, across the meadows, along the Kinzig, like our walks along the Elster. We'd found someone we could talk to, completely naturally . . ."

Carl put the letter down. "As if inspired" and "completely naturally" were two of his mother's favorite expressions. He looked at the envelope: next to the real postmark was a promotional stamp that showed the outline of the Palatinate with the motto "Barbarossa City Gelnhausen: too good to drive through without stopping." But that seemed to be exactly what they had planned, Inge and Walter, despite Barbarossa. And Gelnhausen was not too good for that.

DRINKING FROM THE BOOT

On the day of its first anniversary, the Assel remained closed. "A day just for us, like before," Irina had said to Carl, her

eyes glowing. She meant the pack but also some of the new
staff who had become friends. And a few favorite customers
showed up.

They carried the Shepherd from the stall into the taproom
and set him in a chair. Carl should have known, but when the
Shepherd was surrounded by straw in the familiar setting, what
Hoffi had become after his dive at Mainzer Strasse wasn't as
obvious. His hollow-eyed expression had a terrified, pleading
air. He raised his head and tried to survey the room; a few people
from the old pack were missing. Countless little clumps—of
dirt or feces—were stuck in his long, matted hair. You could see
each of his bones, and under his gray, wrinkled skin they looked
fragile, a sight that called for the old word "spindly" from childhood fairy tales in order to avoid more alarming comparisons.
"Little more than a thread," his mother would have said. Hoffi
also seemed to have shrunk to half his height which provoked
anxiety, not just in Irina, who had persuaded her "brother" (he
had always been her brother, she just hadn't used the word in
a long time) to make this appearance. In any case, the date had
been chosen arbitrarily. No one could say when exactly the Assel
had been founded, on which day this shelter for the working
class had turned into a cellar bar, a café, a "tart dive," a place to
get warm, a cheap snack bar with three kinds of Japanese noodle
soups (and a few other dishes) and, in the end, even an art gallery. And that was just the front half of the Assel. The back half
(Fenske's cellar) had its own history.

Hans rose to speak.

"A year, dear friends. In this time, a decade or more has
passed—you know what I mean. And let's not forget the prehistory, when we took our first steps here below, in the dampness and the darkness, surrounded by squadrons of these
industrious little creatures who crawled from the depths of
the Permian through three hundred million years to us here—to

this wonderful place." He laid his hand on the wall behind the counter and was silent for a moment as if he needed to refocus, then he took a deep breath and resumed: "'Shelter the lost children of a failed revolution,' Little Frank once said over Radio P, but we are not of as melancholy a disposition, my friends—on the contrary, I'd say: Assel means asylum. Asylum for us and for many others. What I mean is: the aguerrillas will win, in their way."

Hans continued in this vein for a while with a slight lisp. He wasn't drunk. He had prepared, he mentioned everyone from the earliest phase by name, even Carl's arrival ("on a cold December night"), his work as a bricklayer, then the phases of the first and second counters, and so on, through the entire history. When sober, his memory was astonishing. In conclusion, Hans thanked the Shepherd and again called the Assel "our U-boat between Cold War and communalism." Pontoon, thought Carl, shouldn't it be pontoon? And why had Hans, who'd always been against anything combative, mentioned the aguerrillas?

The Shepherd smiled bashfully. He nodded in the direction of the counter and said, "Nice." He watched suspiciously as Irina poured him a glass of champagne. He raised his hand defensively and pointed at Dodo. The goat had stayed at his side the entire time. With his bony fingers (they're about to break off, the twigs, thought Carl), he raked the fur on the animal's neck, whereupon the goat stretched, raised its head and slowly rose, so high that Hoffi, the gnome on the large chair, could reach her udder. Carl, the first one to realize how the scene would develop, leaped into the kitchen and the twigs were soon stroking the udder and a thin stream of fresh, warm milk rang on the bottom of the pitcher that Carl held in exactly the right position. He was holding the pitcher and, without raising his head, he could feel the respect. Now there's someone who sees what work needs to be done, "seen work," Carl's father would have said.

They clinked their glasses against the pitcher and toasted each other. And when the Shepherd raised the pitcher to his mouth without a problem and drank, the relief was palpable.

"The Russians asked about you every day. They were worried," Hans claimed, looking closely at Carl. Over spring, Carl's hand had healed well—a writing hand with scars, Carl thought as he entered Fenske's cellar.

In his absence, a small program had become established around the competition and the betting, which had grown to include singing and reciting poems off the cuff. A few of the older Russians, Vassily among them, were embarrassingly well read and always ready to quote a few lines of Goethe or Heine. "I do not know the reason why I am so full of sorrow." Which Hans, without reservation (or batting an eye), called "a form of cultural exchange" that needed, especially now in times of new hostilities, to be fostered again. Because he knew that the Russians were no threat to the Assel (in fact, more of a protection), this development filled him with pride.

"Fenske's cellar was always a kind of historical display case."

Carl, who rarely attempted to contradict Henry, shook his head.

"Everything has changed here except for us, don't you think?"

"And Fenske's boots, his crutches? This whole fantastic space? Someday, in a hundred years, they'll excavate us and wonder what all the things were for."

"Who will excavate us, Hans?"

They stood together at the entrance, waiting for a sign from Vassily.

For several weeks, the older Russians, who still knew who was meant when they toasted Budyonny or Bersarin, no longer held the floor alone. They were often drowned out by the younger men at the table, who only wanted to drink or hold their cockroach races. A few had small, scratched plastic boxes with "their own animals," which they occasionally took out of their pockets. Daddy Vassily called the young Russians "good boys" who didn't have it easy "out there." The good boys wore pants made out of parachute silk and had tattoos on their arms. It turned out that they were mostly Russian construction workers (without papers), living in containers or shacks clustered around the countless new building sites in the city. *Workers*, thought Carl, these are the workers that Hoffi meant, unprotected, underpaid, in the dirt twelve or fourteen hours a day. There was something childlike and forlorn about their round, close-cropped heads, a vulnerable aura in which any conceivable action, however brutal, seemed possible at any time.

The air in the cellar was sour and Carl felt nauseous. Over the table hung the smell of the disinfectant that the Russians used for the uniforms—their trade with jackets and caps was flourishing. And as always, there was some pimp or other at the table, acquiring a Makarov. Carl remembered Vassily's plan for a secret army but in the end that had only been a dream. The Comandante never delivered, despite his elevated Soviet stock, thought Carl. "Kruso was a risk," was Vassily's summary of the story and for a second, Carl wondered what happened to Edgar Bendler, little Ed from Langenberg, the deepest homeland.

Now, Carl was even faster than before. Since he'd started using individual components of his practice gun while writing (carrying them around the apartment, tapping them rhythmically on his hand or squeezing them while walking and talking), he had developed a profound, almost tender relationship to the pieces. It also happened during the contests, as if an electric circuit had been closed: he touched the gun and his lips immediately started moving—he couldn't do anything about it, it just happened, even in the hubbub, in the dark behind the blindfold, alone with a few words on his tongue. "What are you murmuring?" Vassily had asked. "Nothing in particular," Carl had replied. "It's just the thing with the gun." "It's a symbol, Carl." "I know, I know, but for me, it's above all . . ." Material, weight, inner rhythm—a linguistic shape for matter, Carl would have liked to say, although on closer observation, a better name would be a material shape for language. "It is a symbol of our solidarity," Vassily said, "an ancient brotherhood in arms that is now ending. With my army's retreat. But brothers remain brothers, true?"

Vassily liked to speak of the Red Army as if it were his own unit, his rank must have been high. Vassily's esteem for the fact that Carl wrote poetry was as high as the esteem he believed Carl had for the Kalashnikov. Again and again, he had tried to persuade Carl to read aloud "something of his own," but Carl had refused. For Carl, reading his poetry aloud was simply unimaginable. One day Vassily brought a man Carl had often noticed in the Assel up to the bar.

"Oberbaum Press, Berlin and Petersburg," the man said (instead of his name), offering Carl his enormous hand. He was sweating. He was so tall that he almost had to duck beneath the cellar's ceiling—too big for the Assel, thought Carl and felt a stabbing pain in his chest. The publisher's wife was Russian, from St. Petersburg. Vassily joked with her while the publisher looked fixedly at Carl.

"You work here, don't you?"

"Yes, I mean . . ." The music was too loud, the customers, the stabbing pain, everything bothered him. A publisher. In two quick steps, Carl emerged from behind the bar. The tall man pulled him aside.

"I've gotten to know you here," he gestured toward the bar, "as an impressive young man. And Vassily has told me a lot about you. He is very enthusiastic about your—manuscript." His eyes were small and spirited.

"Vassily?"

The publisher made a show of pulling a business card from the pocket of his crumpled suit jacket. He moved both elbows vigorously as if he were preparing to lift off, testing the action of his wings one last time.

"You'll send me something, promise?"

As she turned to go, the woman from St. Petersburg placed her hand on Carl's arm and gave him a warm smile—this all-healing gesture was what was missing for him to be happy.

What the Russian construction workers did not know: the Russian Carl had learned in school was poor, but still good enough for him to understand a few things they spoke about when Vassily was out of earshot. They called Carl "the little Goethe-Nazi," which had alarmed him at first, however it wasn't meant as an insult. They said it approvingly and with a certain admiration, not for Carl as an ersatz Goethe (the symbol of all things intellectual), but for his position in Fenske's cellar, for his obscure connection to Vassily and his closeness to Vassily's daughter Adele (which was no less obscure to Carl). It took Carl some time before he understood this. And then even more time before he understood that it was the last signal to leave the Assel.

To be precise, it was the next to last signal. Carl had just taken up position. Next to him sat Sergey, a very young soldier who gave him a friendly greeting—one of his new challengers. As Adele raised the blindfold to the light (the cellar was still illuminated by the construction lamps from the very first days, which now hung from the ceiling, their large black cones giving the room a casino atmosphere, the 200 watt light bulbs, their chalk-white glow warming the young Russians' close-cropped heads like enormous eggs in an incubator while the rest of the room receded into the void), one of the girls was hit by her

Charlottenburg pimp (protector, husband, housemate, there were several names, sometimes it was more of one, sometimes more of the other or a bit of all at the same time)—in front of everyone, at the table, just like that: left-right, left-right, palm and back of the hand in rapid succession with a sound like whiplashes.

It was Vera from Odessa, cheerful Vera, liked by everyone in the cellar because she sang well and knew lots of songs by heart, even old songs from the Great Patriotic War. Cheerful Vera was sobbing now, then she jumped up and sought refuge with Vassily, which meant: she leaped onto his lap and cowered, suddenly making herself very small. Carl didn't understand much. Vera's exchange with Vassily was short, just a few words and sobs, but like everyone at the table, he caught the tenderness and, yes, beauty of the moment.

And that was probably what tipped the balance. Vassily took the young Charlottenburger to task. Clearly a hothead, the latter misread the situation and insulted Vassily. He yanked at Vera, who did not move an inch from her place on Vassily's lap, so the pimp started ranting about "stupid Russians" who, God knows, didn't belong in Germany anymore, hadn't for a long time now and "should finally get lost, those *shitty liberators*"—and so on. He carried on like this, still yanking on Vera, the "stupid whore" (his words), who sobbed and screamed. The young Russians stared at Vassily and Vassily saw (Carl could observe all this from the head of the table, where he usually stood for his matches) that he had no choice but to give the sign.

The young Russians jumped up and beat the Charlottenburg pimp to a pulp. They stomped on him for a while, then propped him up provisionally again. Vassily slowly rose and whispered something to Vera, who clung to him like a child. Adele, still holding the blindfold, woke from her shock, stroked Vera's cheek and together the women left the cellar.

Since no one was speaking a word, it could not be over yet.

After a while, during which only the pimp's sniveling moans and the usual sounds from the Assel (excessively loud music and yelling) could be heard, Vassily broke the silence.

"Apologies, Carl."

Carl was startled—yes, it was his name: Carl. And he was *also* here, in this cellar, he was one of them. His consciousness seemed swept away. "Which manuscript, Vassily?"

Vassily pushed a glass of goat milk with vodka toward Carl. It was passed, hand to hand, to the end of the table where Carl had taken up position a few minutes, now years, before.

Confused and with a shy that's-not-necessary gesture, Carl shook his head and sat down. Very carefully, he picked up his practice gun and put it on his lap.

"Actually, we were looking forward to your performance after so many weeks. Do you want to leave?"

Again, Carl shook his head. My last night in the Assel, he thought. Now he knew. He took the glass and emptied it in one gulp.

"Svobodan, Sergey," Vassily ordered.

Carl's challenger clicked his heels and left the table. Vassily looked thoughtfully at the groaning Charlottenburger, then he stood up, disappeared into the rear of the cellar and returned with one of Fenske's rubber boots. In front of everyone, Vassily undid his trousers. He ceremoniously brought his dick out and relieved himself. The stream made a dark, roaring sound against the bottom of the boot. One of the young Russians calmly grabbed the Charlottenburger's hair, two others grabbed his arms. Vassily raised the boot (testing the weight) to eye level and gently placed it on the table. Then he went up to Carl, took him (no less gently) by the shoulder and led him outside.

Carl crossed the street and entered the park. The cool night air and a walk. He put his hand into his pocket. The small card was still there, the first business card of his life. Step by step, he felt lighter. He crossed the makeshift metal bridge to Museum Island. The bridge clanged under his feet, the light of the street-lamps in the river. Bode, Pergamon, and the wreck in the middle of the island—these were giant, stranded ships he could talk with. "What brought you here, what storms, and how are you holding up?" This is how Carl talked and he could hardly hear it, but this time he not only surrendered, gabbing, to exhaustion or cozy dawn, this time he surrendered to everything.

"What do you think?" Carl whispered and listened to his footsteps. He classified the things he needed to think about now. First: the publisher. A publisher dammit! Second: that's it for the Assel. Effi would certainly agree. Third: money problems. With the prospect of a book, Carl knew, everything would be easier. A grant, for example. He could submit a few poems, think up a fantastic title and write: "appearing in 1992, Oberbaum Publisher, Berlin." And St. Petersburg!

All of a sudden, his entire life was going in the right direction.

LITTLE GOETHE-NAZI

Effi's door was open. Rico's door was closed and there were voices behind it. Effi's voice and Rico's. Then silence and voices again—soft, whispering, but spectrally amplified by the echo in Rico's bare cell.

There had only ever been one key to Effi's apartment. Effi hadn't seen any reason (or hadn't had the strength) to change that. Carl stepped into Effi's apartment but only two, three steps and without turning on the light. Effi's jackets in the wardrobe, her shoes, the familiar smell. Somewhere in the back, Freddy was sleeping. Just lying there, unaware and unprotected.

Effi and Rico whispering.

Carl had no right to go to Freddy; he suddenly felt seedy, like an intruder. He had no right to turn on the light, not in the entrance hall and even less in the large room, no right to sit on Effi's bed. Actually, he did, but he didn't feel that he had. He could hardly breathe. The fact that they were together, *a couple*, did not exist. Their trips, the nights, the entire year together. He couldn't come up with a single detail he could fall back on, that he could summon, so he had to leave, and he had to leave right now. The idea that Effi might come out of Rico's door now and catch him here, in the darkness of her own hallway, that was unthinkable, appalling, worse than—than?

Why was shame washing over him and not Effi?

Because he was the weaker one.

He went back out into the stairwell and listened.

"Effi?"

He hadn't called especially loud, but loud enough. He had called her name in the direction of the half-opened door, to the empty apartment.

This wasn't a trick, just helplessness—and superstition. As if he'd only just arrived, still halfway on the staircase, as if he hadn't heard the whispering, full of tenderness and *depth*.

Now there was silence in Rico's apartment.

Caught out, thought Carl. How stupid.

And as if it were happening far from him.

He felt like a stranger to himself. This all no longer had anything to do with him, nothing to do with who he actually was. It all disgusted him.

He listened. No more whispering, just the faint ticking of the light timer. Just the control box for the staircase light, next to the toilet. Carl raised his head toward the light and let it dazzle him.

If he were going to leave now, he should pull the door closed so that Freddy would be safe. Carl didn't have the heart to leave him lying there, exposed, unprotected. He'd seen Effi's key in her entrance hall. He would take the key. Or drop it into Rico's mailbox, like a tactful pimp who keeps an eye on everything. And then cashes in. Not like me, thought Carl.

The staircase light went off and the darkness took Carl under its wing. He was not capable of going into the empty apartment again. He deferred the problem and quietly slunk downstairs, but only to the first landing. We hadn't agreed to meet. It's a surprise visit. The usual surprise visit at two in the morning, Carl thought. Because I couldn't stand the wait. Because I didn't move in here, Rico did. Your own fault, Carl Bischoff, you Goethe-Nazi with a publisher.

He pulled the business card from his pocket. It was too dark to read and Carl could only make out the silhouette of a bridge with two towers over the lettering. It was the Oberbaum Bridge. It's the only reason I'm here, Carl thought, because I wanted Effi to know, because it should make her happy, *for him,* that's actually what it was. I'm like a child, Carl thought, a child with no light in the window.

He sat down and leaned his head against the wall. The wall was freezing. The building would remain ice-cold at least until early June, until the thaw worked its way through the front buildings and the courtyards, all the way to the back.

The staircase light clicked on, setting off a gentle movement of shadows: the ass. The pig, that guitar-playing clown—Carl's hatred had grown vague. He searched for some useful rage, but it was too lonely and too late there on the stairs for rage. Still, his heart pounded in his throat.

In some inexplicable way, Carl had known, even as he climbed the stairs. Truth be told, he had already known the evening before and the one before that and on a few earlier ones as well. With this knowledge, Carl had knocked on Effi's door, had heard her shuffling steps, kissed her sad eyes and his hand had been there, on her skin, safe. Only then did relief flood his heart, washing everything away, and he felt his love, utterly clear and without reservation.

They had never really fought, but for weeks the light in Effi's face had seemed to have gone out. Ralf's jump off the roof, his revenge or whatever it should be called: Carl had not been able to console Effi or Effi had not let him (as Carl saw it). Maybe consolation was too little. Effi was gone, she had disappeared to a region Carl did not know how to reach. Effi had never spoken about her mother's death. For Carl it was a sign that silence was best. Not out of consideration, it was just everyday cowardice, which you hardly notice because it's so normal.

They had lain awake the entire night after Ralf's death, as if there were still a hope they might find a space where they could be close again. Carl was exhausted but had not let himself sleep because falling asleep first would be proof that you were the one who was less worried, who was ready to give up. And therefore, the one whose love could not be great enough. And so on.

Carl lay down for a bit on the half-landing. He tried to use his bag as a pillow, but it had nothing soft in it, only the Kashi with its folding stock, which he'd packed as usual. Little Goethe-Nazi. He should have given the gun back, right away, but that wasn't the right time. (Steam had risen from the boot as from a stovepipe. Carl tried to remember what had been so significant in that moment, but he couldn't remember. As if it had all happened a long time ago.)

A few large shadows swayed across the wall. Anyone lying awake right now can hear the rustling of the chestnut trees, thought Carl. He took the Kashi out of his bag and started dismantling it. When he did it this slowly, it seemed almost incomprehensible. Two heavy hands (a bricklayer's hands) doing their puzzling work, as in a dream. An operation that would only make sense decades later as part of the story of a betrayed man.

*

With a light, muffled hammer blow, the staircase light went on. A woman had turned it on. The woman was naked, wearing only a blanket over her shoulders. At first, she didn't see him and Carl didn't see her either because he had fallen asleep. She padded across the hallway into her apartment and after a few seconds she came back, and only then, on the way back to Rico's apartment, did she notice the man with the machine gun. Her scream pierced Carl to the marrow: he leaped up and raised the gun, a reflex from time immemorial.

Effi's skin was white, the harsh light in the staircase made her contour sharp, no matter whatever else there was to discern, Carl knew what Effi looked like *afterwards*.

"The door," Carl stammered, "I mean, I thought—because of Freddy."

Rico was now standing next to Effi in white boxers with a flower pattern. His Karl Valentin face looked polished and suddenly his wide-set eyes were noticeable; he held his hands in the air.

Only then did Carl become aware of the gun. It was an awareness that set in only slowly, unhurriedly: gradually the little lights went on, first one, then two, and so on.

"It's only . . . It was . . . only to practice, Effi, you know that." Carl could explain, he could apologize, but since the lights were now blazing, he slowly swung the muzzle of his gun in Rico's direction.

Effi turned her head to the side and pressed her hands to her face. Carl found it remarkable of her not to say anything. In his thoughts it was bright as day, pure, powerful consciousness, like after an overdose, is how Carl imagined it.

"Do you still love her?" Carl heard the small, slightly circling muzzle ask, but he had probably said it himself, very calmly and clearly and not especially loud, rather softly, despite the hatred coursing in his blood.

Rico's erratic gaze. His head was thrust forward as if he didn't want to miss anything, the shot, for example.

The quarry, when it's listening, Carl thought, and put a foot on the step.

Poor Rico. Didn't know the right answer. Yet again.

"All poets are criminals, Rico, didn't you know? With neither conscience nor morals—that, in a way, is prerequisite for good poetry. Art has to be free, Rico, to state it clearly for once. You should have taken that into consideration, I mean, *with a campaign like that*, I mean, if you're going to pull off something like that. First, you move in here, you plant yourself in a well-feathered nest and play the troubadour and then . . ."

A small, muffled bang and it went dark.

"It's just the light timer, Rico. You're not dead yet."

For a few seconds, they stood there immobile: Effi and Rico next to each other on the upper landing and Carl on the half-landing, invisibly united in the darkness.

Carl felt very tired all of a sudden. And at a loss.

Rico bolted into his apartment and slammed the door. The sound of banging set in, something was being hastily shoved into the entrance hall.

"So he does have some furniture," Carl said.

"Mama? Mama!"

Effi turned the light on and Carl saw that she was freezing.

"You have to go to Freddy."

Effi tried to hold the blanket closed.

"Freddy called you."

"Mama? Is Carl there?"

The freezing air from the courtyard and the rustling of the chestnut tree. Carl squatted down and stowed the gun in his bag. The battle was over.

ARE YOU THINKING OF?

Effi came that afternoon. She hugged him and then they slept together. Carl acted coldly and let Effi do all the things he could never get enough of. She scooted onto him and he could feel her slender body moving carefully on top of him, asking for forgiveness. She could only say it when she was very close, her mouth next to his ear, in a whisper, and then she repeated it again and again. He left her alone with it, not saying a word. He humiliated her.

To hold onto a wound (or hurt) even through an orgasm is difficult but it can be done. The first requirement is concentration, the suppression of certain reflexes that the void between two lovers in crisis automatically elicits (the natural wish for reconciliation and togetherness). Still, the right to atonement gets used up at some point. The guilt fades and the guilt-fuck (a repulsive word and not how Carl thought but he knew that it was what people said) loses its appeal.

After three days, Effi gave up. Carl didn't move. He lay on his side and watched her zigzag out of the room, almost stumbling, watched her gather her things and disappear into the corridor. He heard her jerky breathing, and he heard the door click shut and then it was over.

For a while, Carl tried out hate fantasies. Accusations that were fierce and irrefutable. Yet the hurt was acid and ate its way deeper. At some point Carl could hardly move—he just lay there on his mattress-raft, moored to a dead black-and-white television in the middle of a room which, strictly speaking, was no less bare than Rico's monastery cell. In one of his fantasies, Carl shot him. In sustained firing, the weapon inevitably pulls upwards, Carl had been told by Lieutenant Gawrence, his company commander in the military, and Section Commander Junghanss had explained the rest. As he fired constantly, Carl noticed something odd: he didn't hate Rico.

Carl remained on his raft for a week, letting himself drift. He was a river pirate on the Mississippi, and he ignored the knocking on his door. Now and then, he would drag himself to the kitchen to transfer something from his provisions to his bed; the food cupboard under the kitchen window was full. A few months earlier, Carl had decided to overcome his disgust and use the cupboard. His compromise: the left side with the old preserves still belonged to Lappke (Lappke's Anchor jars with their mysterious, numbing essence), in the middle he kept the coal, and on the right side were stacked provisions from the Assel, not just Japanese soups, but also feta cheese (an entire block in plastic wrap), ham, and sometimes even a few pieces of fruit. He ate something, masturbated, and then did it again.

Sex can be a solution, thought Carl. Sex as its own truth, with which he could evade all that he had recently acknowledged: that they'd never been made for each other, that he'd reached rock bottom. But it was too late for that too because he had misused Effi for three days, to exhaustion. He had always misused her for his own ends. He'd turned Effi into Valeska. He'd *rewritten* her and, in so doing, cast her out. Into the realm of literature. Effi—a fiction. Carl now had to admit that that is what she had been for him from the beginning: in the plastic-film room, in her bodysuit, as enchantress, as artist, in bed.

Effi, the Briest. Effi, the beast.

His glance fell on the remains of food around the raft. He liked the sight of it and felt a small, insane cheerfulness that only thrives on despair and loneliness. Even as a child, I liked to be alone, thought Carl. Not from the beginning, perhaps, but he'd made the best of it, and, in fact, he'd managed so well that, whenever the subject had come up (any siblings?), he could convincingly affirm that he'd never wanted it any other way. He had been *very happy* alone with his cowboys and Indians under the table and then his first construction set, followed soon after by a second, third, and fourth with real screws, perforated steel, and his first very own tool.

He swept his hand over the cold floorboards: crumbs of feta clad with lint like tiny dancers.

Leaving the Assel is no longer an option. While working, Carl thinks up stories that allow him to speak to women without being pushy. He gathers three names—Caroline, Jacqueline, and Jenny. He already had Katja from the Krähe. It's the start of a new life, in which everything happens as he wishes. In which he takes what he deserves.

For a time, Carl no longer wants to write. He takes a break. He drinks. He often starts drinking in the afternoon, starting with something simple and light—a glass of wine, for example. Sipping it calmly. Now and again a sherry, interspersed with the wine, otherwise coffee, coffee, coffee, all at the Assel's expense.

He dresses differently. He wears a coat and hat. It doesn't seem ridiculous to him anymore. His coat and hat match, both are made of a gray, gleaming velour that feels nice, almost fresh, doesn't wrinkle and, depending on the direction you brush it, is a dark or light shade. The coat and hat come from the package his mother sent him half a year ago: "A very nice material, Carl, that gives an impression of velvet."

He'll now wear the things from the West.

On the first evening of his new life, he sits with Katja behind the coffee machine in the Krähe. With each beer, a warm look from her dark eyes. He drinks the beer she brings him and puts the crackers she pushes toward him in his mouth. All evening, he has the feeling that they have a lot to say to each other—Katja and he, hadn't he always known? At night, on the way home, he presses his face into her coat, nothing more than that happens. It's three in the morning and Carl is dead tired.

He keeps a certain distance from everything and that does him good, it gives him an overview: if he doesn't want to be, he's not part of this world. If he doesn't want to, he doesn't have to talk to anyone, sleep with anyone, and so on. He sees others at the table as figures, as characters in a large story that is also playing out at the staff table in front of the bar, with Hans and the prostitutes. He now has the distance that he'd lacked earlier, now he has an eye for something he hadn't cared about before.

He talks with one of the women at the working ladies' table and tastes her microwave cocoa; the hot chocolate tastes much better than expected and Carl has to laugh, although he doesn't know why.

"But we're actually friends, Carl, aren't we?" She offers him a special friends' price and they go into the storage room at the back.

Caroline is only eighteen, but she has very precise ideas. What position she wants to lie in and what Carl should do. How long he should keep his hand first above, then below, never the opposite. She tells him, "first above," then, "more here." She takes hold of his hand. As if she'd read the book that Carl's parents had hidden under a new blue anorak as a fourteenth birthday present, without comment. *Are You Already Thinking of Love?* Two words in the title were cant: "already" and "love." They could have been left out.

"Are you thinking of?" would have been enough.

Jenny is different, but Carl forgets the condoms every time. She invites him to her place in a small apartment in a recently constructed building in Marzahn, ninth floor with an elevator and a view of the city. It's bright and clean. A small dining table and behind it a hatch to the kitchen. Carl feels both alien and secure. They lie on the floor and embrace. Jenny makes a nice comment about Carl's dick (she calls it his "sex"). At midnight,

Carl drives back toward the city center to get condoms and something to eat but then only brings the food—two unmanageable kebabs. Fat drips from the tin foil. It's as if they were jinxed.

With Caroline, Carl often sits in the Ici, with Jenny in the Mulackritze. With Jacqueline, he goes to the Sophieneck.

He drinks too much, and money is getting tight. Jacqueline's henna-brown bangs end right above her eyes. She's doing an apprenticeship, in carpentry. She's a woman who doesn't need much prep (this is one of the expressions that have been accompanying Carl lately, he has more of them in his head, it's the language of his campaign, his armor, as it were).

The Sophieneck is well suited: the semi-circular niches with soft upholstery, each table a kind of private room. Most important for Carl: in this café, you can sit very close together, almost intimately, without having to face each other. You can talk without being observed, touch each other, smoke and dream of the world outside, on Grosse Hamburger Strasse.

A red-haired woman enters from the backroom and goes from table to table. "That's the owner," Carl says, "Red Sophie." He knows her from the waiters' gatherings in the Sophien Club.

Jacqueline tells him about her carpentry work. Carl listens to her and for this moment, he's not unhappy, just tired and a little drunk. He absent-mindedly strokes the upholstery, he feels the coarse brown corduroy, he feels a cigarette burn. He tentatively sticks his finger in and it immediately disappears—everywhere those small, soft, surprisingly pleasant dens, thinks Carl, gateways to another world without Effi.

"I'll be right back," Jacqueline says and smiles at him. Carl watches her go. He pulls his finger out of the hole and gets out his wallet. Just to check. Carl is sure that (in the last compartment) there's a banknote, the basis for going out this afternoon and a guarantee of a few more drinks and all that might follow, but his wallet is empty. He goes through his coat pockets, then his pants pockets and then checks his wallet one more time. He stands up and at that very moment the world spins some more, so that he has to take a little sidestep to steady himself.

The wind, the wind—the round bellies lift and reveal the view. Carl stares at the crumbling, gray rear facade of the building across the courtyard; he feels like he is at the bottom of a well. Far above, on the rim of the well, lives a piano player; she practices every day. Carl knows what she looks like, he saw her at her window, at her rotary clothes dryer. Last week he saw her on the street, Prenzlauer Allee, and almost spoke to her. He closes his eyes and again he sees it: how Jacqueline returns, smiling, without any awkwardness. How he leaps up and apologizes: he'd completely forgotten that he was supposed to deliver an important message to friends, friends who live close by on Linien Strasse. While she waits for him to get back, she should "order something nice." "I'll be back in a minute," Carl said. Then he left. He climbed into the Zhiguli and drove home. He crept back into his den, and eventually he fell asleep.

The piano playing breaks off and Carl tries to think a few simple things:

The wind (lifts the bellies). The window (is dirty). The piano player (has dark hair). Jacqueline (is waiting and orders something nice). A farmer (murders his entire family and throws them into the well in front of the house).

Carl once saw it in a film about rural life. One child had survived and climbed—inch by inch—out of the well.

The piano playing starts up again. The bellies rise, and Carl imagines the pianist looking down at him from the rim of the well. He pictures black hair, a smooth, oval face, and a "yes."

"It's not right," Carl murmured (after two more days on his raft) and got annoyed. He pulled himself together, washed with cold water at the small sink set too high and cleaned up his room. He thought of Effi. She did exactly what she never should have. Did exactly what she needed to do to destroy everything. That's exactly what she did, Carl thought.

It took him a while to find the apartment. It had to be the building with the butcher shop, but there were several stair-cases. Carl didn't much like Prenzlauer Allee. He preferred Schönhauser. Better whales than streetcars. He heard the piano. He put his ear to the door and listened. So close! This close, her playing sounded less pure and almost violent, stirring, it penetrated his body and sparked a kind of anticipation, a kind of inner chiming, a thrill, goosebumps. So that he wouldn't have to knock or ring the bell (and stand there like an idiot), he had written a message. He hesitated over leaving the note but he couldn't stay there forever. Holding his breath, he retreated a few steps to the landing.

How strange it was to look down at his own three win-dows from above and how gray and calcified the panes looked. Probably a question of the light, thought Carl. If you could even speak of light in that well-like gloom. The piano stopped—"Der Wanderer," Carl recognized it now. He stared down into the courtyard because there was suddenly something there: a curtain (one of the bellies) had shifted, very slightly but unmistakably, and with it, the hint of a shadow and its shadowy gliding . . .

If that were me, thought Carl.

If that is me, down there, thought Carl, then there's nothing more for me to do here, then I can go. Then I can stop *all this*. Then I'm free.

Normal logic played no role in what Carl was feeling: relief. A state of pre-human calm filled his heart and he wondered, when it came down to it, what he would do with the rest of the day (and then with the rest of his life). A few lies he had forced himself to believe fell away and the truth came to light: that he still loved Effi. And that it didn't need to torment him. That he didn't need to punish himself or Effi for that. He went down the stairs as if in a trance and left the pianist's building.

But that was merely a moment that didn't immediately change the course of his days. He made appointments and visited the small brothels that were now opening up in the back buildings of Friedrichshain and Pankow. Eating his pudding pretzel at the bakery, he read the ads. Tiny pictures in which a kind of Christmas star hid the woman's genitalia. He did his shifts in the Assel and earned the necessary money. Every Wednesday, he played the Goethe-Nazi. He no longer wrote, although he tried now and then. He made attempts, paced around the room, tapping his hand.

Many contradictory things occurred. Carl caught himself walking along Effi's paths, to the kindergarten on Schönhauser Allee or to the store on Wins Strasse. He still thought of it as the *Kaufhalle*, although the name had long been changed to "supermarket." Only when the name had been changed, did the word *Kaufhalle* catch his attention—its sober functionality, the *buying-hall*. Buying, what there was and what you needed, not much, the bare necessities and sometimes a few things above and beyond. The word was cold and gray on the one hand. On the other, it kept to the point. Like the workshop, the buying-hall adhered to its purpose, beyond the will to overabundance that thrummed from the word "super." The culmination of this pretense was the supermarket's name: Kaiser's.

Carl walked along Effi's paths because the old, incorruptible feeling was back: not only his love for Effi, but also the fact that she was the only one *in my entire life*, Carl thought, as if he were suddenly very old. Effi had never said anything about the actual contents of the love letter he wrote her in Gera, just before he left. She'd never answered—she suddenly appeared on Ryke Strasse in the ACUD, in the plastic-film room, on the raft in her bodysuit. Like an apparition, invoked by intense longing, a product of his most secret desires, a fiction (yes, there it was again). This is why Carl shadowed Effi: he had to see her, in the flesh, he needed proof that she existed. That it wasn't all just a dream.

Instead of Effi, he meets Rico on Husemann Strasse, the only well-lit street in the neighborhood. Carl is on the way from the 1900 to the Franz Club for a last drink and to dreamily watch the dancers. Rico is coming toward him on the other side of the street—maybe from precisely there, Carl thinks, he could ask him about it: who's playing in Franz tonight, Rico? Carl is wearing his gray, velour coat, the foreignness of which suddenly burns his shoulders and what, exactly, is that on his head, a hat that gives an impression of velvet? Rico recognizes him nonetheless and turns toward him. Taking a step into the road, he nods in greeting, which completely throws Carl. Does Rico have Stockholm syndrome? Or does he just want to flatten Carl? Carl picks up his pace and lowers his eyes. Out of the corner of his eye, Rico's jacket with its colorful stripes like a child's pinwheel—Carl passes him and a sense of defeat washes over him.

DO COME

When Carl returned home in the morning, his mailbox was open. Someone had pulled out the wooden clamp. Bright and strange like an object from a better world, an envelope with two stickers leaned against the side of the box. The red sticker said, "Eilzustellung / Express Delivery," the blue one "Mit Luftpost / PAR AVION." Carl recognized his mother's handwriting. She still wrote O for *Osten* before his address, but on the back there was no W, the entire return address was missing and, despite his (for weeks now) desolate state (once again he'd been out walking

all night) Carl saw in this a sign a *situation*. In the postmark's circular ruins, Carl made out the word "Cologne." He immediately
tore the letter open, but it was too dark to read in the staircase.
The light no longer worked.

In the envelope there was money wrapped in two sheets
of paper, two large, stiff bills, which Carl fingered incredulously. His parents had often enclosed money, but much smaller
amounts. It reminded Carl a little of earlier times when his
grandmother would slip him *a little something*. At some point,
Carl had started to plan on the money and to speculate on the
expected sum, which Grandma Luzie (that was her name) kept
ready for him on the top shelf of the kitchen cupboard next to
the coffee. Yes, he had expected it, but then was always *really
happy*.

The letter was short and serious. Everything is happening
very quickly now, his mother wrote. "After thirteen months
of waiting, we've finally received a favorable decision, which
means we need to discuss everything with you as expeditiously
as possible." That was Inge's way of talking in charged situations
and "expeditiously" betrayed the strain his mother was under.

A white static had started up in Carl's head, he was still
thirsty. He dropped onto his workbench and looked at the letter:
a "decision," suddenly "positive" . . . His parents' mystery started
to take its final shape and he didn't have anything to drink in the
house. The game show went into its last round, for which the
contestant (who'd anticipated something but, unable to believe it,
had kept silent) urgently needed something to drink. Carl knelt
down in front of the store cupboard and grabbed one of Lappke's
Anchor jars; he opened it and, without hesitating, brought it to
his lips; he didn't mind the little bit of crumbly white topping,
it was probably not mold at all.

In the second part of the letter, Carl learned that EMI
Electrola was his father's new company. This week Walter is

completing a course at EMI, his mother wrote, which is why she could not come to see Carl in Berlin as planned.

"We had actually firmly planned to visit, Carl."

Fright and relief at once.

The meeting in which his parents would "explain everything" was going to happen in Frankfurt—not in Gelnhausen. Gelnhausen no longer mattered. Most important was to discuss their next steps (there they were again, the steps, their half-visible, half-invisible way of growing ever more distant) with him personally "in depth and calmly," not in a letter, it wasn't really possible to discuss it in a letter. And, of course, they must finally see each other again *as a family*, after such a long time. "We're really looking forward to that, dear Carl!"

Carl took another swig from Lappke's preserves and with his tongue he squished a plum that had slid into his mouth. In an indescribably delectable way, the plum numbed his gums and immediately the rest of him a little, too.

The money was intended for the trip to Frankfurt and for the telegram with which Carl was to confirm he was coming "as expeditiously as possible," (once again this strange word that actually sounded like an expedition). On an additional sheet, his father had drawn up a small, neat table of possible train connections from Berlin to Frankfurt. Walter's handwriting— Carl had almost forgotten it, this was the first time his father had written him.

Now you can just go to Frankfurt (across the border, Carl thought, or rather this thought dozed away) without being shot— wasn't that still completely mind-boggling? His parents wanted him to "suggest times to meet" because only two days were possible, strictly speaking, the coming weekend—that is how urgent it all was.

On the additional page there were further details, also in his father's handwriting: an address for EMI, a guesthouse with a house number and the porter's telephone number, just in case. Along with directions. And then, in closing, his mother again: "Please, do come . . ."

With a last effort of concentration, Carl scrawled the travel times onto a page of a calendar he had drawn himself, which lay open on his workbench. The month was empty, the week white, there was only this one appointment. Then he dug the old telegram envelope out from the bottom of the pile of his parent's letters, pulled out the telegram and carefully unfolded the page; the thin, crumbly, barely legible paper: "we need help please do come immediately your parents."

How long had it been?

He tried to calculate. He took a swig of the plum compote.

"Sixteen months."

In smaller writing and to the side, on the outer edge of the letter, his mother had noted once more: "Herewith 200 marks." The word *herewith* hummed to him from an even earlier, older layer (compared to *expeditiously*); to Carl's ears it had the sound of a long dead or mostly extinct language, a sediment from Inge's younger years as a secretary in a construction company whose premises were regularly flooded by the White Elster. Carl remembered the deserted, graveled company grounds. Two fenced-in shacks and a machine shop: Gera Construction Equipment. As a child, he had played there when he was sick, but *not too sick*, outside Inge's window. The gravel, the stones, their gray luster in the sun, it all meant something and now and again his mother had looked out the window and praised him for being such a good boy.

The construction company was Inge's first job after her escape from her family and her parents' farm, "my flight from the stall to the city," is how she sometimes referred to it. So even back then, thought Carl. It had never occurred to him before. He'd always liked hearing this story but had never thought about it much,

415

about *his parents' life journey.* Where it would take them next is what they wanted to tell him, Inge and Walter, in Frankfurt— which was rather strange, wasn't it?

Carl was no longer thirsty, there was just the rustling in his head. Without taking off his shoes, Carl flopped down on the raft and buried his head in his pillow. Ahoy.

HAMMER DRILL

Luckily there was always a magical woman he could watch in secret and that would have been enough, for this evening, too, until he noticed Ragna among the dancers—where had she been all this time? He went right up to her, made a few wooden dancing movements with his arms, back and forth, like an alcoholic locomotive, but then it wasn't Ragna. Embarrassed, Carl maneuvered his way back to his glass at the bar, without arm movements.

Maybe Ragna had heard about his screw-up and was avoiding him—as a precaution, thought Carl, because she knows what could *happen* to us.

He only had to walk down Schönhauser Allee, but since he was now too drunk for the simple path, he took Sredzki, Knaack, and then Kollwitz Strasse. He was picturing Ragna, her small, sturdy frame. Her fur cap, which she had stopped wearing a long time ago. Black hair, white skin. And the smell of tools, thought Carl, a person like a home.

20 Schönhauser: the first free building in the East, the first inhabited building, the Shepherd had said. The front door was locked and fitted with steel plate and there was no doorbell, of course not. Still, there was a bar, the Precinct, the name a fearlessly cheerful allusion: the precinct police station was one building up the hill.

Without hesitating, Carl entered the bar and recognized its outline from the time when the place was still a defunct store for funeral wreaths and floral arrangements, the *Floristeria*. The counter was covered with bottles and in the back, three dark shapes sat motionless on a threadbare couch. As if sleepwalking, Carl crossed the front and back rooms and found the door to the courtyard. Somewhere out there in the night was the last dirt track in Berlin, which led to the Jewish cemetery. The last escape route, thought Carl.

Inside, only the echo of his footsteps: no one there. Ragna's apartment was not locked and only the magnitude of his disappointment gave him the right to enter. The strength that had carried him to this door (drunken unhappiness turned into longing) vanished immediately. Carl sank into a state in which he saw only a few clear images: his hand on the doorknob, his steps into the unknown interior of the apartment, which must have been the Shepherd's at one point. Something brushed his shoulder and the soft ring of a mobile phone sounded—everything blurred. In the half-light cast by a streetlamp, Carl made out a pair of deer antlers but that must have been an illusion, a strangely branching shadow, perhaps, or some mythical animal on his path. The door to the kitchen. Carl passed it quickly. Raffia mats that crunched softly under his feet like old snow. And a sweet, homey smell that made him feel very tired. Two large, stiff pillows on the floor were the last thing he remembered later. Something constricted his throat. He crouched down, let himself fall and pressed his hands to his face: once again he was the child who was at a complete loss, who wanted to sob everything out.

"There, on the floor," Ragna had said to Kleist in alarm, which is why Kleist crept ahead with the hammer drill in firing position. It was no Multimax multi-purpose tool with a hammer drill function from the DIY store. It was a builder's tool, a power drill for concrete. Even before his fall, the Shepherd had argued for giving up the raids and concentrating only on the Assel (U-boat and shelter for the working class, which would jettison them all soon enough), but now that the pack leader spoke to them only as a shadow, the pack had taken up its old customs again. "It's in their blood, more than serving tables or kitchen duty," Hans said in a half-marveling tone. "They find strength in the hunt and renew the old solidarity."

Kleist turned back one more time and raised his eyebrows. Ragna pointed to an outlet in the hall.

The dye in Kleist's hair reflected the light of the streetlamps; a large, blue moth, making a cautious half-circle. After a while he started to giggle.

"What?" Ragna asked.

"It's your sweetheart. Should I wake him?"

"What sweetheart?"

Without answering, Kleist positioned the hammer drill, five centimeters from Carl's ear. He had threaded the drill's diamond-tipped point through the mat so the raffia would not be damaged and selected the hammer drill function.

"Kleist?" Ragna asked.

Instead of giving her an answer, Kleist turned the drill on.

Scared to death seemed to be the fitting expression if taken seriously. Even later, Carl could only vaguely describe what had happened to him in that instant: he'd been asleep, in a deep sleep, and was scared to death in his sleep—a nightmare from which there was no waking, with no way out. In other words:

First, something tore in his head. Something that made him jump up and threw him against the wall behind him—mouth and eyes wide open: blinded and unable to breathe. Hands pressed against his ears, hands that would have to stay there forever.

After a few seconds, Carl could see again, but he couldn't hear anything, only the wild stampede of his heart trying to find a rhythm it could beat to.

A thundering silent movie was playing in front of his eyes: he saw Ragna, who slapped Kleist in the face and tried to yank a tool out of his hands, it was a powerful tool. He saw Kleist flinch, saw him duck and pull his head in, raising his arms, but more like a child afraid of more blows—while doing so, he bared his teeth and grimaced like a feeble-minded child, who was evading his punishment (as always); these were the exaggerated gestures of a silent movie that make the character even more hateful. The bringer of bad luck, thought Carl, the evil child, but the only subtitle inserted into the film was: *Carl is deaf. Now what?*

Ragna approached him, moving her lips.

"What are you doing here?" Is that what she asked?

She tried to take Carl into her arms, but that was impossible. Carl had become untouchable, a deaf vessel that could shatter at any moment.

Ragna's face before his eyes, her lips, which had opened and closed once more: "Carl."

"Ragna," Carl answered and took fright—his voice! It didn't emerge from him, it just faded away dully in the cavity of his soundproof skull. He dropped to his knees and now Ragna took him in her arms.

On the first day, sign language helps, on the second Carl can understand a word here and there, or at least he imagines he can. Ragna brings what he needs, no alcohol, she makes sure of that. Carl shivers from cold and sweats all night long. His heart races and he can't sleep. "It's just withdrawal," Ragna said. She had led him to her bed, like a child. With an elegant movement, she spread out a foam-rubber mattress, on which she has slept since then, next to Carl.

For a few days, Carl stays in bed even though he's not actually sick, *just deaf*. He is completely enclosed, as if submerged, without sound. His voice is trapped inside him. It's a kind of afterlife, Carl thinks. Sometimes there is only a soft roar and a knocking, very close, but it comes from inside him, it's his blood.

He is apathetic after the shock. The shock has reduced him, intimidated him. He is submissive and easily handled. Here with Ragna, in her bed, he feels the temptation to give everything up, to no longer (never again) be responsible, especially not for his misfortune. What good to him is—his love? None. Forget it all. And the thought that this was punishment. For what? For not having truly loved. For not knowing what love is.

A bare bulb hangs from the ceiling. Henry's studio is on the floor above. Henry visits Carl and talks to Ragna, at least their lips move. Later, Henry brings a few things that Ragna needs for her *treatment*. She massages Carl's temples with a salve, she strokes his forehead and moves her lips. She conscientiously shines a light on his ears. It's pleasant. Carl keeps his eyes on her hands, on her smooth, black hair. A special tea is brewed somewhere outside, maybe by Henry, and he is told to bite on a root, Ragna shows him how: she first puts the root in her own mouth, then in his; the biting and chewing brings movement into Carl's skull; Ragna nods at him encouragingly, her gaze full of praise and severity. Why aren't we together, Carl would like to ask her now, but he doesn't want to hear the muffled echo in his head. Losing your voice means losing everything. Walking and talking is what summons the words and the words are the poem. Writing without talking is inconceivable. Thinking is just the process of correction; first talk, then think, that's the secret. First the music . . .

It's the only thing that I've truly understood since I've been here, in Berlin, Carl thinks, and he thinks *Berlin* and pictures it once again: the way Ragna surveyed him back then, behind the

screen, when he was weak and feverish and he finally understands that, too: it was a kind of treatment, a way of healing
him, nothing more. A favor for a friend. Ragna is his friend in
this city.

Carl watches as Ragna stuffs a pile of finely minced onion into
two children's socks (her own socks, it turns out), which she then
presses against his deaf ears with an elastic band; Carl now looks
like he has a head injury, a war wound. When the man with the
head bandage is alone, he overcomes his inclinations and speaks
softly to himself; he listens to the monster in his head and hopes
for his voice's return. I'll never write again, thinks Carl.

On the fourth day, Ragna drips an oil that contains silver into
his ear. Carl saw the label on the small bottle, written in Russian.
Ragna can't read it, but Carl can. "From Vassily," Ragna writes
on a scrap of paper and taps on the bottle. Carl is touched. He
takes the note and slips it under his pillow. Later in the day,
Hans, Irina, and Little Frank from Radio P come to visit and
Little Frank sets a tiny radio he'd built himself next to Carl's
bed; only then does he realize his faux pas—and they all laugh,
even Carl. His laughter sounds monstrous, as if someone were
drowning in his head.

Ragna heats the Russian oil in a spoon, like someone cooking
drugs. She uses a pipette to drip it into his ear. He has to lie still
on his side. If my eardrum is ruptured, the silver will flow right
into my brain and silver-plate the madness, Carl thinks. And the
unwritten poems. But the oil helps, Carl can feel it immediately,
something in his head melts.

In the middle of the night, Kleist suddenly appears in his
room; he stands naked next to Ragna's mattress, next to Carl's
bed. Carl wants to scream, but can't make a sound, as in a dream.
Kleist is really very thin—and he's a woman, a girl.

The next morning, with a soft plop, the world returns to Carl's
head. Something warm drips out of his ear, which he gratefully

rubs between his fingers. Kleist is lying next to Ragna. In her arms. Carl closes his eyes again and waits. Then he gets up as quietly as possible, gathers his things and slinks out the door and upstairs to Henry's.

"Didn't you know, Carl?"

Henry is amazed.

"Hoffi was in love with Kleist from the very first day. And to the last one, in a sense, until his fall. But Kleist . . . She's still just a kid, what is there to say? I think she slept with all of us here, only not with Hoffi, because he—because he was the Shepherd, you see?"

"And I am, I mean, I was almost in love with Ragna," Carl stammered. Now he could admit it.

"Almost?" Henry murmured. "Everyone could see you were, my friend. Even Kleist."

"You think?"

"Where is your head, Carl?"

"That's what my mother always said."

My mother, Carl thought.

THE PLASTIC-FILM ROOM

He hadn't thought of her. The flash of memory: as if something were communicating with him through a narrow channel from *another* life, in any case not from his. And almost as if he'd never had parents.

I forgot my parents, Carl thought. The time set for their "discussion about everything" had passed, it was yesterday.

"Do come."

And yet, he had taken their request *seriously*. He'd chosen a train, sent a telegram—and then failed to go. He held the thought gingerly, then reformulated it: I was deaf. It was the drill, the shock ... The story didn't excuse him, on the contrary, it showed what had become of him. An erratic guy who hung about with shady characters. That would be the truth from his parents' perspective.

He went to the post office to send a telegram, but what should he write? "Sorry I forgot you." Or: "I was deaf." In that case, it was better to lie: "Border unexpectedly closed again." Or the truth as a bad poem? "Dear parents, I'm now sober. And empty. The music is over. Speech dwells with me no more."

Carl tore up the telegram form, ordered a long-distance call and went into the small gray booth in the corner; it was as if he were returning to the good old days of the Bethmann calls, the days of departure, filled with love and intent on solitude. For the first time since he had come to Berlin, Carl felt a longing for Gera: maybe his writing would have gone better there? He thought of his poem about the soldiers in the U-boat. Written in Halle, revised in Gera, printed in Berlin. It still seemed like a miracle to him. He called the number on the letterhead of the EMI Electrola stationery that his parents had used for their letter. As if they didn't have any other paper to hand, thought Carl. As if they had already started on their way.

The connection was bad. Just crackling and static and sometimes a faint voice emerged from other conversations, somewhere in the country, somewhere in the lives of people who knew nothing about him. Maybe they can sense something, thought Carl. Maybe his silence slowly trickled into the singsong of their trivialities and saturated their sentences with helplessness, despair, and gravity until they finally fell silent. His call was forwarded twice, then a voice:

"Bischoff? Mr. Bischoff! Your parents are ..."

Then the connection was interrupted for a long time. Carl tried again and then several more times. A connection could not be restored and the woman behind the counter just shrugged.

"Calls to the West are difficult again these days, young man. New cables, construction everywhere. Maybe you can try from somewhere in the West, Bornholmer Strasse, maybe, the booth right on the other side of the border is supposed to be good. Secret tip."

On the way home, he met Effi. She was walking directly toward him, like in a dream, a desired vision, a Fata Morgana. Carl tried to look serious and aggrieved, which he failed to do; he would rather open his arms, embrace Effi and hold her, hold her, but she turned and pushed a door open hard.

Her slender, suddenly energetic figure, which drove him crazy. Carl couldn't help but follow her as he so often had in the previous days: Effi and Freddy on the street in front of him, their ambling looked sad and aimless, but they followed their usual paths, they managed fine, without Carl. A thought that drove him closer to them. He tried to take up their rhythm, cozying up to them until the moment when he had to tear himself away and stagger into some side street, to get some distance on some dead end.

Only in the stairwell did Carl recognize the building. It was number thirteen. There was construction in the front, the back building seemed unchanged. A dead bird lay on the stairs; a window was missing in the plastic-film room and the wind had shredded the film; there were pigeon droppings everywhere. Otherwise, everything was as it had been. Exactly as she had been back then, Effi was sitting on the chair, which stood in the same place near the wall, and she wore the same sailor sweater with the same epaulets, only it wasn't as dark as it had been over a year ago, it was day, not night, but in these courtyards it was never really light.

"You need to close the door, Carl."

Effi's voice.

"Why is it all—what's with the new gallery?"

"They moved."

"Effi, I . . ."

"I think it's hard for both of us, Carl. And since you're always following me, looking miserable, I thought this would be an opportunity."

Carl made a dismissive gesture and shook his head.

"I'm not talking about a new beginning, Carl. But an opportunity. Freddy is sad, too. Did you really think we wouldn't notice you?"

"What about Rico?"

"Hang on, hang on. Promise me that we'll leave on good terms when this here is over."

"This here?"

Her small, round head, her medium-length, rather greasy hair dangling over her cheeks. Carl realized that he had admired Effi, but also underappreciated her, maybe even scorned her, or both at once if that's possible in life.

"I can't bear seeing dead people, Carl."

"Who can?"

"No, no—I'm sorry, I apologize."

"You don't need to apologize. I was stupid and . . ."

"And you still are." Effi stretched and laid the palms of her hands on her thighs.

"Things didn't go well with us. I should have told you everything from the beginning. Then we could have gone our separate ways. That would have been better."

Effi sat ramrod straight. Carl looked at her incredulously.

"I didn't always think that. Sometimes I thought you'd need me. I thought I had a duty to you, I thought I was meant to show you something, to make you . . . more mature. What can I say?"

It was as if she were looking down at him even though Carl was standing at the wall next to the door.

"It's the plunging shadow I always see out of the corner of my eye and it's really making me crazy, Carl."

"Ralf? You mean Ralf?"

"Had he really given up? Or is this what he wanted? To pass us, so that we'd find him in the courtyard? I mean, *have to find him*, dead in the courtyard."

Effi looked at the floor, at her shoes. Then she raised her head and looked at Carl or just past him. She sat on the chair as stiffly as she had back then in the plastic-film room, as if she were fulfilling a task (a specific task, written down on a note next to the chair), as if she were portraying something as part of an installation, an artwork, the name of which Carl had never learned—it all became suddenly clear to him. He had never asked and Effi had never talked about it (as was her way). Carl tried to catch her eye. He wanted to surrender, he was ready, and then Effi started talking, precisely with this sentence:

"I never told you about it and you never asked. We never talked about it because it was the only possibility, I mean for the two of us, as a couple."

Effi cleared her throat.

"You know that my mother, I mean, Mama . . ."

Effi was now smiling like a child who has a secret she is only barely keeping.

"You probably already knew back then, like everyone at school did, word got around fast as it does when something like that happens. There were all kinds of stories, the strangest things. Even at the time, no one ever asked me about it, I mean *how* it was—no one dared. My father didn't either. Not even the police. Maybe because I was a child. Maybe because they already had what they needed. Naturally I didn't want to talk to anyone about it and I don't want to today either, do you understand, Carl? There's no point. It's always there and talking about it won't make it any less. For a time, I was able to find a space in which it didn't constantly recur. A space like this one here. This is the space where I actually live."

"You live . . . here?"

"No, I—no idea, Carl. I have no idea how I can make you understand. No idea!" She laughed, short and impatient, it was actually not laughter, just an odd noise. "Poor Carl, you've fallen in love with a madwoman." Her expression changed abruptly, the old disdain resurfacing.

"You know Sylvia Plath?"

"What about her?"

"That's how she did it."

"Who?"

"My mother. Mama. Just less perfectly. That's why I know about Sylvia Plath, because she did it the same way. I thought I could learn something about it from her, but there was nothing."

A slate-gray light fell into the room. Effi's voice sounded hoarse.

"It was on a Friday. I came home from school. I always had my own key, on a string around my neck, we all did then, didn't we? That string around our necks. And was happy to be a latchkey kid. It was nice having that small, pointy piece of metal against my skin."

Effi touched her chest. She seemed to be talking to herself, no longer to Carl, and it was also not a memory, not a story, but just what happened in that moment.

"The door was locked, as always, but there were a few coats and jackets on the carpet that I had to push aside first. It was the same with the kitchen door, very unusual. Then I saw her, on the floor in front of the stove, the oven was open. Her legs were bent, her skirt had ridden up. Her head lay on the oven door. She's resting, taking a nap, I thought, but her face looked displeased. I said, 'Mama,' at first more as a question, 'Mama?' When you're a child, you don't know much about death yet and

I didn't recognize it. First that and besides: death is completely implausible on your mother's face, if you know what I mean. That's why I said, maybe a hundred times, 'Mama,' while her face remained so displeased. Her eyes were wide open, and she was trying to fish a crumb out of the left corner of her mouth with her tongue. It looked like she was rather irritated that she couldn't manage it, you understand, that's how I saw it at first. And for a pretty long time, I think. Her contorted face—like one of those children's birthday party games with food."

Effi fell silent. "But that's not what it's about. Those are just images in my head. And things we never talk about, that we lock up inside and are forever in our memory. So then: why does Mama make a face like that when I come home? Why, when she knows, knows exactly, that I come home from school at exactly this time every Friday afternoon? When she knows this, I mean . . . That's what I have wondered about since then, Carl, constantly, again and again, my whole life, but not as if I wanted an answer, understand? I think I absolutely did not want to know, never, I *never really* asked myself the question. Until a month ago. When Ralf lay dead in the courtyard on Schliemann Strasse. Why is he lying there when he knows that we're coming?"

"Effi!"

"Did Mama plan it too, from the start? Did she want *me* to find her, her oldest child? Yes? And then I find her and then it turns out that once again her eldest doesn't understand anything, that I can't handle it."

Her voice slips and a single, violent sob wells up from some depth inside her. "Which is why I always want to apologize, to ask forgiveness for not being able to make her happy, for her life being so difficult because of us, unbearable, actually, although—"

"Although you're the best, Effi, the most lovable."

Carl hugged her tightly, he wanted to feel her, felt her warmth, which he missed so much, her smell, and her despair.

"No, actually, not."

That was the moment. Carl saw how Effi came apart, the gray light from the courtyard on her face.

"And you know it, Carl. But I did try. Even if you don't believe it."

She walked past him, moving quickly to the door.

"Please sit down and stay a bit longer."

"Effi?"

"It's my own room. You can have it if you want."

PART IX

STAR 111

As the engines whipped the grass next to the runway, uncovering the grass's pale side, Carl tried to understand the pilot's announcement. He was in an airplane for the first time in his life.

It was an Air France plane, and it would fly thirteen hours from Frankfurt to Los Angeles on the trail of his parents' mystery. Strange enough, but he was too tired to ponder it further. At the moment, the chicken with rice, the red wine, and the stewardess who was serving it to him were all more important; for dessert there was coffee and a small cookie: that was flying. It lifted you out of everything. After a few weeks, during which Carl tried in vain to find his way back into something he could have called his daily life, he was all too ready for this trip.

He pulled his father's letter from the large, padded EMI Electrola company envelope, which had also contained his ticket. It hadn't been sent by mail, instead a messenger had brought the envelope to Carl's door and handed it to him almost solemnly. Inge had "completely fallen apart" after he missed the meeting in Frankfurt, Walter wrote, so he was taking it on himself to inform Carl about the most important aspects of their emigration.

Carl reread the rather sober report sent to "make him aware," as his father put it, of the "seriousness of this step." First the application for a working visa "in the States" (which they had already sent in the early days in Gelnhausen, the precondition naturally being German citizenship), then the so-called Immigration Act under Ronald Reagan, a comprehensive immigration law reform in November 1990, which doubled their chances, and finally the job offer in Cologne. Until then the process had only advanced in fits and starts or not at all. Only after EMI had guaranteed his employment and taken over the cost of the visa ("we probably couldn't have managed it alone"), did everything go very quickly. EMI had also booked and paid for their flights and for that reason alone, rescheduling them was simply impossible, "which your mother could barely cope with after you failed to show up, dear Carl. She wanted to refuse to fly!"

His father's letter was matter of fact, but tender, too. Why it all had to happen is something he did not explain. Step by step and in detail, Walter explained the mechanics of their immigration, essentially no differently than he had described on their Sundays in the garage the operation of a four-stroke engine, which was constructed completely logically and yet (in the case of the Zhiguli) was embedded in a large field of uncertainties and was a row that required a great deal of patience to hoe. Walter displayed this patience. And, if Carl understood the details correctly, EMI was particularly interested in Pascal, a programming language which Carl's father had used to develop software for controlling large electronic display screens. He'd written the program that allowed colors to merge or a rose to bloom in fifteen seconds, none of his short electronic films lasted longer than that. "Before, no one had asked me about the things we worked on at the IFAM in Gera in the late eighties, but the Americans in Cologne were only interested in that. They were downright enthusiastic, almost excessively so, especially because of the rose. They didn't care where I came from," Carl's father wrote and concluded his letter:

"All the rest in the personal conversation that we'd like to have with you very soon!"

How familiar this language was to Carl. The formal, wooden aspects were just the surface of a bashful love, Carl knew this

very well. What was hidden behind "the IFAM" was not something he needed to know. "My Parents' Unknown Life," thought
Carl—as if it were the title of this story. And perhaps the point
at which the child finally rose up and demanded information.
On the plane, a second round of coffee was served, but Carl
had fallen asleep.

Malibu—didn't it sound like a name one had heard before,
in childhood fairy tales, perhaps? Inge had prepared Carl's
favorite dish, roast potatoes and fried eggs. "It's called 'sunny
side up' here," his father said with an embarrassed smile. It
was strange for Carl (and sad, actually) to see Inge and Walter
surrounded by this strange furniture. The thick layer of dust on
the bottom shelf of the small table in front of the couch was
also strange. Along with the light, spotted rug, the unfamiliar
smell left by the previous occupant, also an employee of the
company, which owned the house. A wooden staircase led up
to the bedrooms.

10 Heathercliff Road, Malibu—the address was stuck next to
a sketched map on the dashboard of the Suzuki in which Carl's
parents picked him up from the airport. "It's from our very first
days," had been his father's explanation. "It's not so easy to drive
the right way here, especially in the fog." They had driven through
two thick, snow-white clouds, like in a dream. Only once did
Carl glimpse the ocean and a broad pier built on piles as thick
as tree trunks that extended far out over the water. Pacific Coast
Highway—the words on a sign at the side of the road gave this
unreality a name.

"The Way of My Parents," thought Carl and he told them
about the drawing on the wall over his workbench, on which he'd
plotted all the steps of their odyssey from Giessen to Meerholz.
"Malibu is missing," Carl said, "but the page is too small anyway."
He meant it in a conciliatory way, but the tension that had not

diminished since their first, uncertain hug at the airport turned into something else.

"Ah!" his mother cried with a burst of laughter (the way you laugh when you don't know how to continue, with which sentence, with which life).

"A workbench," his father repeated, shaking his head enthusiastically. "Carl has his *own* workbench!" It sounded triumphant (the final triumph of all their days in the garage), he truly seemed delighted about it, but didn't ask any questions, so Carl could omit mentioning that his workbench was just a writing surface—that poems were created there, nothing else.

The building was an ugly cube. His father called it, in English, an *apartment building*. It was no more than one hundred meters from the highway. Walter told Carl about the area. He wore a white shirt with short sleeves, the lenses of his glasses cleared in the electric light. Carl, dead tired from his trip, tried hard to be attentive. Walter was serious. He looked older but not unhappy. He had become even smaller. "Well, you're becoming ever less," Carl's grandmother had often said. It was one of her expressions—ever less.

They walked around the building and Carl's father showed him the garage, full of old appliances and equipment, a freezer, a television, various office devices, among them an Olivetti Lettera.

"Does the typewriter work?" Carl asked.

"We'll take a look at it, son, first thing tomorrow. I still have a few tools."

"Son"—it sounded unfamiliar, strange, and even a bit much, although it did give Carl a warm feeling. Experience told him that closeness was only possible in areas dear to his father's heart. It was the only way to explain the countless hours they had spent together in the garage, united in the ritual of eternal care and maintenance. It was the ritual of their togetherness, conducted in silence as a rule, except for a few isolated words here and there, embellishment of the silence.

"I'll clean up the garage if we end up staying. Then I'll buy a car of my own. In any case, not an automatic!" His father listed a few cars that would be acceptable, four or five models, and only at the end of the list did he ask:

"How's the Zhiguli, Carl?"

Carl had decided to tell them everything—the first, cold days in Berlin, sleeping in the car, the illegal taxi nights, the ambush by the Milva mafia, and finally the new 1200 cc engine that Adele and the Russians had installed in the Zhiguli, a detail Carl had discussed at length and in great detail with his father in his imagination—but he said none of it.

"Good. It's good."

Not much more happened that evening. His father soon disappeared upstairs, and his mother made up a bed for Carl on the sofa. It was the most attractive piece of furniture in the room, wide, soft, upholstered in brown corduroy.

"You need to reach out to him a bit, too," his mother said softly. She held two wine glasses and an open bottle. She seemed younger, even more athletic. She still wore her hair short, only the blond hue was new, blond streaks she called highlights. That her hair had not turned gray was a family trait. "We royalty don't go gray," she'd often said—her maiden name was König.

"Walter would like to talk to you tomorrow and—explain everything. That's his plan. And you know how he is, he wants everything to go just as arranged."

They sat together for a moment on the carpet next to the open terrace door. The idea that his father had *arranged* something unsettled Carl. In the parking lot across the way, the Suzuki shone in the moonlight. Next to it stood a small, metallic blue Mazda, his mother's car as it turned out. She was already driving her own car.

For some reason, Carl had the feeling that his mother fit much better into this foreign environment; she's *flexible* and makes her decisions *strategically*, thought Carl. Inge's favorite Thuringian sayings were very Californian. When he was a child, it was difficult for Carl to see his parents as two different people because they always, as they often emphasized, came to the same conclusions *independently from each other*, especially in matters that concerned him: "We are independently of the same opinion that . . ." For Carl, who had discipline problems, who skipped after-school programs, forgot his homework or crawled around in garbage cans, this was a kind of proof of God's existence: tied to the usual punishments, being grounded or losing television privileges or both at once, the sentence was always unanimous. His parents—two separate people, but the plural in the expression was atrophied and stunted (like an organ with no function)—his parents were *one*. This was not necessarily a bad thing, as long as they loved each other and, out of this profound mutuality, also loved him, the child Carl, the child. He was the offspring, an offshoot of this love, from which everything stemmed. On the one hand, this was good, on the other it also meant a certain loneliness, since it was as if Carl was not close to his parents in the same way that Inge and Walter were close to each other. More precisely, he stood facing them, on the other shore of their love, where there was no one but him, no brother or sister.

"Down there is the ocean," Inge said and pointed to a small, paved street that disappeared between bare hills. A light, warm wind blew, and they could hear the highway.

"Do you know how great our longing was?"

Carl didn't know how to answer. He took a sip, then emptied his glass.

"Sometimes it's very difficult. Walter is very busy, of course, and I take the burden off of him as much as I can. He manages, just, from day to day. I mean, ever since the people at EMI discovered what he can do—and now, of course, he wants to show them. In Cologne they had him do a few strange tests and filmed him as he did them, for an entire week. In the end, they even wanted him to play something for them, on the accordion. They were enchanted, those Hollywood people. Can you imagine, Carl?"

The way his mother was talking to him confused Carl: first, just the two of them and second, a bit too sadly for a long-wished-for reunion. Carl replied, a few sentences. He tried to orient himself in his words, but it all sounded strange. Was his mother now lonely, too, and is that why she was sitting with him here before going to bed?

Inge stood up and so did Carl, then they hugged.

"Good night, Carl. I hope you're able to sleep."

He'd forgotten how short his mother was. She kissed his cheek, her hand on the back of his head; Carl had trouble tolerating it.

Sitting in the car next to Walter was very familiar. It was an intimacy that allowed Carl to slip back into a childlike silence while his father talked about the company and his work. His boss's name was Laura Ter Neden; he said her complete name several times. As far as Carl understood, Walter wrote animation programs. He had the language for it in his head and the Americans had good computers. Most of his colleagues knew about the Fall of the Wall, but otherwise . . . Bare hills and a few palm trees. Carl had seen a hummingbird in the hibiscus shrubs in the parking lot. He stared out over the water, the ocean, the Pacific, ultimately it was pure poetry.

Somewhere on Sunset Boulevard (Carl had read the street sign and thought, here it is, and now I'm here too) his father fell silent. Something in his face had changed.

"This was not our first attempt, Carl."

He cleared his throat, lowered his head and for a moment it looked like he wanted to rest his forehead on the steering wheel.

"We tried once before."

His father spoke so softly that Carl had to bend toward him.

"Before you were born. I had a, how should I put it, an *engagement*."

He smiled bashfully and shook his head. He didn't know where to begin.

"In '61, when the news came, the border closing—we had simply waited too long. But we tried again, two days later on 15 August, through the forest behind Sonneberg, you know . . ."

His last words were a mere whisper.

"We had relatives there, that was our pretext—visiting family and a walk out in nature. We almost made it, but then . . . It was just too much for Inge, in the forest, just too much . . ."

He reached for the gearshift, looked in the rearview mirror (nervously, as if there were someone behind him) and then back at the road, ahead at what he had planned.

"What engagement?" Carl asked, alarmed; he had never seen his father in tears.

They turned and drove along a sagging chain-link fence, behind which was a parking lot. The area looked rundown. "This is our bar," his father pointed at a door garlanded with strings of lights across from the parking lot, "but first we'll go see Bill."

Carl noticed the stars only when passersby stopped to look at them. His father paid no attention to them. In front of his chest, he held a package wrapped in brown paper that Inge had given him. The Walk of Fame was a normal sidewalk, sometimes wider, sometimes less so. There were construction sites here and there and the stars in the pavement, one after another. The sun illuminated the rose-colored stone and the golden spikes. Carl tried to read the names on the stars, but his father was walking too fast—until he stopped abruptly. Walter carefully tore open

the package and handed the paper to Carl. It was a small bouquet of flowers and branches from the hummingbird shrub, with
golden thistle and a bit of steppe grass.

"Didn't Inge make it lovely?"

He set the bouquet right on the star and Carl read the name:
Bill Haley. His head lowered, Walter stood there for a while.
Two, three minutes in the scorching sun. It was, in fact, very
hot on the sidewalk, but Carl decided to stay next to his father.
He had the feeling he needed to stand by him, without really
knowing what for.

People swerved around them; a few looked curiously at the
man standing at Haley's star as at his grave; a woman in white
shorts took a picture. Walter didn't seem to notice, or he didn't
care. Carl looked down the street, he didn't know what to do with
himself. He wasn't used to his father behaving strangely or mys-
teriously and he decided to be mature, whatever Walter told him.

"There's no grave, so we use the star."

On the way back to the car, Walter laid his hand on Carl's
shoulder. He spoke very softly as if this was the opening of the
secret he would finally reveal to Carl.

"Haley's ashes were lost. They weren't handled very carefully.
Maybe they're still somewhere, in a coffee can in some garage in
Texas or Mexico City. A few people claim the ashes were strewn
over the Gulf of Mexico."

"Bill Haley's ashes?"

His father's smell. The touch. Walter took Carl by the arm
and guided him toward a side street.

"When Bill was four years old, a pediatrician accidentally sev-
ered the optic nerve in his left eye. Things like that were always
happening to him, but he still made it."

The bar was very narrow and windowless. Essentially, it was
just a long counter with a few silver-framed pictures of musicians hanging over it, along with an evacuation plan. The drinks

menu offered one hundred kinds of beer, even Köstritzer, their hometown beer, which his father ordered for them.

"Köstritzer in California, isn't that unbelievable, Carl?"

Carl's confused look.

"I'm sorry, Carl, I know, I'm sorry . . . I promised Inge, I'd be quick with Bill. To you it must all seem—strange. But first, to you! Thanks for coming. For taking it on, I mean—all of it."

Walter made a vague gesture with his bottle and drank. He tried to put his arm around Carl, but for that he would have had to get up from his barstool.

"I played the accordion my entire childhood, as you know." Carl didn't know but he nodded attentively and looked at his father's face, which appeared much more alive than it had the day before, almost lively, and this was unusual, too.

"After the end of the war, I started taking lessons—1946, I was seven years old. In the beginning, I didn't particularly want to. I was the only boy in the village who had to learn an instrument. My mother wanted to turn me into some kind of child prodigy, which must have been strange in our family, in which they were all weavers or dairy men and later uranium miners. On every birthday I was given candy and sheet music, at every Christmas a gingerbread house and sheet music, and the sheet music was always for a new, more complicated piece. Where they found the money for it, I don't know. My accordion was used, a black marbled Weltmeister Excelsior, the bellows already had tears, but my father glued onto them some kind of linen that would *never become brittle*, as he always stressed, your grandfather, Carl!"

Carl shivered. The bar was air-conditioned and the beer ice-cold. They were the only guests. It's still early in the day, thought Carl. It looked like his father intended to tell him everything, from the very beginning, the entire story.

"I got a feel for rhythm and beat, and also learned to sing. I took lessons from the Scheffels, who had a saddlery. We paid in goat milk and eggs, sometimes a butchered chicken or even a rabbit. The accordion was so heavy that I couldn't carry it alone, at least not all the way to the Scheffels'. Each time I had to find a solution, a borrowed handcart, or someone passing by from the village would help me. My job was to become a prodigy, but I mostly had to manage that on my own."

He cleared his throat and fell silent.

"Goat milk is good," Carl murmured.

"The poor man's cow. She fed us for years. The milk was rich and . . ."

"Silky."

Surprised and with a hint of suspicion in the corner of his eye, Walter looked at Carl.

Yes, I know a goat, too, Carl would have liked to say, but they could talk about that later.

"After a few years, I joined the Wismut company orchestra, back when the company mined uranium right next to our front door, piling up huge mountains of rock and tailings. When the wind blew, fine dust from the slag heaps blew into the village. The dust was everywhere, on the furniture, the bedsheets, the food. Even the magic eye of our radio, which glowed so beautifully when the reception was good, had a layer of dust. Every evening, I sat in the kitchen and listened to AFN, the American Forces Network—or Radio Luxembourg. Not sure if Chris Howland, a favorite of ours, was already broadcasting then. Howland played rockabilly, rhythm and blues, Western swing—all the cowboy music. At fifteen, I saw myself as a cowboy going out in the world. What I wanted most were a hat and a pair of cowboy boots. My mother said I was crazy. She was disappointed that the child prodigy story never worked out the way she'd imagined it."

Walter drained his glass and refilled it.

"Köstritzer in California. It makes you want to smoke a cigarette."

Carl pulled an opened pack of f6s from his shirt pocket and slid it over the counter. Carefully, as if handling a precious object, Walter picked up the pack.

"Good old f6s. I used to smoke them too. Then I quit, the habit just ended without my deciding to stop—strange, isn't it?"

"Your last pack sat in the cabinet, almost full, in the drawer under the record player. I started smoking with those cigarettes."

"What?"

"I always shook the pack so that it still looked full. Of course, after a while that didn't work anymore."

"I never noticed."

"You stopped and I started. With the same pack."

"Like a relay race. And now you're giving me the cig back. A new round, all over again, right?" Walter adroitly fished a cigarette out of the pack and Carl lit it.

"But you couldn't have been much older than fifteen at the time?"

Carl shrugged and looked his father in the eye. It was their best moment since he'd arrived.

"What can I say. I heard Bill Haley for the first time back then. Howland or whoever played Haley. For hours, I tried to play his music, my heart nearly burst. Haley had an accordion in his band and even a mandolin and that, after all, was almost like us in the orchestra: eight accordions, eight mandolins, and drums, can you imagine, son? Accordion and Mandolin Orchestra of the SDAG Wismut, but most people called us The Uranium Boys. We got everything from the Russians, sheet music, music stands, and eighty bass accordions that gleamed gold. We were driven around the country in buses, to Weida, Berga, all the way to Schlema for the Wismut finals. And we were really good. 'When black coveralls descend in droves below ground, summer or winter, all you'll hear are merry sounds,' pretty strong stuff, right? The miners went nuts, endless encores. This was when we started playing rhythm and blues in secret in the community center in Katzendorf, like a secret society. And AFN played Haley, 'Crazy Man, Crazy' and 'Rock Around the Clock,' I think they played them a hundred times a day."

His father took a drink and slowly pushed his bottle over to Carl's.

"I don't know if it can be explained. My heart was racing, and I could hardly breathe. You had to move to keep from exploding. Jump around, break something. My mother saw me in that state once, in front of the radio, I didn't care. I wasn't there in her dump of a village anymore, I was far away, on another planet. That was the music that made us see what we had to destroy and where the journey was headed, farther and farther away. Eventually there were a few bands that played some pretty good rock 'n' roll. Kurt Henkels imitated Haley, then Fips Fleischer, who was friends with Louis Armstrong, but there were smaller combos, too, who played in Berga or Seelingstädt, the Renft combo, the Echo Quintet and whatever else they were called."

Walter blew smoke and took a deep breath.

"One day, our orchestra leader came to visit and started talking about me studying music—in Weimar! Studying was not something my parents knew anything about. No one in our family had ever gone to college. That their child prodigy fantasy could lead to a degree was not something my mother had considered, strangely enough. She wanted her little genius, ready-made, nicely dressed with his hair neatly parted, mostly to show off to the neighbors—what good was that if I was in Weimar? And so I started an apprenticeship in weaving, in the same factory as my mother. In the bus we sat next to each other, she . . ."

Walter stopped talking, his gaze became absent. Something happened to him or he suddenly lost the thread. They could hear the ice machine under the counter. They were still the only guests.

"She . . ."

"When I was on the night shift," Walter suddenly picked up the story, "I danced: rock 'n' roll along the looms. A loom is very loud with a monotonous beat, rhythmic, that was the drums. I sang the melody and marched up and down the aisle between the machines, left foot kick, right foot kick, two machines left, two machines right, and I was a star on the stage."

His father stopped. He carefully tapped the ash off. He was enjoying his f6 and a smile flitted across his face.

"When the Echos played in Linda bei Weide, that was the first time I saw Inge. Her flared skirt with a wide red belt, her sun-tanned skin—from working in the fields, but of course I didn't know that. She was a fantastic dancer, she was the best. She gradually taught me the steps, just through motions and eye contact—she would nod, I'd do something intuitively, then she'd laugh. The second time, I could do it better . . . That's how we got to know each other, through music. We were pretty inventive. Over time, we thought up our own moves. Inge jumped up onto me and I held her for a while, on my hip so that she hovered next to me, almost weightless . . ." Walter spun on his barstool and an implied Inge hovered in his arm. "We had the same sense of rhythm, I'd say, that was the foundation. That is the foundation for everything, Carl. For music and laughter."

Walter's passion. It was unusual for Carl to see his father like this. They'd never talked about things like this. And now he was talking about them, in this strange depopulated bar in this foreign land.

"Have I talked about Bill Haley?"

"Yes, Papa, earlier." Carl had said Papa, just like that.

"The thing with Bill Haley, it was '58. Haley was playing with the Comets in Berlin, in the Sportspalast. We'd planned it for a long time and had already crossed the border that morning in the S-Bahn, at rush hour. We left my motorcycle in the East. Inge wore her dress with the wide red belt. She looked stunning and was exuberant. From the very beginning she wanted to be right up front. The Comets with their stiff, checkered jackets—they didn't look as crazy as we'd imagined, but their music exploded everything. Some people in the audience brought drumsticks and they drummed on the stage. We were with those who were dancing, below in the aisle at first. After a few songs, several dancers jumped onto the stage and kept dancing up there and, what can I say, we were up there, too. Surely the craziest thing we've ever done."

"I doubt it," Carl murmured, but his father didn't react.

"At one point, we were dancing right in front of Haley. His blind eye twitched, he didn't look particularly happy, they hardly had any room left for their own show. Then things got hectic. The guys with the drumsticks started beating on the instruments, one of them got in the pianist's way. That was Johnny Grande, who usually played accordion, my role model in a way. Apparently, he was the only Comet who could read music. Below, they trashed the space and that was the end. The band fled from the stage, the hooligans destroyed everything left on stage, even the piano. Inge caught a drumstick on her temple—in the end we just ran. Down below the police had marched into the hall, the West Berlin police, some on horses!"

Walter took another cigarette. He held the pack out to Carl.

"What happened next—hard to describe. A door behind the stage and then a labyrinth, changing rooms, washrooms, toilets, we wandered around down there, it was pretty dark everywhere. Inge was crying, she was in pain. I turned toward her, and someone grabbed me and threw me onto the floor. He immediately had control of me and forced me to my knees, some kind of bodyguard, probably. And then I saw Bill. Bill Haley. He stood there like an apparition, in the door of his changing room. He was beside himself and yelling at us. Bill Haley, Carl, do you understand? I think he still had the fear in his bones. He was yelling from fear, in his checkered suit jacket, the spit curl on his forehead and his blind eye, it was a crazy sight. I had trouble with my English, but the man, the gorilla holding me down, translated. Bill wanted to know why these Nazis who stormed his stage all looked like Elvis Presley. Inge, still behind me, was crying, her entire body trembling, and Bill repeated his Elvis Presley question. I had no idea where he was going with that, and I still don't. Then Inge started talking. She said, 'We love rock 'n' roll, it's our life. We love Bill Haley and his Comets.' It sounded sharp, almost defiant, even though she was crying. And then she said that her husband played rock 'n' roll, too, on his accordion.

"It was a bit much of her to say that with Haley standing right in front of us. The guy holding me translated and Bill told him to let me go. *Her husband!* We weren't even engaged."

He drained his glass in one gulp. That memory still brought a smile to his face.

"Another beer, maybe?"

Carl waved the bartender over. He understood that this was his job now.

"Bill liked Inge, maybe that tipped the scales. He invited us to his hotel. We talked—we understood each other well and when we didn't, his gorilla translated. Bill was still outraged. And puzzled and, yes . . . kind. He was kind and clever and almost shy, I'd say. Like a man from a laboratory who, after a few years of hard work, had discovered the formula for rock 'n' roll and couldn't quite understand what he was setting loose on the world with it. Who didn't understand why the FBI was tailing him. Who didn't understand why they were calling him a sorcerer, a rock 'n' roll gangster, and whatever else they called him. I believe that for Bill it was always only about the music. And in any case, he wasn't really made for the stage. He was no pretty boy. No pelvic thrusts.

"In his hotel, he showed us the room with his instruments. They had an extra room for them, and from then on, it was a dream. Outside the window, the city lights. And Bill, half lying on the bed, and his bass player, who started to play something, that's how it began. And then Bill, who said that I should pick up the accordion. We went back and forth for a while, but then I played—I played for Bill Haley, Carl."

Walter took a drink and wiped his lips. His eyes shone.

"'Great fingerwork, Wolter,' that's what Bill said, again and again, at least ten times in a row—he praised me. I know I didn't deserve it, but I felt good. Maybe I was never that good again. He said that he'd been thinking about bringing an accordion back into the band for a long time, to integrate it completely and return to a more acoustic lineup. I believe he was thinking about his roots. It probably had something to do with Elvis. Bill said that I looked like Orbison, Roy Orbison, the same quiff, the same ducktail, black-framed glasses . . ."

Carl's father fell silent, and his gaze was lost somewhere between the gleaming bottles behind the bar.

"Bill said, *Stay.* He wanted to keep us there, Carl. I had the middle shift the following day, my mother had the early shift. She would have been the first to notice if I didn't come back."

His father took a piece of plastic from his linen jacket pocket, tapped on it and shook his head. Then he set it beside Carl's glass. As Carl picked it up, Walter kept his eyes on it. It was a worn autograph card laminated in plastic. Bill Haley on the front, with his skewed eye and the spit curl on his forehead, which at first glance looked like a small hook that had been painted on. He wore a velvet suit, a bow tie, and a pocket handkerchief. "To sweet Inge and Walter! Bill!" On the back was a handwritten address in Texas.

"He wanted us to come. And we wanted to go. Inge wanted to go right away."

Walter hummed something softly to himself and played piano on the bar.

"I worked out for Inge how we should save up first and prepare everything so that we'd have a good start—in America. First this and then that. At some point, I began to wonder if Bill could have meant it seriously, with us. Maybe I sensed something or maybe I didn't, who could know today; thirty-three years change things. In any case, it was the wrong question. He did mean it seriously, in his way. Sometimes I think that he needed us more than we could imagine. He wanted a good experience after the disaster that night. And there we were, two greenhorns from the provinces."

Standing up, Walter knocked his barstool over, Carl caught it.

"Bill started playing in different bands at nineteen—exactly the age I was then. Nineteen years old and full of dreams."

Walter wiped the laminated card on his sleeve and slipped it back into his jacket pocket.

When they stepped out on the street, it was still light. A cloying mugginess hung over the parking lot, but Carl shivered, and the beer brought on a slight dizziness. What was he feeling now? The prolonging of an ancient loneliness, without end. What had he expected? Some kind of reward? For being worried and writing letters (even if they were filled with lies) (but not only)? Or for being desperate over the missed meeting in Frankfurt and now having come *all the way here*, the entire long trek to this bleak side street at the other end of the world?

"So quiet, Carl?"

"What can I say? Bill Haley is dead, you're here. Rock 'n' roll will never die . . ."

His voice sounded unfamiliar. Maybe he'd hoped they'd reunite here, as a family. But actually, the opposite was the case. Carl, their child, had no role in this story.

"Bill died ten years ago. But it wasn't about him or any engagement anymore. You know us, Carl, we're your parents. It's not our way to be bitter our entire lives. But that's exactly it, I mean, we tried not to resent the situation forever . . . We knew that was the only way. To not think about it, not talk about it. Only after people started escaping via Hungary did your mother say it."

"Say what?"

"That I should play something. On the accordion. After nearly thirty years." He smiled bashfully. "It's probably childish, I know."

"No," Carl murmured. Suddenly he felt sorry for his father. Carl wanted to hear it, but also didn't. His unfamiliar parents. Everything was mixed-up. He was their child, but his father was a child, too.

"I think that at first Inge wanted to laugh a bit at how badly I played after such a long time, hitting the wrong notes. My fingers kept getting muddled. Then she jumped up to dance, you know your mother, how much energy she has, but in the end she just stood there, in the middle of the room, crying. She didn't move and didn't look at me. She just wept."

They turned, heading downtown. The sun set.

"I think we were both surprised. I mean, that everything suddenly came flooding back. That evening we talked about it until late at night. I found my sheet music, we played and listened to the records from that time. I believe your mother was already sure that we'd leave."

"And Gera? Your life in Gera?"

His father looked embarrassed again, but his voice was calm and steady, and he seemed completely sober again.

"It wasn't about Bill anymore, of course it wasn't. All of a sudden, we had this chance. For a few seconds, our cage stood open, that's how we thought back then, you know. And then it wasn't about anything else. Only about finally crossing the border. It was about us being the ones to decide. That this is *our* life."

"And before . . . It wasn't?"

"It no longer meant—as much. You weren't living at home anymore and we'd hardly been in touch for a long time. Of course, we had doubts, I mean . . ."

Walter fell silent and Carl looked out the side window.

"Why did you never tell me about it? Never."

"Superstition. Fear. We couldn't talk about it until . . . Until we were sure that this time it would work. That this time we could do it."

Carl still couldn't see what he might like about this city. He didn't like cities, not even Berlin, he now realized.

Inge looked pale, almost terrified. She hugged Carl and tried to look into his eyes. They'd planned an "evening together," Walter had said. First a concert, then dinner in Little Japan.

The entrance to the Downtown Playhouse looked temporary, like a warehouse door. In the foyer, they met *friends*, whom Carl's father had gotten to know through the company, during his work for the studios. Their names were Anna and Jack, and they were introduced to Carl as *musicians*. Carl learned that Jack played the cello and that Anna was a renowned singer. She wore long, black false eyelashes and silver eyeliner around her dark eyes. She asked Carl how he liked being in Los Angeles.

Inge was nervous. She tried to read Carl's face and when he noticed, he couldn't help but smile at her. It was more of a mechanical response and, actually, everyone was smiling. Anna and Jack were planning on founding a band with Walter on the *Schifferklavier*; she used the German word for accordion and tried to speak a little German. Carl's father would also sing—in the band. Carl initially thought they were going to make fun of him (or of his father), but they were serious. They

liked German, its exotic sound, "the sound of a German voice,"
Anna said.

Jack was also called Sound Jack. "In the company, he does
the same thing I do, but for sound," Carl's father explained.
"He writes the sound program; I write the image program." Jack
protested and they discussed it. Even as a child, Carl was always
amazed at how effortlessly one sentence could follow another
when adults met. There was that melody of conversation, which
everyone knew and merely had to sing along to. No one was left
hanging: it all sounded effusive. Carl smiled again and answered
a question. It was the first time that he saw his parents so clearly
from the outside. Maybe it was the first time he actually saw
them as other people and for a moment he was no longer their
child. No longer the self-evident truth of things that are simply
what they are—normal, inconsequential, nothing that needs
to be pondered. Because that, thought Carl, is the meaning of
family: a survival unit that ensures that what is real remains
unrecognized.

Then the concert: three guitars, percussion. "The best here,"
his father had said. Carl was so disoriented in Little Japan that
he ordered a Chinese beer. "Oh, Carl, no!" Anna cried. Carl
blushed and apologized. The waiter kept a straight face.

They were joined by other *friends*. A woman named Fee sat
next to Carl. She was his age and German, and Carl felt relieved.
He liked her gentle horse face. It turned out that Fee's father was
also a musician—with the Berlin Philharmonic. "Musician and
insect collector," Fee said, briefly catching his eye. She occasionally visited her father in Berlin.

She's got things the right way round, thought Carl. The child
sets off for the wide world, not the parents, parents who, in any
case, had already traveled everywhere: insect hunting in Africa,
Australia, even Greenland, with their daughter named Fee,
who was now telling him that she was heading into the desert

the next morning, on an assignment from her agency to film a communist leader.

"A secret meeting, in his camp."

During the meal, Carl half turned toward Fee to avoid the conversation at the table. He was tired.

Fee now told Carl that actually she made movies and she named a title. Carl pictured his mother in Gera, standing alone in the living room and weeping (instead of dancing). He glanced over at her; Inge laughed and raised her eyebrows, which she often did when questioning something. His father was talking to Sound Jack, trying to explain something. His English sounded Thuringian.

Carl had four more days. Now and again, he drove into the city in his mother's Mazda, but he spent most of his time on the beach, "below," as his mother called it. The city was "above."

It felt good to be alone in the car. It's a little like the early days in Berlin, thought Carl, which wasn't true. He hadn't taken this trip on his own initiative and there was no pack to pick him up off the street and what for anyway? He was here as his parents' guest, *at home* in a certain sense. "The tolerant Pacific air makes logic seem so silly," Carl had read in Auden, he couldn't remember which poem. Auden wasn't one of his favorites, but you have to read everything, for later, to make your own way.

"Upon what man it fall . . . That he should leave his house . . ." That was Auden, too, a poem with the strange title "The Wanderer," about a man nothing could hold, who always had to move on. The poem was a kind of prayer for protection and a blessing.

Driving had something pleasantly monotonous and irresponsible about it. The so-called freeway—you merged onto it and became a part of something. Here, you just drove straight ahead for a long time, turned and then drove straight ahead again without anything outside the window ever seeming to change. Everywhere the same sad one-story buildings, bungalows with grills on their doors, advertisements, movie houses, parks, and supermarkets, and a few scruffy, gray palm trees, interspersed with shimmering heat that made everything flow together and become unfathomable. And so, Carl found it difficult to discern details; in any case, his notebook remained empty. The good thing about driving was that everything slipped by, soft, rhythmic, meaningless, so that you could turn on the radio and hum to yourself.

He found LACMA, but then didn't feel like visiting a museum. He wandered between the sculptures in the garden for a while. An ecstatic Orpheus by Rodin, holding his lyre and singing. If that's the truth, Carl thought, and turned away. He walked toward the construction site behind the sculpture garden. He tried not to think about why the construction site interested him more than the Rodin. It turned out not to be a construction site at all, just a tar-filled hole, surrounded by fencing. The midday sun burned and in its light a numbness filled him. Carl carefully shook his head back and forth, he swallowed, moved his tongue and felt the shackles. If he only stared, without thinking, he felt better. The tar welled up right out of the ground, a hollow filled with pitch; he'd never seen anything like it. He could neither turn away nor grasp any particular idea; there was no definition of him to start from, his substance was indeterminable; he was now in his mid-twenties, and he was nothing.

Before sunset, Carl drove to the beach. He paid the seven-dollar parking fee and pulled his car into the row nearest the ocean. A line of orange beacon lights glowed over the hill of Santa Monica Bay. The sun went down and poured all the remaining light on the large windows of the bungalows.

The beach was almost empty at this hour. Aside from him, there was only a very thin, old woman who stalked through the knee-deep water with emphatic nimbleness, making small, ridiculous jumps. And another, even older woman who photographed her as she leaped. The younger old woman hopped, stretched out her arms and played at being a breakwater, again and again, wave after wave. Now and then, she spun around and made a threatening gesture at the older old woman: no pictures! Her anger was feigned, it was impossible not to notice. Mother and daughter, thought Carl. As if on command, the older old woman (the mother who pampers her to death) lifted the camera to her eye, but only briefly. As soon as the woman breaking the waves started hopping again, the older woman took pictures.

Carl felt his hatred. He hated the woman in the waves and the way she did her best to pose like a twelve-year-old. And he hated her mother, the falsity of her kindness, and he would have liked to hit her in the face. He hated the whole hypocritical scene. Carl lowered his eyes and stared at his towel. His hatred was pure and clear, and it was going to explode: he jumped up and after running a few steps, it burst out of him—excessive laughter, much too loud.

I was never happy as a child, isn't that the truth, Carl thought.

Around midnight, the sprinkler turned on. The yapping of the neighborhood dogs drove a coyote back to the desert. "At night, the coyotes drink from the fountains," Carl's father had told him. Around two o'clock, it grew quiet, and the roar of the Pacific was audible in the house.

His father knelt next to the star. He had his tools and a kind of pit lamp. He groaned and grew impatient. Carl, who was behind him the whole time, watching everything closely, tried to help him; he was someone who sees what work needs to be done, a construction worker. Together they lifted the star (which weighed more than a drain cover) out of the sidewalk and tilted it carefully on its side, on the old garage blanket that Walter had spread out for the purpose. The precious star. A few brown slugs were stuck to the back. "Slugs," stated his father. "Bill would not have liked that." Shaking his head, he plucked off the slugs and threw them in the gutter.

The grave was deep. His father's arm disappeared completely into it; his cheek was pressed to the ground. He grimaced, showing his teeth, as always when something required effort or complete concentration. Carl grimaced automatically and his teeth showed, too. His father carefully brought something wrapped in moldy, gray felt up to the light.

"The ashes have disappeared," his father said softly. "No ashes, no bones—this is all we have." He gently opened the felt and something golden shone in it. It was their old portable radio with the golden screen over the speaker. Carl recognized it immediately. Above the gold was the white, lightly notched tuning dial, which was already slightly discolored and worn. Not surprising, thought Carl. Every morning and every evening, the radio had stood on their dining table. The small wooden case with the golden screen had been the secret center of their family life— when did it disappear and why in the world had he not noticed?

"Does it still work?" Carl whispered.

His father took a corner of the felt cloth and rubbed the golden screen, whereupon the radio began to play softly. Some writing became visible, too, a small label with the inscription Star 111.

"Star 111," his father murmured, "from the Star Radio Company." He touched the label, as if reading it were not enough.

Walter groaned, rose laboriously and stood for a moment before the open grave, motionless, his head lowered. Carl understood and joined his father.

"You were there, too, back then," he finally said to Carl. Then (as if he were the ghost of this past), his father pointed out over the fields, where the Walk of Fame disappeared between the hills—it was a field path, on which Carl saw the familiar shapes of his parents approaching; their outlines gradually became clearer. His mother had met his father at the train station. She was pushing a baby carriage. His father walked next to her, cradling the radio in his arms. Carl saw the baby in the carriage, who could be none other than himself (plump and with eyes wide open). He saw dusk falling over the east Thuringian hills and saw how the radio's light illuminated his father's face. The light and the music, which only now reached his ears.

"What did we listen to?" Carl asked.

"Which station is it set to, son?" his father asked.

Carl knelt down to read the dial. A dark, gluey lava oozed out of the pit; it had already caught the radio, it welled up and Carl watched as it began flooding the Walk of Fame.

A few seconds of suffocation, then Carl made the transition. He lay on the broad sofa next to the dust-covered coffee table, and it was Sunday, his last day in Malibu.

He got up and went out onto the terrace. The sun was dazzling. Two hummingbirds that looked like insects buzzed in the shrubbery behind the parking lot. He heard his mother's voice, then the music started up again. It was the music from his dream, it came from the garage, blues, powerful but restrained blues, if that's possible, rhythmic but tender; his father was playing the accordion. Following a sudden fit of longing, Carl went to the garage, his bare feet in grass that felt artificial, like rubber. He opened the side door and just stood there, in his underwear, like a child woken by a bad dream in the middle of the night who wants to be comforted.

The Sunset Restaurant looked like a train station hall filled with white plastic chairs. In the aquarium near the entrance, live crabs were piled up, inextricably tangled with each other. At first glance, they formed a single body, a gleaming brown lump of unfortunate life bristling all over with antennae and eyes.

For their last evening, Inge had reserved three seats on the terrace—a "nice table," as she called it. The restaurant was part of the residential complex and the beach was also private. The breakers below the Sunset were illuminated by halogen flood-lights. The menu explained about Humaliwo, a Chumash village. The name meant "where the surf sounds loudly." Two thousand years later Humaliwo became Malibu.

"What are your plans, Carl?"

After all that had happened, the old parental question. A few overweight seagulls reeled toward them and, with effort, veered away. Only now, as Carl worked out the parental version of his answer—according to which resuming his studies was not out of the question, after all, the German Literature Institute was not far from the restaurant where he "was earning some extra income" as they already knew, then something about his daily life and so on (not a word about Effi, his accident, his failures)—did the pain of the affront reach him.

"And you? We won't see each other again for a few years, will we? Or not at all? Am I supposed to serve as the rearguard that long?"

"Carl!"

"Walter *never* played accordion for me, not once. I didn't even know what was in that case in the cellar."

"No, you didn't, Carl," Inge said.

"Rearguard is probably the wrong word," Walter said.

They've always lived their own life, thought Carl, he should have known when they went away and left everything behind, he should have understood at least that much. Instead, he felt hurt like a child, which was simply ridiculous.

Inge reached across the table for his hand, but Carl leaned back.

"And? What are your plans? Wasn't Haley in Mexico in his later years?"

Carl's father ignored the biting tone of the questions and talked about Bill Haley, Haley in Mexico. Carl listened to him for a while and then stopped. A seagull sat on the neighboring table, staring at him, fixedly, lurking.

I was excluded, thought Carl, whereas Inge and Walter were in on the secret for all that time, in as deep as possible. Only now did he understand: they had never told him a thing and lived an alternate life. A good, acceptable, and, in any case, not unhappy life, just a constrained one. With a move from the country to the city, with studies, professions, and their child Carl. It was anchored to him, too, this second-best life. It corresponded to an underlying feeling of his childhood: the feeling of representing someone or something, never being completely and fully the one meant—not *in himself* or however he could put it. The long afternoons in his childhood room, alone. A decor with cowboys and Indians, an endless battle in endless monologues. Enrolled in school at six, with attention difficulties and discipline problems, teachers' visits to his parents, love dependent on performance and some incredible effort that was simply too much for him. He had the photographs from the album in mind: father, mother, and a child. A child with an exhausted expression and the feeling of being *instead of*, without knowing anything more about it, just the feeling.

After dinner, his father suggested "going out for short stroll" along the beach. Carl plodded ahead, then stopped and looked out over the water to let his parents pass him. He wouldn't look at them and he knew they must find it childish and obstinate of him. They paused for a moment but then walked on, quickly and without turning around once.

They are twice as old as I am, thought Carl, with twice the energy. (And double the courage if he were being honest.) He still couldn't bring it together: his parents and these two rock 'n' rollers. He wondered if they still danced now and then. If Inge still *jumped up onto* him and then *hovered.* He would have liked to admire this couple. He'd have liked to find it all adventurous. The never-abandoned dream—or what was their story about? About which longing? About two people, in any case, who never complained, not to this day, thought Carl. About two people who left, following their dream like an ancient pledge.

His parents' mystery and how it marched on, a hundred meters ahead of him, along the beach. Like way back when we walked along the Elsterdamm, when I was a kid, thought Carl. The child had grown, but the fairy tale of the place where one feels at home still beat in his heart, there where one's parents live. Isn't that how it was? Lost in thought, Carl slowed. The sand near the water was now pleasantly cool and his feet sinking into it made him tired.

His mother stopped and turned back. She waved at Carl and pointed at a tree that grew out over the cliffs, twenty or thirty meters above them. Carl approached and saw that the tree was swaying in the wind, but very slowly, as if in slow motion. It was bathed in light, evening light, its leaves were made of light and they moved, slowly, the light moved in the tree.

"The fact that we were allowed to see this, that's the thing," his mother said softly. "It shows how well things are going for us."

Carl turned away and closed his eyes.

"When Walter needs more time in the evenings, I sometimes come here alone." Carl's mother looked at him, a look he did not want to return under any circumstances. The negative of the tree of light glowed on his retina, as if branded on.

"First, we tried to just forget, and we almost separated. We felt guilty toward each other. Your father was too hesitant back then, after the thing with Bill. Bill liked us for whatever reason. We could have left right away. That would have been best. Maybe we were too young. Later, I was the one who became afraid, in the middle of the forest, at the border, although we'd almost made it. But even so, it was actually already too late."

"Too late. Two years before I was born," Carl murmured.

"Imagine, if I'd been pregnant in prison . . ."

She fell silent and took Carl's arm. Carl tried to figure out what his mother had meant. Why did she say that? He closed his eyes and saw the tree of light. He couldn't remember what the actual question had been. His anger seemed to have dissipated, evaporated in the sun, and what he felt was a diffuse sense of depth and abyss, as if he were that tree above him, right where the cliff was crumbling away.

"Inge!"

His father approached and Carl freed his arm. Walter looked up at the tree which had now turned completely to gold. For a time, none of them said anything. The sun was already very low. The wind picked up. It slowly grew colder.

"Do you two remember our portable radio?" Carl asked.

"The Star 111. A transistor," his father said.

"Where is it now?"

Walter shook his head.

"At the time, we always had it with us," his mother said. "The radio and the three of us on every Sunday outing. You sat in the handcart, Carl, a pillow behind your back and the radio on your lap . . ."

"Three frequencies," his father said earnestly, "and a retractable antenna. It was an excellent radio."

"Where is it now?" Carl asked again.

"There was a little flap on the back of the case that had to be opened occasionally; that's where you put the flat batteries. It was our connection to the world."

"And then?" Carl asked.

Walter, who had heard it as a technical question, explained: "First, you had to bend the batteries' contact tongues up slightly, one short and one long. You had to think counterintuitively."

"Counterintuitively?"

"The short tongue was positive, the long one negative."

"When did we get the radio?"

"It was our first acquisition as a family," his father replied.

Acquisition as a family: the expression was very familiar to Carl and for a moment he wondered if it was still used or if it had disappeared with the objects it had once described.

"At the time, when I bought the radio, we still lived in the country. To celebrate, Inge had met my train at the station and crossed the fields with you in the wagon. Buses didn't run in the evening. It must have been the autumn of '64. I was in my first year at university. We listened to the radio all the way home. It was already dark, and we had to take care not to get lost in the dark. The radio had a leather strap, so that it really looked like a small suitcase. Sometimes I wore the strap over my shoulder, pretty casually, sometimes I held the radio in my arm. Sometimes we sang aloud, at the top of our voices in the darkness and danced a few steps in the middle of the field. The radio was our only light, Star 111. And you were there, in the handcart."

"I was there?"

"You were there. You were *always* there."

"What did we listen to?"

"Radio Luxembourg. Or AFN. The Beatles had just had their first hits. 'Love, Love Me, Do' and so on. That beat everything. You cheered and stuck your little fists out of the wagon. It looked very funny."

Walter laughed and Inge laughed, too, in her mischievous way, wrinkling her nose, and then Carl laughed as well.

"AFN played them all. Chuck Berry, Jerry Lee Lewis, also Johnny Cash and Ray Charles, who were played less often after they did time in prison. Buddy Holly, who died in an airplane crash. Or Little Richard, the songs from before he claimed rock 'n' roll was the devil's music."

Walter talked and Carl stared at him. This was his father. There was a lot that Carl did not know. He didn't know much about himself, either. Not even that he'd been a Beatles fan.

They walked next to each other along the beach in silence for a while. After a few minutes, Carl asked his parents to leave him on his own. "Is that OK?"

He had the feeling that they were secretly following him at first, but when he turned around, he was alone. He wandered aimlessly. He stopped thinking and felt relief—a fine drizzle on his head, he shivered, and had to stand still and close his eyes for a moment.

The roar of the surf, the sea spray in the moonlight, bluish and as if lit from inside. The wind was pleasant, the coolness on his forehead. He walked on and fished a diving mask out of the water, the lens clouded with salt or from being ground in the surf. Carl put it on for a moment and listened: he heard the roar, the eternal noise that embraced him benevolently and took him away. It was a form of profound trust—and abandonment. Trust in one's own abandonment, if such a thing is possible, thought Carl.

He came to a section of the shore on which several dark, mute figures sat and stared out at the ocean. Each one sat alone, isolated, but there seemed to be something that connected them, invisibly.

These are the dead, Carl suddenly realized. The dead before their departure. And it was strange, how uninhibitedly you could walk between them.

He took off his shoes and took a few steps out into the water. He stood and slowly sank in the sand. One wave and another—it was nice. He was standing firmly now. The horizon stretching out before his eyes and fine, sandy mud between his toes. He hummed "Love, Love Me Do" softly into the surf. He swayed very lightly to the beat of the tides. Wasn't it wonderful to be alone?

EPILOGUE

THE INVINCIBLE A

(Carl's Report)

I saw the Assel for the last time on 21 May 2009, just before it vanished completely. The building was already covered with scaffolding, but there were still tables and benches on the sidewalk. I went down the stairs and crept like a thief through the dim rooms, which seemed larger than before because the wall of Fenske's cellar had been removed, but I only realized that later. It was strange to be down there again after so many years. "There's nothing more silent than a reunion with a building site"—who was it who said that? Some contented animal deep in the earth.

There was no one behind the bar and no one at the tables; maybe guests were few at this hour (early afternoon). Everything looked normal and *smudge-proof*—the old tables were covered with a thick layer of clear varnish. On each one was a large menu, handwritten and laminated—a greasy piece of plastic, already crumbling around the edges, as if gnawed on.

The Assel was the first of its kind. After it, restaurants, cafés, and a few kosher shops opened in quick succession. At night, the area was still flooded with tourists who wanted to view the streetwalkers from a safe distance. These weren't clients (maybe in the next life). The tourist guides dubbed Oranienburger Strasse the "Vile Mile," and generally mentioned the Assel as the "first post-Wall bar" or a "trendy hangout."

It smelled of moldy dampness, that hadn't changed. Judging by the menu, the U-boat of the early years had become a mixture of diner and Italian, but the name was the same: The Assel. Outside, above the flight of brick steps leading underground, the name was written in that shaky, spindly Assel lettering that actually did come from the very first days but now looked artificial and incongruous, or as if this were the entrance to a cheap haunted house.

Back then, after my return from Los Angeles and, yes, already on the flight home, the voice of consolation and reconciliation reached me: what had actually happened? I would take care of Effi, support her, because now I knew. Effi's trauma, or whatever the right word for it is. We could talk about all of it. And about the question of what it really means to be together. And why we were never actually *really together* and what had kept us from that. And what, despite it all, the future could hold for us—because of our love.

When I got to her place, she was no longer in her apartment. The door was unlocked. Clothing was strewn everywhere, on the floor and on the bed, as if she'd just been there. On the easel was the picture of the woman who was Effi, the eternal image, the eternal Effi with the necklace that she had taken or quoted from a Matisse portrait called *L'Asie*, as I knew since Paris. She led me to this painting and showed it to me, back then, full of reverence, in the Musée d'Orsay. "It actually hangs in Texas," Effi had said.

A few weeks later, I received mail from Greece. The return address was I. K., Taverna Odysseas, 70 009 Lendas / Diskos, CRETE. She was there with Freddy—and Rico. For an indefinite period, "at least for the summer." Three pages folded twice and closely written on both sides: this was her letter. They had a bamboo hut on the beach; they had built shelves of bamboo and a clay oven but cooked over an open fire "down by the water," in the bay "behind the lion." The lion was a cliff, Effi wrote, a spit of land that extended far into the water. The shortest way to the village was over the lion—and so on. She also wrote about the sun in her letter and about the moon, the heat, the stars, and the sultriness, and about who stopped by their hut every day—why was she telling me this? Effi had never talked much; now she was describing everything in minute detail and as if it were important to me. The stamp showed an ancient mosaic, in which two naked hunters slew a deer. Rico was only mentioned indirectly. "Some people have set themselves up here for a long stay, and you can tell. They're calm, they let the days pass, *and I'm getting it all more and more.*"

Whatever she meant by this, it was enough to strike a particular chord in me, at first barely audible. A small, evil melody that gave me the strength to see the only woman I'd been in love with until then as a stranger, with whom I never wanted to have anything to do again.

Still, a photo of Effi hung on my wall for years, in the corridor, behind the door. Evidently there is a faithfulness that runs deeper, down near the roots and beyond those feelings that rule our decisions—an attachment that persists, that can hardly be explained. Its inviolability (and preciousness) comes from the fact that things happened to *us.*

The photo shows Effi toward the end of her school years, in one of her appearances as a magician in a polka-dot skirt and sailor blouse, a kind of disguise, maybe. It was always my favorite photograph, hard to say why. Probably the girlishness of her stance, the gentleness, her defenseless smile—I wanted to see it, I wanted it *for me*— precisely that. It revealed what I could be for her if we were together or were truly *together.* Effi is reading a note, her head tilted. She reads and marvels. It's a staged marveling. No idea what magical message she'd just received. At her feet and all around her, cloths and crumpled papers are strewn, the battlefield at the end of her performance. Effi could make things disappear and reappear. "How did you do that?"

I asked her once. "Magician's secret," was Effi's answer. And, in fact, she never spoke about it, just as she never spoke about the picture on her easel or about herself. And it did no good to ask. Actually, I never had the feeling I knew her, or when I did, it was only a pretense to reassure myself and because things simply wouldn't work otherwise. I may have been too intrusive sometimes, but more out of the fear of losing her, even though I never actually had her.

"Well? Where's the woman now, where?"

"Gone, she's gone!"

The old magic trick.

Ryke Strasse 1992. Old Knospe's flower bed was in bloom. It was now tended by two punks from Oldenburg who had moved into the cold, very damp apartment on the ground floor (condemned by the authorities, it was always said)—with a legitimate lease, word of which got around. Whenever I passed by, the door was open, "to let out the damp" the Oldenburgers explained. Open doors and damp walls didn't bother them and the two new residents from the north actually did change the climate inside the building. They were unusually friendly and not only to old Knospe ("a real Berliner!"), whom they carried downstairs and back up several times a day. They took all of her suggestions seriously and took *notes*: their plan was "a real garden" and "their own vegetables." They swept the courtyard and cleaned up the small bomb crater copse, where quite a bit of garbage and excrement had collected over the years. With surprising care and skill, the young Oldenburgers put up a temporary fence around the collapsed spot with the dead in the vaults below (this was the image that often, irresistibly, came to my mind after Wrubel's fall into the old air-raid shelter—whether it corresponded to reality or not can no longer be established) and staged parties in the courtyard, to which every single resident in number 27 was invited. Then they would build a campfire and grill, and Sonie would place the expensive speakers of his Rema-Andante stereo in the open window.

Old Knospe wore a thin, slightly bleached summer dress. Not only her flower beds, but she, too, had blossomed in these days. Finally, we all sat together in some large, soft, reclining chairs from the eighties that had suddenly started piling up on the streets and sidewalks for the bulky waste collection and could be dragged home by anyone passing by. Indoors seemed to have become outdoors as if some absurd switch had taken place, an exodus that shamelessly exposed the intimacy of the old life. At least one of these chairs was always close at hand, as were complete three-piece upholstered suites that had been cast out—all ripped open, splashed with dirt—in the heat of the moment or as if contaminated. As if the old coziness were poisoned by the fact that it had existed: a previous life, a previous country.

When old Knospe started in, everyone around the fire fell silent: she knew the stories. First the story of the old building manager named Dahms, who lived in Kreuzberg, Diefenbach Strasse, who had specifically taken over buildings owned by Jews, among them "our ruin, which hadn't always been one," as Mrs. Knospe put it. Then the story of Dr. Lewin—Max Lewin, the owner of the building at 27 Ryke Strasse.

"A doctor, he lived on Warschauer Strasse and died in a concentration camp."

"Was murdered," corrected Sonie, the second-oldest resident in this housing community, which was revealing itself in these days to be an actual community. The old woman nodded and sipped the wine the Oldenburgers had poured for her; she liked to drink, and drank fast, leaving the meat from the grill untouched. I didn't see her eat a bite of it.

Lewin's children, Erik and Ernst, who had appeared on Ryke Strasse "sometime after '45," had told her the whole story. One of them emigrated to Palestine, the other lives in Switzerland, Knospe murmured, and stared into the fire.

"That's war, children. It destroys everything."

Darkness had fallen but it was still warm when Charlotte Knospe, who had lived at 27 Ryke Strasse for sixty-one years, began listing, floor by floor, the names of the tenants who had been in the cellar when the bomb hit the front of the building: "On the ground floor were the Bernsdorffs, very nice people, I have to say. On the left, Franke, on the right, Gärtner, and then on the second floor Hinz, Klemmt, and Pagallies, the old master tailor . . ."

The truth is, I have to admit, I didn't remember a single one of these names when I started writing this report. But the Oldenburgers, who still spoke of "Mother Knospe" and absorbed everything Mother Knospe offered them for their new lives in the East, had taken notes: I just had to find them, which wasn't easy. None of the people from that time lived on Ryke Strasse any longer and the small copse was cleared out long ago and newly planted. Only in the gap next to 27 (number 28 also "fell" in the war) can you find remains of the old building's stones between the roots, as if half-pushed up by invisible hands—real stumbling blocks, if you're not careful.

After a while, it was good to get up from sitting near the fire. I crossed the small copse to the street and walked down Ryke to the water tower, as if it were necessary to report and discuss the latest state of things there, too. This was my spot, my mooring, the lighthouse and haven for my monologues. I circled the tower and its island, now as solitary as myself, several times. I still held my monologues, endless and more or less out loud, and sometimes it was surprising to hear what surfaced, what stole out of the center of my vague thoughts, there, under the trees, in the shadow of the watchman. Now and then, Effi was the subject.

"We were never truly intimate with each other, never intimate, though," I chattered to myself and listened to the trees and I knew that it was over, finito. Effi was sitting in a bamboo hut on the island of Crete, on the beach, and was probably *cheerful.*

So I made my rounds as a roaring came from under the cobblestones, and suddenly there was the smell of fish and fish scales glittered on the stones. I followed their trace to the gray steel gate on Belforter Strasse, which promised an entrance to the center of the island. I pressed my ear to the gate and there it was: the roar. The underground ocean.

A few matters that concerned only me became clear: first, I wanted a lease (like the Oldenburgers had), I didn't want to be *illegal* anymore. Maybe only because I felt older and, as they say, "more sensible," but maybe also because in the meantime the first buildings, just a few doors down, had been "completely renovated." Their absurd and, in the grayness of the street, surreal brightness (beige, yellow, or ochre-colored) dazzled the eyes and heralded the coming of a time in which there would no longer be any room for good old illegality, not for how I got my apartment, nor for unlicensed taxis, and definitely not for bars without permits or unlicensed butchering in back courtyards: all this would soon be over.

Across from the small bomb crater copse, there was now a trendy café I'd never seen anyone set foot in. The woman who worked there as the waitress stood in the doorway for a cigarette several times a day, whatever the weather. She wore sweaters of every color that looked eccentric but also handmade, essentially sad. When I sat on the toilet, I would watch her through the small, arrow-slit-shaped window. The new era had started its work on the sweater-woman, too. The new era was making her nervous, too.

Second, I planned on writing various publishers, including, finally, Oberbaum Berlin and St. Petersburg. It was simply a matter of finding the courage, of taking the next step despite all my doubts. I couldn't go on like that forever, besieged by my twenty poems, those small, aggressive, much-rewritten poetic battle troops.

Third, Dodo. I would take care of Dodo. Goat, apartment, and publisher—three tasks I would set out to accomplish and, if possible, complete successfully. I looked up at the tower lights, which promised me the necessary support. Only here at the water tower was Berlin completely on my side. Only here had I really *gained a foothold*, in the sound of my footfall on my walks around this island from Ryke to Knaack Strasse, from Knaack to Diedenhofer, from Diedenhofer to Belforter, from Belforter to Kolmarer and from there back to Knaack, Knaack, Knaack, and so on, ten, twelve laps until I was tired, tired enough, and could go back home.

One warm day that summer, which no one can date precisely now, the Shepherd disappeared from his stall (from Dodo's stall, to be precise)—after which the goat seemed confused. Following the breakup of the Fenske cellar group, goat milk was rarely requested, and no one felt truly responsible for the animal. At night, Dodo stood among the tables as if lost and all the guests felt they should touch her. The most shameless of them jokingly mistreated her; they shooed the creature through the rooms and again and again there was one who tried to ride her. "Pamplona for the poor," Hans had said but didn't stop them. He had, in a countermove of sorts, begun to drink very heavily.

"They put the goat on the bar and then . . ." He didn't finish, he only shook his head.

One night, after a few Tullamore Dews, the best whiskey the Assel stocked, Hans aired his suspicion: the Shepherd may have been "accidentally discarded" by the new waitstaff (there was a constant stream of new waiters), completely unintentionally, just "in the general zeal" during the monthly mucking out of the stall which was one of the day shift's duties. Presumably he had still been "in there somewhere," in the dirty, old straw, and the new waitstaff, who knew of the Shepherd and his story only through hearsay, had probably overlooked him, so very thin and stringy and nearly invisible Hoffi (Hans now said *Hoffi*, using the good, old name) had become.

"Almost like in 'The Hunger Artist,'" Hans said in a whisper—and wept. This was odd, since he had done nothing to protect (nor had anyone from the old pack) this last phase of the Shepherd's life, his burrowing into the straw. Hans now had the Assel, and he had his gallery on August Strasse or wherever; he was there every night in front of the bar or behind it, but he had not been to see Hoffi in the stall for weeks.

Of course, I checked the place where the old straw (the dung) was usually unloaded; it was the old bomb crater with the half-buried birch tree. The straw was now just a foul, rotting mess. For whatever reason—I picked up a small birch branch and poked around in it. I was alone. In this corner of Krausnick Park (which the surrounding residents, led by an extended series of surprisingly well-organized subbotniks, had, over time, cleared bit by bit), the untended copse still grew thickly enough, so no one could see me. I carefully poked a bit deeper; I smelled the sweetish odor of rot. I breathed mold and then, this was no dream, I heard the voice, Hoffi's voice—there was no doubt—and it was neither soft or faint, instead it was hard and clear. It was an isolated initial sound, a syllable beginning with an "a" sound, various syllables in fact: "an, ad, ack," and so on and so forth in an endless sequence: "ab, aff, adj . . ." The birds nearby fell silent as if amazed and suddenly the world was listening, as if expecting (finally) the magic word it had been waiting for, that everyone had always been waiting for.

"This is our A, the invincible A," the Shepherd had once said. "It stands for a beginning—*Anfang*, for Assel, for the activity of workers, for the aguerrillas," or words to that effect.

"What, Hoffi, what?" I asked impatiently (awful, stupid impatience) and kept poking, without being able to see the Shepherd. He was nothing more than an awareness, an outline in the mold, the writing of spores in the straw, deciphered with the respect in which I still held him, as dubious as he may have seemed at that moment.

"Please speak . . ."

I don't know how better to describe it. Suddenly it seemed as if everything depended on this last message.

"What, what?" I called and plunged my stick into the straw and at that very moment, the "A" fell silent—forever.

The landlord Alfred Wrubel received me in his mezzanine floor apartment on Wolliner Strasse. He led the way, limping. The apartment looked shabby. Gray curtains in front of the windows, a table, a glass-fronted cabinet. Wrubel said he lived there with his sister.

He appeared suspicious, shy, almost fearful, but soon understood that I could not have been the one who had written WRUBEL—CAPITALIST PIG in blood red letters on the wall over the mailboxes. I won his confidence and he explained that up until last year he had lived in the countryside, but fate had made him the representative of a community of heirs, made up of twelve parties, most of whom were poor, he emphasized.

Whatever circumstances led to this community of heirs (had Dr. Lewin's children died or did they sell?), Wrubel's account of them sounded confused and contradictory. But ultimately they were not the point, the lease was. It took me a while to understand that I had to sign a rider to the contract. It declared that I accepted the building's current condition (dire, fragile, more or less in danger of collapse). As tenant, I waived all rights to make claims or "demands relating to this matter." The codicil also contained a list of around eighty meticulously described deficiencies which I have kept as the most precise description of the building at 27 Ryke Strasse. Certainly, the items on the list were familiar to me—the roof caving in around the chimney, the leakage current caused by dampness in the walls which bathed the stairwells at night with a magical bluish light, the rickety windows, jammed doors, and so on. Perhaps Wrubel had no idea how long I had already been a sailor on this wreck without a lease. He didn't know how happy I was to get the lease.

He limped into the next room—a brief murmur, then he returned with the papers. He lightly knocked on his bad leg: a fall into the cellar air-raid shelter, a complicated break. The shock had probably made him forget that I was among those who pulled him out of the cellar. I felt sorry for him, more so even than before. He didn't seem helpless but was marked as someone who had lived through too much and I was a hair's breadth from asking him if it was because of the dead, if he'd actually seen them and if that was why he had screamed down there.

The rent for my apartment rose from the former 31.80 deutschmarks to 143.25 deutschmarks. The base rent had risen by one mark per square meter, Wrubel explained, and added to that were the "operating costs," a concept I knew nothing about at the time. What was that supposed to include (in a building like this) and why in advance?

The cover of the lease was a copy of an ancient form which referred to the "peace rent" and "repairs undertaken by the tenant in 1914"—Wrubel had drawn a neat line with a pen and ruler through these ancient sentences and apologized for them. "We use the pre-war contracts. The new template from Alscher Property Management is completely useless for us. Alscher completely destroyed our buildings, especially the buildings owned by Jews," Wrubel murmured. I entered my date of birth, wrote waiter as my profession and for place of employment gave the address of the Assel on Oranienburger Strasse, which Wrubel—who knows why—acknowledged with a faint smile. Someday I would specify writer, in that moment I believed in the possibility again; I had secured my den with the window onto the courtyard and the workbench for working.

The rapid, overheated years 1991 and 1992 were followed by two slower, almost serene years. By then I was one of the older ones in the Assel. This seniority and a certain reserve (I was considered taciturn and kept my distance from the hubbub at the bar) gained me a measure of respect. I belonged and yet could still keep to myself—an ideal situation which I had constantly tried to create since childhood: I had by now understood this and a few other things about myself. "What do you want to be when you grow up?" The old teacher's question was suddenly being asked again. I now saw that the world around me was immensely significant, it was crazy stuff, good material and I would never find better. Not even in my fantasies about the ideal poetic existence, which on closer examination followed more abstract, fundamentally primitive melodies. I also saw the longing hidden behind it. The idea of saving oneself *beyond*, of escaping everything into another realm of poetry. (In order to return to this dreary, squalid world one day but now untouchable, protected as if bathed in dragon's blood. For instance.) At the same time, there was neither a higher nor a rational (lower) reason for poetry. Feeling compelled to write poetry was an uncertain and hardly awful fate, almost viable, in fact. At least compared to other addictions. For a thirty-year-old, this is no insignificant realization, but something was missing; I hadn't discovered it yet—my own life, in short. It sounds strange, I know, and nothing could seem more absurd to me when I think back today on those years.

In the summer of 1994, I worked my last shifts. For several weeks, I had only signed up for kitchen duties. On the refrigerator lay Ulrich Zieger's *Three Poets' Doubtful Fame*, a slender, black volume with French flaps that I had just started reading and next to it the notepad on which the waiters scribbled their orders: Japanese noodle soup, salad with feta cheese or without, flatbread with ham, potato soup, and so on, all manageable because essentially pre-made (except for the salad, which I had to prep by the bucketful). So I often had enough time for my own things. Sometimes I'd go into the storeroom in the back and leaf through the books that customers had forgotten or intentionally left behind over the years. A small, crude library had come together in this way; it filled an entire vegetable crate. When there were bookmarks, I opened the book to that page and read. Whatever customer had stopped reading at that passage, I continued the story from there, at least for a while. It had something to do with humility. And possibly reconciliation. As if I had to make up for something. (To these books? To stories in general? Because I had previously held in contempt everything that was written clearly, and hence was conventional and inferior?) Maybe I no longer believed that I myself could be a writer one day. In any case, I had become more patient. I took time and then I saw what happened: I began to understand what I read in the storeroom.

There were afternoons in which hours passed without any orders. Then I would go to the high basement window and lay my cheek on the cool, white tiled windowsill. I remained basically invisible, with my eyes just above street level. I saw the sky over the city, the trees in the park and, in front of them, the streetcar's overhead wires. I saw the kindergarten diagonally across the way and the children at the fence, pressing their faces against the chain links; the street was more interesting than their jungle gym. I saw legs, shoes, the stream of passersby, and at night, when my shift was over, I saw the patent leather boots of the working lady whose spot was in front of my window and whose name was Dora. I'd only have to stretch out my hand to touch her boots.

It was a good, old, almost childlike tiredness that enveloped me there at the window. It was the first time in a long while that I felt calm, maybe the first time in my life.

After Ryke Strasse was connected to Berlin's telephone network (in that phase, the building was held together only by the thin, gleaming telephone wires), I would call my parents in America at least once a month. At first, owning my own telephone felt strange and, yes, almost sensational, but in the end, I hardly used it otherwise.

Inge and Walter? I believe they felt good in California. My father had his band (and his work); my mother had started her own exercise group and worked as a trainer or dance instructor for the women of Malibu, four times a week in the garage, which Walter had converted to a fitness studio for her. When I called Malibu, it was my mother who did the talking (my father stayed in the background, following developments from there, which was no different, actually, than it had ever been with or without a telephone. The division of roles was set).

In general, my parents called me. They assumed the cost. Inge had already set the volume on their telephone to high. When she forgot, she would say, "Wait, Carl, I'm going to turn it up," and her voice would immediately become distant, sound tinny, and be difficult to understand. For this reason, I first thought I'd misheard when she told me they had used their American money to buy a German apartment—in Gera! Not just any apartment. They bought *their own apartment*—with the help of Schenkendorff, the spokesperson for the new community of owners.

"Do you want to come back?"

"Maybe." (Her voice quivered.) "Maybe we'll be home soon, Carl. What do you think?"

*

On 31 August 1994, Vassily returned to the Assel one last time; the date is written in my notebook. It was the day of the farewell parade, the Russians' last march in Berlin. "The red star is going home," or something to that effect was written in the newspapers. I had kitchen duty and was daydreaming while looking out at the street. First, I saw only his trouser legs with the broad red stripe on the side, which officers of high rank wear—that is, I saw a man in uniform who approached slowly then stood still; I didn't know it was Vassily, none of us had ever seen him like this.

When I came out front, Irina and Hans were sitting at a table with Vassily. The Assel was empty, the entire street seemed very quiet, as if it were early morning. Vassily had lots of small insignia and golden buttons on his chest. He showed us who he was, actually. Something we basically already knew. He gave a crooked smile when I saluted him and offered me his hand.

Hans had started talking. He was lisping markedly, his tongue was still asleep, but he felt he had to speak. He told us that he had resolved not to spend nights drinking anymore. "More sleep, less alcohol, Vassily, and then . . ." For him, the general was like a benevolent father who helped his child show his best side. Irina stood up and made coffee, which she served with brandy; her hands trembled, which I had never seen before.

"What happens now—for you, Vassily?"

The general undid his belt with the golden star and slowly rolled it into a snail, which he gently put on the table.

"'We're pulling out, and yet our songs remain,' not a bad line, right, Carl? Of course, it sounds better in Russian."

He leaned back and closed his eyes.

"Our duty done! Goodbye, Berlin! Our hearts are set for home . . ."

It was the official farewell song.

"Written by Colonel Luschetzky, a poet I admire greatly," Vassily said. "We're singing it today. And you are all invited!"

Just then, guests entered the Assel and ordered something to eat, so I had to return to the kitchen. A few minutes later, Vassily stood next to me and asked about the gun. I hadn't thought of it for a long time. The Kashi was gathering dust somewhere, in my cupboard or under the workbench.

"I don't know where . . ."

"I assume it's where you always keep it, isn't it, Carlo?"

I nodded. I didn't know what to say.

"Then don't worry if you don't find it when you go home tonight."

He patted my shoulder. A few of the insignia on ribbons clinked faintly. Then we talked a bit more—I've forgotten about what. I had to work, and the microwave was humming. Finally, Vassily asked about the poems, something no one else did. It was typical of him. He wanted to know. Like many Russians of his generation, he was well versed in poetry. He had grown up with it, he had read Mayakovsky and heard Yevtushenko "when I was in Moscow," Vassily said.

I had to admit that I had not yet had a book published. I did not tell him that for some time now all I did was sit at my workbench and paint nice arcs. No writing, no words, just beautiful arcs on brown parchment, sandwich paper, actually. I used the brush and ink from the calligraphy kit that I had brought back from Paris. There was a special posture you had to assume (sitting up straight, but relaxed), a posture of contemplation which included an even, serene way of breathing. In this manner, I drew arcs (the Dresden painter Hermann Glöckner, whom I revered, would have called them "sweeps") and waited for a meaning that would at some point stream out from me. I was in midst of my calligraphy phase, which I didn't see as a crisis but as a new beginning. It was, in any case, the opposite of walking, talking, and tapping.

This was not something I could tell Vassily. He would neither have understood nor approved of it, especially not of the waiting. As a man of action, Vassily could not understand why I hadn't gotten in touch with "our friend" at Oberbaum Berlin and St. Petersburg, and on that quiet, sunny morning I no longer quite knew myself. It was so fundamentally contrary to what I actually wanted (and repeatedly resolved to pursue).

I couldn't look Vassily in the face. He was giving me an inquiring look. I wanted to say something lighthearted, amusing, about Adele's Lada repair shop, perhaps, or the Kashi circus in Fenske's cellar, a little gossip about old times, but could not say a word. All of a sudden it was obvious, and I could no longer deny it: I was afraid. And, in fact, this fear had always been there, a shame that I couldn't overcome, that kept me from letting go of the manuscript and exposing myself. The fear, then, of having my own deficiency set in print, black on white and for eternity. I was afraid of a disaster. What else could explain my inability for years to write more than twenty poems? My manuscript hadn't grown, my fear had—secretly and silently. Fear of the book I longed for, of failure, although it was necessary. But who could you be (in this life), aged thirty, without a book?

Vassily shook his head. He took the receipt pad from on top of the refrigerator and wrote down a phone number. A mafia number, I thought.

"Don't be so fearful, Carlo. You were always too timid with your poems," Vassily said and put the pad back on the refrigerator. The general had read my mind. In the half-light of the kitchen, his medals shone like a golden shield on his chest.

Dodo came in and trotted up to Vassily. The general knelt down and took hold of the goat's beard, he tugged and shook it gently, then lay his forehead against the goat's. This was his farewell.

*

Dodo was active at twilight. Late afternoon, she started look-ing for food and always came to me in the kitchen just before closing. I would make her a bowl of Japanese noodle soup and a salad. I know that goats are herbivores, but Dodo especially liked noodles. I think it was because of some spice that she had become addicted to (the straw and seagrass mattresses were long gone), a kind of Maggi that had been added liberally to the freeze-dried noodles, probably as a preservative.

"How are you, Dodo?" I whispered and the goat blinked at me. Her coat had lost its sheen. Dodo had grown old. I think we were both thinking of Hoffi at that moment. It was past time to keep the promise I had made to myself (and the trees near the water tower) years earlier. I packed my shoulder bag, quickly added a few more cans of soup and got a rope, which I tied to Dodo's collar. We left the Assel together. No one thought anything of it. We crossed the street, I opened the Zhiguli's door and pulled the goat into the car. It wasn't easy, even though Dodo didn't really resist. Her hooves crossed and she got stuck. She wasn't a dog, which immediately understands on the first try how to make itself comfortable on the back seat of a car. Goats want to keep standing. Dodo tried to stay upright for a while but then gave up, and by the time we got to the Tierpark zoo, she looked quite comfortable, lying there with her front legs folded and leaning back (almost casually). Like a sphinx on a Sunday drive.

I turned into a side street directly across from the Tierpark. The goat stretched her neck and tried to lick my cheek.

"Dodo!"

I was spooked. I had sounded exactly like my father: the usual tension in the car, the drive from Gera to the Hermsdorfer interchange, for example, with Sunday dinner at the highway rest stop—in 1970 that was still a pleasant outing, and the rest stop had a tolerable restaurant . . .

The last visitors exited the park and strolled toward the

streetcar stop, and as darkness slowly fell, I started looking for a section of the fence that was rickety or low enough. I hadn't thought this (crucial) step through very thoroughly.

When I returned to the car, the goat was watching me through the rear window. Her head: like a funny little mascot on the rear deck. It occurred to me that my aunt had kept a little tiger in this spot in her blue Skoda. One day, someone broke into her car and tore the tiger to shreds—a completely pointless act. I wondered if I shouldn't stop the whole thing and take Dodo back. When I got into the car, Dodo sat up.

"The wild times are over, aren't they?"

In the rearview mirror, the goat. She looked at me: innocent, trusting, and as if she had even less of an idea than I did who could have just said that.

"Dodo?"

Dodo was silent.

Looking back now, it doesn't matter whether Dodo spoke or not. What's important is what I heard then. And that in that very moment many things suddenly came together—I can only describe it this vaguely. On top of that, there was Dodo's smell, which was making my eyes water.

"Let's go."

Together, we walked round the edge of the park. The animals' night noises, their breathing in sleep. A hoof stamped, a branch creaked like a shot, but softly.

At some point, Dodo stopped. She refused to move. I understood. First, I took the welding goggles off her. Then I undid the rope from her collar and took the collar off, too. Dodo had already begun to rise, initially only halfway up, to make it easier for me, and when I was finally done, everything went very quickly. The fence was high, but Dodo cleared it, landing slowly, hooves quiet, on the other side. She raised her head once more, then disappeared into the darkness.

On the way back, I knew that my time in the Assel was up. I suddenly understood that. As if there were no longer any reason to go there again.

Today, there is still a building at 21 Oranienburger Strasse. When I pass by, I check the house number and its location by certain trees that were across the street in the park back then. Apart from the location—nothing else remains. Even the basement, the old den, is gone. Its ceiling was torn down, the shelter broken up, the U-boat blown up. Through wide panes of glass in the facade, there is a full view of a well-lit, high-ceilinged space, all the way down to the building's foundations. The old refuge has become a kind of aquarium. Why remains a mystery. A few pieces of furniture stand, scattered about in the room, without price tags. I have never seen a customer or a salesman there—not a single person, just a box of glass and stone, in which a few pieces of furniture drift.

ACKNOWLEDGMENTS

I would like to thank my parents, Ingrid Seiler and Reinhard Seiler, for their patience and generosity—this book is dedicated to them. I also thank my former Assel colleagues, Inés Suarez, Johann Christoph Riedel, Susann Grubba, Dirk Uhlig, Hans Pfeifer, and Frank Weisleder, for answering countless questions. For conversations and suggestions, my thanks to Jens Thiele, Peter Walther, and Tobias Wangermann. The photographer Andreas Münstermann has my thanks for opening his picture archive, which brought Ryke Strasse in all its particularity to my eyes once more. Rita Damm of the DEFA Foundation has my thanks for the digitalization and loan of the Wydoks collection in the film archive. Kristina Dörlitz and Frauke Pahlke provided me with valuable support in my research. Special thanks go to my editor, Doris Plöschberger. On top of all this good fortune, I have a supreme good fortune for which I cannot express my gratitude because it is beyond thanks—and yet: thank you, Charlotta, for everything.

The lines of Gennadi Luschetzky's "Farewell Song of the Russian Soldier" were taken [and translated into English] from Hans-Joachim Jung's German translation. The author of the poetry collection *Kastanienallee* is Elke Erb; the poem quoted is titled "KASTANIENALLEE, bewohnt." The *Wegweiser für Übersiedler aus der DDR* (*Guide for Migrants from the GDR*, issued by Wolfgang Schäuble as Interior Minister) was published in 1989 and, along with the sentence quoted above, has a ready supply of other valuable pieces of advice. I owe the phrase "thickening fog of confusion" to Frank Heibert's translation of Richard Ford's *Canada*. I have also quoted individual phrases or lines by Thomas Wolfe, William Butler Yeats, Hannah Arendt, Wolfgang Hilbig, Heiner Müller, Hans Arp, Goethe, Roland Barthes, Franz Kafka, Stefan George, and Thomas Tranströmer.

RAYS FROM ANOTHER STAR

A Translator's Afterword

The novel *Star 111* takes its title from an iconic East German transistor radio, a device that awakened the protagonist Carl Bischoff to the world when he was a child and that was at the heart of one of his small family's few rituals. The image of this portable radio captures the contrary energies that animate Seiler's highly autobiographical work—the centrifugal force of historical upheaval and the centripetal force of introspection and artistic self-definition.

An expansive portrait of a poet as a young man, *Star 111* captures the brief season of utopian anarchy in Berlin immediately following the collapse of the GDR. Through the adventures and misadventures of assorted idealists, artists, idlers, and eccentrics, this novel evokes the heady atmosphere of hope and disorientation, of revolutionary utopianism and opportunism that filled the dilapidated former capital in 1990. Seiler conveys the sense of liberation and possibility felt both by the East Germans who left for the West and by those who stayed behind, yet he resists sentimentalizing the experiences of either group. The result is an intimate study of political romanticism in a time of upheaval and the suffering it inevitably entails but often disregards.

In the three decades since the Fall of the Berlin Wall, the capacious genre of the *Wenderoman*, novels dealing with the collapse of the GDR and the aftermath, has become firmly established in contemporary German literature. Seiler's latest addition to this genre is unusual in that it narrows a broader historical view to an intent focus on the personal. By interweaving the *éducation sentimental* and the political awakening of the aspiring poet, Seiler has created an engaging hybrid *Wenderoman* and *Bildungsroman*. A parallel narrative strand follows Carl's parents' belated flight over the disintegrating border to face awakenings and disillusionments of their own, and offers a nuanced account of an older generation's experience of the era.

One of Germany's most prominent poets, Seiler established himself as a major novelist with his 2014 debut *Kruso*. That novel, set in the summer of 1989 on the Baltic island of Hiddensee, mirrors the downfall of the GDR through the dissolution of a group of outcasts and idealists making their various bids for freedom. A popular destination for dissidents, Hiddensee was not only an oasis of liberty, it was the launching point of a dangerous escape route for East Germans fleeing to Denmark. More than 5,600 East Germans attempted to cross the 40 kilometer channel between 1961 and 1989, but fewer than 1,000 made it. Focused on this small cosmos, *Kruso* records the real human cost of utopian dreams.

Seiler's second novel, *Star 111*, forms a diptych with *Kruso*, portraying the East Berlin underground bar and squatter scenes in the months between the Fall of the Wall and reunification, a time that seemed filled with opportunities to establish social and economic systems other than actually existing socialism or capitalism. "The whole world is being redistributed these days," the hapless Carl is told when he washes up in Berlin after his parents abruptly leave for the West. He is taken in by a group of dissidents, punks, artists, and revolutionaries gathered around Hoffi, a charismatic, messianic leader nicknamed the "Shepherd," because he guards not only his flock of misfits but also his pet goat Dodo, the group's mascot and source of milk. This group—Carl's "pack," part cult, part band of urban guerrillas—are united in following Hoffi's principle that "each and every one is equal and equally worthy, although in the current situation, workers must receive special attention." Their mission is to "sabotage the breeding ground of capital through immediate redistribution" by occupying hundreds of abandoned buildings—in their words "making them livable"—a mission they finance by stealing tools and material from West German construction sites, running unlicensed bars, and selling bits of the Wall, both real and counterfeit, to tourists and foreign speculators. Carl, a trained bricklayer, soon becomes an essential member of the pack and helps them build their figurative and literal bulwarks against the looming capitalist takeover.

At heart a loner, Carl gradually distances himself from them in order to pursue his dream of becoming a poet. He watches from the periphery as the tight-knit group begins to fray when jealousies, ambitions, and appetites take their toll. His personal liberation from expectations, from dominant ideologies and group think, and from self-doubt, is hard-won. *Star 111* is the chronicle of an individual establishing a foothold in a time of upheaval and negotiating the pull of and disenchantment with new perspectives and ideologies. "It was as if the world had fallen into an extremely sensitive, uncertain state," Carl muses, "as if you were only just beginning to exist."

The novel's primary setting is the Prenzlauer Berg and Kollwitzkiez districts, and the topography of East Berlin—the hastily abandoned apartments, the overgrown craters left by Allied bombs, the makeshift bars and restaurants established in derelict storefronts—forms a crucial backdrop to the political atmosphere engendered there in the year and a half following the Fall of the Wall. Indeed, a central theme in *Star 111* is the transformation of the Berlin-Mitte cityscape and the way history is preserved or erased in private and public spaces. One of Lutz Seiler's greatest gifts as a writer—and a major source of headaches for his translators—is his ability to capture the minutiae and texture of a vanished world in rhythmic, lyrical prose. Both *Kruso* and *Star 111* are like time capsules that envelop the reader in sounds, smells, and sights, as well as social atmospheres and assumptions that are, for better or worse, things of the past.

In translating this novel, I tried to capture the many registers of Lutz Seiler's prose: the differing tenors of East and West German bureaucratese; the idiolects of the individual characters or social groups; the changes rung on particular words with their multiple meanings; and most importantly the lines of poems by Hans Arp, Novalis, Elke Erb, Baudelaire, Yeats, Goethe, Barthes, and many others that rattle around in Carl's head or echo through the narrative. In his prose as in his poetry, sound echoes and underpins sense.

Still, his dexterity in playing with sound and sense occasionally eluded my grasp. In several passages, Seiler both draws out multiple shadings of a word's meaning and mines that word's onomatopoeic potential to create an expansive atmosphere or sound symbol that can stretch over pages. One of the most engaging examples of this is in the opening of the chapter "From Another Star." Carl has finally found his own territory, his "claim," from which he can begin prospecting for an authentic, creative existence as a poet. The water tower on Knaack Strasse becomes both guardian and lighthouse of his imagined island. A key word in this extended maritime symbol is *Rauschen*, which in German covers a span of noises from roaring, murmuring, hissing, and rustling to whispering and soughing, but also a rush or sweep, not to mention intoxication—all of which are overtly or implicitly significant in each use of the word. Throughout the novel, the *Rauschen* of pine and chestnut trees as well as of the cobblestones communicates with Carl in a way that is central to his poetic development. However, while trees can make a rustling sound, cars driving over cobblestones do not. They rumble or murmur. Accordingly, I had to alternate in English between the word's multiple meanings, sacrificing some of the novel's internal echoes to the imagery.

Despite—or more likely because of—these difficulties, it was a joy to immerse myself in the rhythm of his sentences and refashion them in English and I hope readers will share this joy.

My translation has benefited enormously from Stefan Tobler's patient and exacting editing, although any oversights or lapses are mine alone. I am grateful for Lutz Seiler's generous answers to my many questions about historical particulars and stylistic choices that are crucial to the texture of the narrative. A residency at the American Academy in Berlin in the spring of 2022 allowed me to search for traces of Carl Bischoff's haunts and research the city's more ephemeral social and political history at the close of the twentieth century. No detail about Berlin or the GDR was too small or obscure for the Academy's librarian, Ilya Oehring, to find and bring to light.

TESS LEWIS

New York, March 2023

LUTZ SEILER (b. 1963) was born in Gera, Thuringia, and today lives in Wilhelmshorst, near Berlin, and in Stockholm. After an apprenticeship in construction, he worked as a carpenter and bricklayer. Since 1997, he has been the literary director and custodian of the Peter Huchel Haus. His essays, poems, stories, and novels have been translated into twenty-five languages and won many prizes, including the Leipzig Book Fair Prize, the Ingeborg Bachmann Prize, the German Book Prize, and, in 2023, the prestigious Georg-Büchner Prize.

TESS LEWIS is a writer and a translator from French and German. Her essays and reviews have appeared in a number of publications, including *Granta, Bookforum*, and the *Los Angeles Review of Books*. She has translated works by Peter Handke, Philippe Jaccottet, and Montaigne, as well as a novel by Ernst Jünger and a collection of essays by Walter Benjamin for NYRB classics. Her translation of Lutz Seiler's debut novel, *Kruso*, was the runner-up in the 2018 Schlegel-Tieck Prize. She is a Guggenheim and a Berlin Prize Fellow and a 2023 Scholar of Note at the American Library in Paris.